The Magical Reality of
Annabel Jones

ALSO BY ANDRENA WOODHAMS

The Extraordinary Awakening of Annabel Jones

Overall, a damned good novel, well-written and engaging. It's written with a real insight into human nature through the eyes of tantric therapy. I personally found it to be a therapeutic read and will no doubt read it again.

Malcolm Horsnell, Professor Emeritus, McMaster University

Read this book for a deeper understanding of tantric practice, appreciating it for the love, healing, and deep forgiveness it provides. Superb story, deeper truths.

Andrea Kay O'Loughlin, Teacher

A nitty-gritty feast of honesty and sophisticated drama-with-purpose. The core theme—the waking-up process of a contemporary woman—is unstinting in accurate descriptions of the intense sensations and emotions that accompany such a foray into the deep self. Bringing these often ineffable feelings to consciousness and weaving them into a dramatic love story made this a book I couldn't put down.

Constance Walsh, International Consultant

A wonderful book that demonstrates the value of the freedom of spirit and mind. Andrena has such clarity of expression and is totally original in her approach. I enjoyed this book from start to finish.

Elizabeth Gage, Jewelry Designer

It weaves the visible and invisible, energy and matter, the inner and outer parts of a journey with great style and courage, a treat for all to read.

Calixte Stamp, Licensed Mental Health Counselor

The Magical Reality of Annabel Jones

Andrena Woodhams

yinbound books

PUBLISHED BY
Yinbound Books

Copyright © 2022 Andrena Woodhams
www.andrenawoodhams.com

ISBN: 978-0-9911599-2-5

LCCN: 2022905790

Front cover image: *Lady with Fan* by Gustav Klimt
Back cover photo: Carlotta Cardana
Cover and interior design: Arik Shimansky

FOR ARIK

You are more wonderful than my wildest dreams

Walk as if you are kissing the earth with your feet

Thich Nhat Hanh

CONTENTS

Inspired by a true story

FIRE
India

The morning breezes have secrets to tell. Don't go back to sleep
—RUMI

It's dawn. My husband places his finger to his lips. "Listen. It's the sound of infinity."

To experience the Taj Mahal is romantic, but to have it to ourselves is spine-tingling. We face each other, so close that I can feel the warmth of his breath. As Eugen's fingers intertwine with mine, our wedding bands glint in a pale shaft of morning light. Looking up, I see it's filtering from the Mihrab-shaped windows above our heads.

I blink, waiting for my eyes to get used to the darkness. We are standing in an octagonal room layered with balustrades that stretch up toward the domed ceiling. Like the petals of a flower, each wall is pierced by a door leading to smaller chambers. The marble walls are deceptive; the closer I look, the more details I can see. Flower motifs are chiseled into every surface. Everywhere are tulips and daffodils; irises and narcissi; curly foliage inlaid with precious jewels that glitter in scintillating colors of red, yellow, and green.

Closing my eyes, I feel the softness of the weathered marble under my feet. The pre-dawn silence is so rich it is palpable. High above us

1

in the Taj Mahal's dome, I can detect a staccato chirping. A door closing in the distance. Then, there is something else. It is a sound like rushing water. It comes from everywhere and nowhere.

Eugen smiles when he sees that I hear it. "The sound of infinity is only for those who take the time to listen." He takes my hands in his. "That is why I want to perform our ceremony here. You see, the Taj is far more than a monument to love. It is man's greatest offering to all that is feminine."

My body shivers when he says this. Here we are, he a Viennese from an old titled Austrian family, I an American born in Kansas; we met in London and live in Vienna. We are too old to have children, too young to retire, but brave enough to act upon love. We gaze at each other for what seems like eternity. And with that, we begin to recite our vows.

I used to see life as a random series of events that were as disconnected from each other as I was disconnected from myself. But once Eugen entered my life, I began to see things differently. He taught me that it was my perception that made me feel small. When I press my nose too close to the screen, everything seems random. But when I pull back and look at the same situation from afar, the haphazard color pixels form a pattern. From this perspective, the story of my life isn't aimless and flat. It is a journey with dimensions and depth, and this journey is taking me somewhere.

But I never thought it would take me here. Emerging from the womb-like interior, I breathe in the smell of daybreak in India—the heady scent of flower blossoms, the sweet smell of early morning fires, the wild scents of nature—and think, *This is the best day of my life.*

The sun is just appearing on the horizon as we walk outside. The dome keeps changing color; it was grayish white when we arrived, now it's pale pink. Its milky marble comes from the Indian city of Makrana. The inlaid jade from China. The lapis lazuli from Afghanistan. The sapphires from Sri Lanka. I can't imagine a more perfect place to begin our marriage than here.

Eugen hooks his thumbs underneath the stretch waistband and hikes them above his hips. "My trousers. They must have stretched."

I put my hands around his waist. "You've lost weight, that's all." He smiles, opening his arms so that I can nuzzle against his chest. "There is another reason we got married here, isn't there?"

"Besides the romantic one?" He strokes my hair. "Yes. It makes things easier."

I was afraid of that. "Wouldn't it have been better to let your family know?"

He sighs and pulls back so that he can look at me. "Oh Annabel. With my family…"

"They can't be worse than mine."

"You would be surprised." He stretches his long arms toward the sky. "*Komm.* Let's get some breakfast."

Just then, the tiles underneath me start to tilt. I close my eyes and try to steady myself, but my legs buckle and the ground comes up to meet me. When I open my eyes again, I'm in a sitting position with a worried husband staring down at me.

"Another spell?"

I nod. "It will pass."

He shades his eyes with his hand. "You need to hydrate. I'll run and get some water."

I shake my head. "I'm fine. Really." I give him my hand. "Just help me up."

Instead of pulling me up, he bends down. "Let me take care of you. I'll be back in no time."

I relent, caressing his cheek with my finger. As I stroke it, I can feel his cheekbones protruding. "Just this once," I tease. "But still. You're too thin. You'll need feeding up when we get back to Vienna."

He stands up again and gives his tall body a shake. "It's a deal." His eyes twinkle as he says this. "You can do anything you want with me when we get back to Vienna. From now on, I am yours."

We say I love you and he turns and bounds with his usual enthusiasm down the stone steps toward the gardens below. I watch him become a speck that gets smaller and smaller and soon he is out of sight.

Once he's gone, I bring my legs to my chest as I gaze up at the dome of the Taj Mahal. Love. It has been a difficult word for me. Letting another in behind the walls I've built to shelter me from my past has not been easy. No matter how much love I feel, it's never enough for my unsteady soul. Because when there is love, there will be heartbreak.

I wonder if the fifth emperor of the Mughal Empire in India, Shah Jahan, knew that when he met his wife, Arjumand Banu, in 1607. From all accounts, it was love at first sight. When they married, Jahan named her Mumtaz Mahal, or the Exalted One of the Palace. Mumtaz was beautiful, intelligent, and kind, and her husband adored her. The empress accompanied her husband on his military campaigns, and it was there, in the Deccan plains, that she died giving birth to their fourteenth child. The devastated emperor retreated into his tent for eight days, and when he re-emerged, his back was bent, he wore glasses and his hair had turned white. For over two decades he poured his soul into creating a monument dedicated to his beloved wife. Four hundred years later, millions of people visit this architectural wonder to celebrate love. And now, two of those millions of people are us.

A troop of monkeys scampers by, tails in the air. The waft of flowers from the garden is intoxicating. Time moves at a different pace here. It is pliable and dreamy and incapable of progressing in a linear manner, causing seconds to fade into minutes. My eyelids feel like heavy blankets. They flutter once, twice, and I'm out.

The morning hush is broken by the call of a peacock. With a start, my eyes open. I must have dozed off. I pat my trousers and remember Eugen has my phone. The dreamlike quality of the Taj is gone, transformed into hordes of tourists taking selfies. I wander through the crowd milling around the dome. Within minutes I'm hot and sweaty, and Eugen is still nowhere to be seen. I will myself to take a deep breath while I retrace my steps to where we last saw each other.

I'm scanning the gardens below when my heart catches. There he

4

is. Head and shoulders above the crowd. Walking up the steps far below me. I call his name, but he can't hear me, so I stand on tiptoes, waving my hands above my head. He stops when he hears my voice. Looking up, our eyes lock. He holds up two water bottles and gives me a thumbs up. I point to the bottom of the stairs. *I'll come to you,* I mouth, and he nods and turns to head back down the stairs.

Everything happens in slow motion after that. He does this strange motion, as if one moment he's standing, and the next, he's falling backwards. His head does a bouncing movement as it hits the stone step. This recollection is more like a photograph than a memory. Then his long body slides like a slithering snake down the steps and comes to rest at the bottom.

People are running toward him from all directions. I hear someone screaming and realize it's me—one long cry of pain, twisting in the sky and the heavens beyond. A crowd has formed around him like black, sticky flies. Dust and heat swirl like a windstorm with him at the fulcrum. When I finally reach him, he's on his back, arms flung outward like Christ on the cross. His eyes are open, staring into the void. My gaze falls on my phone, the glass screen cracked against the stone upon impact. In that instant, these shards shatter my consciousness and I know he is dead.

Confusion. Voices screaming. People try to pull me away from his body. Blood is everywhere, on his shirt, on my hands, seeping into the soggy earth. I'm in an ambulance, rocking side to side. The wailing siren hurts my ears. Hands push me here, guide me there. There are certain things I must do. I need to wait. I give our married names, Annabel and Eugen Vasoy, to the doctors. I'm given a copy of a police report. His death certificate. Shock. Disbelief. And then, just when it seems that the nightmare will never end, I'm back at our hotel, lying on our bed, arms and legs spread like the Vitruvian man.

I am oblivious to everything around me: the soft crisp sheets, the wall-to-wall windows with a clear view of the Taj, the vases of flowers, the Persian carpets, the bowls of fruit, the antiques. A breakfast tray the manager must have sent up sits untouched on the table.

My fingers flex in the empty air. Without my phone, I feel helpless. I sit up and pick up the hotel phone and call the one person whose number I know by heart.

My best friend's voice sounds as if it is coming from a million miles away.

"Bloody hell, Annabel." I hear steps followed by the sound of a door closing. "You went to India to get married, not to attend a funeral." Chloe's voice catches when she realizes that humor might not be the best way to comfort a woman who has just lost her husband hours after exchanging her vows. Chloe blames a lot of things on her upbringing. It was the school of the stiff upper lip, she called it. She has never been one of those people who handle emotions well. Then again, neither am I.

Grief comes in waves. It eliminates the complexities of daily life. It tightens my throat. In the distance, I hear laughing at the pool, the distant traffic, the bells of a temple. It's not right. None of this is right. Everyone needs to stop, grieve, pause. A life has just been snuffed out. How dare everything go on as before? My skin feels clammy.

"Let me start again," she begins, but I interrupt her.

"Are you still at work?" It's a rhetorical question. I already know the answer. Of course she's at work. She's always at work now that Jean Luc is gone.

Chloe More-Hamilton is a full-time friend, a full-time literary agent, and, until six months ago, was a full-time wife, until her ophthalmologist husband took a job at a hospital in San Francisco. Chloe was supposed to go live with him, but the days turned to weeks turned to months and she's now still in London, working harder than ever.

"Sometimes I wonder why I'm married to a man who works halfway around the world."

"Perhaps it's to escape a wife who won't stop giving him a hard time."

"You try being a faithful wife for a year," she huffs.

I keep my voice level. "Be grateful you are a wife."

I hear an intake of breath. "How insensitive can I be?" There is a long pause, and when she next speaks, her voice is softer. "You know I get this way when I'm upset. I'm worried you are going to go into war correspondent mode, pretending you can handle it."

"But I can handle it."

"Mm-hm. I thought so. That means you are already in war correspondent mode and don't even know it. Have you eaten? You need to eat. Order something warm. I know. Tea. But don't bother ordering chai. Hotel chai is terrible. All Indian tea served in hotels is terrible. They use Lipton's, can you believe it? Who uses tea bags anymore anyway?"

"Sixty-one billion Brits, apparently."

"Once a journalist always a journalist. How you can fill that brain of yours with all those facts and figures I'll never know. Promise me to get some food in you, okay?"

I can't even think of food right now, but I don't tell her that. I scrunch the pillow behind my head and lean back against the headboard and close my eyes, letting her voice wash over me. Suddenly there is a pause and I realize she must have asked me a question. I open my eyes. "What?"

"I said have you read the will?"

"How can you think of that at a time like this?" I whisper.

She harrumphs. "Because it's exactly at times like this that you need to think of that. Especially with that mother-in-law of yours. You need to tie your camel tight."

That's one of the favorite sayings she learned from the tantra course where she met Jean Luc. *Trust in God and tie your camel tight.* Eugen was an expert in trusting in God. He was also a self-proclaimed expert in knowing himself, but I set him straight on that. It's easy to think you know yourself when you are born with a family trust and a palace. I close my eyes.

"Okay. Fire away."

"Bank accounts."

I sigh. "We each have our own. A joint account for the gallery."

7

"Who funded this joint bank account?"

I get quiet. "My savings."

"Right. There went your savings. What about your apartment?"

"It's owned by the family foundation."

"That means his family will do everything they can to get you out of there. Austrian courts might not even accept the certificate from your marriage in Delhi."

"But it's legal."

"When it comes to money, old families can be brutal. They won't give a damn that you are Eugen's lawful wife. Even if you counter-sue."

"Which I wouldn't."

"Doesn't matter. It wouldn't stick in court anyway." I hear her flicking her pencil against the edge of her desk. "How much longer are you going to be in India?"

"A few more days. The hotel contacted Lucy as soon as they found out about the accident. Apparently she dropped everything and is on her way here now." When she doesn't respond, I add, "You know, Lucy is the one who arranged for us to do our ceremony at the Taj."

I hear a satisfied hunh. "Eugen's kick-ass travel specialist in Delhi. I'll ask the hotel to give me her contact details. I don't want her to let you out of her sight until you get on that plane back to Vienna. "

I can hear her brain spinning. "Christiane can pick you up from the airport. What else do you need?"

"Don't worry," I say, but by now even I know I'm lying. I put my head in my hands as another wave of grief hit me. I clear my throat. "This was supposed to be the journey of a lifetime."

"Oh my poor friend," Chloe answers. "I'm afraid your journey has only just begun."

I hang up and look down at myself. I try to scrape a brown smudge from my shirt with my fingernail but stop when I realize it's blood. Walking to the bathroom, I peel it off, together with my rumpled and stained skirt, and drop them in the trash on the way. Standing under the shower, I turn the water on full. Droplets pound my head like tiny bullets. They stream down my face and over my body, dribbling in rivulets onto my feet.

I gaze at the water running down my legs for so long I have to remind myself that these feet belong to me. Grabbing the loofah, I begin to scrub my skin, hard, hoping I can remove the emptiness I feel. His death invades my pores. I shut my eyes, trying to push the memories away, but it doesn't work. I miss Eugen so much it hurts.

Turning off the shower, I get out, and am drying myself when I hear a knock, followed by the sound of the bell. Throwing on the first thing I can find, I follow my feet to the door and open it. Standing in front of me is Eugen's travel agent, Lucy. Her long blond hair is in disarray, her eyes wide, her round, moon-shaped face filled with concern. She must have left her office in Delhi in no time flat. She throws her arms around me.

"I've just been to the hospital."

"They let you in?"

"I said Eugen was my brother." Her eyes cloud over with pain. "They said he died on impact."

My voice sounds hollow in my ears. "It happened right in front of me."

"Oh fuck." Her eyes brim with tears.

She puts an arm around me and guides me to the sofa. "Are you okay?" She takes a tissue and dabs my forehead. It comes away damp.

I touch my forehead. "I just got out of the shower. I guess I stayed longer than I should."

For a moment neither of us says anything. She breaks the silence by handing me a plastic bag. "A man from the morgue gave me this."

I peer inside. It's Eugen's wedding ring and a crumpled note. It looks like a crib sheet for our vows.

"My phone?"

"This is India. It's gone. I'll get you another one."

My gaze goes beyond her toward the picture windows. In the distance, the Taj Mahal appears above the dark green forest like a white, shimmering crown. "What were we thinking of, having a private wedding ceremony at the Taj? It's a mausoleum. Not a place to get married. Someone told Eugen not to do this. Said it would bring us bad luck."

She pulls a notebook and a pen from her bag. "Don't go there. Woulda shoulda coulda doesn't help anyone. You got married there because you loved each other." She hands me the pen. "I want you to make a list of the people who need to be contacted." When she sees the blank look on my face, her voice softens. "Just do the best you can."

I take the notebook and pen from her with a docility that surprises me. It takes a few seconds before my brain kicks into gear. "They are all in Vienna," I say, scribbling names and addresses down. "Eugen's family—I'd suggest his sister Lili."

"And your family?"

The word hovers in the air between us. A normal response would be to say yes. But my family? Those lonely years in Kansas beckon, but there is only so much pain I can handle right now. "I haven't spoken to them in years."

She takes the notebook and pen from me. "There's something else. A wandering sadhu wants to see you," she says, stuffing both into her bag. "He has been sitting by the entrance gate for most of the day."

I wipe a few beads of sweat from my brow. "A sadhu?"

"It's a holy man," she explains. She closes her bag, then fiddles with the clasp, as if she's uncomfortable with what she is telling me.

I look down at my lap. "I'm not even sure I know what a sadhu is."

"It's a person who has renounced his worldly life and possessions. They vow to wander naked the rest of their lives, pondering God."

My eyes drift beyond her. "As if there is a God."

A wave of sadness crosses her face. "Oh, Annabel." She puts her hand on mine. It feels cool to the touch. "You might as well give it a try. What can you lose?"

My shoulders sag. "Might as well. I've lost everything else."

Her eyes look pained. When she next speaks, her voice is professional. "I'll ask for him to be sent up." She stands up, pulls her Indian kurta over her hips, then swings her bag onto her shoulder.

10

"And another thing. There was a news crew at the Taj this morning. They captured everything so it's been on the news. Flowers have been coming in from all over. I'll have them sent up to your room."

Fifteen minutes later, the doorbell rings. Lucy opens the door. Standing on the threshold is a wiry man, naked to the waist, and a bellboy. The sadhu's dust-colored dreadlocks are coiled like a turban on top of his head. His forehead is streaked with ash. A cream-colored beard hangs like a rope from his chin. His face is leathery from the sun and so gaunt his cheekbones protrude. He pulsates raw, wild energy, but it's his eyes that stand out the most. They shine with the vibrancy of the sun.

Lucy gives a tip to the bellboy, who bows, closing the door behind him. The sadhu walks into the room as if he owns it. If the opulence bothers him, he doesn't show it. He heads in the direction of the terrace and stands by the glass door. His bare feet seem to hardly touch the carpet.

Lucy scurries up to him and slides open the door. The heat hits us like a furnace. Surprisingly agile for a man his age, the sadhu slips outside and drops into a cross-legged position. He points at the ground in front of him.

"Sit down," he says, looking up at me. Judging from his accent, he's educated.

I place a chair cushion on the ground and sit cross-legged in front of him. After the air-conditioned interior, the dry Indian heat is stifling. I feel dopey. It takes all my energy not to put my forehead on the floor and fall asleep.

His gaze is unwavering. "I am saying my mid-morning prayers by the river. I see a man walking on the water toward me. He is tall." He points to the wedding ring on my left finger. "He is wearing a ring like that. He insists that I give you this message." He turns and says something in Hindi to Lucy.

"He wants you to sit shiva," Lucy says, pulling a chair up to sit next to me.

I don't know what is more unbelievable. That a sadhu could have seen Eugen after he died, or that he wants me to perform a Jewish ritual for one of the most Catholic families in Austria. "You mean the god Shiva?"

"That's what I thought," Lucy says. "But he says no."

"But Eugen isn't Jewish."

"It doesn't matter. I just know you must sit with him before he is cremated."

"That means she would have to do it tonight," Lucy says slowly.

I look at Lucy. I can't believe she is taking this man seriously. Spend the night with Eugen's body in a hotel?

"Wear the clothes you planned to wear to celebrate tonight," the saddhu continues.

"But they're white," I stutter.

"Mourning dress *is* white in India," Lucy explains.

The sadhu ignores her. "Then travel to Varanasi. Give his ashes to Ma Ganga."

I give the sadhu an odd look. How did he know that Eugen wanted his ashes spread on the Ganges? I remember him telling me this once. When I asked him why he didn't put his death wishes in his will, he explained it would be a waste of time. Austrians need a body to mourn. The Viennese even have a name for it: *Eine schöne Leiche*. A beautiful corpse.

"His family wouldn't like that," I tell the sadhu.

He throws me a fierce look. "He has set you free. You must do the same for him."

The sadhu's confident tone of voice irritates me. "Free? What are you talking about?"

The sadhu frowns. "To fulfill your dharma."

"Dharma?" I ask, not understanding.

Lucy leans forward. "Dharma is one of those Indian words that's hard to translate. It's the reason why you were born."

I find my back stiffening. "I don't know my dharma."

The sadhu stares at me in disbelief. What he is asking is so obvious to him that he can barely contain his frustration. "How can you not

12

know your dharma? Without understanding yourself, what is the use of understanding the world?"

We are at a cultural crossroads. Here is a man who has got rid of all his possessions so that he can wander nearly naked the rest of his life pondering God. I am a Western-educated woman who has spent most of her life gathering possessions to enjoy the comfort of it. I've had to do a lot of work on myself. But it was all for one purpose, and that was to find a husband.

"I've just fulfilled my dharma, or whatever you want to call it. He just died."

The sadhu's eyes burn into mine. "Look at me."

A trickle of sweat runs down my back. I know what he wants. He wants to gaze with me. Eugen and I used to do this in tantra. When a student gazes into a teacher's eyes, the teacher acts like a tuning fork, raising the student's consciousness to the level of the teacher. All sorts of things can occur when this happens. Emotions locked into the muscle tissues may come up to be felt. In my current frame of mind, I might turn into a raging volcano. "I can't," I whisper.

His eyes beckon. "Do not fight your destiny."

There was a strange sense of inevitability when Eugen told me he wanted to get married in India. I bring my eyes up to his. The sadhu's face is as emotionless as a mirror. I gulp as the familiar tingling races through my entire body. Then, suddenly, a sadness so deep I'm afraid it will swallow me whole bursts up my throat like a high-pressure water valve. I collapse in heart-wrenching sobs. Like a drowning woman, I feel it all, the emptiness, the desperation, the anger that my soulmate is no more.

I'm still sobbing quietly when a tissue is placed in my hand. I take it and wipe the tears away, but they keep welling in my eyes and spilling down my cheeks, dripping onto my shirt, my hands, the floor. Time and time again I wipe my eyes, but it's no good. I feel like I'm leaking. When I finally look up again, the sadhu is looking at me. There is a depth of compassion in his eyes that I didn't see before.

My eyes flick to the Taj Mahal. I can feel Shah Jahan's loneliness in my soul. "It's love," I whisper.

He nods. "Your husband is gone, but his love will always be with you. He loved you even before you were born, and this love will continue with you far after you die."

"But my childhood," I whisper.

He shakes his head. "Everything is exactly as it needs to be."

I'm still quietly crying when I hear him leave.

The next thing I know, Lucy is bending down next to me. "Are you okay?"

I look up at her, my voice barely a whisper. "Do what he says. Then get me back to Vienna. I want to go home."

"I'll get on it right away." She tiptoes off the terrace, sliding the door shut behind her. I hear the door click and the silence of the Taj returns.

My childhood. I haven't thought of that in a long time. In fact, I haven't thought of anything that happened during my formative years for such a long time it is like recalling the life of someone else. I suppose it's because when I moved to Europe, I wanted to put everything behind me. I've been running for so long I have never bothered to examine what I left behind.

I was born in Kansas, an unexpected accident who appeared years after my brother. When Peter left for college, I should have been sent away to boarding school. But for some reason—I think it's because my parents never bothered to think about it—I was pawned off onto neighbors or left on my own for months at a time.

I don't remember much from that time, probably because that was when the sexual abuse occurred. It was one of my father's sleazy tennis buddies who offered to look in on me while they were away. It happened so often that Flora Mae, our Black housekeeper, decided that enough was enough and began to take me home with her after work.

I loved Flora Mae. She was tall, like a model, and wore her white maid's outfit like an African queen. Her home, a ramshackle house with faded yellow paint and a sagging porch on what my parents referred to as the wrong side of town, became my home away from home every time my parents were away. For two years I lived this way. Life at Flora Mae's was simple, but solid, and I soaked up the attention like a biscuit soaks up gravy. I'm going to dance at your wedding, she always used to tell me, and now, thinking back to our civil service in Delhi, I wish she had.

It was only when I became withdrawn and my grades plummeted that my parents, who knew nothing of the abuse, realized it might not be a good idea to leave a girl to fend for herself at such a young age. Not knowing what to do, they followed my brother Peter's advice and sent me to live with a Brazilian family in Rio de Janeiro who ran what he told them was a family-run institution that would help my spiritual growth.

But my family had made a mistake. My mild-mannered Brazilian mother, Dona Mathilde, didn't run a spiritual institution, but a *spiritista* society that doubled as a charity for the poor. There was no church, no Sermon on the Mount, no one telling me what to do. Just Dona Mathilde, who spoke with a quiet voice and wore pale cotton dresses rather than sequined high-heeled flashers, like most of the Brazilians I knew. The night I arrived, I remember gazing out my bedroom window at the tropical forests, listening to the sound of the surf and thinking that I had died and gone to heaven.

But I'll never forget when Dona Mathilde told me that she conducted séances. She gave me a little sugar water to calm me down the first time I encountered a spirit wandering the corridor. She taught me how to clean my energy when I came back from a party; how to defend myself from Macumba black magic; and how to participate in Umbanda, or white-magic ritual. Just like Dorothy in *The Wizard of* Oz, my life had turned from black and white to Technicolor. I even had my own wizard. Her name was Dona Mathilde.

Images of my forbidden childhood in Brazil come tumbling up from the depths within me. I close my eyes and sink into them. After being kept locked away for so long, it feels as comfortable as a warm bath.

It is six months since I've arrived in Rio de Janeiro. Dona Mathilde thinks my Portuguese is good enough for me to observe my first séance. I hurriedly pull on a pair of jeans and a T-shirt as members of Dona Mathilde's Spiritist society arrive. They are eight in all. They mill around the mahogany table, then take their seats. I'm not allowed to sit at the table because Dona Mathilde thinks I'm not strong enough to hold my own amongst the spirits, so I perch on a chair in the corner of the dining room, cuddling my knees to my chest and resting my chin on them.

Dona Mathilde walks to the head of the table and asks everyone to close their eyes. Then she prays to God, explaining that a local has taken ill. His doctor can't find anything wrong with him. His wife is worried. They need help.

Everyone closes their eyes and places their hands, palms up, on the table in front of them. Suddenly, a current sweeps through the room, causing the people seated at the table to sway, as if in a breeze. One of the men—a mild-mannered lawyer with a mustache—pushes his arms out in front of him and shouts *Idiotas*!

Dona Mathilde opens her eyes. "Who are you?"

I look at the lawyer. Although he is speaking, his eyes remain closed. But it's the way he holds his features. It's like someone else is using his body to speak, and this spirit, or soul, is angry. I'm amazed as I hear him spit, "You think you're something special, don't you?"

Dona Mathilde tilts her head, as if she is listening to something only she can hear. She pauses and asks, "How did you die?"

His words explode like a shotgun. "I'M—NOT—DEAD!"

I glance at the others. Heads bowed, mouths and arms relaxed, they remain with their eyes closed like open vessels. His aggression flows right through them.

Dona Mathilde's voice brings me back to the present. "What happened?"

The moment she asks the lawyer this question, the man's face

16

becomes blank. "I was driving a car. There was a loud noise. And then everything went black."

I rub my eyes. I now understood what Dona Mathilde meant when she said I wasn't ready to sit at the table. I hadn't expected a séance to be a democratically open forum for any soul to pass through—especially ones who didn't know that they were dead. *How could he not know he was dead?* I rack my brain for an answer. *I bet it was a car accident.*

Dona Mathilde keeps her eyes glued on the man. "Open your eyes. There is a tunnel, and at the end there is a very bright light. Can you see it?"

The man wags his head back and forth. "There's nothing out there."

Dona Mathilde continues to talk, her voice even and low. "Walk toward the light. This will help you. Walk toward the light."

He won't do it, so Dona Mathilde stops talking and sighs. She drops her head, then simply, but with authority, asks the soul to leave.

With a sharp movement, the man's head drops forward, and the spirit is gone. I'm still staring at the man for the longest time, trying to understand what is now different, when another soul comes in and enters the body of another person sitting at the table. However this time, it is easy to see that this soul is an old man.

"And who are you?" Dona Mathilde asks.

The man gives a gentle laugh. "Ai-yai. It didn't matter much who I was when I was alive, so it doesn't matter now that I'm dead."

Although the owner of the body is cultured, this spirit isn't. He speaks like an illiterate Brazilian, dropping consonants and adding others where they don't belong.

"I was a *faxineiro*," he says. "A street sweeper. I suppose you could call me the street sweeper of the skies." He laughs at his joke, then stops, as if he doesn't want to be disrespectful. "I don't want to take up too much of your time. I wasn't good with words when I was alive, and I'm not any better now." He pauses. "That soul is in pain. I just wanted you to know I'll keep an eye on him."

Dona Mathilde smiles. We all smile. "*Obrigada*. Thank you."

17

"You are doing a good job," he adds. "God bless you all."

I want to hug him. But he is gone, as light and airy as the wind. After a short moment, a third spirit arrives, one who had been a doctor in a previous lifetime and enters the body of one of the women sitting at the table. He states the ill man has something wrong with his liver. It's not serious, but it will take time to heal.

Dona Mathilde finishes the séance with a prayer. Everyone opens their eyes, and the maid comes in with steaming cups of *cafezinhos* and plates of pound cake with condensed milk frosting. It is as normal as a town hall meeting.

Brazil taught me that a person's body and a person's soul are two separate entities. While a person is on this earth, the soul wears a meat suit, as Native Americans call it. It is a good idea to take care of a meat suit, feed it well, give it plenty of sleep, wash and bathe and adorn it because it is home on earth. And listen to it. Especially listen to it because it holds a lot of wisdom in those old bones. *The wisdom of the ages is inside you*, Dona Mathilde used to say. *All you need to do is go within.*

Bouquets from well-wishers and friends arrive throughout the day. Many of the flowers and cards come from people I have never heard of. Clearly, Eugen has made as much of an impact on others' lives as he has made on mine. Each bouquet, each card, each telephone call brings a fresh flood of tears.

The rest of the day doesn't progress in a linear, normal fashion, but shapes itself against the emotions that rise in my breast. I see Eugen everywhere I look. I wander from window to window, try to take a nap and fail, open and close drawers, bring pieces of his clothing under my nose. The reminders of Eugen's presence—his electric toothbrush resting next to the sink, his canvas toiletries bag hanging on the back door, his lungi folded next to the shower, call out to me of a life that is no more. I lie on the bed and wrap my arms tightly around myself, rocking like a baby. *I'll get over this*, I keep repeating. But deep down, I know I'm lying.

For as long as I can remember, I had harbored the dream of meeting my prince charming. My longing was so strong that when I met Pat Rodegast, a well-respected medium, I asked her precisely this question. To my surprise, she said yes, and described him: six inches taller than me, dark hair, good looking, sharp features. At the end of my session, she placed her card in my hands. "I am going to give you my address," she told me. "I have never seen such a clear picture of a person who will be your mate this life. When you meet him, let me know."

Her words burned into my heart. I waited for years, but nothing happened. So then, when Eugen walked into my television studio in London, I knew it was him. After all those years of waiting, I had found my prince at last.

I had already moved from London to Vienna by the time Eugen discovered that Vandana, his ex-wife, was dying of cancer. Eugen had to be there for Vandana *and* me, something neither of us handled well. Those difficult years broke us apart, then brought us back together even more deeply than before.

Transitioning from career journalist to chatelaine wasn't as easy as I had hoped it to be. It was me who came up with the idea to replenish the family's dwindling financial resources by transforming the ground floor of the palace into an art gallery. This is how Eugen presented our India trip to his mother: a buying trip to acquire furniture for the gallery. Our trip to India was both romantic and pragmatic. That was just like us: I was the pragmatist, Eugen, the romantic. He was a gentleman in the true sense of the word. A gentle man.

I open my eyes with a start. I must have fallen asleep. I leap out of bed, not understanding why I am alone, and when I remember, I drop onto the bed again with my head in my hands. I don't know how I do it, but by the time Lucy knocks at the door, I am washed, dressed, and perfumed, wearing a flowing white gown with a white shawl around my shoulders.

We give each other a teary hug, then walk down the corridor. "The news report of Eugen's death has moved hearts everywhere," she tells me. "So be prepared."

"For what?"

As we walk into the lobby, a doorman, wearing white gloves and a turban with a tail trailing down his back like a long white snake, opens the door and a blast of warm air hits me. I squint into the darkness. In front of me, dozens of women are singing and clapping. When they see me, their movements intensify.

"They have been pouring into the hotel grounds all day," Lucy explains as we stand on the steps, staring at the scene in front of us. I feel like I've landed in a Bollywood movie.

"Please Ma'am," the doorman says. "Leave your shoes here. I will arrange to have them delivered to your room."

Removing my sandals, I hand them to him, give Lucy a hug, put my hands in the prayer position and walk down the steps. The petals underneath my tired feet feel soft and forgiving. When I reach the last step, the women separate, creating a pathway. As I walk through them, hands caress my arms, my face, my back.

It feels as if I am entering a birth canal. With each touch of a hand, with each caress, I feel that something is happening within me. I am no longer one woman in pain, I'm all women in pain. The pain is so deep it hurts to breathe. And yet it feels as if a salve is being applied to my wound, transforming it into something greater than myself. And it is because of these women. We don't know each other and yet we do. We are living from that place within ourselves where love meets pain. I understand, with each step, you can't have one without the other.

By the time I reach the private guest suite where Eugen's body lies, I'm a woman I don't recognize. A woman accepting all that is being given to her. Even death. I walk up flower-strewn steps and arrive at a door. On either side, bronze bowls with floating white rose petals grace the entrance. I open the door and step inside.

Everything is bathed in candlelight. Sticks of incense waft long smoky spirals in the corners. The atmosphere is so thick I feel like I could swim in it. There, on the bed, as if on a dais, is Eugen. Dressed in a white sheet and laid out as if he is in state, the body has been oiled, the hair washed, the blood scrubbed away.

I sit on a chair and put my hands on my lap, rubbing one thumb over the other, just as Eugen used to do. Hours pass. Sometimes, when the candles flicker just so, I delude myself for one brief second into thinking that he's sleeping. Any minute, he'll open his eyes and sit up, and we'll laugh about what a pickle we've gotten ourselves into. But I know that my eyes are playing tricks on me. Those eyes won't look upon anyone ever again.

When the night turns darkest, I wrap myself in my shawl, overwhelmed by drowsiness. My eyelids, as heavy as drapes, drop, and I fall into a place where I'm neither awake nor asleep. I'm aware of my breath, the gentle hum of the air conditioner, and a presence I can only describe as angelic. The night passes, and when I open my eyes again, it is over. I put my hand on his and feel his skin, now cold. The Eugen I know is no more.

The first fingers of dawn are spreading across the sky by the time I leave the room. I close the door quietly and step into the garden. The light is a pinkish hue; the smell of morning dew is in the air. The candles have gone out, and the women in white have left. In the distance, I hear golf buggies and people chatting, and I know that these are the tourists leaving the hotel on their way to the Taj. It's hard to believe that Eugen and I were among them just yesterday.

Making my way through the gardens back to the hotel, a plethora of conflicting emotions washes away the last vestiges of inner turmoil. Eugen may be dead, but he still lives in my heart. And there he will remain for the rest of my life. With that realization firmly within my breast, I trudge back into the land of the living.

The train to Varanasi rocks from side to side, slows down with a long sigh, and then, with a shudder, is off again. Lucy and I are facing a man with kohl-lined eyes who is talking to a young man wearing a light beard. Both men are dressed in white cloth. One piece is wrapped around the waist, another around the shoulders. A long, thin white thread loops over one shoulder and crosses their chests. Their foreheads are smeared with thick streaks of sandalwood.

They are poor Brahmins, Lucy tells me. They earn their living by officiating at the many rituals common in India: births, marriages, coming of age. And death. Especially death. This is probably why they are on this train. Varanasi is India's city of death.

Just then, Lucy's phone starts to vibrate. As she picks it up and begins to talk, I turn to look out the window. A man is driving a moped while his wife, saffron sari blowing in the wind, sits sideways on the back with a baby in one arm. A child balances between the handlebars. A solid mass of cars weaves easily around them, like a river flowing around a stone.

I now understand why Eugen loved it here. Our world may be cleaner, but there is a vibrancy here that is sorely lacking in the West. I see the glow of a field worker wrapped in scarlet, garishly painted shrines, and sunsets in hot pink and orange. Everywhere I look, people are sitting, lying, squatting, standing, running, balancing bundles on their head, weaving through traffic, always going somewhere—by foot, bicycle, car, bus, tuk-tuk, and motorbike. Trucks painted like gypsy caravans pound the road parallel to the railway tracks, each with beads dangling from rearview mirrors and plasticized images of gods and gurus flapping in the wind. Just then the train rattles to a stop. In the now-silent compartment, bits of Lucy's conversation float toward me, and I realize it has something to do with me.

She hangs up the phone and collapses into her seat. "Eugen's family didn't know you were getting married, did they?"

When I shake my head she shakes her head too. "That's what I was afraid of."

Just then, Lucy's phone vibrates again. She picks it up, listens for a few seconds, then presses the mute button. "It's your mother-in-law."

She hands me the phone. Before I answer it, I rest it against my trouser leg and lower my voice. "You did send the ashes to Vienna, right?"

She nods. "They received the package this morning."

"And they were put in an urn just like the one we have?"

"Identical." Her eyes scrunch together. "Are you sure you're up for this?"

I nod, then take a deep breath, and place the phone on speaker. "Maria Eugenia, how are you?"

Her voice is so loud it blares from the phone like a bull horn. "How do you expect me to be when I have just learned you had my son cremated?"

I quickly take it off speaker and press the phone to my ear. *Stepson,* I think, but some things are best left unsaid. I gaze out the window, trying to find the calm I had only a few minutes ago. "I was following his wishes."

"What do you know about his wishes?" she snaps. "His body should have been returned to Vienna to be buried in our family crypt."

I consider several responses before deciding that the truth is the best. "But you have the ashes."

She speaks as if she didn't even hear me. "Ashes? Ashes?" Her voice raises an octave. "How dare you cremate the body! What you did is illegal. A decision like that can only be made by a member of the family."

Asserting myself with Eugen's stepmother has never been easy. "I am family."

Her laugh sounds like a bark. "You aren't going to tell me that you think that little ceremony you did at the Taj Mahal counts as anything."

Sweat drips down my back. "But the civil ceremony we performed in Delhi last week does."

She wasn't expecting that. I remember all the times I spent trying to coax Eugen into telling our wedding plans to his family. He flatly refused, and so I acquiesced. But now I want to kick myself. For our stupidity. Our naivety. Our selfishness. No matter how awful this woman is, she had the right to know that her stepson was getting married. It's this thought that gives me the courage to say what I'm about to say.

"Had I, or Eugen, known what was going to happen, we wouldn't have done what we did. Of course we should have told you. I see that now. But there's nothing I can do to change the past except to apologize and say I am sorry. I really am." Her shocked silence gives me the courage to continue. "I am his wife. Or I was, anyway. And you are my mother-in-law. We are going to have to find a way to work this out between us."

And then the screaming begins. It's just like one of my father's rages. It sounds like a combination between a banshee and a siren. Eugen always hinted at his stepmother's emotional instability, and now I see he wasn't exaggerating. Lucy watches me interject a few times, but it's pointless. She's going to scream until she's spent.

Taking the phone from my ear, I press the speaker button. Her voice, now blasting from the phone's speaker, spouts accusations and swear words so loud that everyone in our compartment looks at me. I put the phone a foot in front of my mouth.

"Hello?" my mouth says. "I can't hear you." As I speak, I push the phone farther away from me so that my voice will sound faint. "Hello, hello?" By now, I'm holding the phone as far away as I can. Then I press the button to end the call.

"It's the only way to deal with a rant," I explain, handing the phone to Lucy.

She gives me an appreciative look. "Sounds like you're talking from experience."

"I am."

Just then the train jerks, causing the passengers to sway, and, with a loud complaining screech, continues on its way to Varanasi.

The name Varanasi comes from two rivers, one called the Varuna in the north, the other the now-dry Assi in the south. In between these two rivers is a four-mile crescent less than a mile wide. This is where the ancient city lies. On one side is the city, on the other, the Ganges. Its banks are lined with stone steps leading down to the river called ghats. This is where the cremation pyres lie.

Varanasi was Eugen's favorite city in India. I remember him telling me that it is every Hindu's wish to be cremated and to have their ashes scattered over the sacred waters. I had hoped to like Varanasi, too. After all, it is the oldest continually inhabited city in the world. But nothing prepares me for what I see.

In Varanasi, death isn't mourned, it's celebrated. Funeral pyres burn continuously. Standing on one of the ghats, overlooking the Ganges, a constant smudge of orange flames and the smell of putrefying flesh makes me want to throw up. All around me are religious rituals, hair-cutting ceremonies, funeral ceremonies. Mourners in white-peaked Nehru caps. Cows wander amongst the pyres. Children snap selfies with their departed grandparents who are carried in bike rickshaws through the warren of sunless streets. But it's the bodies that bother me most. They line the ghats. Float in the river. Are lifted on stretchers, tottering high above the crowds like suitcases, as pallbearers maneuver their way through the crowds. Every time a bell rings in the street, another mummy-like body, covered with garlands of orange and red marigolds and wrapped in a white cloth, is carried by. There are so many bodies being cremated I can't keep track.

And all of this is happening on the banks of the same river where men in shorts wash to purify themselves.

The filth, the pollution, the heat, the deafening honking horns, the crowds of people, the smell of urine, chip away at my boundaries. I feel every bone in my body raging at God for putting me in such a situation. Only a few days ago, I was a bride experiencing the happiest day of her life. Now I'm just one more person who has come to deposit the ashes of a burnt body into a river. *What am I doing here?* I want to scream and swear at the same time.

Toward the end of the day, Lucy and I sit at the edge of the Ganges near the ghats. I can't get the images of the bodies out of my mind. It's been hard enough to accept death by spending a night with Eugen's perfumed body. But to witness this casual acceptance of death is more than I can bear. I rub the skin on my arm, and when I pull my fingers away, I see the skin is gray. I look at Lucy questioningly.

"It's ash," Lucy says.

"From where?"

She points to the ghats.

I want to crawl out of my skin. "This is human ash?"

Lucy gives a weary sigh. "It happens every time I'm here."

I close my eyes and try to think of something, anything, but the reality in which I find myself. Dust to dust. Ashes to ashes. Is this what life is all about? To end up scattered on some dirty river? Everywhere I look I see Kali, the black-faced, tongue-lolling goddess, taunting me.

Life isn't fair, she whispers. There's no love here. There's no beauty here either. I gaze at an old woman wearing a dirty white sari. One bony hand is stretched out, palm up, in the universal sign of begging. Her eyes are clouded with cataracts. Her forehead is smeared with white paint.

"She's a Varanasi widow," Lucy says, taking her sunglasses off. "They come from all over India to live at ashrams here."

"But why?"

"When a woman's husband dies, her life becomes meaningless."

"So she comes here?" I say, turning to gaze at the woman. "Willingly?"

"It's the only place that will accept her." She opens her purse and pulls out a wad of rupee bills. "Animals are treated better than most women in India." She peels off a few bills and hands them to the woman, who slips them into her sari so fast it's almost as if nothing happened.

"But what about their families? Their children?"

Lucy fiddles with the clasp of her purse. "They are often the ones who expel them."

I stare at the woman. She was once a daughter, a wife, a mother, even a grandmother. She should be with her family. I feel something stir within me. My chest is so tight I can hardly breathe. It's rage. Rage to see a society mistreat a woman whose only crime is to have blind trust in her family. They should be taking care of her, making her last days comfortable. Instead, she is on a ghat, overlooking the river where one day she, too, will be scattered.

"How did our world become so misogynistic?" I whisper.

The woman lifts her hand toward me, cupped upward. I bend down to eye level and place my hand on her cheek. Her skin is remarkably soft. She looks up and our eyes meet.

I expect to see sadness. Despair. A mournful resignation. I expect to see—myself. A widow whose life has no more meaning. Instead, her eyes shine like the sadhu. Her serenity jars me out of my anger and self-pity. It tells me that there is something more here that I am not seeing. If she can do it, I think, getting wearily onto my feet, so can I.

It is dusk. The sun is a golden marble resting in a tangerine-colored evening sky. I'm standing on the shores of India's holiest river, listening to melodic chanting punctuated by dozens of low, haunting calls from conch shells. The otherworldly sounds reverberate in the air. It is *aarti*, the evening fire ritual performed daily to show gratitude to Mother Ganga, which is what the Indians call the Ganges. The air still stinks. My feet squelch over paving stones that are wet with paan spittle that looks like blood. I see women washing clothes in an oily, polluted river. Tourists snapping photos. But then, watching men standing, waist deep, eyes closed and hands in prayer, lost in meditation, I can connect with something that transcends the ugliness. The devotion of the singing and the drums vibrates in every cell of my body.

I take the urn containing Eugen's ashes from Lucy. Bending on my knees, I scatter the ashes onto the river's surface, then stand up as Lucy hands me a leaf shaped into the form of a boat. Lighting a tiny candle, I place it inside. Then, as gently as holding a newborn baby, I place the boat on the waters and let it go.

The little boat floats away from me, its candle flickering like a mast in the darkness. I look through the ash, through the gray smog, and beyond to the endless muddy waters of the Ganges. My life as I know it is over. And I'm in limbo, waiting for my new one to begin.

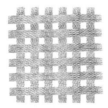

DARKNESS

Vienna

Each person comes into this world with a specific destiny—he has something to fulfill, some message has to be delivered, some work has to be completed. You are not here accidentally—you are here meaningfully. There is a purpose behind you. The whole intends to do something through you
—Osho

The heaviness of Vienna envelops me as soon as the plane lands. After weeks of living in soft silks and cottons, my sweater and boots feel heavy; the cold grayness dampens my soul. The corridors of Vienna's dreary new airport feel interminable as I make my way through the crowds.

When the automatic doors to the arrivals area whoosh open, my eyes rake the expectant faces, instinctively scanning for Eugen's shock of gray hair. But there is only an empty space where he would have been. He always insisted on picking me up at the airport if he could. It's only a fifteen-minute drive, he used to say. You moved here for me, so that's the least I can do.

I did move to Vienna to be with him. I gave up my career, too. But that was part of the package of being with someone from an old

European family. At first, like many Americans, the history and the traditions touched a romantic nerve in me. I was fascinated by it all and thought I could do my bit to help bring the family into the twenty-first century. However, it didn't take long before reality set in. The city palace and the castle in Styria lost their glamour once I realized what it cost to maintain them. I began to understand just how heavy these piles of stones weighed upon everyone, especially Eugen, who was the only male heir. Over time, experience taught me how unspoken rules held everyone in their places, and with that, I began to appreciate Eugen's ability to work with everyone in the family, including his stepmother, Maria Eugenia.

Eugen was only eight years old when his mother Magdalena died of a hornet sting while vacationing at their family hunting estate in Styria. Eight years later, a distant friend of the family, Maria Eugenia, ensnared Eugen's father Georg. Eighteen months later, Lili was born. When Georg died of what Maria Eugenia referred to as a wasting disease, it left Eugen, not yet twenty, burdened with a stepmother eight years older than him and a baby sister young enough to be his daughter.

I was still a journalist working in London when Eugen proposed marriage and I accepted it. Still, it was hard to go from Annabel Jones from CNN to become Eugen's live-in fiancée; from interviewing entrepreneurs to renovating leaky roofs; from being fiercely independent to living under the watchful eyes of a stepmother who believed families like his weren't supposed to marry foreigners like me unless they came with hefty bank accounts. Desperate to show my worth, I sank my savings into our apartment and from that moment on, Vienna became my home.

And it still is. Looking up at the large clock in the airport's main hall, I see that Christiane should be arriving any minute. Christiane moved from New York to Vienna with her Austrian husband Otto, who was working in Manhattan at the time. Otto happened to also be Eugen's lawyer, so it didn't take long for us to become fast friends.

I reluctantly leave the warmth of the airport and walk outside, only to reel backward as the icy wind hits me in the face. I stamp my feet, the air biting my lungs with each breath. Just when I'm about to go back inside, a station wagon screeches up and Christiane, bundled in layers of dark green with a bright tartan scarf wrapped around her neck, leaps out and swoops me into her arms. In the process, she drops everything she's holding: her phone, her wallet, her gloves, even her keys. One after the other they fall, making plopping noises on the frozen asphalt. As words pours out of her mouth like a waterfall—she always has some sort of excuse as to why she's late, so I don't even listen—we bend down simultaneously to pick everything up and accidentally bump heads. Startled, we catch eyes and burst into laughter. That's what we always do. Laugh. Even when we both want to cry. I fall into her arms and bury myself against her coat, letting the thick loden wool dry the wetness on my cheeks. Hugging her feels like falling into a puffy duvet.

If there is a word I could use to describe Christiane, it would be round. Her body is as plump as a melon, her face is shaped like a full moon, and even her hands and feet are graced with pleasant curves that make everyone want to snuggle her. We gather Christiane's things, then spend the next few minutes trying to find room in the trunk for my bag. As she shuffles canning jars, cooking magazines, newspapers, gardening gloves, grocery bags, gumboots, umbrellas—at least three, two of which look pretty dodgy to me—she rambles on about the latest scandal at the opera house, what films are showing at the cinema, and the new exhibitions in Vienna's Museum Quarter. I know what's she's doing. She's trying to distract me the only way she knows how: with conversation. By the time we get underway, my ears are stuffed with words and my fingers are so cold I can barely buckle myself in. Teeth chattering, I slide down in the seat and put my hands under my legs to warm them.

"We're going to Attersee," Christiane says, as the car speeds up. "Otto is away skiing, so we've got the chalet to ourselves." She bites her lip when she sees the dismay on my face. "It wasn't my idea. The palace has had an infestation of rats. It's being fumigated over the holidays. Lili sent Darinka by with a few bags. They're on the back seat."

Glancing at the back seat, I see two large suitcases. Attached to their handles are labels in Darinka's large block handwriting.

"I assume she's gone home to Bratislava?" I stretch my legs in front of me and hear a tinny rattle from a soda can rolling about under my feet.

"With her family. She was in a horrible state when I told her the news." She gives a sideways glance. "So was I."

I stuff the can into the side pocket. "How is Maria Eugenia taking it?"

She overtakes a truck ten times our size with a naughty glint in her eye. "A perfect show of mourning at the funeral. You should have seen it. There she was, shrouded in the finest black lace, surrounded by her circle of sycophants, the perfect mother in mourning."

"Stepmother," I correct.

"Funny how she forgets this minor point when it doesn't suit her. She's only eight years older than Eugen is, for Christ's sake. And then there was Lili, hiding away in the corner, crying her eyes out."

Just thinking of Eugen's younger sister makes me feel as if I'm melting. "Poor Lili. Eugen was her only sibling. She must be devastated."

Christiane shrugs. "I have to admit her tears looked genuine. I can't tell you how angry I was to hear Maria Eugenia insinuate it might have been your fault."

My head whips in her direction. "My fault?"

"You know how she does it. A simple gesture. The rolling of eyes. She is the mistress of insinuation."

Just the mention of Maria Eugenia's name makes my stomach knot. "You know I had the body cremated."

"Ooohhh, yes," she says, stretching out the words. "That information was made perfectly clear. His funeral urn was placed in great ceremony in the family crypt."

"*One* of the funeral urns," I say. When she gives me a curious look, I add, "The crematorium in India prepared two. One with the real ashes and the other with, well, ashes." I flash her a guilty look. "Don't ask me who got which."

Christiane covers her mouth, but she can't help herself and lets out a giggle.

"Glad to see you still have some spunk left in you. What a dreadful family. Eugen was the nicest of the lot. He must have taken after his father. Or his mother; what was her name?"

"Magdalena," I say.

"Apparently she was lovely. How Georg could have gone from her to Maria Eugenia is beyond me. But my God, that woman can move mountains when she wants to. You should have seen how she browbeat the entire city to attend the funeral. People came in from all over Europe."

I pull my earlobe. "Did you have to go?"

"I could hardly not go. Otto made sure of that. Bloody freezing it was, too." Christiane shifts the gears. "Now close your eyes and get some sleep." She reaches over and pats my leg. "Remember. Never fear, girlfriends are here."

The following morning, I wake before dawn. Even before I open my eyes, I feel them: tiny bubbles pouring into my head and down into my body. This has been happening every morning since Eugen died. Dona Mathilde, who knew about these things, told me not to worry when this happens, because it's just my energy returning into my body.

According to Dona Mathilde, our energy, or souls, leaves our bodies at night. It returns the moment the body awakes. That's what the effervescent bubbles are: my energy is returning to my body.

I didn't believe her until early one morning in Vienna a few years ago. Eugen and I had separated and I was opening the drawers of my soul, pulling out everything that I had inside me and examining it. It's hard work, uncovering the unconscious patterns and dynamics that run one's life. I was so miserable that all I wanted to do was lie back and sleep, which is why I crashed into bed late at night. I was lying on my back, my eyes closed, just about to fall asleep, when I felt myself floating upwards. I was moving so fast that my mind screamed, *Watch out, we're going to hit the ceiling!* But the moment this thought appeared, I was back in my bed again. Under the duvet. With my eyes closed. I pulled my hands from under the covers as my mind went round in circles, trying to figure out what had just happened. Finally I came to the only conclusion possible.

I am not my body. I can't be, or else I wouldn't have felt myself floating up to the ceiling. I had even looked down and seen my body falling asleep under the covers. The experience was so odd I wrote it all down in my dream book. It's a good thing, too, because the next morning, when I read what I had written, I was shocked to discover my mind had erased the entire episode from my memory. If I hadn't written it down, I would never have remembered it.

This was when I began to understand that my mind is not a friend on the journey to becoming self-aware. Eugen was right: the mind is an excellent servant but a terrible master. Memories of Eugen coddle me as I yawn and sit up in bed. After the long flight from India, I'm feeling disembodied. Placing my feet on the floor, I wait until I can feel the ground through the soles of my feet, then slowly get up.

Wrapping myself in a bathrobe, I make a cup of tea and curl up on the sofa, gazing mindlessly into the inky night. Christiane's home, a converted farmhouse on Attersee, or Lake Atter in English, is in my opinion one of the most beautiful spots on earth. In front of me is a hillside covered by an eiderdown of snow. Far below, the lake snuggles against the mountain, wearing a forest of fir trees like the edging on a granite coat.

The mug warms my hands as I watch the Big Dipper fading into the horizon. This constellation has meant so many different things to different peoples. *How much of what we believe to be reality is myth*, I think. Since time began, we have been making up stories to explain the unknown.

Death. It's the final unknown. It's not a comma, or even a semicolon. It's a full stop. The life of Eugen von und zu Vasoy is over. Underneath his portrait hanging in the atrium of the Palace Vasoy will be a small brass plaque inscribed with two dates: born and died. To see a life bookended like that—he was just fifty-two, for goodness' sake—feels so wrong. If I had thought things were difficult in India, it was nothing compared to what Austria's going to be. Eugen was a man with so much presence that his absence will be screaming at me for years to come. I put my cup down and head to my room to get dressed. A walk will do me good.

The sun is hovering above the horizon by the time I make it out the door. Slipping on my gloves, I begin to walk, my breath floating like a dragon's tail in the air. Down I go, snow crunching underfoot, past the fields and the farms nestled like toy houses in the nooks of the valley. By the time I reach the lake, the mist has risen, the water sparkling like a coat of diamonds. As my muscles warm up, my stride gets longer, my breathing more regular.

I'm just about to turn back when a muffled roar cuts into my awareness. In the distance, a tiny speck is coming my way. As it gets bigger, I see it's a car, so I stand by the side of the road to let it pass. Instead, it slows and the window glides down.

"A lift, madame? We've got *Topfengolatsche* pastries, fresh from the baker."

A man's hand dangles a paper bag out the opened window. Squinting in the sun's rays, I look at the driver. He has freshly shaven cheeks and black hair brushed back to reveal a high forehead. He takes off his sunglasses and flashes me a smile.

I blink, not believing who is in front of me. "Jean Luc?" My lips are so cold I can barely get the words out.

Before I can say anything more, the passenger door flies open, and out pops Chloe. She rushes around the front of the car, a long taupe cashmere sweater floating behind her, and throws herself into my arms. At that moment, the sun streaks across the fields, showering the car with its rays, and for the first time in a long while, I feel its warmth against my bruised soul.

Soon we're back in the chalet, stamping our feet and hanging up our coats and scarves before following the aroma of freshly brewed coffee into the kitchen. We find Christiane, wrapped in a blue bathrobe and matching furry slippers, bustling amongst the pots and pans of last night's dinner. She fluffs the foam in a pot of steamed milk with one hand while stirring a pan of scrambled eggs with the other. Putting the wooden spoon down, she hands me a cup of hot cocoa.

"Do you like your surprise?"

"You knew they were coming?" It's a stupid question, I know, but I can't help it.

"Knew they were coming? I organized it," Christiane says, picking up the spoon again. "Behind this chaos lies a creative mind."

She waves the spoon in the air to indicate where I can sit, but it isn't easy. Every possible space is covered with clutter: empty Nespresso capsules; rolls of wrapping paper, ribbons, and tape; CDs; a broken cup with the handle and a tub of super glue resting inside; bottles of dried spices; even a bowl with turmeric and ginger roots long past their sell-by dates.

"She was the one who invited us," Chloe says as she watches Christiane open a cupboard and pull out two cups. "As we're heading to Kitzbühel, it's right on the way."

She holds the cups while Christiane pours coffee into them, then takes them in one hand and pulls me into the sitting room.

Just then, Jean Luc walks in and drops three bunches of roses on the dining room table. "Gifts for the three graces," he says, pulling off his ski jacket. "The pink ones are for Christiane, the white ones for Annabel, and the red roses," he says, walking over and kissing Chloe on the back of her neck, "are for my wife."

Not many men would dare to bring roses to three women, but that's Jean Luc. I frown when I see Chloe raise a suspicious eyebrow. "Trying to soften me up, are you?"

Christiane, who has just walked in from the kitchen with a tray of glasses, places them on the table. "Chloe, just say thank you." She scoops up her flowers in her arms and buries her nose in the petals. "So this is what it feels like to receive roses."

Chloe looks up sharply. "Doesn't Otto give you flowers?"

"You've got to be kidding." Christiane places the roses on the table, then disappears into the never-never land of clutter under the table. For a second, all we can see are her furry slippers, then an arm appears and she passes up three glass vases.

"Every man knows women love flowers," Jean Luc answers, taking the vases from her and helping her off the floor. He pulls a piece of fluff from her hair.

"French men maybe," Christiane says, dusting herself off as Jean Luc throws the fluff in the waste basket under the table. "But not Austrians. Because Otto doesn't like food, I eat for the both of us." She tightens the belt around her robe and retreats into the kitchen.

Chloe watches her leave, then places her roses inside a vase, arranging the tallest, most closed buds in the middle.

"Go on," I say to Chloe. "Be nice for once."

She looks guilty. "I'm not being rude, I'm being firm." Then, like a sleek panther, she throws herself in his arms and covers him with kisses. "The truth is, I hate being apart. You can't make love to roses, you know."

"I wouldn't even try," Jean Luc says, running a hand through her hair. "But sometimes those thorns of yours can draw blood."

As I pick up my roses, I spot a small card resting amongst the petals. Pulling it out, I read, "Love is timeless. Death does not separate the Lover from the Beloved." Roses. They have always meant something to me, ever since Eugen and I smelled roses when we first hugged. It blew my mind, smelling roses where there were none, but Eugen explained to me that what was happening was a siddhi. It was one of my senses extending far behind the accepted norms. The one thing I never understood, however, is why it happened. For a second, I close my eyes, willing the rising tide of tears inside me to descend again. It doesn't work. Out it comes, welling up over my eyelids and dripping in rivulets down my cheeks.

Jean Luc pulls a tissue from his pocket and dabs my eyes. "Khalil Gibran has a better way with words than I ever will."

I take the tissue from him, blow my nose, and throw it away in the waste paper basket. Then, placing my roses in a glass vase, I walk into the kitchen to fill it with water, then return to the sitting room. "So

37

how is San Francisco?"

Jean Luc is helping Chloe arrange the flower vases under the windowsill. "I'm loving it," he says, glancing at Chloe. "I only wish I had my wife by my side."

"Compromise is part of marriage," Christiane says as she walks in, her arms full of cups and saucers. "I had to give up my job when I came here to marry Otto." She motions for us to sit down. "Let's eat."

"You see?" Jean Luc says as he pulls out a chair for me, then helps Chloe sit down. "They made it work."

As usual, Christiane has prepared a feast. There is freshly squeezed orange juice, bowls of yoghurt and muesli, slices of tangy sourdough which jostle in a basket of puffy rolls with stars cut into their faces. As Chloe arranges the platters on the table, Christiane makes one more round into the kitchen and returns with a platter of scrambled eggs and grilled slices of bacon in one hand and a bowl of mushrooms in the other. Most of the chopped parsley she sprinkles on the eggs floats onto the tablecloth.

Soon the noise of people eating fills the room. Even though the food is delicious, I'm having a hard time swallowing. Everything keeps getting stuck in my throat. Pushing my plate away, I begin the laborious and painful process of recounting the story of Eugen's death. It takes me over a half an hour, umpteen tears, and a box of tissues to do it. When I finish, everyone's emotions are running so high that no one can find any words. A hush descends upon the table.

Finally, Chloe breaks the silence by pushing my plate in front of me. "Eat."

I look down at my plate as if it is a foreign object. "I can't. I'm not hungry." I push it towards Christiane and change the subject. "How's your diet coming?"

Christiane spears a piece of bacon from my plate. "Let's not mention the war."

I tilt my head. "Did you make an appointment to see Mildred?"

She turns the bacon this way and that as if deciding how to eat it. "I tried, but she told me my body was too hot and sweaty to work on." She finally breaks it in half and puts the entire piece in her mouth. "It wasn't my fault that I was running late. I couldn't find a parking place anywhere."

Jean Luc finishes his coffee and puts the cup down. "Mildred? Isn't she the Filipina healer you work with?"

I nod. "One of Vienna's greatest secrets. I've got an appointment next week. I can make one for you if you wish."

Christiane wipes her mouth with her napkin. "I can't afford such a luxury."

I wonder if Christiane realizes that the thick padding of fat around her chest is what the Austrian psychiatrist Wilhelm Reich called body armor. Inches thick, it's how her body protects her sensitive heart. Then again, I wouldn't mind a little padding around my heart right now. My body aches so much it hurts. I put my head in my hands as tears flow down my cheeks like a running stream.

I hear chairs scraping. Dishes being moved out of the way. Urgent whispering. When I next look up, Christiane is pulling tissues out of a box by her side by the handful.

She twists a tissue between her fingers. "I can't imagine the pain that you're going through," she whispers, dabbing it under my eyes. "So just know I've got two shoulders you can cry on. And I've got two hands that will cook for you."

"And she's got ample kilos to share with you if you need fattening up," Chloe says, appearing out of nowhere with another box of tissues. "Dab under your eyes, too, Christiane. Your mascara is running everywhere."

Jean Luc scoots closer to Christiane. "Ignore my wife. She's forgotten her manners," he says, pulling a tissue from the box Chloe is holding. With surgical precision, he wipes away the mascara from under Christiane's eyes, then tosses the blackened tissue into the waste paper basket.

"Vienna's not the place for you right now." Chloe slips onto the bench next to Jean Luc and leans against him. "So Jean Luc and I have come up with an idea. We both think you should go to California."

I run a hand through my hair. "To do what?"

"Well, for one, to keep me company," Jean Luc says. "You need time to heal. And California is a great place to do it." Jean Luc's eyes begin to shine. "Besides. I've met someone who may be able to help you. An underground shaman."

I'm not even sure what a shaman does, but I don't want to get into that now. The idea of letting anyone in right now is more than I can bear. A curtain descends, cutting me off from them, from the world, from myself. "I'm fine. Really."

I feel a light pressure on my arm and look back to see Chloe's hand on it. Her wedding ring glitters in the pale winter sunlight. "Don't try to bludgeon your way through this."

"I'm not bludgeoning my way through anything," I say, shaking her off. I'm desperate to get back to my room. I'm so tired I can barely keep my eyes open. "Which reminds me." I force myself to sit up straight and turn to Christiane. "Do you have an extra set of keys to my apartment? Mine are at the bottom of my suitcase."

Christiane starts to place the plates in a pile. "Keys," she mutters, glancing at the toppling pile of paper on her desk. "I remember you gave me a spare set once."

I will myself not to place my head in my hands again. I know if I do, I'll fall asleep. "I just wish we could have gone home before coming here."

Jean Luc picks up the pile of plates and hands them to Chloe, who disappears into the kitchen just as Christiane slips under the table. After a few minutes, she appears again, a set of keys in her hand. "There is a method to my madness."

Chloe returns from the kitchen, wiping her hands on a dish towel. She sits down at the table. "I don't get it. Why didn't you go home first?"

"We would have," Christiane explains, handing me the keys. "Lili called and said the palace was being fumigated over the holidays."

Jean Luc frowns. "I didn't think anything happened in Vienna over the Christmas holidays."

Chloe throws the dish towel on the table. "It doesn't. Even banks and grocery stores are closed." She stares at Christine. "And yet home fumigation services are working normally?"

Christiane nods, but as she does, I can see that she, too, realizes something is up. For a moment, the only thing is the sound of Chloe's nails drumming on the table.

Jean Luc comes from behind me and gently rests his hands on my shoulders. "Annabel, *chérie*. Who else has a set of keys?"

I think for a moment. "Darinka. The concierge. And Maria Eugenia." Then the realization hits, and a bolt of lightning goes through me. I leap up so fast from the table I nearly take the tablecloth with me. "I've got to get back to Vienna. And pronto."

As soon as Chloe and Jean Luc leave, Christiane and I are in the car, racing back to Vienna. By the time we arrive, it's midnight. As Christiane's station wagon idles on the street, the solid green gate opens with an ominous creak. Passing through an entrance, two large stone Atlas figures, their muscular arms shouldering the heavy masonry, throw flickering shadows upon us. Christiane maneuvers the car into the courtyard and even before she parks, I've jumped out and am running up the steps, taking two at a time, while pulling the elusive keys from my purse.

Heaving open the great, two-story door, the entrance hall envelops me as if I'm an inconsequential ant. Running up the massive marble staircase, I hear the door shut behind me with a dull thud.

On the third floor, I unlock the door to my apartment with shaking hands. Fumbling in the dark along the edge of the wall, my fingers find the light switch and I flick it on. I blink, not wanting to believe what my eyes are telling me. There are no carpets on the floor. No paintings on the wall. No furniture filling the massive rooms. The bathroom, our bedroom, the library, the office, the guest bedrooms— all are as empty as an abandoned warehouse.

Silently I tiptoe through the empty rooms, hoping against hope to find something, anything, to indicate that this was my home. I am still wandering from room to room when I hear a sound behind me. It's Christiane. She is as pale as a ghost.

41

"What the —" Christiane begins.

As Christiane whips out her phone, I feel like I'm tumbling into oblivion. My purse drops—*bang!*—on the floor. I look at it, not understanding how it got there. My entire body is shaking. The room begins to spin as my legs buckle underneath me and the floor comes rushing up to meet me with a bump. I am still on the floor, staring into space, when Christiane comes rushing over.

"Eugen always tried to shield you from his family. But now that he's gone, prepare yourself. The knives are out."

"But where will I go?" I whisper as Christiane helps me up.

"I'll tell you exactly where you will go," Christiane says, putting an arm around me. "From now on, my home is your home." She feels as solid as mother earth. Leaning my head on her shoulder, she inches me, step by step, to the door. Out into the icy foyer we go, then make our way down the marble steps, our footsteps clattering into the emptiness around us. At the bottom, Christiane glares at a painting of a Vasoy ancestor sitting pompously in a gilded frame on the landing. When she looks at me, her eyes are glittering with anger. "Now let's get out of here before I rip one of their damned ancestor portraits to shreds."

I wake up to silence. In Vienna, the city of music, even stillness is loud. The hush pervades the ancient stone walls, ricochets along the cobblestone streets, permeates the slumbering serenity that heralds the beginning of the year. I open my eyes to see floor-to-ceiling bookcases crammed with books and magazines. A desk under a massive window overlooking the Belvedere gardens. A pull-out sofa, which is where I'm sleeping. I'm in Christiane's library-cum-guest room. As my memories of the past twenty-four hours come flooding into my consciousness, I remember why. With a sinking heart, I realize that my territory, which only a few weeks ago was a loving husband, a beautiful home, and an exciting future, has been reduced to two suitcases, a sofa bed, and five hangers on a coat rack.

I'm still groggy as I take a bath, then I retire to my room to put what is left of my life in order, while Christiane goes shopping for food. But it's no good. After thirty minutes of trying to squeeze my clothing between piles of books, papers, staplers, business cards and the largest collection of old computer cables I have ever seen, I give up. Trying to unpack feels like trying to build a house in quicksand. Every time I make a neat tidy pile, the clutter absorbs it.

I collapse on the still unmade bed. I'm too irritated to sit still, too exhausted to sleep, and too angry to speak to anyone, especially someone I love. Anger is one of the emotions I always find challenging. It has taken me years to be able to move beyond the comfortable position of family pacifier to see that I was afraid of anger, and it has taken even longer to express it responsibly. Thrusting my feet into my boots, I grab my coat and hat and run down the stairs and into the street.

Outside, the cold air on my cheeks feels good. My feet wander the streets, hoping to find their way to somewhere that will help orient me in a future that is empty. I cross a massive square with statues heralding a war victory, walk along a curved pedestrian street lined with shops and cafés, and before I know it, I'm standing in the one place I knew I was heading all the time.

Herr Dietmayer's *Trafik*, one of Vienna's hundreds of newspaper shops that dot every street corner, is a hole in the wall, barely large enough for two or three people to stand inside. Opening the narrow glass door, a bell tinkles, and I walk in.

Although the shop is crammed with newspapers and magazines, the atmosphere is congenial and warm. Other Trafiks smell of stale tobacco, but everything in this one seems different, more alive. I breathe in a citrusy smell and see a basket of fresh lemons on the countertop and hear the strains of the famous waltz *Wiener Blut* floating in the air.

Standing behind the counter, a squat Buddha-like man with a balding head and kind eyes is cutting a ribbon from a pile of newspapers with a quick upper movement of his Swiss army knife when he sees me.

"Annabelchen! You're back." He hands me a copy of my favorite

43

newspaper. "It's on me."

I shake my head.

He stops speaking and looks at me, really looks at me. His eyes rest on my face, my hodgepodge of clothing, the sadness in my eyes, and he nods. "So it's true." Reaching under the countertop, he lowers the music. "Lock the door. You need a cup of tea."

In all of Vienna, it is only here, in this newspaper temple stand, that I can let my guard down. I've known Karl since I arrived in Vienna, first as a newspaper seller, then, as a source of common sense and wisdom, and lastly as a spiritual teacher. He's an underground wise man that professes to sell magazines, but in truth gives away so much more. As I lock the door, he busies himself under the counter and appears with two steaming mugs of tea, each with a stick of cinnamon in it. Pieces of lemon peel, cut in the shape of stars, float on top.

"Lemon balm, melissa, and mint," he says. "Good for those who are concerned about the radical changes in their life and not knowing what will happen in the future."

"That's me in a nutshell," I say, as I remove my coat.

Karl pulls two chairs out from behind a niche in the wall and opens them so that we can sit facing each other. I reach up to take the cups from the counter as Karl eases himself down on a chair. I give him his tea and we gaze into our cups, taking little sips as we listen to the music. I appreciate that he doesn't fill the air with words. I haven't been here more than a few minutes and I can already feel my blood pressure lowering.

"This reminds me of our first morning in Delhi," I say. "Eugen and I had a cup of street masala chai in these little clay cups that you break on the ground when you've finished. It's part of a tea-drinking ceremony. The chai wallah poured the tea in a creamy waterfall right into our cups without spilling a single drop." My throat chokes up so much I can't finish the sentence.

"*Bhar*," Karl says, talking so that I don't have to. "Eugen must have done his homework. It's rare for street vendors to use them anymore." He puts his mug down. "So tell me. How are you feeling right now?"

44

"Guilty," I whisper. "I feel guilty that Eugen is dead and I'm alive."

"That's part of mourning," he says. "But you know that already."

I nod. "Don't worry. I know there is nothing much you can say. I'm getting used to these silences."

He nods. "Good. So let's fill it with useful words. How's his family taking it?"

"My mother-in-law thinks I cremated the body so they couldn't have it."

"Then she doesn't know her son. Nor do they know the woman he married."

"She's got her revenge," I say. "I've come home to an empty apartment."

He sits up. "What do you mean?"

"The apartment is empty."

His face darkens. "So Eugen wasn't exaggerating when he said his family was difficult. Where are you living?"

"With Christiane and Otto."

His forehead wrinkles where his hair once grew. "So that's why your energy is short-circuiting. You looked like a firecracker when you walked in."

"Is it that obvious?"

"It is when you can see energy."

His acknowledgement of my feelings opens a door within me. I squeeze my eyes together, but it doesn't work. Hot, angry tears pour down my cheeks.

"I've never felt such anger, Karl," I say, wiping my cheek with my finger. "I'll never get through it."

He hands me a tissue. "I'm not surprised."

I purse my lips, but it's no good. "But what can I do with it?" I burst out. "I don't want to pound pillows anymore. I've done enough primal screams. And I don't want to dump my anger onto others. There's already too much unconscious anger in the world." I dab my eyes as I speak, but it's no good. The tears splash onto my lap, dribble onto the floor. I keep trying to stop them, but it seems to be a never-ending flood.

"Just feel it," Karl says.

I look at him through my tears. "And then what?"

His eyes deepen. "You can harness it to heal."

"I can't believe anger can heal anything," I say, wiping my face on my sleeve. "It certainly didn't do my family any good."

His eyes hold mine. "So let's go back there for a moment. When you were a young girl, what was the one thing you wanted more than anything else in the world?"

I think of those long, lonely days in Kansas. "To belong," I whisper. "I wanted a home. A family. And a man who loves me. And I got what I wanted, Karl. I was happy. We were happy. What was wrong with that?"

If he notices my eyes flashing with anger, he ignores it. "And now?"

I dab my eyes one last time. "I've got nothing."

"No," he says, his eyes on mine. "Examine what's left over."

Karl always does this. Asks me a question that pulls me out of my mental state. He's forcing me to look at the situation from a different viewpoint. A larger one. As the minutes pass, I feel a fury of emotional waves crash through me. At first my chest puffs up. My face twitches as thoughts come and go, some accusatory, others angry. My mouth twists and I bite my lower lip, and then something happens. My shoulders slump, allowing the anxiousness that I was holding on them to roll off like a long, gentle wave.

I sink in my chair. "I'm back with this hole inside me and I've got nothing to fill it with." My words choke in my throat. "Why did this have to happen to me?"

"For you," he says gently, taking the crumpled tissues from me and tossing them into an empty box in the corner by our feet.

I stop. "What do you mean, for me?"

"Things don't happen to you. They happen for you." Karl's eyes deepen when he sees the pain in my eyes. "All of this—me, Vienna, Eugen, his family, your past—are all here to help you do the most important thing that you can ever do in this lifetime."

"Which is?"

"To wake up, Annabelchen."

46

The way he says my name—Annabelchen, little Annabel—does it. I breathe out, and with it goes all my anger. "What do you mean, wake up?"

"Well," he says, pointing at my cup and indicating I should drink from it. "You know when you are asleep. And you wake up. It's like that. Spiritual awareness works backwards. You are only aware that you had been sleeping when you start to wake up."

Just then a man bangs on the door. Karl stands up, carefully maneuvering his prosthetic leg into place. "Do you know," he says, taking my cup from me and placing it alongside his on the shelf behind the counter, "In the twenty years since I opened this shop, people have gone from wanting to buy newspapers to looking for ways to improve their health and the health of the planet. People need tools to live a different way. They want to feel healthy, in body, soul, and spirit. Deep down everyone is feeling the call to wake up, whether they recognize it or not."

By the tone of his voice, I recognize that my time alone with him is over. I stand up and help him fold up the chairs. "So what are you going to do about it?" I ask.

Karl reaches up to adjust one of the prayer flags on the ceiling. "I'm going to open a new shop. One that doesn't rely upon selling cigarettes for a living. Besides." He lowers his arms. "I couldn't sell anything that I know is bad for people's health anyway."

He opens the countertop and slips behind it, lowers it again and takes a few lemons from the basket by the shelf. "Consider these little packages of sunshine a gift to help your body wake up, too." He wraps the lemons in a piece of used newspaper which he folds like origami. "Drink a large glass of water with a squeeze of lemon when you wake up, on an empty stomach. It'll spring clean your liver."

"Liver?"

He hands me the package. "That's where the body holds anger, by the way."

As I place it in my bag, I notice I feel lighter, as if someone has taken a heavy load off my back. I can't help giving him a look of amazement. "How do you do it?"

He gives me an innocent grin, then limps past me and, with a quick twist, opens the door. Outside, an old man wearing a felt hat and loden coat is waiting, an ancient dachshund by his feet.

"Every time I come in here, I'm upset. And every time I leave, I feel restored." Zipping up my coat, I flatten myself against the wall to let the man walk by, pulling the dog behind him. He tilts his hat in my direction and smiles and we greet each other.

"*Guten Morgan!* How is little Hansi?" I hear as Karl bends over the countertop to smile at the dog.

I take a copy of my favorite newspaper from the shelf. "This new shop. What will it be called?"

He smiles. "The Wake Up Shop." He reaches over and squeezes my hand, and before I know it I'm out the door and on my way home again.

"You want to do what?" Christiane says, with a look of horror on her face.

I take a stack of *New Yorker* magazines off the chair and hand them to her. For years Christiane has been complaining to me that she needs help with her clutter, so I might as well try. Besides, I've got to do something or I will explode. "Let's start with these. Put them in the trash."

She practically shrieks in horror. "Not my *New Yorkers!*" She takes them from me, hugging them to her chest like a baby.

"Do you really need them?" I ask gently.

"They reassure me," she cries. "Remind me of who I am." She puts them on the table. Before I know it, she's sitting on the table and pulling out her reading glasses as she flips through the pages.

I know I'm pushing up against her boundaries but I need to make a breakthrough or back off. "Those magazines aren't a protection; they are a prison."

"You don't think I've tried?" she cries, jumping up. "Of course I want to be clear of all this. But as soon as I try, a wet blanket covers me and I'm asleep before I know it."

"That's resistance," I say. "If you had parents who constantly ran over your boundaries, you had to set up defense mechanisms to protect yourself. There are breathing techniques you can learn that can help you power your way through it."

Her eyes mist. "Breathing won't work. And I'm not going to study tantra."

"Do you know what happened to me when I began tantra? Sleep. I was yawning so much I couldn't speak. My teacher thought I was hilarious." I glance at her and see she's listening, so I continue. "How would you feel if all of this was gone, and you were free? Free to do whatever you wanted to do. Who knows, perhaps finding another outlet for your cooking rather than trying to force it on the one person who doesn't care about food?"

She starts to say something, stops, wanders around the kitchen, puts her hands on her hips and opens the freezer door. "I want to eat a bagful of Snickers."

I pull her away from the refrigerator and close the freezer door. "We just need to find another way." I stop, wracking my brain to remember the exercises that I learned during all my years of breaking through my own barriers. "What do you love to do?"

A smile bursts on her face. "That's easy. Cooking."

"If you love cooking so much, why do you work in a museum?"

"Why?" She gives me a blank look. "I suppose it's because my father did. He was the most amazing collector." Her eyes start to brim with tears. She blinks furiously, but it's no good. "My mother eventually left him because of it."

This realization has destabilized her. She closes her eyes for so long I'm almost wondering if there isn't something wrong. By the time she opens them again, there is a glint in her eye I haven't seen before. "I can't bear it any longer."

I look around us. "This mess?"

She frowns. "No. Me." She looks up, takes a deep breath, wipes her hair from her forehead and gazes at the magazines. Then she picks the stack up, holds it over the trash can, and lets them go. The solid clang reverberates in the silence between us. "Let's do it," she says.

"Quick. Before I change my mind."

This is how our great clutter-buster clear-out begins. The secret to clearing, I tell her, is not to look too closely at what we're throwing out. In the beginning, I send her off to buy materials, but when she returns with industrial-size garbage bags and smelling suspiciously of chocolate, I recognize that the best thing we can do for our friendship is for her to make us lunch.

Eventually, we find our rhythm. I case out a room, Christiane flutters here and there like a nervous bird, pointing to what she wants to keep. By the next day, the apartment looks like a bomb has gone off in a paper factory. We plough ahead from dawn to dusk. In the evening, we collapse in bed, and when we wake up, we begin again. There are the occasional setbacks, such as the night when I catch Christiane in the hallway, pulling a broken saucer out of the trash. She drops it as casually as she can and looks at me as if I had caught her stealing. "Cup of tea?" she says. "I was just getting one."

From then on, I call the men from the charity shop to come twice a day, once in the morning and once in the evening. After four days we are there. One hundred and fifty industrial-size bags of clutter, sixty banana boxes, and countless meltdowns later, Christiane's apartment has grown wings.

Healing is a two-way process. I don't know who is more transformed, Christiane or me. The look on Otto's face when he opens the door makes it all worth it. I've never seen such a smile. And best of all, it's directed at Christiane.

By the time the sixth of January arrives—Three Kings Day is the official end of the Christmas holidays in Austria—I have a phone that's brand new and a body that's falling apart. My back is aching from Christiane's pull-out sofa, my arms sore from the clear out, and I haven't slept properly since Eugen's death. Thank goodness for Mildred.

Mildred is one of life's amazing characters. Under five foot tall, with jet black hair, eyes that glitter like obsidian, and vaguely smelling of Austrian pumpkinseed oil, which is what she uses when she does her energy massages, Mildred is one of Vienna's rare treasures. Most tourists come here to visit its museums, or to attend an opera, or simply to sit in a café and soak up the atmosphere, but there is also a constant stream of people who come here from all over the world to visit this tiny Filipina.

Portraits of a doe-eyed Virgin Mary and serene saints watch me as I enter Mildred's home in Hietzing, a short tram ride out of town. Within seconds, a bamboo curtain rattles and Mildred bustles out of a treatment room. She's wearing flip-flops and her habitual clear plastic apron over a cotton housedress.

"Hello hello. In here," she says, pointing to another room next to the kitchen. "Clothes off and on the table."

No words of condolence, no wishing me a happy new year. That's Mildred. Then again, not many people could manage a schedule like hers. Like today. It's eight o'clock in the morning on a major holiday and she's already seen her first patient. Mildred works all day long, seven days a week, often in twelve-hour shifts, and there is still a two-month waiting list to see her. I've met healers like this over the years, and understand them, too, thanks to Dona Mathilde.

Dona Mathilde categorized healers into two groups: there are Healers with a capital H, and then there are those who heal. Narrow and deep is how Dona Mathilde used to describe a Healer with a capital H. They do what they are born to do—heal—and nothing else. Mildred is a Healer with a capital H. They are an extraordinary lot, Healers. I've learned to ignore their private lives because they rarely have them. But I consider them to be a gift to humanity, so even if Mildred is brusque, I take it all in my stride. Her wisdom is far greater than her manners.

The treatment room is dark and as warm as a womb. Two clocks sit on the shelf, each set ten minutes earlier than the actual time, and below them, next to the shelves of cartons of massage oil and packages of paper towels, are shelf after shelf of CDs. I take my sheet from my bag—if I didn't come with it, she wouldn't see me—place it on the massage table, then slip off my clothes and lie face up on the

51

table. Within a few minutes Mildred arrives and begins to slather my body with pumpkin oil. She then pops a CD into the small portable player in the corner and out croons a French romantic song. Returning to the table, she gives my right hip a satisfied prod. "Finally. Your right hip is open." She moves my leg on its axis, tutting to herself, then places her fingers in a V and begins to massage my stomach as if her hand is a hoe and my belly is a field she wants to plough. "I have been waiting for years for this. What has happened that shocked your system?"

"Eugen died."

"What?!" No tears. No shock. Nothing but a grunt as she continues working on my internal organs, as she calls them. "No wonder you are so tight here. I can hardly get in. You are like a greased pig. How?"

"He fell down the steps of the Taj Mahal," I say, pausing as a shot of pain runs through my heart. I could swear my stomach is wanting to pull away from her hands, but I keep myself firmly on the table and breathe, trying to work with her rather than resist her.

"Hunh," she answers. "He was not like you. He couldn't take the pain."

I'm trying not to take this seemingly insensitive remark personally. "What do you know about it? He hit his neck on a step."

She pushes down on my stomach. Instantly I groan as a shiver of pain shoots up to my heart. "He could not take the pain of working with me."

"But you are the one who inflicts pain," I say, groaning as her fingers work their way up the insides of my thighs. Within seconds she is trying to coax what feels to be a rope under my skin into another position in my leg. Mildred calls these ropes energy lines, and she is busy re-aligning them so that my energy will start to flow again. I lift my head up from the table to look at her. She is working with her eyes closed.

"What are you doing now?"

"Once you have so much tension in the muscle, the muscle shrinks," she explains. "And the electrical wirings also shrink and get dry. And then, while it is shrinking, from year to year, the opening of

52

the pelvic bone here is becoming narrow."

"But how do you know this?"

She opens her eyes. "I am only telling you what I have experienced for thirty-two years. You don't need a machine to see this."

"Sometimes when you work on me, I have bruises afterwards for weeks."

"That is because you have a stubborn body," she answers, gently pushing my forehead so that my head rests back on the table again. "Do not hold your breath."

Easier said than done. I take a few deep breaths and close my eyes as Mildred's voice float over me.

"People do not understand that it is through pain that I work." She stops talking as I turn onto my back. "I take on the pain of the body when I begin to work on it. That is how I know where to go. I feel it in my heart, here." She stops and taps her heart. "I follow my feelings. That feels better, I say, so I follow wherever my fingers go to release the pain in me. So when Eugen stopped seeing me, I told him do not do this."

I sit up again. "Eugen stopped seeing you?"

She nods. "A year ago. I still have the pain in my heart, and I can do nothing about it. I cry and I cry until I can release it. It is very painful. So that is why I do not take a person back if they stop working with me. I cannot take the pain."

I hear a small explosion in my belly, Instantly, tears roll down my cheeks.

"There!" She gives a cry of satisfaction as she rubs her fingers over the same spot. Where, a second ago, it felt as if she had been trying to dig out a stone from under my skin, now this point is soft and supple.

"Good," she says. "I will stop. Your body is swelling, so it is healing."

"How do you know when a body is too tired to heal?" I ask.

"Because it will not go glug-glug when I touch it," she says, cleaning her hands with disinfectant.

"What about hopeless cases?"

Mildred pulls my sheet over me, tucking it under me as if it were the softest of eiderdown quilts. She dries her hands on a paper towel.

53

"I love hopeless cases."

"Why?"

"Nothing like thinking you are going to die to make a person open up to a new way of seeing life," she says, kissing me on the forehead. "He was not well, Annabel. Do not mourn that he died."

Before I can answer, she is off to see her next patient.

After the session with Mildred, it's time to head to the palace to meet Darinka. I feel like one of the walking war wounded as I slowly let myself in through the main gate and trudge up the grand staircase to the third floor.

The apartment is as silent as a tomb. There is no sound of Eugen whistling as he makes his morning cup of coffee, no radio playing classical music in the kitchen, no tinkling of the hot water filling the ancient radiators. Just the sound of the furnace blasting heat through the large, empty rooms. Every house has its idiosyncratic sounds and I know them all because I have lived with them here, day in and day out, for nearly a decade.

I sit on the parquet floor in our bedroom, hugging my legs with my arms, my chin resting on my knees, and stare at the emptiness around me. My mind so filled with the past that there is no room for the present. Our bed was—I turn my face slightly to the right—over there, facing the window overlooking the courtyard. Beyond the window are the steeples and onion domes of Vienna. A higgledy-piggledy patchwork of roofs stretches as far as I can see.

I listen to the trams skimming along their tracks. The birdsong in the courtyard. The call of a worker on the street below. When the bell of St Stephens begins to gong, I know it is coming up to nine o'clock. I get up and brush the dust off my jeans. Darinka will be here any second now.

I can still hear Mildred's voice. *Eugen was not well, Annabel.* It's true. My stomach gives an uncomfortable rumble that is more than just the fact that I haven't had breakfast. I'm just hitching my rucksack on my back when Darinka walks in. Her eyes are red with tears, her short blond hair is tucked in wisps behind her ears. We both look up when there is a whirring sound above us. There, high up, near the ceiling. Something is flying round and round the chandelier. It's a tiny bat.

"*Fledermaus*," Darinka says.

I watch the little black dot sweeping in concentric circles. "I've never seen a bat in here before."

"He has been here since Herr Prinz died," she says.

I gaze at Darinka with heaviness in my soul. We never talk much—I don't think she can communicate with anyone as her German isn't very good.

"*Schnell*," she whispers and waves for me to follow her out the door.

When we pass Maria Eugenia's apartment, she puts her finger to her lips.

"Prinzessin is back."

On the ground floor, instead of turning toward the main door, we double back on ourselves and go through a hidden door at the back of the building. At the end of a smaller courtyard is a long low building with tufts of weeds growing from the roof. With telltale signs of dampness and a sagging roof, this small building is the one part of the complex I always avoided.

"Are they in here?" I ask.

Darinka nods as she thrusts a heavy key in the rusty lock. A second later, I hear a click and the door opens.

We slip inside. Nearly windowless, the room is completely dark. Shapes begin to form in the gloom like gray ghosts. I hold my breath, but when Darinka snaps on the light, I see it's only my furniture, which has been covered with sheets. I lift one, then the other, and peer underneath. An entire life—gone. I remember many years ago I read Sogyal Rinpoche's book, *The Tibetan Book of Living and Dying*, and being surprised at the number of meditations on death. At the time, I remember thinking, *Who wants to do that?* If I had understood the premise of the book a little more then, I'd be having an easier time now, first with Eugen's death, and now with the death of our life together.

Darinka shakes her head, then says the only word she can find in her limited German to express what she feels. "*Katastrophe.*" She gives my hand a squeeze, then trudges with heavy steps into the courtyard and is gone.

I'm wandering through the shed, opening a drawer here, peering in a carton there, when a noise startles me. Turning my head, I look toward the door and see a person slipping through it. I would recognize that silhouette anywhere. It's Maria Eugenia.

As always, Eugen's stepmother is dressed impeccably, her blond hair, with never a strand out of place, is coiffed on the top of her head. A dark green and burgundy Hermes scarf is tied around her neck; a loden cape hangs loosely on her shoulders. There's no doubt about it; she is, and will always be, a beautiful woman. Her features are fine, her movements graceful, her skin the most wonderful shade of alabaster. Nearly sixty, she hardly has a wrinkle.

She looks like one of the family portraits of ancestors lining the staircase and is about as approachable. Maria Eugenia is the matriarch of an old European family, and she never let me forget it. No matter how well I dressed, or how hard I tried, I was, and would always be, in her eyes, a Kansas hick. Even though Eugen never admitted it, I knew she didn't like me. But I didn't realize just how much until now.

When Maria Eugenia sees me, she stops. For a moment neither of us says anything. The stillness is broken by the sound of footsteps. Behind her, Darinka appears. Her face is a deep chartreuse.

Maria Eugenia's presence is as icy as the December wind. "You," she says to Darinka, using the informal *du* instead of *Sie*, an insult since they are the same age. "Your services are no longer required. Give me your keys and leave."

Darinka gasps. The heavy keys hit the floor. I call out Darinka's name, but she has already turned and fled.

"There but for the grace of God go I," I say, watching her retreating back.

Maria Eugenia waves her hand and dismisses Darinka as easily as she would a waiter. "She's just a cleaning lady. She can get another job."

"Maria Eugenia," I begin. "We've got to pull together to get through this."

She rests a graceful hand on her hip. "How can you say that, having just returned from India. Don't you know it was the worst place for a dying man to go?"

"Dying?" Images flood my mind. His clothes hanging off him. His interminable energy flagging. The puffiness around his ankles that never went away. I hear Mildred's voice again. *He was not well.*

I hear words that make my blood run cold. "He was diagnosed with the same wasting illness his father had. It was only a matter of time."

All I can do is stutter. "But he never said anything to me. I didn't know."

She gives me a wan smile. "Makes you wonder what other secrets he may have had that you don't know about, doesn't it?"

"What do you mean by that? I loved Eugen with all my heart."

She gives a short, sharp exhale. "Did you now? So why didn't you get married here? I can't really believe you got married there anyway."

Trying to keep myself under control, I blurt out, "I'll prove it to you." I reach down to the rucksack by my feet. My fingers tremble as they undo the loops and pull out the plastic folder that holds the documents I have for Otto. I flip through them until I find what I'm looking for: our marriage certificate from New Delhi. As I hand it to her, my eyes catch hers. She turns it in her hands, raises it to the light, then runs her finger over the official stamps. Then, before I can do anything, her fingers tear it, once, twice, three times.

"No!" I cry, but it's too late. The pieces fall like teardrops onto the floor. I fall on my knees and begin to sweep up the scraps with my forearms. Dust is everywhere. On my hands and arms, my legs and shoes, on my face. I brush it from my forehead, taste it on my tongue.

For a moment, Maria Eugenia stares at me. She then slowly drops lower as if she is about to curtsy. I hear a whisper. "Do you know the only thing worse than a gold digger, Annabel?" She is so close I can feel her breath on my neck. "An unsuccessful gold digger."

Just then I hear a noise. Maria Eugenia quickly stands up, removes a handkerchief from inside her cuff and wipes her fingers on it, then pushes it up her sleeve again as she breaks into a steely smile. "Lili, darling, look who I've found here."

I look up through my disheveled hair to see Eugen's younger sister, Lili. She's wearing gumboots and a dark green jacket. Her mane of brown hair falls around her shoulders like a thick brown shawl. She stares at me as if I'm a Martian.

"Lili," I say, "Please help me. There was a terrible mistake."

Her eyes catch her mother's, and I could swear that I see Maria Eugenia give a brief shake of her head as she waves for Lili to get behind her.

Not knowing what to do, I continue to scoop the last bits of my precious certificate into my rucksack when Maria Eugenia does something bizarre. She gives me an almost motherly gaze. Moistening a fingertip with her lips and pressing it to my cheek, she turns her index finger over to show me, on the tip, a stray eyelash. "We are happy to keep your things here till the end of the year without charge. That should give you enough time to settle elsewhere. Lili, please take the keys from Miss Jones and show her the door." She then glides out of the cellar and is gone.

I start to say something, but Lili interrupts me. "How could you do this," she hisses. "Getting married and not telling us." She is so angry I can hear the tremor in her voice. She pushes a strand of hair away from her face. "To think I trusted you."

I stand up and close my rucksack with a firm pull of the strap, then swing it on my back. "I wanted to tell you. But Eugen made me promise not to."

"Don't blame my brother," she says, flipping off the light and storming out into the courtyard.

"Lili," I say again, trotting after her. In my post-Mildred state, I feel like my body is a sack of potatoes. "You can trust me."

I watch Lili press the fob and the heavy green door swings open.

She breathes out sharply. "You know perfectly well you can't trust anyone in this family. It's a rat's warren of smoke and mirrors and lies."

"Lili," I say, reaching out to touch her sleeve, but she steps back as if I were a leper.

"Please don't take this the wrong way. But the sooner you leave our lives, the better." Turning on her heels, she walks away as the gate swings shut with a shuddering, low bang.

"You look like you need a drink," Otto says, after opening the door to his office and seeing a bedraggled me in front of him. Christiane's husband is a thin, wiry man with round glasses that sit on his nose like a silver figure eight. His body straightens in military fashion and he clicks his heels in an old-fashioned *Küss die Hand*, or kiss the hand greeting, but when he raises my hand to kiss the back of it, I pull it away.

"I think I'd better wash it first," I say.

He glances at my hands, grimaces, then points me to the washroom. Inside, I splash some cold water on my face, run a brush through my hair, and when I next stand in front of him, feeling a little more refreshed, he helps me with my coat, which he hangs on the wooden coat rack by the door.

Otto used to be a partner in one of Vienna's most well-respected law firms, before taking early retirement to open his own practice with one criterion: he would only take clients he liked. To everyone's surprise, including his own, it worked. Otto has become one of the most sought-after lawyers in town. As we sit down at the mahogany table in his meeting room, he takes a bottle of sparkling water from the tray in front of him and pours out two glasses. I run my fingers through my hair before taking the glass from him.

He pulls a scrap from my hair and gives it to me. "And this was?"

I turn my rucksack upside down and we watch bits of paper floating like confetti out of it. "Our marriage certificate. I made the mistake of showing it to Maria Eugenia."

He sighs as he looks through the pieces. "This is the original, I suppose. I'm sure we'll be able to rectify this eventually."

I slump in my chair. "Does that mean I should negate everything she says?"

Otto looks up. "Such as?"

I sweep my gaze around the room, trying to manage the surge of emotion tumbling inside me. "Such as Eugen knew he was dying?"

He taps his fingers on the table for a good minute before answering. "I suspected as much," he says with a sigh. "So when Eugen mentioned he wanted to get his papers in order, I was determined to help him manage it."

"And did you?"

"You know how stubborn Eugen could be," he says, pulling a thick folder towards him. The red and white ribbon and waxed seal tell me that it is important enough to have been officially notarized. "But happily I did." He points out the standard clauses of a will, the address of the palace, my name, Lili's and Maria Eugenia's name, but when he flips to the end, there is only a blank space.

The room tilts underneath me. "He didn't sign the will?" I whisper.

Otto clears his throat. "He was supposed to."

I close my eyes. I've had to process so much information my head is spinning. "But why?" I ask.

"Why what?"

"Why didn't he tell me that he was ill?"

Otto looks embarrassed for Eugen. "He wanted to protect you."

"That's not protection, that's cowardice." I say this with more force than I had intended. "He didn't trust me, that's clear."

"Of course he trusted you."

I frown. "Oh really? And yet he didn't tell me he was ill, but he told his stepmother."

He taps the edges before putting it back into its folder. "Don't be so sure he did. A woman like that wouldn't think twice about snooping in your home while you are away."

"Now I know why Eugen used to keep his private things under lock and key." I pause. "When he remembered."

Otto tries a different tack. "If you had known your life with Eugen

60

would be cut short, would you have done anything differently?"

I rub my hand along the wooden armrest of my chair, feeling the soft polished wood. "No. Not really. I would have opened my heart sooner. Loved him more. Spent less time working and more time having fun."

Otto's expression softens. "Don't be too hard on men. We are emotional cowards. Why accept pain now when we can avoid it is our motto. I'm sure that's why God gave childbirth to women. If it had been in men's hands our race would have been extinct long ago." He waits for me to smile, and when I do, he smiles at me, putting his elbows on the table and resting his chin lightly on top of his clasped hands.

"I suggest you lay low. Let Maria Eugenia think she's won the battle. Yes, you could order an injunction, but until we have more clarity, I don't think that would be a good idea. Sometimes the best action is no action."

I slump in the chair, staring at my hands as if they are foreign objects. "I can't stay in your apartment forever."

"How about renting somewhere in Vienna?"

I shake my head. "With my possessions in storage? That would be hell."

"What about your parents in America?" he asks. "Can't you go home?"

"Home," I say, my voice echoing in my ears. "I don't know why everyone always talks about home."

"That's because," Otto says gently, "they normally have one."

I stop talking, listening to the grandfather clock in the hallway bonging the hour in slow, steady rhythm. I'm feeling something. It's like a pull, tugging at me to remember something. My mind flips through the past few days of conversations and then I remember. It was a conversation with Jean Luc. "But I can go to California, I suppose."

"Weren't you born in California?"

"No, Kansas. It's about as far from California as —"

"— Togoland is from Vienna?"

Otto smiles, then his eyes flit to his watch which indicates that our time is up. He gathers the papers in front of him and taps them into a tidy pile and puts them all in a folder with my name on it.

Otto opens the door and we walk into the hallway.

"You know, I don't think I've ever felt this way," I say as he helps me put on my coat. "I don't even know who I am anymore."

"I can tell you who you are," he says, putting a hand lightly on my back as he guides me to the door. "You are a friend who may have just saved our marriage. So just between you and me, I'm going to waive my fees till this is sorted out."

It's moments like these that I appreciate that Otto is not only my lawyer, but a friend. I hug him so tight that his glasses wobble on his nose.

"Go to California," he says as he opens the door. "If there is one place in the world you can go to find yourself again, it will be there."

SPACE

San Francisco

Show me a sane man and I will cure him for you
—Carl Jung

I squint in the sunshine. The daylight in California is so radiant I can hardly see. It's not just sunshine, it's a luminosity I have never seen before. The skyline of San Francisco spreads in front of me as Jean Luc and I drive toward the Golden Gate Bridge. As his car crests the hill, a mantel of white fog rolls back and San Francisco's iconic landmark appears. It glows burnt orange against an intensely blue sky.

We had hoped that Chloe would join us, but her last-minute literary deal ruined that. It's a pity, really. Marin County, where Jean Luc has been living for nearly seven months now, feels so alive. The cars are sleeker and faster, the joggers look energetic and fit. Even the sky glows a deeper blue. Listening to the rhythmic kabam-kabum-kabum underneath us, I slip my hand through the sunroof, feeling the rush of cool air as the car drives over the bridge. On either side of us, patches of sunlight burst from behind the fog, sprinkling millions of glittering diamonds into the blue sky.

We arrive at Jean Luc's home, a two-story white wooden cottage in a lovely hilly area across the Golden Gate Bridge from San Francisco. Within walking distance is an old-fashioned main street with a grocery store, a local diner, a sushi restaurant, a gas station, and a paper shop. On the hill, a mission school bell chimes on the hour.

Eugen's death couldn't have caught me at a more precarious time financially. I had just poured my savings into renovating our home. Eugen was going to pay me back once he received his rents, but of course that isn't going to happen now that the bank accounts have been seized by Maria Eugenia. Officially, according to Austrian law, we never married. This means that until I can prove I'm his legal wife, I have no nest egg to fall back on. Otto says he will investigate recovering my home, but that doesn't look promising. Not if Maria Eugenia gets her way. So until the travel insurance money comes through—if the insurance money comes through—I'm on a short leash. Both Jean Luc and Chloe have offered to lend me money, but I don't want to feel like a charity case. However, although I don't have much money, I do have time. Lots of it.

I remember talking with Jean Luc about what to do with all this free time while we were on the plane to San Francisco. While Jean Luc flipped through an in-flight magazine filled with glossy images of suntanned skiers with white smiles and mirrored sunglasses, I'd been trying to create a *To Do* list for my US trip. I hadn't got any further than *Get More Sleep* when I gave up and closed my notebook. Releasing the seatbelt, I leaned my seat back as far as it would go.

"All I wanted was to go home, Jean Luc. Now I can't even do that. But to learn Eugen was dying." My voice trailed. "Did you know?"

Jean Luc stopped flipping through the magazine and stuffed it in the seat pocket in front of him. "Eugen told me he wasn't feeling well."

I turned to him. "When?"

"The last time you both were in London. So I suggested he get a physical."

"So that's why he had one," I said slowly.

He turned to me. "He didn't tell you, I see."

"No," I answered. "But he did begin to talk of marriage around

64

then." I bit my lower lip. "Why couldn't he have just been straight with me?"

Jean Luc released his seatbelt and stretched his legs out in front of him. "It's part of our stupid masculine attitude that is drummed into us since we were small. We men feel like we must always have everything under control, which of course we can't. I think it's one of the reasons men get angry all the time. If something doesn't go our way, we feel like we've lost the battle."

I slipped my shoes off and picked up my notebook and pen. "But nothing is under our control," I answered. "There is nothing like death to prove that one." I opened the notebook and glared at the empty pages. "So you tell me. How do I go about finding meaning in a life that has none?"

Jean Luc leaned over and closed my notebook. "You'll find meaning again, but you won't achieve it that way."

"Okay. Then how?"

"By doing nothing."

I rubbed my neck. "I'd feel guilty if I did nothing."

"Then don't listen to your mind," he told me, glancing at the notebook in my hand. "Guilt is one of the best tools it uses to keep itself in the driver's seat."

I fiddled with the pen in my hand. "I know, I know. The mind is an excellent servant and a horrible master," I answered, kicking my tote further under the seat. "My problem is that I know all of this. I studied it. Eugen and I spent most of our time together discussing these principles. I could have written a book on how to find personal peace. But Eugen's death has made me aware that I've been spouting words I've picked up from others but don't have a clue what they mean."

My eyes looked beyond him toward the window. I didn't want to admit it, but I felt like a fool. I had slogged through my issues around sexuality so that my relationship with Eugen could grow and flourish. Marrying Eugen was proof that I had succeeded. All I had to do was apply myself, and I could make anything happen. "I should have brought water with us when we went to the Taj," I muttered.

Jean Luc gave me a gentle smile. "You're not blaming yourself for his death, are you?"

"No," I answered, a bit too quickly. "Well, sometimes. Okay. Most of the time. I'm just so angry at myself. Why did my body have to pick that moment to feel dizzy."

Jean Luc gave me a sharp look. "You were dizzy?"

I shrugged. "It's been happening on and off for months. Eugen used to call them my spells."

Jean Luc's gaze intensified. "Remind me what happens when you have a spell?"

"I become dopey and confused. And when it happens, there is nothing I can do about it. I simply need to sit or lie down until it's over."

Jean Luc was paying close attention to my every word. "How long has this been happening?"

I stopped to think. "Just after I began working on myself. But it's intensified after Eugen's death. It's like getting a massive power surge."

He nodded. "Somatic body therapy. Reichian work with Val. Energy work in tantra. Breath work. Yoga. That could do it."

Just then, a cabin attendant took our orders for drinks. As Jean Luc passed me a glass of water, the plane jumped, spilling a few drops. I took a napkin from the cabin attendant with a nod of thanks and began to dab the edge of the seat. "I know it sounds ridiculous," I said, crumpling the napkin up and handing it back to the attendant. "But it's like I'm dying."

I could have sworn Jean Luc was amused by my comment. "You're not dying. You're waking up."

I glared at him. "Have you been talking to Karl?"

Jean Luc's tone lowered into the professional-doctor-speaking-to-patient voice. "Waking up is a spiritual term. Cassandra, the shaman I've been working with, is doing a lot of journeys with people who are doing just that."

"Cassandra? Isn't that a Greek princess who told prophecies that no one believed?"

"Trojan, actually. She rejected Apollo's advances, which is why he cursed her. Which is probably what you want to do with life now. It's a typical reaction in the wake up process."

"Come on, Jean Luc. What's happening to me isn't spiritual. It's physical."

"Waking up *is* physical," he answered. Jean Luc reached over and lowered my tray, then his. "When life begins to push you around, it wants to wake you up. It wants everyone on this planet to wake up. And it will keep making things uncomfortable for all of us until we do."

I shook my head and put my tray up again. "Thanks. I'm not hungry."

Jean Luc shook his head. "You need to eat."

I frowned. "There's a lot of things I should do. But do you know how I really feel? I'm tired. Tired of digging around in myself. Tired of being sad, or angry, or fearful, or any of these damned emotions that keep sweeping through me day in and day out. Eugen and I had a life. We loved each other. We were building a life together. Now he's dead and I'm having weird things happening to me and you are trying to tell me that this is part of some preordained wake-up process." I watched him pick up his knife and fork and begin to eat. Just the smell of food made me nauseous.

Jean Luc put his silverware down and stared at me for the longest time. Then, just as I was about to say something more, he pulled his phone out from the inside pocket of his jacket, swiped it a few times. "How about a complete medical physical when you arrive?"

Reassuring images of doctors in white coats, stethoscopes around their necks, nodding in sympathy, swirled around me. "Thanks," I said quietly. I watched him spend a few minutes taking notes, then he put the phone back in his pocket and patted it.

"I'll do it first thing upon our arrival." Then he reached over and took the pen from my hand, put the cap back on and turned my notebook upside down. "Now how about giving yourself a little of what you wrote on your list. Get some sleep."

And so I start my life in the US as a lab rat. I'm pulled, I'm pricked, I'm run through scanners and machines. Squeezed and prodded like a greased pig. They take blood from my arm. Tap my knees. Make me pee in a cup. Take stool samples. Inject concoctions into my system that make me radioactive. I run on treadmills. Read eye charts. Listen to beeps and tones through headphones. Sit for endless hours in waiting rooms in front of blaring televisions that I can't turn off. Every single orifice in my body is examined, looked at, listened to, prodded, or poked. I am run through more strange-looking machines than a science fiction movie. I run from one doctor to another, one clinic to another, one hospital to another, and finally, after two weeks, I receive the results.

"Healthy," the doctor says, as he gazes at me over a pair of black-rimmed reading glasses. They are so thick they make his eyes look bulbous, like a frog. Jean Luc and I are sitting in a sleek glass-fronted clinic in downtown San Francisco. Medical certificates jockey with graduation degrees and school photos of smiling children on the walls. I watch the doctor scratch his neck as he gazes at the lab reports on his desk.

"No medications?"

"None," I say.

"Not even vitamins? Aspirin? Painkillers? Sleeping pills?"

I glance at Jean Luc. "Is that so unusual?"

"In this country it is," Jean Luc answers.

The doctor pulls a pen from his white lab coat pocket, taps it a few times on his desk, and then begins to write on a pad of paper in front of him. "Heart like a twenty-year-old. No alcohol. Doesn't smoke. Exercises six times a week. If you are worried about those dizzy spells of yours, it's probably because of the loss you have suffered. Anti-depressants will help." He scribbles on a prescription pad.

I leap to my feet. "How can you prescribe a mood-altering drug without even asking me?"

"Thank you, doctor, I'll handle things from here," Jean Luc says, taking the prescription from the doctor's outstretched hand. I throw a fierce look at the doctor as Jean Luc hurries me out of the room.

When we get into the car, I put my arms straight out, elbows down, and gaze at the black and blue marks on my veins. "Just look at me! I look like I've been in a war. I've got bandages from all the places where I was pricked with needles. My stomach is upset from the things I've had to drink. I can't even sit down properly because of all those injections I had."

Jean Luc smiles to himself as he starts the car and noses it into the afternoon traffic.

"Good thing you got me out of there," I say, studying the prescription in my hand. "He's prescribed enough medications that I could open my own pharmacy. All that for a little dizziness?"

Jean Luc changes gear and the car picks up speed and heads along Highway 100 towards the bridge to Sausalito. I fold the paper with the prescriptions in half and place it in my purse. He glances at me while driving.

"We can stop at a pharmacy to get the prescription filled. Antidepressants may even lessen the symptoms."

I cross my arms. "No way."

The car hums along the highway on our way home. All I want to do when I get there is crawl into bed and sleep. Sleep. I close my eyes and lean my head against the head rest.

"I'll manage it," I say. "I always do."

Determination. Distraction. Denial. I employ them all while sitting at Jean Luc's local café, listening to the repeated schlock-whizz sound of the barista making espressos behind the counter while I sip my mocha. It's too loud here, so I find a table in the corner and focus on downloading apps into my new phone. But it's not much better here, either. No matter where I go, there is too much noise. Next to me, a man yells into his cellphone. Behind me, two women in business suits chat in shrill voices over a laptop computer. Techies in T-shirts huddle around a corner table. After slow, sedate Vienna, the

United States feels like living at the end of a bungee cord.

One day, when I'm driving back to Jean Luc's early to beat the afternoon traffic, the familiar tingling in my fingers begins. I know what this means. A spell is coming. Within minutes, I'm so sleepy I can hardly keep my eyes open. I shake my head, slap my cheeks, wiggle my fingers, but it's no good. The surging energy overwhelms my system, fogging my brain. I feel so sluggish I nearly run off the road. I barely have the energy to pull the car over, turn the engine off, stumble outside, and flop on the grass before I'm out cold.

A man's voice wakes me. "Are you OK?"

I open my eyes to see a young man on a racing bike, gazing down at me. I sit up, blinking as I try to get my bearings. I have no idea where I am. I glance at the car. The door is open. He helps me up, and I wobble toward the car. The keys are still in the ignition. My purse is on the passenger seat. I take my phone out and do a double take: thirty minutes have gone by.

"I'm fine, really," I tell the biker. My lips can barely form the words. It takes a few minutes before he is reassured enough to pedal away. I'm not sure how I get home, but I do, crawling out of the car and collapsing on the sofa. This is where Jean Luc finds me, staring into the void, when he arrives home.

"How do you feel now?" he asks when I tell him what happened. He puts his fingers on my pulse, then checks to see if I have a fever.

I rub my hands together. The prickling sensations have subsided. "Odd," I say.

He goes to the kitchen to make two cups of tea, then comes back, hands me one, and sits across from me and smiles. "So. Still think waking up isn't real?"

Sometimes, when I'm tossing and turning at 4 a.m., trying to make sense in a world that no longer has any meaning, I think about death.

Death is relative, Dona Mathilde used to say. We die all the time. Lots of deaths. That's how we grow.

"But why do we have to die?" I remember asking her.

As Dona Mathilde considered my questions, her eyebrows rose and she gave me the vague, open-ended stare that always occurred when she wasn't speaking from herself, but from somewhere in her that held a larger wisdom. "You'll die, that's a fact," she said softly. "Your body will. It is skin and bones and you must take care of it the best you can so that you can live long and well. But who you are doesn't die." She smiled when she saw the look on my face. "But you knew that already, didn't you?"

It was early evening and we were walking home along the streets in the hills above Rio de Janeiro, where we had been purchasing musical instruments—a *cuíca*, a drum with a stick poking out of the middle of it; a whistle; and an *agogô*, which looked like a pincer with two bells on the ends—for her Spiritist society to make a *batucada*, or drum section, to play in carnival. Even though carnival was still a few days away, people were already gathering outside bars to drink *caipirinhas* and shots of *cachaça*, dressed in the bright greens and yellows and reds of the different samba schools. I breathed in the smoky sweet smell from the charcoal fires of the street vendors and felt the syncopated beat of drums move my body with its earthy rhythms.

As we walked, I noticed that the crowd in front of us was parting in two to avoid something resting on the ground near the gutter. I stopped to look and saw that it was a dead rose and a candle that had been burnt to the nib.

I was about to nudge the rose into the gutter when Dona Mathilde stopped me.

Her eyes glittered like obsidian. "Don't. It is *macumba*, dark energy. Watch."

On either side of us, I was surprised to see the crowd avoiding the rose like water flowing around a rock.

Instinctively I reached out to hold her hand. "I didn't think you believe in macumba."

Her eyes deepened. "It's not a question of belief, but of respect. I respect macumba because I respect darkness."

My hand tightened in hers. "But you don't have any darkness in

71

you."

She laughed. "We all have darkness, little one. It's only when you can accept your own darkness that you are free."

"Free from what?"

"Fear. A person who can't accept their own shadow is attracted by the shadow in others," she told me. "Which is why, one day, you will need to find your own."

"But if there is a God," I remember saying as we headed toward home. "Why would he make a world that has darkness? Why can't we all be born perfect?"

"We are perfect," she began, but then saw that I wasn't understanding. "Because it teaches us to be compassionate," she said, squeezing my hand gently as we picked our way along the cobblestones.

"Even with bad people?" I asked.

"With everyone." She patted my hand with hers. "Especially with yourself."

By the time February rolls around, gone are my hopes of anything that resembles a normal life. If I hadn't had Jean Luc guiding me, I would have thought I was going crazy. Before I arrived in California, I had a hard time not doing exercise. Now I can hardly get out of bed. The light-headedness can come over me at any time, and if I am not near a place where I can lie down, I'm in trouble.

Otto calls. Karl texts me. Christiane sends me emails. Chloe calls, but she is fighting so much with Jean Luc—I hear them bickering on the phone most mornings—I avoid answering my phone. I drift away from my friends, and I no longer care. I can't talk to them about what is happening, yet it's so encompassing that I can't talk about anything else.

The process continues. Days go by—or is it weeks? No, it's a month, but time no longer has a hold over me. I have to remember to eat, and when I do, everything tastes like plastic. Lying on the sofa, my limbs draped like lifeless appendages over the sides, I listen to the internal chatter looping around my head like a bad soap opera. I'm overwhelmed by a yearning to go home, but the problem is that I don't know where that home is. I miss Vienna, I miss London, I miss Eugen, I miss my friends, but it's deeper than that. It is like an itch I can't scratch. I stop watching videos, can't bear to listen to music. I feel like crying and screaming at the same time. All I can do is sit. And wait.

I might have waited forever—I have little desire to do anything else—if Jean Luc hadn't walked into his living room one evening with a container of roasted vegetables in one hand and a cup of tea in the other. He sits down and opens the carton of food, then gets out plates and cutlery and begins to serve me. He's in a chatty mood this evening, which suits me fine because I don't have a single thing to say.

"Do you remember that shaman I told you about? The one who does journeys?"

He had mentioned journeys a number of times, *en passant*, just like he mentioned waking up *en passant*, but since I didn't understand the term, I ignored it just as I would an irritating fly, hoping it would go away.

"She has just written me. She'll be in San Francisco this weekend. I know you said you didn't want to meet her, but I think you should."

I look up from the sofa, where I am spending another whacked-out moment. My eyes are as hollow as I feel.

"You're not getting better, that's for sure."

My shoulders drop. I know when I'm beaten. "Will it help?"

If he can feel me wavering, he doesn't show it. "It might."

And that is how I am introduced to shamanism.

"So how do shamans work?" I ask Jean Luc, as the waitress comes up and takes our order. We've just finished a walk along the quay in Sausalito and are sitting at a window table in Jean Luc's favorite sushi restaurant. A young Japanese man dressed in a crisp white apron fills our ceramic cups with popped rice tea and leaves the teapot on the table.

Jean Luc picks up a menu, pretending to study it even though he knows every item by heart. "They help a person enter an altered state of consciousness." He puts the menu down and calls the server over so that we can order.

I take a sip of tea, then sit, staring at my cup while cradling it between my hands. "And how does a shaman do this?"

He puts the menu down. "They use sound. Movement. Dance. Breath."

A server, a dainty Japanese woman with the loveliest ivory skin, comes by to take our order. We watch her leave, then I hold my teacup out to Jean Luc. "And how does your shaman work?"

He pours me more tea with surgical precision. "Mostly with phone sessions."

I take a sip, hoping my relief isn't too apparent. "For a minute I was afraid you were going to say she uses drugs."

"Well, she does use ayahuasca."

I stop unwrapping the pair of lacquer chopsticks from my cloth napkin. "You pay someone to help you trip?"

Jean Luc starts to laugh. "A trip is recreational. A journey with Cassandra is sacred."

I take a sip of tea, trying to keep the suspicion from my voice. "I don't do drugs. Never have."

He takes the napkin from my hand, pulls the chopsticks out of their wrapper, flips the napkin open and hands both back to me. "Eat. You're too thin. Besides. Ayahuasca isn't a drug. It's an entheogen."

A server places a plate of tempura on the table between us. I take a bite. "What's the difference?"

The transformation from Jean Luc, friend and husband of Chloe, to medical professional, is so quick I hardly even notice it. Jean Luc sits a little straighter in his chair and puts the chopsticks down next to his plate. "An entheogen, my dear Annabel, is a psycho-active substance that is used in sacred ceremonies to induce spiritual experiences."

I put my chopsticks down. "In other words, it's a drug."

74

Jean Luc's hands begin to chop in the air like surgical knives. "Let's look at your definition of drugs. "Painkillers, sleeping pills, anti-depressants. They all need a prescription. What other drugs are freely available to us? Ah yes, nicotine and alcohol."

"Which are off limits to minors."

He nods. "And coffee, tea and sugar can be consumed by anyone."

I hold my cup between my fingers, staring at the tea leaves floating inside. "I'm talking about serious drugs. You know my brother died of a drug overdose."

Out of nowhere a big bubble of sadness swells within me, sadness that I didn't even know I had, and tears gush in rivulets down my cheeks. "Why bother to love, when we are all going to die anyway?"

Jean Luc waits for my tears to run their course, then digs in his pocket and hands me a tissue. "Let's go home, shall we?" he says quietly. "I'll call Cassandra and tell her that you aren't interested." He raises his hand for the check, then gives the waitress his credit card.

I take the tissue, wipe away my tears, and then stare at this man in front of me who is Chloe's husband. I've known Jean Luc for over five years now. Every time he has suggested something to me, it has been worth it. Jean Luc is a seeker. That's what he had in common with Eugen. Eugen would do this. He would have done anything that would have taken him deeper into himself. My heart begins to pound. "Did it make a difference in your life?"

He nods. "It's the deepest work I know."

"Peter took LSD to avoid himself, not to go deeper into himself." I look up. "So if you think I should meet her, I would be foolish to say no."

Jean Luc studies me. "*À quelque chose malheur est bon.* Your English expression is much more poetic. Every cloud has a, how do you say it in English? A silver lining. You, my dear Annabel," he says as he helps me get up from the table, "are about to change your life."

Cassandra, mistress of the magical, isn't how I expect her to be. Tall and slim, with long dark hair and dressed in flowing dark fabrics, a beautiful cashmere shawl draped over one shoulder, she's sophisticated and attractive. The house where she's staying is set in a Japanese rock garden surrounded by shady trees. Inside, it is open plan and contemporary, with panoramic views of San Francisco Bay.

As I watch Cassandra walk through the entrance hall to greet me, her hand, as light as a fluttering dove, trails along the wall to balance her. She floats so lightly toward me I hardly hear the tapping of her cane. Vaguely, I remember Jean Luc telling me that she has severe physical limitations. Only once, when we hug, do I glance down at her feet to see why she can't walk well, but once we begin to talk, I forget about her appearance and never think about it again. Carefully, she lowers her body onto a chair and places her cane underneath the seat. She then invites me to pull up a chair in front of her, which I do. My stomach gives a nervous flutter.

"I'm so sorry to hear about your husband," Cassandra says, breaking the silence. Her voice is low and pleasurably deep.

When I gaze in her eyes, I can feel these aren't just words. She means it. "Thanks. It's been hard."

She nods, studying me. "Tell me a little about yourself. Do you have a family?"

"One brother," I say. "He died of a drug overdose."

She gives me a noncommittal smile. "Were you close?"

I look beyond her. "Very."

She nods. "And your parents. Are they in Austria, too?"

My eyes run from one side of the room to the other. I feel a claustrophobic twinge in my gut. "No, just me. They live in Kansas."

She continues to study me. "Are you going to see them while you're here?"

I squirm in my chair. I don't know why she's asking me about things other than my current pain. I change the subject. "I'd rather focus on the present, if you don't mind."

For a split second, I think Cassandra is going to ask me more, but then she flows with my request, and her gaze softens.

"I'm afraid I can't bring back your husband. Or your brother. Or your home. But what I can do is help you make a shift inside yourself

76

so that you aren't dependent upon external things for your happiness."

"And how do you do this?"

"I call the process journeywork."

I respond with an uneasy look. "You can understand why I'm not keen on drugs."

She gives me a look of sympathy. "I'm not keen on the drug culture either."

"So how did you get involved?"

She gives her legs a gentle pat. "I came down with a deteriorating joint condition when I was twenty. There was nothing the doctors could do."

"That must have been horrible."

She nods. "It was. Until then, I had been a professional athlete. I spent years in the 'why me' phase."

I lean back in my chair. "What happened?"

She adjusts the cushion behind her back. "I saw a friend of mine start to change before my eyes. She was becoming more open, more loving, more relaxed. When she told me she was working with ayahuasca, I wasn't interested because I was anti-substance. But I kept seeing her change, so finally I did my first journey. It was transformative. I had the experience that everything was God. Western medicine, holistic medicine, one wasn't better than the other. I came out of my journey open to seeing what Western medicine could do for me."

"And it changed you?"

"It changed my consciousness."

"And your body?"

She shrugs. "There isn't much more doctors can do."

"So why do anything at all?"

She shakes her head. "I might still feel pain, but I no longer suffer." She smiles when she sees I'm not following her. "It's an inside job."

Even though I'm not sure what Cassandra means by this, as the minutes tick by, I do find something is happening to me. I'm not sure if it's because of the sound of her voice or her presence. Soon I'm feeling as if I'm in the most comfortable of beds, surrounded by puffy pillows and soft cushions. I'm so relaxed that when she asks if we can do a little energy work, I don't even think twice. At her request, I sit up, put my feet flat on the floor, rest my spine against the back of the chair, and close my eyes.

I hear her voice. "What are you aware of?"

For a moment, I don't speak. My awareness is nowhere. I'm floating. It's only after a few moments that I start to distinguish noises around me: the humming of the refrigerator in the kitchen, the sound of a pigeon cooing in the garden, a leaf blower somewhere far away. I keep taking a breath, then another and another, as she requests. She tells me to concentrate on feeling the soles of my feet resting on the floor.

I hear her voice again. "What are you aware of now?"

Tingling. Then, as soon as my mind registers that I'm feeling something, it stops. It takes a few minutes for me to relax again. Finally, after some time, warmth envelops my feet. I feel a vertical pull downward from the center of my body. It makes me feel heavy. Not a bad heaviness. I feel relaxed, but aware, as if I'm connected to everything around me. I feel better than I have felt since Eugen died.

When I open my eyes, Cassandra is still in front of me, but she looks different. Or maybe it is I who am looking at her differently.

"That was it?" I ask.

She laughs. "You've just done a mini journey."

"Where?"

"Down," she says. "Inside yourself."

By the time Jean Luc comes to pick me up, we are chatting as if we've known each other all our lives. I realize that whatever she has to offer, I want it.

"I'll do it," I say. Before I know it, we've arranged it all. Cassandra will be coming to the house the following evening. Jean Luc will be assisting her. We all get up to say our goodbyes. When she hugs me, I feel like the most precious human being in the world.

The following day, I'm lying with my back on the grass, my stomach rumbling with hunger, when Cassandra arrives. She looks radiant in flowing black trousers and a ginger-colored Chinese silk jacket, a paisley scarf thrown over her shoulder. I stand up and she gives me a hug and then rests both hands on her cane. "How are you?"

"Nervous," I answer. I don't want to tell her, but a low, uncomfortable anxiety has been with me all day.

"It's often that way before a journey," she explains, as we slowly walk into the house.

Inside, the drapes are closed to filter out the evening sun's last rays. Candles are flickering in the corner of the room. As Cassandra settles on the sofa, Jean Luc dims the lights, gives me a pillow and a blanket, and gathers candles onto a small tray. He places a glass with a spoon in it and a bottle of water next to Cassandra and sits across from her on the sofa.

"We use psilocybin mushrooms," Cassandra says, stirring some dried brown flakes into a glass of water. "But the main ingredient is ayahuasca. We call her the Mother." She hands a few capsules that look just like vitamins to me with the instructions to swallow them with the water. I do. My reticence is so great I feel as if a part of me is dying with each sip. To say I'm petrified is an understatement. The earthy taste of the mushrooms catches in my throat. I light a candle, speak my intention, and lie down on the floor. Jean Luc places a duvet over me and tucks me in.

They settle on either side of me and I close my eyes as the music begins. A soft drumbeat and the low, repetitive voice of a Tibetan chant flood my ears. Time passes. One piece of music ends, another begins. This happens time and time again until the CD ends. My eyes open.

To my surprise, the room is dark. The flickering candlelight draws wavering shadows on the walls. Cassandra puts a hand on my shoulder. "Is everything all right?"

I quell an urge to sit up. Instead, I close my eyes and the music begins again. It's a beautiful Russian choral piece. During Glasnost, I spent a few months in St Petersburg in the wintertime to learn

Russian. It was so cold that the only thing there was to do was to go to a concert every night, and I used to listen to music just like this. I'm sifting through memories of St Petersburg in the wintry light when something twinkles at the edge of my inner vision. My mind is tracing the harmonious voices when my image of the blue Smolny Cathedral shatters, kaleidoscope-like.

In its wake, I tumble into a world governed by forces I have never experienced before. It is free of the division of the five senses. It is the union of everything I have ever known. I surrender to the experience, the music becoming my guide. My senses open like flowers into richness beyond description; my linear world detonates into depth. It is a world of unfathomable colors, shapes, and forms, jewels of sapphire and lapis lazuli and glittering golds, scintillating shapes, and dazzling rays infinitely brighter than the sun.

Time becomes as infinite as the ocean. Everywhere I look behind my closed eyes, the incessant blue of the sky beckons. Clouds roll into infinity.

I feel alive, wonderfully alive, free of all fears in a world that has no beginning or end. It is a world boundless in creativity and form, more delicious than anything I have ever tasted, smelled, touched. It is freedom from everything I knew that created restriction. I am everywhere and everything; I am all that I see, all that I experience. Nothing lies outside of me; everything is within. The universe is eternal, and it is all within me. This is where I came from before I was born and where I will return after I die. Consciousness. Before, it was a word. Now it is reality.

The music changes into the heavy, syncopated beat of an African drum and I fall into deep darkness that throbs with the endless cycles of life. I am the insect that crawls in the earth, the worms that eat the rotting wood of the forest floor, all that crawls and slithers and clicks in the night.

Then the music changes, and now I head into my body. Here, too, I find the pulsating forces of life. I wander through my veins and flow along the blood that surges and pounds in rhythm with my heartbeat. I rest in my heart, sensing it relax and contract, and I see that it, too, is a microcosm of the pulsation of life itself.

It is all so weird and wonderful and fascinating that I feel sad when I hear the music end. The silence is heavy, each second oozing with eternity. I am aware of every particle of dust in the room and beyond that, of everything forever into the cosmos. I am the minimum and the maximum; I am everything and nothing and the space in between.

I open my eyes. Cassandra is in front of me. I turn my head and see Jean Luc. They are both gazing at me.

I try to say something, but instead I start to laugh.

"Have you got the cosmic joke?" Cassandra asks.

I can't stop laughing. I've been afraid all my life, and I now know that there is nothing to be afraid of. Dona Mathilde always said the world was inside me, but I didn't believe her. I try to think of my greatest fear: death. But there isn't any death. I shed my body, but that doesn't mean I disappear. I can't disappear—it's physically impossible.

Words can't describe the feeling of relief that washes over me. Just think, all these years I've been listening to my mind as if it were God. But I am endless, bountiful love. That's all I am. That's all everyone is.

Cassandra and Jean Luc help me sit up. I feel clumsy and heavy.

"Can you sit up and look at me?" Cassandra asks.

My body sags under its weight, and as soon as I close my eyes, I am back flying the free and open skies of consciousness.

"You are you, and I am me. Can you feel where you end and I begin?"

I look at her, confused. "But we are all one."

"Feel your boundaries." When I do nothing, she turns to Jean Luc. "Put your hands on her belly to help bring her back into her body."

"You are you, and I am me," Cassandra repeats.

With a sigh, I concentrate my gaze, and discover I'm leaking. My energy keeps seeping away from me, drifting toward Jean Luc and Cassandra. It feels like water running out of a sieve.

It reminds me of when I was a child, looking in the mirror while

81

trying to teach myself to wiggle my ears. The subtlety of trying to find the exact muscle to make my ear do a micro-movement was exasperating. This is the same thing, but instead of muscles, I'm trying to bring my energy inside myself rather than letting it drain out of me. Finally, by concentrating on my belly, I feel myself spiral down toward my center like water going down a drain. That's it! But the moment I relax, it begins to seep upward again. I recognize that this happens on a regular basis in my relationships. I lose myself in other people. The only difference between those incidents and now is that I can feel it.

Boundaries. I thought it had to do with body language, like crossing my arms when I want to signal people to stay away. But this is physical: If I am in my body, no one else can be there. When I am home in myself, no one else can squat.

Cassandra's voice again. "Who are you?"

I look at her in absolute horror. Me? There's a me?

"I don't remember."

"Well, look at yourself," Cassandra answers. "Are you a man or a woman?"

I look down. Why look at that—I have a body! My eyes roam over the long appendages that are my arms, the even longer appendages that are my legs, and the thickness of my torso. There's a pause when I can't grasp what this has to do with me, and then, like a bubble from consciousness, up comes a thought: *This is my body.*

I feel as if I've won the lottery. "Why, it's a nice body, too. Strong!" I pat my arms and my legs in awe, then pull up my trouser leg and stare in wonder at my bare feet.

I can't understand why they think this is funny. All these fingers and toes and tendons. The way the skin is smooth and elastic and warm to the touch. The way it's pulled over the bones. The way my wrist can bend back and forth. How each knuckle of each finger can work independently of the other. What engineering! What perfection!

I hear Cassandra talking to Jean Luc. "This is like experiencing a birth." She turns back to me. "It is a nice body," she says. "Are you a

82

man or a woman?"

I stop examining my toes and look up at her. "A man or a woman?"

I look down at my body, and to my surprise, I register that I have long legs with thin ankles. And my hands! Why, my hands, with their slender fingers are—feminine! A nanosecond while my mind scrambles through its memory banks to recall what this means. I put my hands to my head to feel my hair, soft and curly, then over my face to feel a small nose, large eyes, and mouth. My skin is soft and supple. "Why, I'm a woman," I answer. "A woman."

As soon as this registers with my brain, a deep, heavy pain wells up in my stomach. It's so deep that I can't take it, so I close my eyes and flit off into the cosmos.

"Whoops, you're gone again," Cassandra says. "What made you leave?"

"The pain." It's so overwhelming that it takes my breath away.

"Is it the pain of this life, or is it the pain of the Feminine?"

It takes me a second to separate myself from the pain. "It's in the core of my being," I say slowly.

"Then feel it," Cassandra says. "All of it. Go on."

I close my eyes and put my awareness in my lower belly. It is mind-numbing in intensity and deeper than my bones. It is in the fabric of my being. For a moment, it's too much, but then I open wider and embrace it. The pain doesn't disappear, but it's within me, rather than outside me. Like coming up for air after a long deep swim in dark murky waters, I open my eyes and feel myself slip a fraction of an inch deeper into my body.

Cassandra looks into my eyes. "Your joy is not to be found outside you."

A wave of nausea punches me in the stomach. I throw myself on my side until my stomach calms down. I know that they won't force me to do anything I don't want to, so after a few minutes, I sit up, wobbly but determined. "You were saying something that made me ill," I whisper. "What did you say?"

"I said that there is nowhere you can go."

And at that word, I projectile vomit. Within seconds a pot is shoved underneath me. I hang my head over the pot. "It's gone," I say into the pot without a twinge of embarrassment. I wipe my mouth, sit up, and gaze directly into Cassandra's eyes, like a warrior in battle. "Say it again. Say it to my face."

"Your joy is within you," she says, looking me in the eyes.

I stare deeply into her eyes, nodding my head. "I get it. I get it now."

Cassandra looks at Jean Luc. "She's in her body, just like that."

It's true. Instead of floating vaporously outside my anchor of flesh, I have slipped into my body as if it's an envelope. It feels incredible! No wonder I used to suffer from cold feet. I hadn't spent much time in them. An enormous wave of heat overwhelms me, so I throw my pullover off my shoulders. I feel more present than I ever have in my life.

"And Eugen? Can you hold him in your heart?"

"He is always with me." What I thought was my heart was only the tip of an iceberg. I hug my legs and rock back and forth as I vacuum bits of me hanging out in the ether.

"Are you still here?"

I look up, still hugging my legs. "There's so much of me, I can't seem to get all of me into this little body." It feels like trying to put an ocean into a milk bottle.

Now that I am in my body, everything is richer, more vibrant. Cassandra radiates a golden glow that is awe-inspiring. Every pore in her skin, every hair on her head, every wrinkle around her eyes is luminous.

Another wave of heat engulfs me as I slip deeper into my body. I could do this forever, but finally I hear Cassandra tell Jean Luc that I've done enough. I check with my body and know she's right. Although my mind is clear, my body is tired. Jean Luc helps me to my bedroom and puts me, fully clothed, to bed. I hear the refrigerator opening and the kettle boiling, but I soon forget them. I'm too busy with myself. I spend hours rocking myself as a mother would a newborn child. How I love my body! A car roars past. What's that? Then somewhere from my memory bank, I remember. Oh yes, we have cars now. So much energy that my body feels like a large heat lamp. And so the night passes.

Then, just as I start to feel the edge of sleep, I feel the pain of living in a body that will die. Then I switch perspectives and drop into Consciousness. I am the consciousness that lives in my body and I am Consciousness which is everything. I am everything. I want to dance on the lawn in celebration. *I'm awake!* I think. I can't wait to tell Jean Luc and Karl. But then I stop. What does it matter?

And with that, I fall asleep.

The sound of voices wakes me up. I open my eyes. For a long time, I stare at the ceiling, my mind a blank screen. A bubble rises in my consciousness, and with it comes a thought: I'm Annabel. And I am in California. And with that thought, my mind takes over, busily trying to erase everything from the night before. *Awake, huh?* I swing out of bed and place both feet firmly on the floor. My body feels like a sack of potatoes. Vertigo follows me as I make my way into the kitchen. I pause and take a deep breath before peering around the corner. Jean Luc and Cassandra are chatting in the kitchen. They look showered and refreshed and very much alive.

Unlike me.

"Uh, good morning," I say. My voice skips and growls like a spluttering engine. I feel lightheaded and wobbly, and most of all, embarrassed. I'm not used to baring my soul. It was raw, unfiltered, and that makes me feel insecure.

Cassandra looks into my eyes before giving me a hug. "You need protein."

Soon, I'm sitting before a feast of eggs with a few slices of avocado on the side. My body says that it's hungry, but I am not hungry. How strange to coordinate two different things that I used to consider as one: my body and me. The textures and smells are as funny as I feel. After the intense reality of last night, this three-dimensional world is insipid. In fact, I'm not even sure whether I like being here at all.

"I want you to get just how much you did last night," Cassandra says.

I furrow my brow. "How do you know? You didn't take the ayahuasca."

"The dimensions you traveled to aren't the result of the ayahuasca," Cassandra says. "Everywhere you went was real."

The heaviness inside me lifts. "You mean it wasn't the ayahuasca?"

Cassandra nods for Jean Luc to bring up a chair. Soon, we're facing each other and she is doing with me the same thing that she did when we first met. She asks me to take a breath, and then another, and to follow the breath back down into my body.

I take a deep breath, and another, and in a few minutes, I feel a whoosh inside of me, as if a trapdoor has opened in my solar plexus. A feeling of warm honey begins to drift down along my spine into the area of my hips. My legs begin to tingle and the soles of my feet begin to get hot.

"There you go," she says. She watches me as I try to keep my energy down low, but sometimes it goes up into my head again.

"It's like taking baby steps," she explains. "You are learning to use a new muscle. Now. Connect with your center first, and then open your eyes."

When I open my eyes, it feels as if I'm opening the curtains on a stage.

"What a journey," I say as I stand up. Even though it's time for her to go, I find myself being sad not to see her again. "Oh well," I say. "Back to reality again."

But now it is Cassandra who laughs. "Your real journey begins now."

WIND

Joshua Tree

Be still. Stillness reveals the secrets of eternity
—Lao Tzu

At first, it's bliss. I'm walking slower, eating slower, even thinking slower. *Is this how other people live?* I wonder. Just as I'm about to write all my friends to get on a plane and do this amazing thing called a journey, something happens. A week later, I wake up to find that the bliss has faded. And in its place, I feel pain.

It's everywhere. When I see a bulldozer clearing a field, I cry as the are trees being pulled out by their roots. I give a few coins to a homeless man and tears run down my face when I read the abandonment in his eyes. Standing in line for my morning chai tea latte, I look into a woman's eyes and can feel her broken heart. Soon I have to lower my gaze whenever I go out because every time I catch a person's eye, I feel like I'm tapping into their sadness.

Then the pain becomes physical. I get a yeast infection that won't go away. Canker sores erupt at the back of my throat. I walk around with cannonballs in my thighs, marbles in the bottoms of my feet, a board in my lower back. I can't even do yoga because my neck freezes up as if it is in a vise. Within two weeks of my journey, Jean Luc's porch becomes my territory, migraines and nausea my norm. I go from never having headaches to living on homeopathic migraine pills, from being mostly vegetarian to craving meat, from rarely expressing anger to being consumed by rage.

I'm angry at Eugen for dying. Angry at Maria Eugenia for being a bitch. Angry at Lili for not trusting me. Angry at Chloe and Jean Luc for fighting. Angry at, well, just about anything I think of. I always thought I loved life. Now I'm not sure.

I'm resting in the deck chair outside Jean Luc's house, tears streaming down my face, when I see him walking toward me. He has the phone in his hand. When he sees my tears, he reaches in his back pocket and pulls out a tissue and gives it to me. "What's it this morning?"

"The tree," I say. "It's in pain. Can't you see the electric wires running through its branches?"

He looks at me, then at the tree, then at me again. "You can feel that?"

I wipe away the tears with the back of my hand. "I thought I'd get better after a journey, not worse."

He hands me the phone. "Maybe Cassandra can help." He squeezes my shoulder and goes back into the house.

"Hey!" I hear Cassandra's pleasantly hoarse voice. "How are you?"

"Terrible," I say. "All I can see is pain."

She gives a soft laugh. "Maybe what you're seeing is your pain."

I slide lower in my chair. "My pain? That's impossible."

Rather than answering me, she asks me another question. "What else are you aware of?"

I run my hand through my curls, searching for a way to describe the vast changes that are occurring within me. "It's as if I'm no longer separate from the world."

She gives a gentle laugh. "Maybe you're no longer separate from yourself."

This last sentence circles within my brain a few times before it can compute. "Are you trying to say this pain is mine?"

"You aren't making this up," she answers. "The pain is real.

Sometimes integration can be more difficult than the journey itself."

Integration! Of course. I fall back onto the chair. "So that is what is happening to me." From all the body work I've done over the years, I know integration well. It isn't how far you go, but how much you can hold, a teacher once said to me. My awareness has expanded beyond my usual boundaries, and now my mind is trying to pull it back into the old patterns again. "So this pain has been with me for years. All that is happening is that I am beginning to feel it."

Just then, the neighbor across the street revs up his lawnmower. I'm so sensitive that every sound vibrates in my body. Not being able to stand the noise, I ask Cassandra to hold on and get up from the deck chair and head inside. But as soon as I open the screen door, I'm confronted by a screaming Frenchman pacing back and forth in the kitchen, one hand holding his phone to his ear. Yet another fight with Chloe. I slink downstairs and slip into my room and close the door. "Contact with the outside world right now is excruciating," I say, throwing myself on the bed. "I'm not sure if it wouldn't be easier to live in a cave."

She laughs, but I can tell she knows I'm not exaggerating. "That's why I'm calling. Our casita in Joshua Tree—that's a Southwest term for the small caretaker's cottage—has just become available. It's not expensive." She pauses. "It might give you a little time and space to integrate your journey."

As she fills me in on the details, I hear the thump of footsteps and drawers slamming, followed by a few French expletives. Definitely Chloe. Just the idea of being somewhere alone. In nature. Surrounded by peace and no people to catch eyes with, feels like a balm to my ragged senses.

Before I hang up, I've made my decision. Within a day, I have a flight to Los Angeles, and three days later, I'm on my way to Joshua Tree.

The hot sun, glimmering like a golden fireball suspended in a neon blue sky, beats down upon my rental car as I leave Los Angeles airport and set off in the direction of the desert. As the urban sprawl disappears, I emerge from the pale haze that hugs the city and the land grows more beautiful. My car heads down a highway that flies as straight as an arrow into the horizon. The vast wilderness swallows me up as if I were a mere gnat. It puts my situation in perspective. Comforts me, somehow.

After a few hours' drive, I arrive at Joshua Tree. I encounter the plant that gives the town its name. A Joshua tree isn't a tree, but a cactus that looks like a hand with bent fingers. There are hundreds of them everywhere, rising from the sandy earth, making the landscape look like a Salvador Dali painting. I turn off the highway and bump down a dirt road that ends at a ranch-style wooden gate. Passing through it, I arrive at a large adobe house surrounded by a rickety wooden fence. Behind it is an enormous sandstone cliff. The house's muted eggshell color and large picture windows are a pleasing combination of contemporary-chic-meets-arid-desert.

Cassandra told me she would be on a phone session when I arrived, so I head next door to the casita and park my car. The little adobe house looks like a small red matchbox. As I get out of the car, the silence engulfs me as I pull my suitcase out of the trunk and walk slowly toward the casita. Fishing the key out from underneath the welcome mat, I open the screen door and let myself in.

The casita is tiny and compact, with everything I need: a comfortable bed, a tiny living room, an open kitchen and a wobbly desk in front of the picture window that gazes onto the desert beyond. The burgundy terra-cotta tiles, the soft beige throw blankets, and the roughly hewn wooden walls are cozy without being pretentious. Going through my now habitual feathering of a temporary nest, I open my suitcase and clutch my yoga mat to my chest, wondering whether it should share space with the extra blankets in the sitting room or in the wardrobe in the bedroom. I haven't occupied such a tiny space since my college days. But then, after living in guest bedrooms, first with Christiane, then with Jean Luc, my little home feels like a palace.

By the time I unpack and freshen up, evening has set in. I find a flashlight and make my way to the main house to have dinner with Cassandra. The light is fading fast. A faint smell of burning wood is in the air. Peering in through the kitchen window, I see Cassandra preparing dinner.

The scene is in such a contrast to my old life that I stop to take in the moment. *How did I get here?* I should be in Vienna with Eugen, cataloging the furniture we bought in Rajasthan for our gallery. Instead, I find myself outside the home of a woman I barely know, having done something I don't understand, which involved taking a substance I'm trying hard not to judge.

As I raise my hand to tap on the window, something bats my leg, causing me to jump. On the deck chair right next to me, a large black cat lies on its side, looking pleased that he was able to send me into orbit. His strong body and thick short fur remind me of a miniature black panther.

I bend down and scratch him under his chin. "Hello, what's your name?"

He rubs his cheek against my finger, then gives it a friendly bite. I pull away, but he gently touches my hand with his paw, as if to apologize. I stroke him on the head, listening to his rumbling purr, then stand up and knock on the door.

Cassandra looks up when she hears the knock and waves me inside. We give each other a warm hug. Her home is just like a house in the desert should be; a well-equipped kitchen, a sitting room with tall ceilings, French doors opening onto patios, a few rustic pieces of painted furniture, and loads of skylights. Picture windows frame the landscape like paintings on every wall.

Judging from the smells in the kitchen, dinner is nearly ready. Helping her by setting the table, I see a French grammar workbook on the oak dining table and pick it up. "Are you learning French?"

"I'm a hopeless Francophile," she answers, giving the pot on the stove one more stir, then placing the wooden spoon on the countertop. "I fell in love with France when I was a surfer traveling the world looking for the perfect wave."

Seeing that it is difficult for her to walk with too much in her hands, I wave her on and pick up the pot of stew and follow her into the dining room. "You used to be a surfer?"

"I was a professional athlete," she says, settling onto the chair as I put the pot on the table. "Hard to believe, isn't it?" She gives me a gentle smile as she ladles hearty portions of green chili into my bowl. "Luckily I got pretty early on that I'm not this body." I look at her as she says this, but I'm so tired that my mind doesn't even bother trying to understand. I don't even notice that we barely speak during the meal. It is so quiet I can even hear myself chew.

After dinner, we retire to the sitting room with cups of tea. By now, the moon is high in the sky.

"I don't get it," I say. "I had hoped that after my journey, I would be feeling better. Instead, I'm hurting all over. What am I doing wrong?"

She laughs. "You aren't doing anything wrong," she says. "What you are experiencing is all part of the process of healing. Embodiment is painful, because you are having to feel all the reasons you left your body in the first place. The exhaustion from years of working too hard. Childhood memories. Parts of yourself you'd rather not accept. All the pain you are feeling isn't a result of your journey. It was always there. You are just becoming aware of it, that's all."

"Which is why I'm so tired."

She nods. "And the headaches. Night sweats. Aches and pains. I find bodywork helps. I've got someone I know who is good. I'll put you in touch."

"I thought I am in my body," I say. "Didn't that happen on my journey?"

"Your journey begins now."

"So what do I need to do?"

"Go for walks. Lie on your back on the earth. Sit with yourself. Get to know yourself better. Explore what takes you away from yourself and what brings you deeper inside yourself."

We stop talking as a *yip yip yip* floats toward us. I look toward the

92

window.

"Coyotes," she answers. "They howl every time the moon is full."

Just then, a gust of wind whips through the house, causing the windows to shake and rattle. It startles me, causing me to jump up.

"It's just the wind," Cassandra says, a look of amusement on her face. We say goodnight and I dash to my casita and lock the door, feeling like a true city slicker. Peeling off my clothes, I crawl into bed. My forty nights in the desert have begun.

The night is endless. I'm awake for most of it, staring into the darkness, my ears overwhelmed by the penetrating stillness. Why does the world always feel heaviest in the middle of the night?

When Eugen used to find me curled in a ball under the duvet, watching a movie on my phone because I couldn't sleep, he would gently remove the earplugs, take my phone, and coax me to sit me up to meditate. If you're awake, he would tell me, it's because your mind doesn't want you to go to sleep. So don't get caught up in your mind's drama. So I sit up, pulling the duvet around me in a cocoon, lean against the pillows, and close my eyes. But without Eugen next to me, it's useless. Frustrated, I crawl under the covers, not even daring to get out of bed to go to the bathroom—who knows, maybe scorpions crawl on the floors here at night—and end up sleeping in fits and starts. When I reach my hand over to his side of the bed and feel the cold flat sheets where his warm body would normally be, my longing is so great I cry for hours. I fall into a restless sleep just before dawn.

I wake up to sun streaming in through my window. I'm so tired from the night's battle that it takes me a few seconds to remember where I am. I run through a few points on my gratitude list, but it's not very long, so instead, I decide to look around. The bedroom is small and snug, with not much space apart from the double bed. A spider web floats like a lace handkerchief in the corner of the bedroom window. I snuggle back down into the pocket of warmth, but my curiosity overcomes my tiredness, so I get up and get dressed.

Rolling out my yoga mat in the middle of the living room floor, I collapse on it with an exhausted *oomph*. My body feels cumbersome, as if I am dragging around a lump of flesh. I try to do a few sun salutations, but even that's too much. I sit down, exhausted. Too tired to do any movement poses, I place my legs straight in front of me and fall forward over them, letting my head dangle in the air. Why not try a turtle pose, I think. Normally, I'm always left with my torso hanging in mid-air; my head dangling like a rusty spout, but this time when I bring my shoulders under my bent knees, then slide one arm after the other, palms down, under each leg, everything feels so smooth that it surprises me. Straightening my legs to lever my torso onto the ground, I prepare to feel the usual tightness in my gut that stops me, but this time, like magic, my rounded back becomes the shell, my splayed limbs the four legs of a turtle. I'm still unwinding myself, bewildered by this unexpected fluidity, when I hear a voice.

"A perfect *Kurmasana*." It's Cassandra outside the screen door. She is holding two steaming cups in one hand.

I sit up slowly and wave for her to come in. "I've never been able to do that before."

As she opens the door and walks inside, one arm swings as she gently sways side to side. The black cat I ran into last night on the porch saunters behind her in her wake.

"The turtle is a surrender pose," she says, resting her free hand on the countertop to keep her balance. "So if you couldn't do it before and you can now, looks as if you've done a deep surrender. Shall I come back when you're finished?"

"No, do stay. I'm done anyway," I say, getting up. "Is one for me?"

She nods, giving me one. "I hope you like froth."

"Love it," I say, pulling up a chair for her to sit down. The black cat jumps up next to her and lies against her leg, kneading the rattan with its claws.

I take a sip. "It's delicious. What is it?"

"Chaga latte. It's made from ground chaga mushrooms, hot coconut milk, grated ginger, cinnamon, and raw honey," she says.

I take another sip while leaning over to scratch the top of the cat's head. I'm greeted with a rumbling purr.

She smiles. "Mandu likes you."

"Is that his name?"

"Cat Mandu," she says. The black cat, hearing its name, butts its head against her thigh.

I look back down at the cat again. "Kathmandu. I like it."

She reaches up and wraps the shawl around her against the cool morning air. "What are your plans?" she says.

I go into the bedroom and come back with a notepad entitled *To Accomplish in Joshua Tree*. "Let's see. Two hours of exercise a day, including yoga. I'd like to learn to meditate. Start a journal. If I have the time, I may even explore the region. I heard there are some fascinating Native American ruins near here." I close my book with a satisfied snap.

I'm not sure why she thinks this is so funny. "You do know it's perfectly OK not to have any plans, too."

"I like to keep myself busy."

"Clearly." She hesitates. "I've got a few walking tickets this morning and would be happy to use them to show you around."

Walking tickets, I learn, is her way of measuring how long she can walk before her body gives out. It sounds like a great idea, so I wash out our cups, grab a fleece and we're off.

By now the sun is higher. It's an exquisite morning. The sands are dotted with giant rock formations as smooth and as oddly shaped as loaves of bread. Our boots crunch on the cold crisp ground. We come across wild burrs and watermelons the size of large grapefruits, lying tangled in the sand. The path winds around tumbleweeds and boulders until we reach the top of a rocky cliff.

Around us, on all sides, is the Mojave Desert. We both turn as we hear a distant noise. A tiny black figure is approaching us, hugging the edges of the rocks. As it gets closer, we hear a series of meows getting louder and louder. It's Mandu, trotting toward us as fast as his paws can go. When he arrives, he slows down and saunters casually for the last few paces, pretending he just happened to be passing through. His behavior is so funny we start to laugh. He ignores us and begins winding between our legs, then sits like a bowling pin at our feet.

I bend down to scratch the top of his head and am immediately answered with a purr. He closes his eyes, happily butting my hand. "I've never seen a cat who likes going for walks."

She smiles as she watches us. "Neither have I. But no one has told him that. He's not afraid of dogs, either. Once, a neighbor's German shepherd attacked him. Instead of running, he turned and faced the dog, hissing and throwing punches with his claws. A few well-placed swipes on the nose and the dog turned tail and ran."

We both look down at Mandu. He seems pleased to be the center of attention.

"It's amazing what you can achieve if you aren't afraid," I say, bending down to scratch his head again. For a moment, Cassandra and I gaze at the endless space in front of us.

"So why not live that way?"

I look up. "Live what way?"

"Like Mandu. I'm sure if you ask him, he'll teach you all you need to know."

Leaving me to ponder this thought, she turns to make her way back toward the house. Her body sways like a silk scarf in the wind as she moves down the path, Mandu at her heels. I watch them until they are only tiny figures, a woman and a cat, moving like brushstrokes through an immense palette of beige. She occasionally stops and bends over to stroke him, then the trail turns, and they are out of sight.

Soon, I know where the grocery store is. Where to find the best organic fruit and vegetables. Where to buy gas. Everything lies on the Twentynine Palms Highway except the Joshua Tree public library. As the only source of fast Internet, it becomes my hangout. I devour the books Jean Luc has recommended: *The Teachings of Don Juan* by Carlos Castaneda, *Food of the Gods* by Terence McKenna, Michael Pollan's *How to Change Your Mind*.

Clearly things have moved on since Dona Mathilde and her spiritism days. South American shamans now offer journeys in the jungle. There are shamanic courses, Brazilian churches based around ayahuasca ceremonies, and lots of spiritual tourism to sacred spaces around the world. Clearly, I'm not the only one searching for healing.

About two weeks after I arrive, I'm sitting in the public library when my rucksack begins to vibrate. Opening it, I see it's my phone. Ignoring the stares from the people around me, I answer it in a whisper without seeing who it is.

"Finally," a voice barks. Chloe's clipped British English blasts like a foghorn.

"Tone it down," I whisper as I scoot out of the reading room. Spotting a folding chair by the water cooler, I collapse in it and lift my phone to my ear. "Someone might pull out a gun and shoot me for this."

"Glad you still have a sense of humor," she says. I hear the squeak of a chair which tells me she's still in the office. "Mine disappeared after being on the phone with those damned insurance companies of yours." I hear the rustle of papers. "What a useless bunch they all are. One insurance company doesn't want to release your pay-out because they want proof it's an accident." She snorts in indignation. "As if Eugen wanted to throw himself down the steps. The other won't pay because they don't believe your marriage in Delhi was legit. Bastards."

Thank goodness for Chloe. Once she puts her mind to something, she'll go like a steamroller until she gets the results she wants. It's one of the things that drive me crazy about her, and one of the reasons I love her so.

I hear her tapping her pencil on the table. "We've got to get you some income."

"You're telling me. But I can't. All sorts of strange things are happening to me now. I can't even look at a person without downloading all the pain in their soul."

"Jesus," she answers. "No wonder you had to leave San Francisco. I had thought it was the fights with Jean Luc."

It was that, too, but I don't want to mention that to her. I've already had one blast in my ear too many this morning. "That's how

97

I ended up in Joshua Tree. It's so peaceful here. You'll see it when you come over Easter."

There is a pause on the other end of the line. "I'm not coming. Long flights are bad for the skin. Too dehydrating you know."

"Chloe," I say. "You've got to come. It's not good for your marriage."

I've got a better idea," she says. "You know that Jean Luc's uncle Emil has offered Jean Luc his home in Provence in August." She now goes into the ho-hum mode I know so well. "So how about this? You come to London for the summer. I'll break out the Pimm's. We can enjoy the season in London. I'll get tickets to Wimbledon. Maybe even wangle an invitation to Cowes Week. Then, once it's August, we can go to Provence."

I lean my head against the wall and sigh. The idea of doing anything social makes my head spin. "London sounds great. But this doesn't mean you not coming here. Jean Luc has even arranged a journey for the both of you."

"Drugs aren't my thing, darling."

"Ayahuasca isn't a recreational drug. It's an entheogen."

"Entheogens. Drugs. It's the same thing."

"Not at all. You take drugs all the time. You smoke. You drink alcohol. You eat sugar. You take sleeping pills."

"Anti-depressants too," she adds. "Work like a charm."

I lean back and gaze at the ceiling. "This isn't recreational."

"I'm not going to take LSD like your brother did. Look what happened to him."

Ouch. I wish Chloe would be gentler when she fires those Sagittarian arrows of truth. I run my finger along the edge of the water cooler. "You don't need to remind me how Peter died," I whisper. Instantly Chloe begins to apologize, but I interrupt her. "The decision to work with an entheogen was huge for me. After seeing what drugs did to my brother I made a promise to myself never to touch anything of the sort. But I'm glad I did. It has made a massive impact on my psyche." When she doesn't say anything, I add, "If I can face my fears, you can too."

"It's Jean Luc who needs to face his fears," she says softly. "He's running away. He ran away from Paris. He ran away from London. Now he's running away from me."

"Then follow him." I wait until the wave of defensive excuses peters out. "Maybe he is running away. But if he's taken this job, something in him is propelling him to do it. Find out what it is. Get to know him better. Who knows, you might get to know yourself a bit better in the bargain."

"I know myself."

"I said that once, too," I answer. "And then my life changed."

Her voice catches. "That's the problem. I don't *want* my life to change. I want it just the way it used to be. The way it was. Before . . ." I hear a muffled sob.

"Your miscarriage," I answer.

"And with Jean Luc gone, my chances of becoming pregnant again are nil." She sniffs again. "Oh damn." Then the connection goes. She's hung up.

By the time I get back to the casita, the afternoon has turned hazy. It's nondescript weather, and I'm in a mood to match. Looking for a way to cheer myself up, I knock on Cassandra's door. She's on the sofa, surrounded by balls of colored string and piles of dried stems of sage. She's using the string to tie the leaves into tight bunches that look like little wands. The colorful zigzag patterns made by the string against the silvery leaves is beautiful. Having finished wrapping the string around the sage leaves, her long fingers tie it into a knot. She tugs once or twice to make sure it's tight, then places the wand on the pile next to her.

"Smudge sticks," she explains as I sit down. "I use them to clean the energy of the journey space." She fingers what's left of the sage. "I'll need to collect more of the wild white sage soon."

"I'll get some for you," I say. "I've seen it growing along the path to the ridge."

Happy to do a favor for Cassandra, I walk back to the casita, stuff a plastic bag in my puffer jacket, and set off. The wind, cold and blustery, blows a few tumbleweeds across the path as I start up toward the ridge. After walking for fifteen minutes, I see little tufts of pale green growing in between the dry yellow grasses. It's the wild white sage Cassandra wants. A gust of wind hits me, making my hair fly around my face, so I bury my nose deeper in my puffer and start picking.

Chloe's call has saddened me. She's closing down. I've seen this pattern before. She runs through men like water, and if things continue this way, her marriage won't survive. The relationship will become like a rubber band that has stretched too much, and it won't be able to go back to what it was.

Before I know it, my mind has left Chloe and has latched onto Eugen, then Maria Eugenia, and then it's off, dashing into the never-never land of self-pity. I give an extra hard yank at a sage plant and pull it out of the ground. Wiping my forehead with my arm, I feel the dusty grime from the roots mixing with my sweat and look at the sage in my hands. I haven't been paying the slightest attention to what I've been doing. I cast a glance in my sack, see it's nearly full, then hunch my shoulders against the cold wind and turn back. I want to get back to Cassandra before dark.

By the time I return to the main house, my mind is raging like a storm. Keeping my eyes on the ground, I walk into the house, intent on giving Cassandra the sack of wild sage and scooting out as soon as I can to retreat to the casita and stew in my juices.

Cassandra is sitting on a chair in the living room, still tying the sage into wands. She takes the sack from me, opens it, and peers inside. She pulls one plant out, then another, and looks up at me in confusion. "What have you done?"

Disappointment is written all over her face. I brush my hair from my face. "I went and collected the white sage, just as you asked."

She places a plant on the table in front of her, and stares at it with dismay. Her long fingers gently smooth out the leaves, as if they were made of delicate lace. "Look at this plant. You didn't just pick it. You yanked it out by its roots."

100

It's the only time I have ever seen a flash of irritation on her face. "It's a plant."

She gives me a look of complete bewilderment. "Annabel. A plant is alive. Everything on this planet is alive, just as we are alive." Her eyes demand that I look at her. "Doing this work means to become aware. When you harvest white sage, it's a sacred act. You don't rip up the plant. You take a few stems, leaving enough for the plant to regrow. Instead of harvesting this plant's leaves, you've killed it."

I stare at her in dismay. "That never even crossed my mind."

She gathers the sage on the table and stares at it, as if deciding what she can do. "Separation is an illusion. You are this plant. We are one consciousness." She begins to separate the stems from the roots and places them carefully in a pile next to her. "Luckily, plants are generous and forgiving." She is no longer looking at me, but at the plant in front of her. "I always ask permission of the eldest plant in the area where I intend to collect sage. I take the time to honor each gift that each plant gives me."

I shift from one foot to the other. "And you do that with everything?"

She looks up at me, surprised. "Everything," she says. "The food I eat. The clothes I wear. The books I read. The people I meet. Only when I'm connected inside my own being can I connect with everything else."

Her words hit me between the eyes. None of this has ever occurred to me. I have treated the planet as mine. Plants are there for the picking. People, too. In fact, the entire world is there to serve me, when I want, if I want, and in the quantity I want.

"We get so caught up in our thoughts. Spinning our wheels."

I sit down in front of her. My energy has drained out of me like water from a bathtub. "I'm doing everything I can. I'm going for walks. Trying to meditate, although that's proving useless. Journaling. Yoga. Waking up early. I've got every hour accounted for."

"Why?"

I run my hand over my jeans, dusting off the film of dirt that has accumulated on them. "So I can get there faster I suppose."

"There is no there to get to." Her demeanor softens. "This isn't a practice of getting what you want, or what you think you want. It's not about identifying with your little personality. When you begin to identify with a deeper truth of who you are, everything shifts."

"'I know, I know. I'm waking up."

Her tone is gentle, but her words are firm. "In my experience, there aren't many radical awakenings. Waking up is a daily process of being present, no matter what the circumstances."

"Maybe I should do another journey."

She shakes her head. "You have to do the work. You must do the practices. You must do the inquiry. The plants and teachers are allies, but ultimately it's that commitment to yourself that will make the shifts you are looking for."

"I thought I was doing just that," I say, slowly.

She looks up at me with compassion and, dare I say, a lot of patience. "There is always more to do."

By the time I return to my casita, I feel like a wet rag. Here I am lecturing Chloe to get to know herself, and I realize I've been avoiding doing just that. I had thought I was doing such a good job of keeping myself busy. Now I see it was all about staying in control. Who am I kidding?

I pull out my computer and look at the calendar. My days have been categorized into endless packages of time. Flex! Focus! Free Time! With a look of irritation, I delete them all. I then look at the wall clock above the sink. It's white and round and simple—and it tells the time. That's all I need. I take my phone out and swipe it to off. For the next few weeks, I'm going to see what it's like to just be.

I go to bed early, and when I wake up the next day, I can feel another spell coming on. My heart is stuttering in my chest. And then the buzzing begins, and nothing really matters anymore. Tiny bubbles pour into my body just as the sun begins to rise. Sometimes they gather around my heart, then rush down my legs and fizzle around my feet. Other times, they crash around my ears, which hum and beep and roar. It isn't painful unless I try to resist it, and if that happens, pains shoot through my body like cramps. The streaming continues for hours, and I surrender, surrender, surrender.

You'll never get there, my mind says. But I know better than to listen to its prattle. Cassandra explained that my mind won't be my friend in this battle. And that is what it is: a battle. Waking up means identifying with the parts of me that are far greater than my mind, which is quite a shock, considering that until not too long ago, I thought I *was* my mind. All I know is that when one of these episodes happens, I have no choice but to surrender and let the body do its thing.

When it stops, it leaves me confused and exhausted. Sleep. That's all I want to do. Sleep has been given a bad rap. I remember doing a news report called the sleep loss epidemic. Lack of sleep is considered one of the greatest public health challenges of the twenty-first century. So instead of forcing myself to get out of bed, I decide to do something called a twenty-four-hour sleep. It's a mini digital detox. No radio, no books, no television or computer or Internet. No stimulus whatsoever. No food, either. Just water. Lots of it. This is the best way to give the body time to heal. I throw something on, walk over to let Cassandra know what I'm doing, and crawl back into bed.

At first, my mind revolts. It gives me lists of urgent things that need to be done, such as answer emails, work on my budget, worry about my dwindling finances—anything but stay in bed. However, once I don't give in to my mind, something happens. My body does a reverse gravitational thing and becomes so heavy I can barely make it to the bathroom and back. I sleep all day, get up and have a few glasses of water, and then sleep through the night like a baby. To my surprise, I sleep through the next day, too. Forty-eight hours later, I'm clear-eyed and more refreshed than I've felt in months.

From then on, my life takes on a different rhythm. Mandu, my self-appointed teacher, arrives every morning about an hour after the sun rises. Wherever I go, he trots behind me. If I'm going too fast, he lets me know. Loudly. He knows his limits. He will walk as far as the cliffs, but not beyond. If I want to explore farther, he hangs back and meows to let me know his displeasure. And if I still ignore him, he runs up and bats the back of my calf with his paw. When he sees he has my attention, he falls on his side and gives me a pitiful meow that I can't ignore. Vulnerability, he teaches me, isn't a weakness, but a strength.

He introduces me to his friends, the insects, whom he loves to chase. We say hello to the neighbor's donkey, who brays a melancholy foghorn to us every afternoon. We watch bats, which appear every twilight to pirouette in their evening dance. He shows me how to ask for love when I need it, kneading his paws gently on my chest, eyes closed in blissful ecstasy. Boundaries aren't an issue. Neither is fear. Or expressing his needs. He never seems to be worried about the future. He purrs when he wants to be stroked, ignores me when he wants to be alone, taps my leg with his paw when he wants my attention. He has no problem expressing his rage, either, and will bare his fangs and give a good swipe of his claws at anyone he doesn't want to have around—including me.

We spend hours together, listening to the wind whispering its secrets to us. Occasionally, when we gaze at the landscape, he sits on my lap, eyes closed, paws tucked in, and teaches me the elements of meditation. *Sit quietly*, he purrs. *Close your eyes. And feel.* We lie on a blanket for hours and hours, gazing at the clouds. I never realized how much I took the planet for granted. I've been in my head for so long I forgot I had feet.

With Mandu's help, I work my way through the emotions that have been weighing me down. And when the wind whispers to me at night, reminding me that Eugen is no more, this truth becomes easier to bear. Eugen may be gone, but I'm never alone. I'm surrounded by plants and trees and creatures whose presence can help me along my path. I pound the sand with my boots. Howl at the moon. Dance in my sitting room, feeling the earth's rhythms in my soul. I sit with my sadness. Own it. Become it. And finally, I let it go. And when I do, a deep undertow of time begins, stretching out the days so that they grow longer and longer until I no longer know how many have passed.

As my habits start to fade, rhythms of my own appear. I wake when I want to, sleep when I want to, eat when I want to. I spend time in nature, doing nothing but sitting still and absorbing it in its entirety. I visit an oasis in Cottonwood Springs, an hour's drive away, and sit on the ground, smelling the sweetness of the dried fronds underneath me while gazing at the palm trees towering above me. I spend hours feeling the cool wind on my cheeks. Watching the bees skimming on the trickle of water coming from the rocks. Letting the grains of sand fall from my fingers. Listening to the crickets hum and sing around me. I have been fighting against the rhythms of nature all my life. When I go back to my casita, I push aside the books about spirituality and grief and bereavement and decide to simply receive.

Soon, my bedside table becomes littered with a new type of book. Thanks to Karl, who keeps sending me encouraging texts, I begin to see food not as something which tastes good, but as medicine.

The more I listen to my body, the more interesting life becomes. I realize that I don't need to eat three times a day but only two. I don't want to eat meat and prefer to eat fruits and vegetables. And greens! I can never get enough of them. Spinach, kale, lettuce, mustard leaf, parsley, cilantro, mint. They are all delicious. And water. I used to be a camel. But now, the more water I drink, the thirstier I become. I consume raw food, love my fruit smoothies, and sleep and sleep some more. As the time goes on, I begin to avoid gluten. Reduce dairy. Stop sugar and coffee and tea. And I feel great.

And so life settles down to a rhythm. I attempt to meditate at the crack of dawn, and, if the occasional panic attack overwhelms me, I know I'm in my head again. So I take a long walk in nature to ground myself back in the body; cry or shout or pound my feet to work it through my muscle tissues; sleep, eat, and start all over again. As the days go by, I let go of truckloads of fermented fears. The deeper I go, the more subtle the process becomes. It's hard work, dredging up all these old emotions, and harder yet to feel them. But there is an upside, and I begin to feel it within a few weeks. In these spaces of emptiness within me, something new happens. I awake to the senses.

The first sense to deepen is smell. At the farmer's market I become a bloodhound, sniffing the bottoms of the melons, running my nose along pots of thyme and basil and oregano, waving bunches of fresh cilantro under my nostrils. My lungs never seem large enough to breathe it all in. But the most extraordinary change is my eyesight. It comes in waves, rippling across my field of vision as if the world has been washed. Colors become brighter, textures more intense, details I never saw before stand out, as if I'm looking at the world through a magnifying glass.

Over the next few weeks, these waves of clarity appear for only a few seconds at first, but then they stay for longer. Finally, without being aware of what is happening, they become permanent. The same happens when I'm with Cassandra. Before long, her unconventional wisdom is so much a part of me that I forget that I saw the world in any other way. Everything has a deeper level to it when I'm around her. A walk in the desert isn't just a walk in the desert, it's connecting with the planet. It's feeling her under my feet, sensing the warmth of her breath on my cheeks in the wind, the softness of her tears in the rain, the thunder of her anger in a storm. Recognizing that everything, whether it's the burning heat of the day or the wild storms of spring, is part of the cycle of life. It rains. The sun shines. There's a storm. It's dry. There's a rhythm to everything. And finally, I feel that rhythm within me.

Spring comes to Joshua Tree, and with it, a renewed sense of life. The desert bursts into color. Wildflowers spring out of the ground like gifts from the gods. There are the pale blue faces of the Mojave aster, the intense oranges of the globe mallow; the bright red desert paintbrush. Even the spiky hedgehog and beavertail cacti splashed with pink and magenta pompoms. After a long and difficult winter, it feels good to see everything coming back to life. Including me.

I am on my leather chair on the porch with my tennis shoes propped against the rickety wooden gate in front of me, feeling like a cowboy, when I hear a car door slam. I get up from the deck and see a rental car parked outside the main house. Clouds of dust float upward behind the wheels.

"You're here!" I exclaim when I see Jean Luc getting out. I crane my neck for the familiar profile of tawny hair, but the passenger seat is empty. Jean Luc looks empty, too. He is thinner, less sure of himself. Even his hair, which normally is sleeked back from his forehead, is looking a bit ragged.

Dinner is outside on the deck. The stars are twinkling like fireflies and coyotes are howling in the distance, but Jean Luc is oblivious to it all. The air fills with words, mostly his. Politics, business, sports, we talk about anything except what we are doing right now, which is enjoying a delicious meal with friends.

I think about this as I do the dishes and clean up the kitchen, while Jean Luc, who is planning to journey tomorrow, disappears for his warm-up session with Cassandra. I wonder if I was this disconnected when I arrived. Probably worse. I wipe my hands on the towel and hang it up in the kitchen, then walk back to my casita to retire for the evening with a good book.

But the night calls me, so I put on my jacket and sit outside to gaze at the stars. I've come to love these moments of solitude. The sky is a black blanket above me, the stars twinkling like pinpricks of light. I sit, listening to the distant coyote serenade. I've finally understood why spiritual retreats need to be long. It takes time to slow down. To get out of the mind. And to get into the body. It's where I am now, and it feels good.

I'm sitting quietly, absorbing the sounds of the nighttime, when I hear footsteps coming down the path, and soon I see the glimmer of a flashlight.

"Is there any chance of a cup of tea for a poor Frenchman?"

A more mellow Jean Luc appears at my porch gate. I make the tea and hand him a blanket so we can sit on the porch. For a few moments, neither of us says anything. A cricket begins to chirp.

I catch a glimpse of his face in the moonlight. It's etched in worry. "What's going on?"

He picks up his cup of tea and gazes into it. "Do you know, the Holocene began 11,700 years ago. Now we are living in the Anthropocene. Basically, it's when we humans came to the fore. Thousands of years from now, our descendants—that is, if there are any—will discover a fossilized layer of plastic and chicken bones."

"A sobering thought," I say.

He nods. "When I took this job, I hoped to be part of this movement to help heal the planet. I thought entheogenic substances would be of service. Only when we heal ourselves can we heal the world."

I've learned that when a man does this, it's like emptying out what he has inside of him so that he can get to what is really bothering him. I keep quiet.

He rubs the back of his neck. "But I don't know any longer. My hospital is more interested in profits than healing. My patients take far too many prescriptions. The people I know are either too busy distracting themselves or spiritually bypassing to make any true impact on the world."

"Spiritually bypassing?"

Jean Luc stretches his legs out in front of him. "It's a way of sidestepping the uncomfortable issues a person needs to deal with. It's everywhere—even with yoga moms and tantra and spiritual communities, whom I have always considered my tribe. It hurts me to see that the same people who claim to be focused on health and well-being are just as angry as their enemies. It doesn't matter which side of the political spectrum they are. People don't want to wake up, Annabel. They are determined to stay asleep."

"Jean Luc," I say, quietly. "What does this have to do with you?"

He gives me a sheepish look. "Am I lecturing again?" He takes another sip of tea. "Maybe it's me who has been doing some spiritual bypassing. I recognized this when Cassandra told me I had to stop microdosing if I wanted to do a journey. Fat lot of good that did me."

I turn to look at him. "Microdosing?"

He shrugs. "It's nothing, really. Friends and colleagues do it all the time." When I don't say anything, he explains that microdosing is taking small amounts of LSD on a regular basis. "It's micro amounts, really," he adds. "It doesn't make you high."

I don't want to judge him, but it's hard. "Is that why you've been arguing with Chloe?"

"She's deeply opposed to this. Thinks I'm doing it to avoid my issues."

I try to keep my voice level. "Are you?"

His gaze goes beyond me toward the hills. "All I know is that I've been running all my life. Running from France. Running from London. Running from my marriage. I've been running so far and for so long I've got nowhere else to go."

"And that includes your marriage," I say.

He expels a little air in a typical French pah. "I should never have married Chloe."

Even though I've been expecting this sentence to come out of his mouth for months, it's still challenging when I hear it. "Why?"

"Because she doesn't have the depth," he says. "Val had so much more depth, Annabel. I thought I could find it in Chloe. Now I'm not sure. I couldn't tell her this of course. I don't want to hurt her."

Val, Jean Luc's ex-girlfriend, is the most amazing Reichian therapist, and lives in London. Chloe always felt threatened by her, and now I know why. "Don't want to hurt her, or are you afraid she will leave you if she knows what you really are thinking?"

He runs his hands through his hair. "I don't know. That's why I'm in one country, with a wife in another, and my heart —"

"With Val?"

He puts his head in his hands. "I don't know anymore."

"Do you love Chloe?" I ask gently.

"I know I was in love with Chloe." He looks up and catches my eyes. "She got pregnant, we got married."

"Then came the miscarriage," I say.

"Then came the miscarriage," he repeats.

"America isn't the only place that's lost its internal compass."

His eyes cloud over when he hears this. He puts his hands on his legs and stands up. "I'm not even sure why I came here," he says.

"Chloe isn't here, so it's pointless. I'm going home."

I stand up. "No," I say. The words tumble out of my mouth. "I'll journey with you."

"You?"

I nod. "You've always been there for me. Now I can be here for you."

Jean Luc crosses his arms, studying me like a doctor assessing a new patient. For the first time since he arrived, he seems relieved. "You'd do that?"

I think back to my journey. "Of course I will," I say. "Besides, what is there to be afraid of?"

By sunset the following day, we're ready. Piles of blankets and pillows are in the corner. Candles burn around the room. Cool desert air wafts in from the open doors. Golden fingers of sunlight stretch like multicolored streamers across the powder-blue sky. Within minutes, the sun slides behind the horizon, the color fades, and the evening sets in. It's time for the journey to begin.

The double journey with Jean Luc is not at all what I expected. It is the journey of light and dark. To my surprise, Jean Luc spends most of the night sitting on the sofa, discussing lightness as if it were a theme in an amusement park.

However, the ayahuasca certainly has taken affect with me. I spend my journey on the floor, floundering about in the one place I have spent most of my life avoiding: darkness.

"*Ah bien sûr.*" I hear Jean Luc saying to Cassandra. "I can see what you are pointing out. Yes. I've killed people. I have mutilated and shot and murdered and tortured people."

I roll over on my side and hold my stomach. Where are those endless skies? The interconnectivity and harmony of it all? This journey is nothing like my previous one. I can't find any joy at all. I look up, begging Jean Luc and Cassandra to help me. "Um, excuse me. I'm having a hard time listening to this conversation. Can we change the subject?"

Jean Luc looks at me as if I were a child. "You know perfectly well that you've killed people too."

I know that! I roll into a ball, trying not to hear his words. But it's no good. All I have to do is close my eyes and all the visions of every horrible thing I've ever done throughout eons flash in front of my eyes. Mutilations. Chopping off people's heads. Dismembering them. Poisoning them. Torturing them. Tearing them apart limb by limb. It's blood, it's gore, it's gruesome—and it has all been done by me. I'm watching the worst horror film of my life, and I can't change the channel.

Jean Luc, on the other hand, is having a wonderful time. He says that he can't feel the ayahuasca. Later, once I began to understand how journeys work, I realized that it is because he was resisting. Whatever it was that was coming up, he wasn't going there.

Cassandra asks me if I want to do some work not a moment too soon. Gratefully I accept, but my body is so rubbery that Jean Luc has to prop me up with pillows so I don't fall over. Cassandra later tells me it's because I couldn't hold the energy. Without Jean Luc's help, I flop on my side like a limp balloon.

"What's wrong with me?" I whisper.

"Is this the Mommy-Daddy journey?" In that moment, I understand why she's considered one of the best teachers out there. I collapse from eons of disembodied pain into a single childhood of pain: my own. I've hit cushions to connect with my rage and my sadness. I've read books to be psychologically aware and done enough self-help courses to understand what happened during my childhood and why. My defense mechanism when I was young was to be absent. To remove myself from my body. I did this for so long that this feeling of being disassociated from myself became natural.

All Cassandra needs to do is ask a question about my childhood and I throw up. I throw up so often that it becomes one solid movement of regurgitating pain, over and over again, until I can't believe I have anything left. And then it starts all over.

Cunt! Whore! Bitch! My father's voice screaming at me when I came home just minutes beyond my midnight curfew. The brutality

111

of being sexually abused by a trusted friend of the family. Of being left to fend for myself when I was far too young. Of being beaten and abandoned. My self-worth, both as an individual and as a woman, being systematically erased until I became a Barbie doll aiming to satisfy my parents' unfulfilled ambitions. No wonder I don't know who I am. It was pummeled out of me from the moment I was born.

It takes hours for Cassandra to help me to return, step by step, back to the moment when, in order to survive the trauma, I disconnected from myself. I have been flying, untethered from my essence, for most of my life. I get, to the core of my being, how wounded I am. Like a lotus, I've been struggling to grow toward the sunlight but have never managed because I couldn't establish roots. The roots of a lotus lie deep in the blackness of the mud. And until I can embrace this darkness within me, I will never be able to deepen into myself. No wonder life has been such a struggle. When my journey is over, I'm so physically exhausted that I don't hear their conversations. I can't think of participating in the post-journey soup. I'm out for the rest of the night.

I wake to the sound of my own breathing. There is a stillness within me that I have never felt before. No wonder I could never meditate. Every time my awareness deepened, I felt nauseous. Now I know why. I have been living with a garbage can of rage inside me. I did psychological work to understand it. I even emoted primal screams to express it. But I have never been able to do the simple work of feeling it.

My life can be divided into two parts: before journeywork and after journeywork. Before, I was always chasing. Chasing to be accepted. Chasing to be loved. Chasing to achieve security. Hoping that I could fill it with something—job, house, husband, children. The list was endless. But now that I have entered my black hole, I feel tired, but free. Free enough to do the one thing I have been avoiding for so long.

By the time I arrive at breakfast, Jean Luc is sitting at the kitchen table talking to Cassandra. He has showered, his cheeks freshly shaven, his clean wet hair combed back neatly from his forehead. Judging from the plate in front of him, he has had a massive integration breakfast. He looks as radiant as a teenager.

Unlike me.

"How's the stomach?" Jean Luc says, as I crawl into my chair. Every muscle in my body aches.

Jean Luc goes back to finishing his breakfast. "That was impressive. I didn't know it was physically possible to throw up that much."

I wave away Cassandra's offer of breakfast. "Uh, no thanks."

"Try to eat something," Cassandra says. She gives me a little dry toast, then sits down across from me. "It will ground you."

The toast tastes like plastic. "I'll need all the grounding I can get, especially with the decision I've made."

Both Jean Luc and Cassandra look at me.

"I'm going to visit my parents on my way back to London."

Jean Luc looks at me over his mug. "*Et dis donc.* That is big."

"That's beautiful," Cassandra says.

I turn to Jean Luc. "What about you?"

"Once you left, I found I had a few difficult truths of my own to deal with."

Cassandra turns to him. "Such as?"

He runs his fingers through his wet hair. His face is so relaxed the shadows around his eyes have disappeared. "Such as the world does not need one more tantra teacher. So my plans of running a tantra seminar at my great uncle's place in Provence in August will come to nil. One the other hand, the world needs your teachings. So I have an idea." He leans forward, resting his forearms on the table. " Why don't you come instead?"

Cassandra's eyes widen. She folds and refolds the napkin in front of her. "Thank you, Jean Luc. But I can't. This body is too weak."

He continues to smile. "You love France. You need a holiday. And I am a doctor so I can take care of you in Europe."

"Well," she answers. "I couldn't possibly. I only travel for work."

Jean Luc and I exchange glances.

"Even better," he answers. "Annabel and I know dozens of people who would be interested in your work. The villa can fit us all."

Cassandra shakes her head. "No, both of you. Stop. That's not what I meant."

But Jean Luc isn't paying the slightest attention to what she's saying. Neither am I. In our post-journey state, we are sensitive enough to read energy, and hers is saying yes loud and clear.

Jean Luc smiles. "Annabel knows Provence, and she knows you and your needs," he says, looking Cassandra in the eye. "If we are lucky, we may even convince her to take the job of coordinating this all."

Cassandra can't help herself. "Which month did you say it would be?"

That's when we know it will work.

Before I leave Joshua Tree, it's all arranged. Cassandra will spend the month of August in Provence. The wildcard in all this is Chloe, of course. Although Jean Luc doesn't believe it, I know she will come, even if it is a retreat. I just have to figure out how.

My parents' house in Kansas is a colonial red-brick home with white trim. It has two bay windows in the front and an open porch at the back that overlooks the meadows beyond. My favorite room is the mahogany-paneled library, where my father loved to retreat after work with a single malt. The countryside that surrounds the house is filled with fields of corn and wheat and the occasional pumping jack, swinging like a seesaw.

My decision to come to Kansas has surprised my parents as much as it has surprised me. It's been well over a decade since we last saw each other. As I drive in from the airport, everything seems smaller than I remember. The house is smaller. The city is smaller. Even my parents are smaller. The ogres who lorded over me when I was a child are now old and fragile.

Since I was last here, life has throttled my father. A sailing accident ripped off the fingers on his left hand. His chest was sliced open in quadruple bypass surgery. He has lost most of his money and all his homes, apart from the homestead, and with that, his church has lost interest in him. His English accent is faint. His hair is gone, but his spirit is still feisty. My mother, still an attractive woman in her eighties, is as gentle as a child and as pampered as a Persian cat.

In the decade since we last saw each other, we have each lost what was dear to us. I have lost my husband and the love of my life. My father has lost his money. My mother has lost her youthful beauty. We are all in mourning.

The mornings are defined by religious programming interspersed with FOX News. Music blasts throughout the sound system all day, mostly Mendelssohn and Bruch and Brahms, the long, haunting melodies of the violins deepening my parents' lonely despair. Scrabble is played at night, followed by reruns of *Masterpiece Theatre*.

My father covertly watches me doing yoga from behind the library door.

Initially, we dance and dip to avoid any conversation that could remotely cause contention, but it doesn't take long before this comes to an end. We're sitting on the porch after dinner when the moment of truth arrives. I begin to tell my parents, calmly and succinctly, how I felt when they left me when I was only ten years old. How difficult it was for me to take care of myself. Fend for myself. By the time I mention the words sexual abuse, my father looks like he's going to explode.

Kansas is tornado country. When I was young, I always knew when a tornado could appear because nature would become silent. The stillness wasn't pleasant, it was menacing. So was the flat, yellowish light. Police cars would drive through the neighborhoods, sirens wailing. Radio and television would flash warnings, leaving everyone on tenterhooks, waiting to see what nature would do.

Sometimes, the weather worsened. Thunder growled, lightning flashed, and winds blew in gusts strong enough to tear limbs from trees and roofs from houses. Twisters, as they were known, would sweep across the plains like long, thin black ropes, dancing in the charcoal sky. When they landed, they could easily tear off the roof of one house, leave the next house untouched and destroy a third. The destruction was random, and that's why it was so frightening. That is how my father's anger is. Indiscriminate. Unexpected. And violent.

"Liar!" my father screams as he leaps up from the table. His eyes bulge. Sweat gathers on his forehead. He rushes into the house, my mother fluttering in his wake, trying to appease him.

But now my father is too old to do much damage. It's almost embarrassing to see him as he returns, dragging my suitcase, then stopping to catch his breath as he attempts to throw it at my feet. It makes a clattering noise on the wooden floor. "Take it and be gone." He's shaking so much that he collapses into a chair. "Look at you," he growls. "Coming here begging. You just want money."

I could scream back. Get my revenge for all those years he's treated me this way. But what's the point? What will it give me? A few moments of satisfaction? If I do that, I'm still part of the problem. Fighting anger with anger isn't the solution. I can be bigger than that. I take all those thoughts screaming around my head and stuff them inside me where I can process them later. Then, I pick up the suitcase from the floor and move it out of the way to sit down next to him. "This isn't about money."

"Of course it's about money," my father snaps. "Everything is always about money." His eyes shine with desperation. "I could get you a job at the church. As a secretary. I still have some sway there."

The idea that I would return to Kansas to work for his church is so outrageous I can't think of a reply. My mouth comes to my rescue. "Daddy," it says. "I'm not here to punish you, but to heal me."

He stops, mid-sentence. My response is so far beyond his comprehension that the only thing he can do is stare at me. But I now know the truth. I'll never receive an apology. In fact, I'll never receive many of the things that I had hoped for from this trip. Neither parent is capable of it.

After the blowout, it's like the aftermath of a storm. We cautiously inspect the damage, carefully tiptoeing around each other, throwing out feelers to find safe subjects to talk about. Overly polite to each other, we search to bridge the gaps between us, throwing ropes across schisms as wide as the Grand Canyon to find common ground. We traverse different world views. Political views. Belief systems.

I have faced a lot of adversity, but behind all the languages I speak and the countries I have lived in, I see that, just like Dorothy in *The Wizard of Oz*, my life is all about coming home. But my home isn't here. It never was. And it never will be.

But I'm glad I came, because I now know that the person holding onto the baggage of the past is me. That means it's up to me to let it go.

This entire process that I am in, call it waking up or what you will, is about becoming an adult. Most people in the world—especially many of those who are running our countries and our corporations—are children. My parents are no exception. Rather than becoming adults, they have just become old.

STONE

London

Any fool can know. The point is to understand
—Albert Einstein

Rain pelts against my taxi window as I ride into town from Heathrow airport. Even though it's the beginning of May, the weather is as gray as I feel. After the wild expanse of the desert and the endless plains of Kansas, I find London's drab urban sprawl depressing. I wrap my shawl around my neck and slide deeper into the seat, listening to the sound of the traffic. Everything feels heavy, even the passersby wearing lackluster clothing in grays and blacks. I used to think of Britain as dignified. Orderly. Sedate. Now it just looks tired.

But maybe that's just me. The truth is, I've always loved London. When I first moved here, it represented freedom for me. Because of my English father, I feel comfortable with British habits, such as eating with the knife in the right hand and fork in the left.

After graduating from Columbia Journalism School in New York, I left for London, where, following a stint in various newsrooms, I landed a job at CNN. I loved my fast-paced life as a reporter, breathing every news deadline as if my life depended on it. I loved the sophistication, the cosmopolitan worldview, and the cozy cups of tea in buildings that creaked with age. When I learned I was eligible for a British passport because of my father's nationality, I wasted no time acquiring it. No wonder London feels as comfortable as an old shoe.

My taxi trundles down the tree-lined Ladbroke Grove in Notting Hill and stops in front of a white stucco building with a large portico and peeling ivory columns. I dig in my wallet, feeling the heavy British coins in my hand as I pay, then the driver deposits my suitcases on the porch and drives off with a cheery wave.

I ring the bell and within seconds, the door opens and a tiny woman with wavy gray hair cut into a fashionable French bob throws her arms to the heavens and bustles me into the foyer. Jeanette, who has worked with Chloe for as long as I can remember, is so much a part of Chloe's home that I can't imagine the city without her. We spend a few teary-eyed minutes over Eugen, then move on to subjects most Brits retreat to when they don't know what to say, such as the royals and the weather. Chloe will be back for dinner, she explains, helping me with my suitcases and closing the door.

Although Chloe may think of herself as progressive, when it comes to decoration, she's as traditional as English chintz. As usual, the house is filled with flowers—white flowers in particular. There's a vase of white roses in the entranceway, white geraniums in the flower boxes, and even white magnolia and dogwood trees in the back garden. The house is cluttered in a comfortable way, with scatterings of leather-bound books and an array of exotic objects from her father's army days in the Middle East. The guest room, with its large windows overlooking the communal garden, has been transformed into Jean Luc's study, so Jeanette ushers me into the new guest suite on the lower ground floor to unpack and settle in. She places a dainty vase with a white rose from the garden on my nightstand, then disappears up the stairs to make me a welcoming cup of tea.

The room contains a four-poster bed covered in crisp linens, a silk Kirman oriental carpet, and a large mahogany chest of drawers with brass handles that tinkle when I open them. I wander here and there, opening and closing cupboard doors, trying to decide how much I need to unpack to make myself feel at home, when Chloe's black cat, Olive, walks in and rubs against my legs. Running my hand lightly across her back, I watch her arch in pleasure, so I pick her up and deposit her on the bed. She turns around once and rolls up into a black pillow.

Spotting the gleaming white bathtub in the adjoining bathroom, I can't resist opening the faucets to run a hot bath. After months of showers, the sound of gushing water is reassuringly familiar. I set my cup of tea next to the tub, sprinkle a handful of bath salts in the steaming water, peel off my clothes, and ease myself in. The hot water feels like silk against my travel-worn skin. Taking a sip of tea, I close my eyes, breathe in the smell of roses, and relax into the scent, letting my body unwind while I listen to the faint rumble of traffic in the distance. Even below ground it's impossible to forget that I'm in one of the world's largest metropolises.

Afterwards, I dress warmly and walk upstairs to the kitchen, where Jeanette is setting the table for tonight's dinner. I let her fuss over me, and in no time at all, I'm curled up with a pot of afternoon tea and warm buttered crumpets by the gas fire in the sitting room. I take a bite of a crumpet—the original English muffin, Chloe loves pointing out—and get to work tackling the pile of mail Christiane has forwarded.

I spend the rest of the morning signing checks, chasing insurance companies, and calling banks. Every bill, postcard, and bank statement reminds me of my precarious financial situation. It is mystifying to be back where I began when I moved to Europe twenty years ago. Then, I was spurred on by my dreams. But now, the only thing in front of me is a near-empty bank account. I'm going to have to get a job again, and soon.

Chloe arrives home late. It may be the cold weather, but something about the way she is holding her body—it looks as tight as a wire—tells me she isn't in a good place. We eat a light supper Jeanette has prepared for us and curl up on her overstuffed chairs in the living room. A cold snap has brought winter to London, so the drapes are drawn, heat is blasting through the radiators, and a fire is crackling away in the fireplace. I'm nursing a cup of verbena tea, Chloe a glass of red wine, and we are nibbling on pieces of dark chocolate.

Chloe removes a hair clip with one hand. She gives me a once over as her long tawny hair tumbles down around her shoulders. "Hair blonder. Skin glowing. You're looking well."

Olive jumps into my lap and places herself in a meatloaf position, paws curled neatly underneath her. I scratch her behind the ears. "Thanks. Solitude does wonders."

Chloe eyes Olive's paws kneading my knees in ecstasy. "You were always more of a cat person than I am."

I look up from Olive to find Chloe staring at me. "I never understood why you didn't get a dog."

"Ben's enough," she says, taking a sip of wine.

"I thought he was your mother's dog."

She twirls the glass between her long fingers. "No, he's mine. Or was mine. He has been appropriated by my mother, anyway."

"So how is your mother?" I ask. "It's been ages since I saw her."

"Stuck in deep dark Herefordshire," she answers. "She never comes up to London anymore. Not since my father died, anyway." Her eyes wander past me to study the painting behind my back as if it is the most interesting thing in the room. Leaning back, she sways her head from side to side, as if enjoying the feel of her hair flowing against her back. "But let's get back to you. My life is so boring these days I can't even find words to describe it."

It's always this way. Every time the subject of her mother comes up, she does something to change the subject. True to form, when her eyes wander back to mine, I can feel a wall has descended behind them. "So. What did you do all alone?"

"I was asking a few questions of myself. Reflecting on why I'm here."

She raises her left eyebrow as she stares at me, aghast that I could do such a thing.

"You need to meet a man."

The only communicating I've done in the past six weeks, apart from the few days with my parents, has been with Cassandra and, briefly, Jean Luc. I realize it's going to take some time for me to adjust to social banter. I put my hand out. "Don't even think about it. Men won't be on my radar screen for quite a while."

Chloe pours more wine into her glass, then raises it in a mock toast. "You just need a few distractions and you'll be sorted. Just wait and see."

"But I don't want to be distracted."

"Distractions are what life is all about." She downs the contents, then wipes a trickle of wine away from her lip with a varnished red fingernail.

I tilt my head as I study my friend. "I wouldn't leave Jean Luc alone for too long. I'll never forget what my mother once told me. 'If you don't travel with your husband, someone else will.'"

Chloe gives me a look as if I'm an annoying fly. "God, what a patriarchal statement that is. Let's get this straight. He left me."

I nod. "Maybe you ought to ask yourself why."

Her ho-hum look tells me exactly how she feels about my attempt to analyze her. "You spent far too long alone," she says as she helps herself to more wine. "How long was it, anyway?"

As I glance at the bottle and see that it is already half-empty, Olive gets up and stretches, then jumps off my lap. We watch her slink off.

"Over a month. Forty days to be exact."

"Ah, the proverbial forty days," Chloe says, fluffing her hair with her hand. "Noah's flood was forty days. Jesus spent forty days in the wilderness. Buddha meditated for forty days." She stretches out her legs, kicks off her high heels and tucks her legs underneath her. "Enlightenment! The be all and end all of the spiritual quest."

I take a sip of verbena tea. Enlightenment, Cassandra once told me, isn't what spiritual seekers think it is. Slaying the ego doesn't make a person a superstar. In fact, it's the opposite. It is as if there is

123

no longer anyone home. I remember Eugen telling me about a Swiss friend of his in Saanen who was a friend of the Indian philosopher Krishnamurti. Sometimes when they were driving together, he told Eugen, Krishnamurti would be in the passenger seat, but it felt as if no one was there at all. I often wondered if this is what Cassandra meant. Thinking of Eugen makes me squirm in my chair. "It's strange being in London without Eugen."

Her eyes soften. "You must miss him terribly."

I slip further down into my chair. "I do."

For a moment the only thing I can hear is the crackling of the fire.

My friend lifts her glass up to the light and stares at the liquid. The tone of her voice becomes dreamy. "Do you know what I miss most?" Her eyes swivel to meet mine. "Touch. One day to the next, you no longer have anyone holding you." She brings the wine to her lips and takes a long sip, then places it on the table in front of us.

Feeling the familiar blanket of depression beginning to descend over me, I place my hands on either side of the chair and pull myself into an upright position. Self-pity and jetlag is a dangerous combination. "Let's not go there. It's taking me out of the present moment."

My friend picks up a square of chocolate and breaks it in two. "Ah, the present moment," she says. "That's where all pleasure lies. And that, my dear Annabel, is why I have a plan." She hands me a piece. "Here. Have some. It's good for your libido."

I shake my head. "No thanks, I'd prefer to stick with my tea."

She picks up the bottle and pours herself yet one more glass. "Suit yourself. But don't forget that a woman's female organs dry out if they aren't used on a regular basis." She waggles the glass under my nose. "That is why I'm going back on the market again. I'm tired of waiting for the immaculate conception."

"Chloe!" I say, exasperated.

She gives her mane a good shake. "I have a great life. I'm living in a wonderful house in one of the most fabulous cities in the world. I want my husband back."

I look up from dusting black fur off my jeans. "So why are you pushing him away?"

She looks at me with a defiant air. "What do you mean by that?"

I cast my gaze over the room, wondering why I never saw it before. "Look around. Where is Jean Luc? Where are photos of his family? He moved into your home, in your city. He even adopted most of your friends."

She rolls her eyes. "Well, we had to drop his friends. They were all boring. Just look at Val."

I lean forward in my chair and look around. The cluster of family photographs in the hallway. The invitations on the mantelpiece. The vases of flowers on the tables. Everything around us, from the portraits on the walls to the silver photographs on the mantelpiece is a parody of an English town house. "Why does he have to fit into your life? Why don't you fit a little more into his?"

She rolls her eyes. "Because he's French. And the French are simply far too foreign to be trusted."

I look at my best friend. Really look at her. Her thin hands. Her mouth pursed into a tight line. What I once took as self-assurance, I now realize is insecurity. "If he moved to California, why not go with him. Spend some time figuring out what makes him tick. Ask him what he thinks about trying again for a child. "

She frowns. "What does it matter what Jean Luc thinks? It's my womb."

I close my eyes. Talking to Chloe feels like bouncing on Teflon. "I don't get it. You never wanted to have children anyway."

She glares at me, then slaps her glass on the edge of the table, knocking the bottle of wine as she does. "Aren't I allowed to change my mind?"

I watch, horrified, as the wine bottle sways one way, then the other, like it's drunk. Then, as if in slow motion, it topples over the edge. I leap forward to catch it, but it's too late. With a muffled clunk, it drops on the beige carpet. A large red stain seeps in all directions like a pool of blood.

"Leave it," Chloe says with a wave of her hand.

But I'm already running toward the kitchen. By the time I return with Jeanette's salt cellar and an old tea towel, Chloe is on her feet, examining the now empty bottle of wine. "Such a pity," she murmurs. "That was one of my father's last Chateaux Latours."

But I ignore her. Throwing a handful of salt on the stain, I toss a tea towel on top of it and step on it repeatedly, hoping it will sop up the liquid. "Now all Jeanette has to do is vacuum in the morning."

"I said leave it," Chloe says, dropping the bottle on the floor next to the stain. As I step off the wine-drenched towel, she reaches down and picks it up between two fingers and stares at it with disgust, then drops it like a handkerchief onto the sofa.

"What are you doing?" I cry, snatching the towel from the sofa.

Chloe rips it out of my hands. "Jesus, Annabel. Jeanette will handle it."

I watch in horror as she drops it again on the sofa. "What is wrong with you?"

"There's nothing wrong with me," she says, picking up a paper napkin and wiping her hands delicately, then crumpling it and throwing it on the floor. "That's why I hire a housekeeper. So that she can do the dirty work."

I snatch the napkin from the floor. "Why don't you think about Jeanette for once?"

"Why?" she growls. "She works for me."

"Works *with* you," I snap back, placing it inside my empty teacup. I'm furious at Chloe for treating Jeanette like menial labor. For treating Jean Luc without respect. And for not treating her miscarriage with more dignity. I love my best friend, but right now, I don't like her. "He's your husband, not a lackey. You nearly had a child with him and you lost it. A miscarriage needs to be mourned."

"And what if I didn't miscarry?"

The words are so slurred that I almost think I'm mistaken, but when I see her with her hand over her mouth, I know I'm not.

"What did you just say?"

Chloe looks as if someone has just pricked her side with a pin. The anger fades, and she drops on the sofa and puts her head into her hands. Her hair dangles like long tendrils of seaweed in between her red fingernails. "It was a false pregnancy. Pseudocyesis, the doctor called it." She looks up at me with bloodshot eyes. "I had all the symptoms, the nausea, the fatigue, my breasts were swollen. Even my belly was distended. I could even swear I could hear the baby's heartbeat."

I sit next to her and take her hand. Her fingers are like ice. "But Jean Luc is a doctor. Surely he could spot it."

She turns to me. A tear slips down her cheek. "He didn't. No one did. By the time I found out, it was too late. The wedding plans had already been made."

"So you never told Jean Luc?" I ask quietly.

"And I never will." By now she's crying. "You keep talking about depth and I haven't a clue what you're talking about. I don't know how to dig within myself. Do you know why? Because I've never had to. Unlike you, I didn't have to escape Kansas. I know how to work hard and I have always known where I wanted to go. I was born with a silver spoon in my mouth, and I've been sucking it like sugar ever since."

She jumps up, furiously wiping the tears from under her eyes. A line of mascara runs down her cheek. "So I'm stuck, royally stuck, and fucked up, too, and don't know what to do about it. *That's* why I've got to get pregnant. Somehow, someway. Because without that child, our marriage is finished." And she flees the room.

The following morning, Chloe's rigid, got-it-all-together drawbridge is locked into place with all emotions safely sorted and hidden. Over the next few weeks, we make polite noises to each other but that's it. She doesn't want to get involved in a deep conversation, and I'm not in the mood to force her. Not wanting to stay at home, I make the rounds in London, visiting friends and colleagues for leads that might bring me work. I find a yoga studio. Buy a used bike so I can zip around the streets. But London is changed, so changed. People used to saunter, now they run. It was always expensive, now it's astronomical. When I lived here, everyone I knew was concentrated in a few areas of the city. We drove cars and found parking spaces, too. Wheel clamping had not yet become the norm. Neither had congestion and emission zones, and charges motorists must pay to drive into the city center. Now the pulse of the city has moved to areas I never would have dreamt of setting foot in a decade ago. London used to be an overgrown village. It's now become six hundred square miles of urban sprawl.

I stroll through Hyde Park, escape to a set of adopted parents who live in the country, ride the underground to meet with colleagues to talk about work, have a Reichian bodywork session with Jean Luc's ex, Val. It's she who makes me realize that I don't have the energy for, or the interest in, London. Weaving through the crowds along the busy avenues, plugging a finger into my ears to dampen the whining sirens and the rumbling traffic, I feel like a radio receiver with all the frequencies wide open. My senses are on constant overload, red signals flashing: *Alert! Alert!* I dodge here and there, get on and off buses, switch underground carriages, take taxis, keep my eyes on the sidewalks to avoid exchanging looks with passersby—but it always gets me in the end. I'm an open sponge, absorbing everyone else's mess, and there is nothing I can do to stop it. Every time I spend a few hours outside, I must rush home and lie down to recuperate for hours. London is short-circuiting my system.

Every morning, before the traffic becomes too bad, I get dressed and let myself into the communal garden to do a few yoga stretches while it's still quiet, then I lie with my back on the ground. This is a precious moment for me, smelling the grass and absorbing the strength of the earth underneath me. *No,* I tell myself, *it's not true, it can't be true.* London was my safety net, the one place in the world which felt like home. Chloe's house, my career as a journalist, everything I identified with, was always here. I need to get up, get a job, get back into life. But the more I repeat this, the more I know I'm lying to myself. It's not just the city that's changed. It's me.

One evening, I return home to hear pots and pans banging in the kitchen, which tells me that Jeanette is still here. I find her leaning over the stove, adding handfuls of chopped herbs to a pot of soup. Her eyes flit to the clock on the wall and she gives me a guilty look.

"I know it's late. But if I don't cook, Chloe won't eat, poor girl. She's too thin."

"Chloe's out tonight," I say, as I sit down at the table. I watch her bustling around the kitchen, chattering away like a sparrow in springtime. Within minutes, I have a glass of elderflower cordial in front of me, with fresh slices of lemon floating in it. I love being in the kitchen when Jeanette is cooking. Her body looks as if she's dancing, moving here and there, opening drawers and cupboards, sprinkling a little of this, chopping a little of that, giving me a spoonful of whatever it is she's got going. Jeanette refuses to cook meat—only the occasional fish—but what she really excels at is vegetables. Tonight, it's a Greek spanakopita made with wild garlic rather than spinach and a starter of potato and leek soup. The smells coming from the stove are heavenly.

I had no idea how hungry I am until I sit down. "Wild garlic!" I exclaim, beaming. I was the one who taught her about wild garlic. I learned to forage in Austria, where wild garlic is considered a delicacy. Before Vienna, I had only bought food in supermarkets, but Eugen's father, Georg, changed that. In the autumn, he used to take me into the mountains to pick mushrooms—the curled yellow chanterelles, the sponge-like morels, the stumpy boletus and elegant parasols and even black trumpets. In the spring, we gathered wild garlic leaves before they flowered, while they were still tender, to make pesto. He taught me how to pick nettles without being stung by pinching their leaves firmly, and how to choose the best dandelion leaves for a salad.

"And to think I thought this plant was a weed," Jeanette says as she chops the dark green leaves and throws them into a pot of boiling water. "The life force in wild food is extraordinary. You can feel the energy surging through your body with each bite."

As I watch Jeanette fold the dark green leaves into the pastry, the blue pullover she's wearing slips from her shoulder and to my surprise, I see a tiny mark. "Is that a tattoo?"

Jeanette gives an embarrassed laugh, as if I've caught her doing something she shouldn't have. She places the wooden spoon on the counter and pulls the sweater farther down so I can get a closer look. "It's the Camargue Cross." She runs a finger along the lines of the tattoo as she describes it to me. "You see, the upper part is a three-pronged trident, the lower end, a sea anchor with a heart. It represents three cardinal virtues: The trident is faith, the anchor is hope, and the heart is love."

She pulls the sweater up over her shoulder again and pats it in place, then picks up her spoon and gives the pot in front of her a good stir.

I can't help myself. "Why did you get it?"

She looks surprised. "It reminds me of where I come from."

"But you're not French."

"*Mais oui*," she answers. "Why do you think I can pronounce Jean Luc's name so well?" She smiles when she sees the surprise on my face. "I'm naturalized British. Fred and the children and grandchildren are English. But I'll never forget where I was born."

"Which is?"

"Saintes-Maries-de-la-Mer," she answers me. "It's a little town right in the heart of the Camargue."

Of course she's French, I think to myself, looking at her profile. There has always been an elegance about the way she moves and the clothes she wears. A little make-up. A touch of jewelry. I wonder why I hadn't notice it before.

"You know we're going to Provence in August."

Jeanette touches the spoon to the inside of her wrist, then tastes it. "Provence is sophisticated and gentle. But the Camargue is rough and raw, like your Wild West. It has endless skies and marshes and wildlife, like wild white horses and pink flamingos. It's where the best salt in the world comes from."

"Salt?"

"Salt!" she cries, putting the spoon down next to the stove. "Ninety percent of all sea salt in France comes from our salt marshes," Jeanette

130

explains, as she picks up the salt cellar from the counter. "The best is pure, gray, untreated salt, still in its crystallized form." She removes a handful and runs the crystals through her fingers as she talks, then gives me one so that I can try.

"It tastes like, um, salt."

Her eyes sparkle. "Salt is edible diamonds." She reaches up and opens the cupboard above her head, then takes out a small round canister with a cork top and opens it up. "This is my favorite. It's called *fleur de sel*, or flower salt."

I bend over to examine the salt in the canister. It looks like snowflakes. "What's the difference between this and cooking salt?"

"Goodness gracious! Flower salt is a finishing salt. That means it's not used for cooking but to finish a dish." When she sees I don't understand, she takes a few grains and puts them in the palm of her hand. "When sea water is let into salt flats and the water evaporates, it leaves a fine upper crust. This is flower salt. It's so delicate that it can only be gathered by women. They have a lighter touch, you see, when they rake it in." She puts the flakes back into the canister. "It's different from *nacre de sel*, or mother of pearl salt, which isn't so flaky but has a more rounded texture. The difference between the two is that one is gathered when the wind comes from the west, the other when the wind comes from the east—or is it the opposite?" She wipes her hands on her apron. "Well, one of the two, anyway. I prefer flower salt; it's more flavorful." She laughs. "Salt is one of the most powerful things on this planet. Just think. It's the only part of our planet that we eat." She reaches up and brushes her hair away with her forearm. "Not just for minerals and nutrients. It's a reminder of where we come from." She turns the stove off, then wipes her hands on the dishtowel. '

"Come from?"

Jeanette stops wiping her hands and looks at me, as if my question has such an obvious answer that she can't understand why I would even need to ask it. "She is our mother."

"Our mother?" At first what she says seems to be a non-sequitur. "Oh I see. Mother Earth. Of course."

She brushes her apron to rid it of some of the salt flakes that have fallen on it. "There is so much we say but never really think about, isn't there? It's where we come from when we're born and where we'll return when we die. She is our mother. And we are her children. She nourishes us. Feeds us. Clothes and houses us. She is our only home." She reaches behind her, and with a quick pull of the drawstring, her apron releases. She pulls it over her head and hangs it inside the broom cupboard.

I watch her do one last swipe of the countertop with the dishcloth before preparing to go home. "Remember, the world moves at its own rhythm, not ours. Even though things may seem static to you, they are not. Wheels are turning somewhere, putting everything in place. Then one day something out of the blue will happen and you'll be scrambling to keep up."

I look up at her. "Do you really think so?"

She gives me a gentle smile. "I know so. All you need to do is to be ready."

The following morning, I sit at the kitchen table with Olive curled up on my lap, drinking my morning tea while trying to ignore the jackhammers outside the window. I'm flipping through the classified ads with a distracted air when my phone rings. Christiane's face lights up the screen.

"How are you finding London?"

"Loud," I say. I finish my tea, close the newspaper, and put the cup down on the Prime Minister's face with a sense of satisfaction.

"I'm sure anything's loud after living in the desert."

Outside, an extra-strong burst of metallic rat-a-tat-tat hits my ears. The noise blares like a loudspeaker in my brain. Just then, Jeanette arrives. Taking off her coat and putting it in the closet by the door, she walks over to the window and frowns. Sitting in a meatloaf position in the window box, front paws firmly tucked in, is the neighbor's cat. As black as Olive but double the size, it's been here every morning since I've arrived. I watch her shoo it away, then, using both hands,

132

she shuts the window with a bang and waves me out of the kitchen. Wrapping a soft throw around my shoulders, I pick up the phone and walk into the sitting room and curl up in an armchair and place the phone on speaker.

"Are you enjoying London?"

"Sort of. I've been viewing apartments that are far too expensive to rent. Interviewing for jobs I don't want. Seeing friends I don't have much in common with anymore."

"So come to Austria. In two weeks, Mondsee is hosting the world's first international shamanic symposium." She laughs down the line. "Isn't that outrageous?"

Shamanism isn't exactly in Christiane's line of interest. "How did you find that out?" I ask, pulling the fuzzy bits from the throw.

Her voice bubbles down the line. "I was doing my culture-vulture thing and attended an exhibition on Venus of Willendorf at the Natural History Museum. And who did I run into but that newspaper vendor friend of yours."

My eyes brighten. "Herr Dietmayer? What was he doing there?"

"Attending the same exhibition as I was." She lowers her voice. "What happened to his leg? He has a funny way of walking."

I think of that lovely rolling gait of Karl's. "He lost his leg just below the knee when he was fighting in Cambodia. He was a mercenary."

I hear a gasp down the line. "Hard to believe, isn't it? A Buddhist monk saved him. That's what changed his life. Do you know he's over eighty? I wish I knew his secret."

But I do. Of all the people I know in Vienna, Herr Dietmayer is a man who knows himself. He once told me that spiritual freedom can be reached either by going up or going down, but if you go far enough, both paths reach the same place. It was a hard concept to understand at first, especially when I learned that his path to peace was through war. During the year that Eugen and I separated, Herr Dietmayer was an essential person in my healing. By the time we met, I already had realized that I had hit the end of the road when it came to blaming others for my issues. One of my biggest was sex.

Imagine my surprise when I learned that my news agent happened to be one of Austria's greatest tantra teachers. It was a long grueling path to free myself from the prison of my beliefs regarding sex. Slowly, with the help of tantric therapy, I undid my twisted thoughts, released my judgments, and when, at the end of my struggle, hidden memories of the sexual abuse that had occurred when I was a child began to surface, I could begin to process them and start down the long road toward healing myself.

Out of the corner of my eye, I see Jeanette head upstairs. Thinking of my own healing makes me wonder how Christiane is coming along. "How's the clutter?"

"I'll be attacking Attersee next week. If I focus it will be clean by the time you arrive, so you can see for yourself."

"And your diet?"

"Otto is still giving me a hard time."

"Have you seen Mildred?"

She huffs. "She told me I had to lose five kilos before she worked on me. How presumptuous can a masseuse be?"

"Healer, not masseuse," I say, but I know my words are falling on deaf ears. "All it takes is a decision."

"Easy for you to say. You never had a weight problem. I've given up. I think I'm going to be a voluptuous Venus of Willendorf and that's that."

"Venus of Willendorf?" I ask.

"She's my type of woman. Those glorious melon breasts and rounded belly clearly show where her priorities were. None of this anorexic pubescent teenage-boy look we're all supposed to emulate."

I could swear I can hear her smiling. "You do know what Venus of Willendorf is, right?"

"Of course," I lie.

"That's what I thought. You haven't a clue. Venus of Willendorf is one of the oldest surviving works of art in the world."

I turn my head when I hear the door opening. Jeanette peers in, a mop in her hand. She's on the prowl for a bat which she found in the attic the other day. She waves the mop at me, I wave back and she disappears again. "Venus who?"

"Not who. Where. Willendorf is a village in the Wachau. You know, that lovely spot on the Danube not too far outside Vienna."

"She's Austrian?"

"She's Cro-Magnon. And she is twenty five thousand years old. These little figurines have been found all over the place. Not just in Europe, but in Turkey and the Middle East and even as far away as India. And guess who told me all this?"

"Who?"

"Lili!" Her voice practically explodes down the line. "I had forgotten she works at the Natural History Museum."

"How is she?"

"I think she's a little embarrassed by what happened at the palace."

"So she should be." I gaze out the window, watching trees fluttering their branches in the breeze. The Salzkammergut region is Austria's equivalent of the Lake District in England and is such a beautiful part of the world. So peaceful and quiet. Unlike here. "Do you really think I should come?"

Christiane gives me a surprisingly level-headed answer. "Let's put this into perspective. I run into your friend Karl, who tells me about a shamanic symposium that happens to be right next door. There's a cheap flight from London to Salzburg on Ryanair. You speak German. You are interested in shamanism. And you've got a place to stay. Is there anything else you want?"

"A meeting with Otto?" I ask hopefully.

She laughs. "Done." She rings off, leaving me staring at my phone.

The train picks up speed as it leaves Waterloo station. I've got a two-hour ride ahead of me before I reach Dorset, where a workshop Jean Luc has gifted me as a thank you for helping him organize Provence will be held. I gaze out the window. With London behind me and train stations rolling by like toy villages, my body starts to relax, and my mind, too.

Rather than trying to fit my life back into the box I used to know, why not see what's being offered? I was invited to California to spend time with Jean Luc. I was invited to do a journey with Cassandra. I was invited to spend forty days with her. I've been invited to attend a shamanic symposium in Austria. And I've been invited here, to this breathing workshop. None of this I had to make happen. All I had to do was say yes.

When we arrive, a shuttle is idling outside the station entrance, waiting to take me to a farm set within rolling fields stretching as far as the eye can see. Wisteria floats like a pale blue shawl with tassels over the entrance of the barn where the course will be held. I check in and put my things in my room, then arrive at the barn just as the course facilitator, a tall man with black hair and a salt-and-pepper beard, walks in. He introduces himself, turns on the audio-visual system, and we find our seats.

Breathing, he says, is the cornerstone of life. A person can live for a month without food, weeks without water, but only minutes without air. It's such a basic thing that most of us miss its importance. He isn't teaching a technique, he explains. It's not something to learn. It's about unlearning what we were taught so that our bodies can breathe as they were meant to.

The bald man next to me raises his hand. "But we weren't taught to breathe."

The facilitator smiles. "Is that true?" He points to the screen. The first slide shows a boy facing the camera. He has just taken a deep breath. His chest is puffed up like a body builder, his belly tight, and his arms are splayed wide. Next to him is a second photo of a man in the same pose.

"This is a father and son," he says. "Both were asked to take a deep breath."

"They look like mirror images," a young woman in black leggings says.

The facilitator nods. "They are. A generation apart. We adopt our parents' attitudes. We also adopt their breathing patterns. That's why so often we end up becoming our parents. We unconsciously adopt their patterns. Their dynamics. We even breathe the same way."

He now brings up an image of a woman wearing a tight-fitting dress with high heels and a man wearing a suit and tie. "Because a breath is a full-body experience, it starts in the lower abdomen, fills the belly and arrives at the upper chest. But what happens here?" He points to the belts on the clothes.

"They cinch the waist," I say.

He nods. "This blocks the body's ability to take a full breath. Women's bras tighten around their chests, men's ties tighten around their necks. We wear clothing that inhibits the body from performing the one habit we do about thirty thousand times a day."

"Why would we wear clothing like that?" I ask.

He smiles. "Now that is a good question. Everyone stand up and you'll find out."

We all stand up and look at him, curiously.

"Now take a deep breath. The biggest you can."

I hike up my shoulders and breathe in, just as I saw the boy in the photo do. When I look around, everyone has done the same thing as me.

The facilitator nods. "You've all done what you've been taught. When you breathe in, you tighten your stomach."

"But that's normal," I say.

"Is it?" He gives me a mysterious smile and pulls up a picture of a balloon. "If you breathe in, the belly should expand like a balloon, and shrink when the air is expelled. A breath is like a bellows. Focus on the inhale. The exhale is automatic. Try again."

We all do as he suggests. But it isn't as easy as it looks. Try as I might to let my stomach relax when I inhale, I can't. It feels like coordinating two separate motions that don't mix. Becoming conscious of an unconscious habit is incredibly difficult. After a few minutes, each one of us starts to realize that the facilitator is right.

He smiles when he sees the surprise on our faces. "That's right," he says. "We're breathing against our own nature." This time, we're all more subdued as we sit down.

"But why?" I ask.

"Fear," he says. "It's the mindset of a warrior-based culture. When people believe there isn't enough, they become fearful and will eventually fight each other."

"But isn't that our nature? Survival of the fittest and all that?" the bald man says.

He shakes his head. "No. It's a learned habit."

Now he has all our attention.

"It begins when we're still in the womb," he says. He clicks the teleprompter and we see a newborn connected to its mother via the umbilical cord. "When a baby is born, it's attached to its mother via its umbilical cord." He then shows several slides of women giving birth naturally. "Natural birth attempts to recreate the atmosphere in the womb. The lighting is dim. The temperature is warm. People speak softly to each other. Midwives realize that a baby goes from the self-sufficient atmosphere of a mother's womb, is squeezed through a narrow tube, and arrives in a world of lights and movement and people. It's already traumatized enough by the changes. Therefore they try to make this transition as gentle as possible."

He then shows a photograph of a hand in a plastic glove holding a screaming baby upside down by its feet. "We're taught to treat birth like an emergency. When the baby is born in a loud bright room, rather than letting the umbilical cord naturally seal off, what do we do? We cut it. The baby must either breathe on its own, or it dies." He pauses to let this information sink in. "Think about it. Our first breath on this planet is in fear. Fear that there is not enough oxygen. This mindset—that there is not enough—begins with our first breath." He pauses again. "Then the baby is held upside down and slapped. It's swaddled so it can't move and is placed in a cage. In one fell swoop, the baby is cut off from everything it once knew. And you wonder why we are fear-based?"

"But the placenta can be infected," a woman says. "Or what about if a baby is breech? Or the mother needs a caesarean?"

The facilitator cedes the point. "I'm not saying we shouldn't have facilities in case of an emergency. We've come a long way since women were automatically put under anesthesia and babies were given formula because a mother's milk was considered dangerous."

"That was me," I say.

The facilitator turns to me. "Not just you. It was millions of us born before the millennium. You were never fed your mother's milk. Never suckled your mother's breast. If you have difficulty establishing trust, don't blame yourself."

He turns to the rest of the class. "How can we expect to know our rhythms when we were so brutally cut off from our mothers'? A woman's body and the planet are one. When we are cut off from one, we are cut off from feeling the planet's rhythms within us. And we wonder why the planet is in such a state? It's because we have lost a deeper connection with ourselves."

Our relationship with our bodies reflects our relationship with the planet. I'm still mulling this over when I hear, "Think about it. We do everything to pull away from the earth, rather than to rest on it. We wear heels so that only the toes remained on the earth. We've been taught to develop our minds but remain stunted in our emotional growth. Aggression is fostered through competitive sports. We are taught to suppress our caring natures. This separates us from each other and from the rhythms of our planet. This is how we have been taught for the past two to three thousand years."

"It can't be true," the man next to me says.

The facilitator's eyes skim the crowd. "Let's find out, shall we?"

As we arrange our mats in a circle and lie on our backs, he continues to talk. "A breath is like a wave," he says, as an assistant places boxes of tissues and bottles of water in strategic places around the room. "It ascends and descends through the body, starting in the abdomen, moving into the middle of the chest, and ending in the heart. Then the wave descends from the upper body and downward into the abdomen.

"Focus on the inhale. Relax your jaw. Let the exhale happen naturally," he adds as the music begins. For a few minutes, I close my eyes and breathe as he has shown us. It sounded so easy. All we need to do is breathe for an hour. But it's anything but that. My stomach is so hard it feels like cement. And when I force the breath, my shoulders hike up around my neck and I look as if I've swallowed a watermelon. Finally, after struggling, I hear the facilitator's voice.

"You have an overachiever's breath. All the air is concentrated here," he says, placing a hand on my abdomen. "You're trying to force yourself to breathe. Just relax."

Relaxing is hard work. I keep trying to anticipate what my body wants to do and then help it. Then, after I keep breathing, tiredness sets in that is so powerful I can barely stay awake. Because of my experience with tantra, I know that this is resistance, and know better than to succumb to it. I keep pounding my fists against the mat until, like magic, an invisible belt hitched tightly around my chest loosens a few notches. When this happens, I relax and the body takes over like a well-oiled machine. I take a deep breath, savoring the coolness of the air swirling in my lungs, as my abdomen expands like bellows. My ribcage lifts as the air moves higher into my chest, then the breath leaves through my open mouth with the ease of the outgoing tide.

The wooden floor feels soft and velvety. I lose all sense of time. I am in the same state of relaxed awareness as the journey space. But this time, instead of achieving altered consciousness through an entheogen, I've done it through breathing. This realization itself is worth the entire course. Now I know why Jean Luc wanted me to take it.

I don't know how long I'm in this no-time, no-space mode when something happens. Slowly, without even being aware of it, I sink beyond the me who is lying on a yoga mat in Dorset into another world.

Something flickers. I sense, rather than see, the blackness behind my closed eyes become dense. Heavy. And dark. My brain whirls, trying to make sense of it all. Oh, I see. It is night. Once I understand this, other shapes begin to appear. There, on my left, is an outline of a mountain. No, it is an island because in front of me lies a large body of water. For a moment I search to get my bearings. *Oh!* It is an inlet from the sea, and on my left is a series of islands that dribble into it. The largest is humpbacked, followed by two smaller islands. They remind me of the Loch Ness monster gliding through an inky sea. I am bombarded by smells and sounds and sights and it takes a moment as my brain frantically categorizes them.

I am looking through eyes that aren't my own. They feel massive and bulging and, oh my goodness, do I stink. It comes from the pelt that I am wearing. It is thick and heavy and when I sweat, which I am doing, the fur gives out a disagreeable odor, strong and pungent. My feet are encased in thick moccasin-like boots. Leather cords crisscross up my calves. My legs are thick and strong like tree trunks, and I am wearing something that feels like a metal bowl on my head. It takes a couple of seconds for me to assimilate everything before the moon and stars shift and I understand.

I am a Viking! With that realization, other senses come into focus. My breath is heavy and panting, as if I have run a marathon. The cold—it is winter and there is the crunch of snow underfoot—bites into my exposed cheeks. I am looking at reddish flickers in the distance. I hear yells coming from far away. The sounds echo against the mountains, amplified by the water. Once again there is a moment when my brain lags behind the sensations. It scrambles and sorts everything into something that has meaning, and when it does, a feeling of agony bursts within my breast.

Those shapes in the distance are a fleet of longboats on fire. The screams are my men flinging themselves into the sea. My ships are moored in the harbor and have been caught off guard and attacked. I hear a sharp crack of timber as a mast crashes into the water. I am on a cliff. I must have run up here to help and now it is too late. Tears of frustration burn my cheeks. My people are dying.

A vise squeezes my heart so tight that it takes my breath away. I—am—to—blame. There is only one honorable thing to do. I inhale and step into the inky blackness and cry out something that sounds like *Odin*—only later do I learn this is a Norse God. But instead of falling, time freezes. In this curious space of no-time and no-space, where time can be forwarded or reversed at will, I look at this smelly, enormous Viking frozen in mid-air and make a decision. I have had enough of taking on people's problems. It isn't my fault that my parents are unhappy. I wasn't abandoned when I was young because

I did something wrong. *Can you walk by the wailing woman?* a psychic once asked me. *If you can't it will be your downfall.* When I didn't understand what she meant, she cried with exasperation. *Can't you see that the universe intentionally puts people in difficult situations? Who are you to always try to fix things?*

Don't do it! I cry to the Viking. *It's not your fault. It was never your fault.* He must have heard me because he turns around and looks in my direction. His hair is stringy and matted; his face streaked and bloody. But it is his eyes that hold my attention. The torment in them makes my heart burst. The moment shimmers, and then a miracle happens.

He takes a small, tentative step toward me. The sounds of the night begin to fade; then the world shifts and I am back in Dorset. On my mat, my eyes closed, breathing softly, in a room full of people. But this time, the Viking is with me. He is standing at the end of my mat, his back to me. I feel his integrity. His generosity. His strength. But mostly, I feel his *power.* It stems from his inner compass, the center of himself where he knows the correct thing to do, at all times. He is the tallest of trees, rooted in the ground, he is the gentleness of the wind, dancing with whatever life holds in front of him. He is a person centered in himself, and oh, is he magnificent to behold. He lifts his arms to either side and falls, like a tree crashing into the ground, on top of me. However, instead of the resistance that comes when two bodies meet, his body falls *inside* mine. My senses go into overload, my breathing stretches and groans, but when I relax, my energetic straitjacket expands and I *become* him. When, minutes later, the facilitator asks us to open our eyes, my face is wet with tears.

I'm having breakfast with Chloe on the Monday after getting back from Dorset. Olive is eating her kibble from a bowl on the floor next to us. The neighbor's black cat is sitting outside on the windowsill, watching us. The sun is shining brightly through the kitchen window and making geometric designs on the black-and-white tiled floor. Chloe looks up from her Weetabix.

"Tell me more about this Viking chappie. Do you think he was real?"

"He was as real as my own childhood memories."

I know, by the way Chloe is looking at me, she doesn't believe me. But before I can say anything more, we hear a key in the lock. Simultaneously, we both turn to see the door open, and Jeanette appears. She looks as if she's been walking through a windstorm. Her normally chic hair is tousled like a silvery hedgehog.

Jeanette shuts the door and leans against it. She runs her fingers through her hair, smoothing it in place, then looks toward the kitchen window and sees the neighbor's cat.

"Shoo!" she says, picking up a dishtowel and flicking it against the glass. "Shame on you, squashing the petunias like that."

He yawns and jumps off the windowsill and disappears.

"I don't know what's got into that cat," Jeanette says as she shuts the window. "He's been stalking us since Annabel arrived." She runs her finger over the top of the window and grimaces when she sees it black with soot. "I washed this only last week."

"That's another thing I learned," I say as I watch Jeanette head to the sink and wash her hands. "How to clean your nasal passages."

"Now I would love to learn how to do that," Jeanette says, staring at the dirty water spiraling down the basin. "When I had the twins, I insisted on moving out of London while I was breastfeeding. I didn't want London filth in my milk."

"Oh, to have had a conscious mother like you," I say. "I was raised on bottles and formula." I turn to Chloe, who is finishing her cereal. "What about you?"

But instead of answering, Chloe stares at her spoon as if it is a foreign object. Her stiff demeanor is in such contrast to the relaxed tone of our conversation that I rerun the conversation through my mind, searching for something that I must have said that upset her. Looking for a way to ease the tension, I'm about to say something when Jeanette, wiping her hands on the dishtowel, walks behind Chloe and puts both hands on her shoulders. "Of course you were breastfed, my dear. Why do you think you're so grounded?"

143

Chloe drops her spoon on the table. "What does one thing have to do with the other?"

Jeanette gives a light laugh. "More than you think." She gives Chloe's shoulders a gentle squeeze. "I've known you since you were born."

Chloe snorts. "You've been working for the family for far too long then."

When Chloe treats Jeanette this way it makes me want to cringe, but Jeanette must have the skin of a rhinoceros. Giving herself a shake, she turns the kettle on with a decisive flick of her other hand. "You girls need a cup of tea. Let me make you one."

I give Chloe a little kick under the table and glare at her, but she ignores me and attacks the morning's mail. She pulls a stiff card from the pile with a triumphant air.

"Found it." She turns to me. "It is real. See?" She taps it against her hand. "It makes a noise when it touches my hand." She rubs her finger over the lettering. "And it is embossed. Just like stiffies should be. It says invitation for two."

I take the card from her and read it out loud.

"You are invited to a —" I stop and look up from the card. "A singles party?" The hair on the back of my neck stands on end. "Are you out of your mind?"

Chloe gives me a triumphant smile. "I've decided that you need to meet a man."

Jeanette bursts into laughter. "Oh Mistress Chloe, really."

The kettle starts to whistle but we all ignore it. I give the card back to her as if it is a hot iron. Just the idea of going to a singles drinks party is anathema to me. My body gives an involuntary shudder. "Maybe you need a meet a man. I don't."

But Chloe will have nothing of it. She tosses the card on the table in front of me and grabs her keys. "Be that way," she snaps. "I've got to get to work. Someone has to pay the bills around here." And before I can say anything more, she runs off.

144

Jeanette and I are so shocked we don't say anything. Finally, Jeanette breaks the silence.

"Poor dear. She always gets that way when she's feeling vulnerable."

"She's not the only one."

Jeanette looks at me when I say this, then does something that surprises me. She reaches out and takes hold of my hand. Her skin is white and soft and cool. It puts me off guard to feel her treat me with such gentleness. Her caring gesture unlocks the bolts to a door within my heart, which slides open and before I know it, I'm in tears.

"I can't accept that Eugen is gone," I say, dabbing my eyes with a tissue Jeanette just gave me. I look at her through teary eyes. "Have you had anything like this happen to you? Someone taken away from you whom you loved more than life itself?"

"Yes, I have," she says quietly. "I didn't think I'd ever get over it." She gives my hand one more squeeze before letting it go.

"And did you?"

Her sigh is as soft as a summer breeze. "Yes and no," she says. "I don't think you ever get over something like that. But what does happen is that you learn to live with it." She puts the kettle back on. "Cup of tea? That always puts everything right."

"Thanks," I say, crumpling the tissue with one hand and standing up to throw it away. "How lucky Chloe is to have you."

She opens the cupboard, pulls down a mug, makes a cup of tea, and hands it to me. "No. It's me who is lucky to have her. More than she will ever know." Then, as she turns to wash up, her voice floats over the sound of the water running in the sink. "Now. About this drinks party. I think you should go."

I pick up the invitation to look at it. "Why?"

"Mistress Chloe is more lost than she allows herself to realize. And you, my dear Annabel, are not as lost as Mistress Chloe thinks." She turns the water off and dries her hands on her apron. "All that is gold does not glitter, not all those who wander are lost."

I smile. "J.R.R. Tolkien."

She reaches in the closet and pulls out a cotton scarf. "Nothing is

145

as it seems. Sometimes you think you are doing something for one reason, and only later, you'll discover it was for another." She winks as she wraps it around her neck. "That's why you ought to go to this drinks party. I think this may be one of those times."

It's a warm evening. The lawn in Berkeley Square is so tidy it looks as if it was mown yesterday. I'm walking along a gravel path through the square toward number 50, which is where the party will be held. I spot Chloe standing in front of the house and wave. As she waves back, a black cat darts out from under a parked car. It scoots in front of me so quickly I nearly trip over it, then it disappears through the railings and is gone.

Not being superstitious, it doesn't bother me, but Chloe's eyes, which resemble two ping pong balls, tell me that she might be.

"Did you see that?" she yelps. "A black cat just crossed your path. What did my headmistress at school tell me you need to do? Throw salt over your left shoulder. No, walk backwards ten steps and turn around three times. Or is it thirteen steps? Damn," she says, pulling out her phone and tapping on it furiously.

I squint in the direction the black cat disappeared. "You can't tell me that you really believe in bad luck."

She looks up from her phone, panic written all over her face. "Of course I do. I don't walk under ladders either."

I put my hands on my hips. "Well, if that's the case, I'm in for a bout of bad luck because I have an awful lot of black cats around me at the moment."

She stops typing. "What do you mean by that?"

I turn towards her. "Cat Mandu in Joshua Tree. Olive here. Then there is that black cat hanging around in the flowerbox. Jeanette said it's been around since I arrived."

Chloe makes a last swipe at her phone with a lacquered nail. "Everyone knows that cats are impossible to herd. And yet you think that someone somewhere is placing them in strategic positions so that you can see them." She drops the phone in her purse and snaps it shut. "Girlfriend, you have spent too much time contemplating your navel." She slips her arm into mine. "Which is why I wanted you to come here. These are normal people doing normal things, like meeting men." She inches me towards the door.

Just then, a taxi stops at the curb. Two men, one shaped like a pear and one like an apple, get out and march to the door on unsteady legs.

I glare at Chloe. "All they need is a bloody cane."

Just then, the taxi driver runs up and hands one of the men his cane. He thanks the taxi driver, then hobbles by and rings the doorbell. The door opens, blasting braying cocktail party chit-chat, then he disappears inside.

I turn to my best friend and raise my index finger. "One hour," I say. Then, feeling like I'm about to walk the plank, I follow her inside.

It's a milieu I once knew well: nice, well-meaning people talking about nice, well-informed things in a nice, well-dressed atmosphere. As Chloe flounces in, the entire room stops. In one syncopated movement, most of the men stand a little straighter. It is always this way with Chloe. She has sex appeal, and she knows it. She waves at the hostess and disappears into the crowd, leaving me standing in the middle of the room. Grumbling, I melt against the wall and pull out my phone. It's going to be a long evening.

Just then I look up and see a woman watching me. We catch eyes and smile.

"Were you dragged here by a girlfriend, too?" she asks, and I laugh. As she hands me her card, I notice her eyes are the color of lapis lazuli, with the clearest whites I've ever seen. I'm surprised by the words written on her card. "You are a spiritual healer?"

She takes two glasses of sparkling water from a passing waiter and gives me one. "I'm surprised you even know what it means."

"I was raised by one," I say, putting the card in my purse.

Before we know it, we are talking like long-lost friends. Melissa is American, like me. A widow, like me. Stopped drinking alcohol because her body could no longer take it, like me. Going through a major life transition, like me. After a few minutes I've forgotten Chloe, forgotten London, forgotten everything except our

147

conversation. For the first time since I arrived in London, I'm with someone who understands me. "How did you become a spiritual healer?" I ask.

She takes a sip of water. "It's crazy, isn't it? Frankly, I had never heard of a spiritual healer until I became one."

Finally some interesting conversation. "How did you become one?"

"I was married and living with my husband in London when I began to get ill. No matter what I did, I didn't get any better. Finally, I flew home to Philadelphia for a checkup. That's when I was diagnosed with cancer. One morning, while I was in the hospital, I woke up to see an angel at the foot of the bed. He was the most beautiful being I have ever seen. He told me I was cured, and we had a lot of work to do. And that was that."

Just as I'm about to ask her another question, her body quivers as if an electrical shock has just run through her. When she next looks at me, her eyes have an unnatural sheen. "Who are you really, and what do you want to do here?"

I look at her a moment, trying to discern what has changed. Her body has straightened, her gaze incredibly direct. But it's her voice that gives her away. It's far too loud. "Um, Melissa, is that you?"

"Oh!" Melissa gives an embarrassed laugh. "My angel told me I would be working tonight. Do you mind?"

Here? In a singles drinks party? I feel the familiar tingle in the fingers and remember what I need to do from my days with Dona Mathilde. I look into her eyes—they look clear—and without any input from my brain, my head nods up and down.

"I communicate," I say.

Even before I hand my empty glass to a passing waiter, the angel is back. His tone is stern. "That's only a small part of what you are about to do here."

Melissa butts in. I can tell it's her because the tone of voice is softer, less assertive. "Oh! I'm being shown the word unity."

"You will unify people," the angel declares. "You've done that for many lives. I am being shown a past life. You were in a powerful

148

position, and you think you failed your people. But in the long run, it helped everyone. As a result, you take too much responsibility for others and don't allow them to learn from their mistakes. You need to forgive yourself. Can you do that?"

All of this happens so quickly that I don't even have a chance to react. One moment I'm at a drinks party, wishing I were anywhere but here, the next I'm speaking to an undercover angel who believes I need a course correction.

Just then I feel someone taking me by the arm and I hear a voice I know. "Dear God help us all. We've landed in a dinosaur park." Chloe's words have a mushiness that tells me she has had one glass of champagne too many.

With enormous effort, I drag my eyes away from Melissa, but I can't focus on Chloe's face. I open my mouth, but my lips can't form words. I'm like a fish blowing bubbles.

"Um, excuse me," Melissa says. "Just give us a few minutes."

My eyes swivel back to Melissa as if they are being pulled by magnets. Then everything disappears: Chloe, Melissa, the room, the chatter. By now, I couldn't break our gaze even if I wanted to. The temperature of the room rockets upwards. My forehead breaks out in a sweat. Then, just when I can't stand it any longer, something hits me like a thunderbolt between the eyes and I feel a searing pain. Just like that, the electrical cord that binds us together snaps, and the angel is gone.

This leaves Melissa and I staring at each other. We both burst into laughter.

For a few seconds, I stand there, blinking. It feels like I've dropped into the depths of the sea. Far, far above me, I hear a muted chattering. A hand waves in front of my face. My eyes follow the hand up the arm and I see long, tawny hair. Smooth skin. Long eyelashes framing eyes as wide as saucers. Chloe is standing in front of me waving her hand. "Hello? Earth to Annabel." Her voice sounds as if it is coming from a million miles away.

I rub the spot on my forehead. It feels warm and tender to the touch. "Ow, that hurt."

Chloe glares at Melissa, who grabs a glass of water from a passing waiter. "What did you do to her?"

"Opened her third eye," Melissa says, giving me the glass. "Drink it. You'll need it."

I can barely get the water down without splashing it all over the floor.

Melissa takes the glass from me. "How are you feeling?"

I'm having a hard time finding the muscles to move my mouth. "Strange."

Chloe stares at Melissa as if she is a foreign entity. "Are you trying to tell me that you have just zapped my friend? In a drinks party?"

Melissa shakes her head. "It wasn't me. It was my angel."

As Melissa begins to explain to Chloe what happened, their voices fade in the background. My senses feel as if they have been jumbled about and I can't get them all to work at the same time. I can't focus on what is happening all around me, but when I look at a person, something happens in my forehead. Sometimes, it aches. Other times, it is so pleasurable I can hardly drag my eyes away. I keep turning my head this way and that, staring at the people milling around us. "This is weird. Really weird."

"Jesus, Annabel."

Just then the muscles in my legs give out. They buckle underneath me and the floor nearly comes up to greet me, but I'm caught just in time by Melissa. She looks at Chloe. "You need to get her home."

Chloe, on the other hand, isn't in full working order either. She looks as if she is having an internal storm. Her face gets redder and redder, and I feel my forehead ache. Looking away, I hear her voice. "Why do these things keep happening to you?"

Melissa turns to her. "What things?"

Chloe does this funny dance with her hands. "Like losing your husband on the day you say your vows. Then getting kicked out of your home. And that time in the desert. That Viking chappie. No wonder you have all these black cats following you."

Melissa asks someone to call a taxi, then slowly herds us toward the entrance hall. "Black cats?" she says, trying to repress a smile.

150

"That's a new one to me."

Chloe looks as if she is about to blow a gasket. "But what does this all *mean?*"

Melissa only answers with a Cheshire Cat grin. By the time we get to the door, a taxi is waiting outside. Melissa opens the door while Chloe slips inside, then helps me get in next to her.

Melissa bends down and gazes at both of us. "We need more people like you," she says, then tilts her head as if she is listening to something only she can hear. When she turns, she looks Chloe in the eye. "*Both* of you. So hurry up." She squeezes my arm once, closes the car door, turns and is gone.

WATER

Salzkammergut

Since things neither exist nor do not exist, are neither real nor unreal, are utterly beyond adopting and rejecting—one might as well burst out laughing.
—Longchenpa Rabjampa

It's the colors I've missed most. Here they are again, just as I remembered, the smooth emerald of the fields and the darker olive of the forests. The Alps, dusted with white snow, and the lakes, placidly resting in their mountain homes and glistening sapphire, turquoise, and indigo. To me, the Salzkammergut is one of the most beautiful spots in Europe. As the plane circles above Salzburg, the rays of the morning sun shimmer like diamonds, showering a trail of glitter across the sky. I blink, my eyes watering from the intensity of the sun and the sky after the muted London grays, and stow my conference papers under my seat as we prepare to land.

I've texted Herr Dietmayer to tell him I'll be in Mondsee to attend the shamanic symposium. I also wanted to talk to him about the incident with Melissa. My forehead still hurts occasionally, but apart from that, I can't say I notice a big change in anything but Chloe. I think she is secretly worried I'm going to pull out a magic wand and zap her one, which is pretty funny considering I know about as much as she does.

I rent a car at the airport and drive into Salzburg and park in the underground parking that has been dug into a jagged stone cliff. Walking through the tunnel toward the old town, I meander along the Getreidegasse, the main street that runs through it. I'm surrounded by morning sounds: the shopkeepers rolling their grilles up with a *brrrrrrrrrrrrrr-rap!*, the squeaking of a bicycle bouncing against the cobblestones, and the calls of sparrows darting in the skies. I buy a package of blue, foil-wrapped *Mozartkugel* chocolates—the handmade blue ones from Salzburg and not the commercial red ones from Vienna—then spot a florist shop displaying the most beautiful long-stemmed pink roses. I walk past the shop, but the roses beckon, tugging at me to remember that once the smell of roses was the catalyst that brought Eugen and me together. Acting on a hunch, I go back and buy a dozen, telling myself that they will be a perfect house gift for Christiane. Then, with my arms full of flowers, I walk up four flights of stairs and arrive at Otto's office just as the bells of the Glockenspiel begin to play.

Otto's Salzburg office looks just like a compact version of his office in Vienna: comfortable and traditional, with Persian carpets and the most exquisite round mahogany table in the center of the room. Otto, looking very Austrian in a dark green linen jacket, greets me with a beaming smile and a click of his heels. "You look good. If this is what shamanism does, I want some, too," he says as he closes the door behind me.

While Otto hands the papers from his previous meeting to his legal assistant, I lay the flowers in the middle of the table, then walk to the window to gaze at the imposing fortress which dominates the town. It is obvious, from its rich Baroque architecture, that this was a powerful city when it was built. Salzburg's wealth comes from salt. White gold, they call it. The salt mines located under the mountains gave the city money, status, and its name: Salzburg translates as Fortress of Salt. No wonder there is the expression that a person is worth their salt. Thinking back about what I learned from Jeannette,

154

I make a note to bring some back for her to add to her collection.

The assistant, a bookish young man with a fop of red hair, puts a folder with Vasoy written on it in front of Otto, then returns with a silver tray with coffee and a bowl of Mozartkugeln. Otto pulls out a chair for me and we sit down. I smile when I see the small blue and silver balls in the bowl.

"Only the blue ones of course," Otto says as he takes one and eats it. He crushes the foil into a tiny ball and places it next to his cup as the young man leaves. As I pick up a chocolate, Otto pulls a document from the folder. "Do you remember Eugen left a few things with me before you left for India?" He hands it to me. "I now know why."

I fiddle with the red and white ribbon attached to it. "It looks as if it is part of a will."

He takes a sip of coffee. "It is part of the will. A codicil, to be precise."

Underneath it is a second piece of paper. All those umlauts and dots tell me it's in Hungarian. I look up. "I don't understand what this is."

He finishes his coffee, places the cup in the saucer and pushes it away. "It's a birth certificate."

Now I'm really confused. "Why would Eugen have a photocopy of a Hungarian birth certificate attached to a codicil in his will?"

"Because it's an essential part of this codicil."

I squint at the document. "But Eugen's name is on it. Lili's too."

He nods. "That's because Lili's mother is Hungarian."

I frown. "I don't get it. Maria Eugenia is Lili's mother."

"That's what we've all been led to believe."

I look up to see him studying me, then look down at this paper in my hands that is telling me something that my brain is having a hard time computing. "You mean Lili was adopted?"

"In a manner of speaking."

"Who is her father?"

"Was her father," he says. "He died recently. In India, in fact."

It takes a few seconds before the penny drops, and when it does, the ground nearly falls away from underneath me. "Eugen was Lili's father?" My mind is spinning so fast I'm afraid it's going to fly right out of the room. I start to say something, but Otto puts his hand up.

"It took me a while to verify everything. That's why I didn't want to say anything to you until now." He polishes his round spectacles with his handkerchief then places them back on his nose. "It happened on a family trip to Hungary. Georg and Maria Eugenia took Eugen to visit family relatives on the eastern shores of Lake Balaton. Eugen must have been a rebellious teenager and the family seamstress a real beauty."

Yet one more Vasoy secret hits the dust. Once again I wonder at the psychological workings of a family that is so concerned with keeping up appearances. "I take it Lili doesn't know this."

"Not as far as I am aware," he says. "I didn't know it until Eugen gave me these."

I lean over to examine the document again. "Eszther Szabo," I read. "So that's her real mother. Do we know anything about her?"

He takes the document from me. "Not much. What I do know is that it all began because Maria Eugenia couldn't have children. The moment she learned the seamstress was pregnant, she was back to Hungary like a shot. The poor girl didn't stand a chance. She was dismissed from her job and, without any steady income, took the money as a settlement and disappeared. Maria Eugenia returned to Vienna with a baby in tow and the rest is history."

There is a knock on the door. Otto's assistant barely has time to open it when Christiane rushes in. In her arms is a large tray of bright red strawberries.

"I've just come from the Grunmarkt," she says, wiping the beads of sweat from her brow. I couldn't serve just any dessert. Not with Annabel and Karl coming to dinner."

"Karl?" Otto asks, taking the strawberries from her and putting them on the table.

"Annabel's newsagent friend," Christiane explains as Otto pulls his handkerchief from his pocket and gives it to his wife to dab her brow.

I stand up, but instead of pulling me into her arms, Christiane stands transfixed. The handkerchief flutters from her hand and she lifts the bouquet of roses into her arms.

"You remembered," she whispers, gazing at it if it was a fragile baby. She buries her nose into the petals and gives an audible sigh of pleasure. "Oh *Schatzilein*."

The blood drains from Otto's face. It's clear he has no idea of what is going on. None of us do. Then I remember Christiane's reaction when Jean Luc gave her roses. Otto is useless with dates. He can barely remember his own birthday. Slowly the pieces of the puzzle fall into place. As soon as I can gather my wits, I throw Otto a lifeline.

"Otto was just telling me how he wanted to celebrate that you cleared your clutter," I say, picking the handkerchief up from the floor and handing it to Otto with a meaningful look. "It reminded him of all you did to make your wedding such an amazing event."

Otto's face flushes as he takes the handkerchief and stuffs it back into his pocket again.

"Yes," he says slowly. "Yes," he says again, as it dawns on him what is happening. "Yes," he says once more as his voice strengthens. "Happy anniversary, darling."

Christiane squeezes him so tight I'm afraid that he is going to disappear. Calling the assistant into the office, she gives him the roses to place in some water, then pulls up a chair as he appears with more coffee and chocolates. Only in Austria, I think. Every meeting, whether it is official or with friends, needs to begin and end on a relaxed and friendly basis. *Gemütlichkeit*, it's called. It means coziness or contentedness, and it's an essential part of business and friendship. Feeling the stress of the meeting floating away, I pick up another chocolate from the bowl.

"So what's this you're holding?" Christiane says, pointing to the document clutched in Otto's other hand. He is still in such a fluster that I take it and explain its significance.

Now it's Christiane's turn to be flustered. "Lili is Eugen's daughter?" she says, automatically reaching toward the bowl to grab two more chocolates. "Those Vasoys really are something, aren't they?" She pops one chocolate into her mouth and the second one in

157

her bag. "Are you upset he didn't tell you?"

"Of course I am," I say. "But I'm more upset that Lili won't have known either of her parents. Poor thing."

"Poor thing nothing," Otto says. He places a cube of sugar in his coffee and downs it in one go. "This codicil means that even though Eugen didn't sign the will, it is apparent what his intentions were."

I look up. "Which was?"

"To pass the estate on to Lili."

Christiane rubs her hands with glee. "Oh the press is going to have a field day with this."

I lean back in my chair and look at the ceiling as if I am going to find the answer to the millions of questions floating around my head there. "I don't get it," I say. "Why didn't Eugen leave this in his secret drawer?"

Otto gives me a sharp look. "*What* secret drawer?"

I bring my gaze down to meet his. "In his desk. It was where he put things that he didn't want anyone to know about."

Otto's eyes glitter. "Would Maria Eugenia know about the drawer?"

I shake my head. "I'm not sure. I know about it because Eugen's father showed me how to open it." I smile at the memory. "That was before Eugen inherited the desk, of course. Eugen never realized that I knew."

"I'll bet Maria Eugenia knew," Christiane says, her eyes narrowing as she crumples the foil into a ball and tosses it on the tray next to the coffeepot. "I'll bet that's why she sacked the apartment. She knows this is a losing battle. It's only a matter of time. Especially with that shifty lawyer of hers, what is his name?"

"Jakob Nici," Otto says. "Despicable creature. Lawyers like that are bad for our brand."

Otto is about to put the document back in the folder when Christiane takes it. "Just a minute." Placing it on the table in front of her, she pulls out her phone and snaps a photo of both pages.

"What are you doing?" I ask.

"After Maria Eugenia shredded your marriage certificate, I want to make sure she doesn't do the same thing with this." She swipes her phone a few times, then places it in her purse with a satisfied smile. "I've just sent you the photos. By the way, *Schatzi*. How well do you know Maria Eugenia?"

Otto takes his glasses off his nose and cleans them with his handkerchief. "Well enough that when I left the firm, I chose not to continue as her lawyer. It didn't take long for Jakob to find her. Rich widows are his specialty." His eyes lift to the clock on the wall which tells me it's time to go. We all get up from the table.

"So you're going to finally start the ball rolling?" I ask as I pick up my bag and swing it over my shoulder.

Otto nods. "I'll send Eugen's will to Maria Eugenia next week," he says. "Although I want to warn you. I am not Maria Eugenia's favorite person. Once she learns that I'm representing you, she's going to howl like a banshee."

Christiane hums to herself as she gathers her things. "So let her howl," she says. "After what she's done, it will be music to my ears."

My rental car winds through tidy, well-groomed forests and thirty minutes later, I arrive in Mondsee, a tiny town overlooking a cobalt-blue lake of the same name. Behind the town, the craggy Drachenwand—the Dragon's Wall cliff—ascends vertically from the lakeshore like an oversize film backdrop.

Mondsee—Moon Lake in English—is a collection of buildings surrounding an abbey and a monastery that have been transformed into a hotel conference center. Originally constructed in 739, the two structures dominate the town like twin Goliaths, their ancient towers and steeples thrusting into the sky. As I park my car on a side street, a deep clang reverberates across the town, announcing the hour. I've got just enough time to register before the opening ceremony of the shamanic symposium begins.

As I turn up the main pedestrian thoroughfare, a black cat leaning against the iron grille of a windowsill catches my eye. As I walk by, I could swear it is following me with its eyes. On either side of me are immaculately restored baroque townhouses, some with sloping roofs and eye-slit windows, others with wrought-iron balustrades cascading trails of red and pink geraniums. At the end of the street, the monastery, painted the same shade of ochre as the cathedral, opens into a square with graceful arches surrounding a courtyard. As I cross the square to register for the conference, I smell the freshly mown lawn and listen to the trickle of water in the fountain, and give an involuntary sigh. It is good to have earth under my feet again.

After registering, I hurry into the medieval hall. The large room, with its high ceilings and soaring whitewashed walls, is overflowing with four hundred chattering participants. As I'm looking around, I see a man waving his hand at me from the crowd. When he starts walking toward me, I recognize the rolling gait.

"Karl!" I cry.

I've never seen my favorite newsagent looking so good. Dressed in a long-sleeved white T-shirt and neatly creased beige trousers, Herr Dietmayer's smile is like the sun bursting out on a cloudy day.

"You look *wunderbar*," he says, giving me a quick hug. "*Komm*. I've got seats in the front row. One of the perks of having a handicap."

It's so busy, I don't pay attention to my surroundings as we make our way toward our seats. It's only when we sit down that I notice the woman with thick auburn hair in the chair next to me. When she looks up, my heart skips a beat. It's Lili. I whip around to Karl, only to be given an innocent smile.

As awkward as this is, I'm impressed by Karl's audacity. It's a masterstroke. This is exactly what Lili and I need: to sit with each other, side by side, without words, for an hour. Given the camaraderie of the audience around us, the ice between us is bound to melt.

We murmur a minimal greeting to each other and sit down as the clapping begins. Just then, the conference host walks onto the stage. I place my purse on my lap and sigh deeply, trying to get rid of my nervousness with my exhale.

A round of applause begins as a line of men and women dressed in feathers and bones, shells and stones, animal skins, and bright woven fabrics walks onto the stage. According to the conference

160

papers, they're shamans from Peru, Burma, Korea, Siberia, Norway, the United States, and South Africa. Their faces, with high cheekbones, black hair, and shining eyes, have an earthy indigenous look. Their presence is humble yet powerful. As each shaman is introduced, I feel as if we've been thrown the softest of blankets, coddling us in warmth. They are blessing us, and we feel it. By the time the opening ceremony is over, it's as quiet as a church service.

As the shamans make their way off the stage, the applause breaks the stillness. As I clap, I sneak a glance at Lili. She's holding her hands tightly together, one thumb slowly rubbing the other. It's a nervous tick Eugen used to have. Of course she's like Eugen—she's not his sister. She's his daughter. Pretending to rummage for my phone in my purse, I watch her out of the corner of my eye. Her mane of wavy russet hair and her almond-shaped eyes must come from her Hungarian mother. But her profile, with that lovely nose with its slight ski-slope end, is Eugen through and through.

I feel my heart slide sideways. If she's Eugen's daughter, that means she's my stepdaughter. Already grown up and mature, but a daughter just the same. I always did want a daughter but assumed it would never happen. I'm wallowing in a cloud of childhood wishes that I thought would never come true when I hear a voice.

"Anthropologically, indigenous societies would call these people Elders." Lili's voice is so tight the words sound as if they are being squeezed through her lips.

She's holding the pamphlet so tightly that her long thin fingers are white. With a start, I realize she doesn't know how to handle the situation any better than I do. I can feel my heart thumping in my chest. Ignoring the thoughts swirling around the inside of my skull, I close my eyes and take a deep breath, willing my pounding heart to calm down.

"I'm glad to see you," I say, and I mean it.

Then, right then and there, under the watchful eyes of Karl, Lili does something surprising. She puts her hand behind her neck and rubs it. "I have something to say to you." She looks up from underneath her long hair. "I want to tell you that I'm sorry. I'm

161

embarrassed how I treated you." Her words come in fits and starts, as if she's sitting in the dock of a court and reading the summary of a case of a person awaiting trial. It was the family lawyer, she explains. He had insisted they act quickly to remove everything from Eugen's apartment to protect the family assets. "Or so my mother said," she says. Her eyes travel from Karl's face to mine like a butterfly searching for a place to land. "I was heartbroken and needed to find somewhere to place my anger." She lowers her eyes. "So I put it on you."

"You were in shock, my dear," Karl says, softly.

She turns to him and frowns. "Had I known Mami was intending on moving into the apartment herself, I would have acted differently."

My hands fly up to my mouth, but it's too late. The words shoot out before I can stop them. "Maria Eugenia has moved into my home?"

Lili looks as if she's about to cry. "And that crooked lawyer of hers is in her old apartment one floor below. You don't have to tell me that I'm stupid. I already know."

"I take it that this is the same lawyer who counseled you to kick me out."

Her face reddens. "Jakob Nici. Those buggy eyes of his give me the creeps. If you never forgive me, I'll understand completely."

"Why don't we have lunch tomorrow," I say quietly. "I'm sure we can find a way out of this together."

Her eyes widen. "I couldn't think of anything nicer." And before I can say anything more, she throws herself in my arms and bursts into tears.

"Well done," Karl says, as we drive along a narrow road toward Christiane's chalet. "I don't think I've ever seen an inner tsunami blast through so quickly."

I glance over at him from the driver's seat. "Was it that obvious?"

He smiles. "Never play poker. I could see every thought crossing through your mind."

162

The sun is already low on the horizon as I drive along the road as it winds around the shoreline of Attersee. Each lake in the Salzkammergut has different characteristics, and Mondsee and Attersee are no different. Mondsee, with its craggy cliffs and cobalt waters, is wild and feral, but Attersee, with its farms and alpine chalets lined with balconies of red geraniums, is softer and more genteel. During the grand days of Emperor Franz Josef, when the Austro-Hungarian Empire was one of the most powerful in the world, Attersee, the largest lake in Austria, was the place to escape the heat of Vienna during the summer. I slow down to admire a dock house with painted shutters, then continue to wind my way along its shores.

"Lili really wasn't aware of Maria Eugenia's plans?"

Karl shakes his head. "Lili told me what she knew, and when I met Christiane at Lili's exhibition of Venus of Willendorf, she filled me in on the rest. You must remember that everyone was in shock. All she knew was that you were going on a buying trip in India, and suddenly Eugen was dead. Apparently, the scene her mother threw when the embassy delivered Eugen's ashes was so dramatic that they had to call a doctor to sedate her."

Just the idea of Maria Eugenia playing the victim riles me so much that I change gears too fast and the car revs.

Karl gives me an amused look. "Breathe," he says. He crosses his bad leg over the good one. "It took some time for me to help Lili understand why you both got married in India and didn't tell her. It took longer for her to see that cremating Eugen's body was in accordance with his wishes. But the hardest thing for her to understand was her mother's manipulating. She's a right vixen, that woman. How she could have a daughter as lovely as Lili is beyond me."

My gaze flicks to Karl. Might as well open the Vasoy Pandora's box. Everyone is going to learn this eventually anyway. "She didn't," I say, quietly.

Karl fixes his gaze on me with such intensity that I can feel it on my skin.

I stare at the road in front of me. "Lili is Eugen's daughter." As I tell him the story of how Lili came to be adopted by Maria Eugenia, Karl stares in front of him like a statue. The only movement I see is his hands. They clench and relax, over and over again.

When I'm finished, there is silence. Finally, Karl breaks the lull in the conversation with a cough. "I take it she doesn't know this."

"Not yet."

He turns to me. "That's going to be an interesting lunch you'll both have tomorrow."

The car bumps up a gravel drive, then I pull in front of the chalet and turn off the motor.

We rest a moment inside the car, enjoying the quiet of the countryside.

Before I open the door, I turn to him. "Just a minute. I want to ask you something. Who is Venus of Willendorf?"

He opens the rucksack on his lap. "Don't you know her?"

I shake my head. Karl pulls out his wallet and digs around until he finds what he is looking for. "Then it's time for me to make a proper introduction. She's one of the greatest grandes dames of Europe."

I'm surprised to see him give me a dog-eared photo. "You carry this with you?"

He nods. "I carry a photo of all women who matter to me."

I study the photo. It is a statue of a naked woman. Tight braids of hair wind their way round her head. Her thin arms rest on her massive breasts. She has no eyes, nose, or mouth. Her wide, rounded hips, and her legs, which are strong, end at just above the ankle in a point. Her head is bent downwards, as if she is shy.

"She's beautiful," I say, running my finger over the image. "There is a power to her which I can't describe. Earthy. Real." I hand the photo back to him. Karl carefully places it in his wallet, which he slides into his rucksack, and we get out. Even though he is over eighty years old, he insists on rolling my suitcase behind him as we walk to a wooden arbor. I open the wooden gate underneath it. "So she's an ancient fertility symbol," I say, as we walk through.

He hitches his rucksack onto his back while I pull the gate closed.

"She is more powerful than that. She is the symbol for all the changes that we are seeing around us." Before I can ask any more, he gives me a mysterious smile and we walk into the house.

Christiane, still wearing her favorite gardening dress, a pair of scissors sticking out of the front pocket, is on the terrace deadheading the flowers in her window boxes as we arrive. Her hair is speckled with leaves. It's a beautiful spring evening. Cows moo in the field next door, the smell of freshly cut grass drifts in on the breeze. The chalet, nestled along the green slopes that rise gently from the lake, is awash in a pinkish hue.

"Come see the *Alpenglühen*," she says, waving us onto the terrace. "Quick. Before it disappears."

In front of us, on the opposite side of the lake, the Höllengebirge, a massive cliff of exposed granite, is ablaze with color. Alpenglow, Christiane explains, is an optical phenomenon that occurs when the sun is just below the horizon but shines upon the mountains. It doesn't happen all the time, but when it does, it makes the cliff look like a glowing ember. As Christiane disappears inside the kitchen to make the final preparations for dinner, the beauty of the nature around us is so awe inspiring that we are still standing in front of the cliff, spellbound, when Otto joins us.

"Is it true?" he asks, carefully patting his wet hair in place. His clean soapy smell tells me he's just had a shower. "Is Lili Vasoy really here?"

I grin. "Not only that. I'm having lunch with her tomorrow."

The look on his face is priceless. "How did you arrange that?"

I point to Herr Dietmayer. "Thank him."

As they shake hands, Otto's eyes light up. "I know you. You're the newsagent on the Graben in Vienna. People call your shop a one-stop miracle stop."

Karl laughs. "Temples come in different forms, I suppose."

"Well, you certainly have performed a miracle," Otto says. "It's a game changer."

Just then, a sleek tomcat with thick bristly black fur saunters in front of us and disappears into the kitchen. When Karl and I follow it inside, Christiane is bending down to place a chipped porcelain bowl filled with kibble in front of it. "He's adopted us," Christiane says as she stands up. "We call him Lumumba."

Looking up, I see into the sitting room, where the long-stemmed pink roses are sitting like a crown in the center of the room.

Otto walks in and winks. "I owe you one for today," he whispers in my ear as he picks up my bag.

"What's in there?" Christiane says as Otto disappears up the stairs with my case. She's pointing to the leaves sprouting from Karl's rucksack.

"Celery," Karl says. "It's for my juice. I drink a large glass on an empty stomach every morning."

I pick a few leaves from Christiane's hair. "I started drinking celery juice in Joshua Tree," I say. "It helps the liver cleanse itself. It's helped me lose weight, too."

The last sentence gets Christiane's attention. "Lose weight?"

Karl takes a thumb and hooks it into the waist of his trousers. They look as if they're one size too big. "I used to have a paunch."

She goes to the cupboard and takes out the wine glasses, then places them on a large tray. "How does it work?"

"The celery juice clears you out, that's why," he says. "Think of it as taking an inner shower."

Soon we are sitting around the dining room table having dinner. Above us, candles in the wrought-iron chandelier flicker gently, making the room feel cozy and warm. After I tell them about Joshua Tree and the latest on the Chloe and Jean Luc saga, conversation inevitably leads to Maria Eugenia.

"Weren't you furious?" Christiane says.

"Of course I was," I answer. "Why do you think I helped you clean your apartment?"

She reaches over and serves herself another portion of potatoes. "Well, at least you used that anger effectively. Mine just makes my blood pressure soar."

"It might make you feel better to know that people like Maria Eugenia are having an increasingly difficult time in today's world," Karl intercedes.

Otto pulls the sleeves of his shirt out from underneath his sweater. "What do you mean by 'people like Maria Eugenia'?"

Karl takes a sip of wine. "Because she's a dinosaur. People like her thrive on war, and that's not the answer to our world today." When he sees our faces, he laughs. "Let me explain things in a different way." He puts the glass on the table so that his hands can be free. "By now I assume all of you realize that everything is energy. And it moves in complimentary but opposite ways called yin and yang. It's the natural ebb and flow of the world. People like Maria Eugenia are overly yang."

"But she's a woman," Christiane says. "I thought yang is masculine."

He opens his hands wide. "Men usually have more yang and females more yin. But we need both. Now every 2,150 years or so, we enter a new astronomical age. The Age of Aquarius is yin. And this is affecting us a lot more than we can imagine."

Otto stares at Karl. "And what happened the last time this transition occurred?"

"Well, for one, four of the world's five major religions began." He stops talking as we all absorb this. "So did our modern calendar."

Christiane nods her head. "Fascinating. Zero AD was around 2,000 years ago."

"But AD means anno domini, or in the year of our lord," Otto says slowly. "That's when Jesus was born."

"I'm not confirming or denying Jesus' legitimacy," Karl says. "I'm just showing the impact of this last shift on our consciousness."

Otto is running the tip of his finger round the edge of his wine glass. "But what is happening now is a result of technological advances."

"Maybe it's the opposite," Karl says quietly. "Maybe our technological advances are a result of this shift." He pauses, as if weighing how he is going to continue his conversation. "Everything

167

comes from consciousness. If a person has an idea, they are just the funnel for that idea. That is why often the same idea is reproduced in different parts of the world. It bubbles up in consciousness waiting for a person to run with it."

"You are saying we are now reacting to a motor that is running on a different fuel than before. And this fuel is yin or feminine. Difficult to comprehend, but I can at least grasp it," Otto says.

"The internet is the best example," Karl answers. "It's yin. So are artificial intelligence, social media, and all communication." He sits up and plants both of his feet on the floor and straightens his back against the chair. "Yin is non-hierarchical. Non-aggressive. Non-linear. Intuitive. Can't be controlled. Which is why entrenched yang entities such as dictatorships are having such a difficult time. Because they thrive on control and separation. They will continue to have a difficult time because separation isn't the name of the game anymore. To exist in this free-flowing non-hierarchical yin world, a person needs to be centered."

"I still am not sure I understand the difference," Otto says.

Karl nods. "This understanding doesn't happen overnight. Let me tell you how I first learned it. When I returned from Cambodia, life wasn't easy. Suddenly even the simplest of movements—walking— was a challenge. I had to find a new way of being with myself and the world that would bring me peace rather than anger. This is why I began to study tai chi at my sport club. My teacher was a soft-spoken man called Master Chan. One day during our class, two youngsters swaggered in and were making a right stink of themselves. When Master Chan realized they weren't going to stop, he asked one of the men to push him down. We were horrified, of course, but when the man—who was double the size and half the age of Master Chan— charged, rather than pushing Master Chan down, he boomeranged against the wall. It angered him so much that he tried again, hoping to catch Master Chan off guard, but he only flew against the opposite wall. His friend was laughing so hard that Master Chan offered that both of them try together."

"What happened?" Christiane asks. Her eyes are as big as saucers.

168

Karl laughs. "They bounced off him as if he was made of rubber. It was one of the most extraordinary feats of strength and dexterity that I have ever seen. But here is what I found interesting. During the entire demonstration, Master Chan never raised his voice. Never got out of breath. Never got angry. When it was over, he bowed to the young men and continued the class without another glance in their direction."

Otto gives him a confused look. "But how did he do it?"

Karl puts both hands on the table and gets up. "Let me show you." He asks Otto to stand up and face him.

Otto stands up with a wary air. "You aren't going to throw me across the room, are you?"

He shakes his head no, then taps his own shoulder. "Push me here."

Otto places his hand on Karl's shoulder and pushes. Karl's body doesn't move an inch. It is as solid as cement.

"You see?" Karl says. "This is how we fight. Yang against yang. Brute force against brute force. Now push my shoulder again."

Otto complies, but this time, as soon as his hand touches Karl's shoulder, Otto is propelled backward so fast it's like he's been pushed in the chest. If Karl hadn't reached out to steady him, he would have flown against the wall.

Otto's eyes are shining. I've never seen him like this. He's so excited that he keeps taking his glasses off and cleaning them and putting them back on his nose, and then cleaning them all over again. "That was amazing," he cries. "How did you do that?"

"I didn't do anything," Karl says. Christiane wants to have a go and the same thing happens to her. We are all laughing as they sit down again.

"It looked effortless," Otto says.

"It was effortless," Karl answers as he settles back down on his chair. The fact that this eighty-something man with a prosthetic leg could do this so easily doesn't pass anyone by. Christiane fills his glass with water, and he drinks the entire thing in one go. All energy work requires lots of water, he explains as he puts the glass down and asks her to fill it up again, which she does. "Rather than fight you, I surrendered to you. That's yin. It looks weak, but it's anything but that. It's the most underused energy of the planet."

Otto stuffs his handkerchief back in his pocket. "But if this is the case, why doesn't everyone use it?"

Karl smiles. "Because most people are still living from a yang mindset. It's all about dominating. Winners and losers. Master Chan, however, didn't need to win. There was no ego. He simply remained centered and let the youngsters defeat themselves."

"Centered," Otto says. "That's how you must be when you fight in court. I call it Softly softly catchee monkey."

Karl finishes the water and places the empty glass in front of him. "That's what I did with Lili. I listened to her. Didn't make her wrong. I saw she was caught up in a dynamic of fear woven by her mother. It took time, but slowly I helped her unwind the fear that held her in its talons so she could begin to see the situation clearly. It wasn't easy. That poor girl has been under her mother's thumb for so long she hasn't developed the ability to see for herself yet. But there is an inner strength within her. In time, she'll get it."

By now it's getting late. We all get up and bring the dishes into the kitchen. By the time we return to the table, Otto is holding a tray of homemade schnapps. He pours it into four small glasses, then clinks his glass against each of ours. Then, he downs the contents which makes his body do a little shiver and his eyes water. "I'm looking forward to catching this monkey," he says. "She's been on the rampage for too long already."

The following morning, when I walk into the Norwegian shaman's class, Lili is already there. It's difficult to sit inside on such a beautiful morning, but we do, scraping our chairs around the man in a semi-circle.

The Norwegian is contained, even shy. He studied with the Sámi, he explains, which is the ethnic name for the indigenous people better known as Laplanders.

The Sámi call him a *noaidi*, he says, as he lifts an oval-shaped flat drum made of reindeer skin stretched over a thin ring of bentwood. This, he explains, is a noaidi's most prized possession. In the old days, ceremonial drums were used to tap the rhythms of the planet so the Sámi could know when to move and where to hunt in the wilderness.

He turns the drum around so we can see it. "Every ceremonial drum has its own personality and spirit. This one was crafted by my teacher." He pulls out a drumstick and holds the drum in his left hand. "Now. I would like you to close your eyes and listen."

Sunlight streams through the oversize windows. A hush descends upon the classroom. I close my eyes as the noaidi begins to play a slow, syncopated rhythm. *Bam-bam-bam-bam-bam-bam-bam-bam.* After a few moments, I start to distinguish the superficial noises—a bird singing, someone talking in the courtyard, the hum of the lights—from an underlying layer of silence. But this silence isn't an absence of sound, it's an emptiness that is full. After a while, I'm aware of something moving inside it, in and out. When I strain to listen to it, it slips away. It's like waiting for a butterfly to land. I can't grab hold of it, I must relax into it.

Finally, I'm able to distinguish what it is: drums. Not the drum the noaidi is playing, but a different drumbeat. It's coming from nowhere and everywhere at the same time. It's accompanied by low, deep chanting.

Then the noaidi's drum gets louder, as if it's being amplified inside my ears. The sound encapsulates me. I become it, and when I do, I realize it's a heartbeat. Not my heartbeat, but the heartbeat of the planet. In that moment, an awareness hits me: The planet is alive. Just as I'm alive. We—humans and animals and plants and everything on this earth—are part of a cosmic union that is constantly pulsating. Expansion, contraction, expansion, contraction. That's the movement of life. As I blend into this cosmic heartbeat, the sense of "I" melts, and when it does, the walls of separation that differentiate me from my environment melt and I become one with it all. I'm floating in this feeling of perfect unity, when I hear, as if it's coming from far away, the Norwegian's voice, asking us to open our eyes.

When I open my eyes, we are all staring into space with glazed expressions. In no time at all, the room is filled with a burst of a furious chatter. It cuts the peacefulness like a knife. *No!* I think, as words zing around the room like buzzing flies. It's so jarring, I close my eyes again and sink into the depths of myself. When I finally do open my eyes, everyone is gone except the noaidi. For a second I stare at my feet. Then I look up. "When you were playing your drums, I heard something else. Chanting."

His gaze becomes more intense. "You heard that?"

I nod. "As if there were men sitting around a camp fire." I hesitate before continuing. "I'm not sure, but I could swear I even heard the fire crackling."

An inner light dances in his eyes. "Welcome," he says, smiling. And we pick up our belongings and walk out the door.

Outside, Lili is waiting for me. Casually dressed in a soft camel jacket and jeans, her hair in a loose ponytail, she's much more relaxed than yesterday. The noaidi says his goodbyes and we turn and walk down the stairs and head into town for lunch.

It's only a few steps to Marktplaz, the pedestrian street in Mondsee where the restaurants are. Clusters of tables with large umbrellas spill onto both sides of the street. We choose a table away from the crowds and sit down. Clouds gathering behind the Drachenwand cliff tell me it may storm later on.

As we give the waitress our orders, a black cat slinks around the corner, saunters under Lili's chair, and flops on its side. I'm staring at it when I hear Lili's voice.

"I heard you speaking to the shaman. Could you really hear things when we meditated? I mean chanting and all that?"

"I think so," I say. I could swear the black cat looks up at me when I say this. Staring at it, I add, "Maybe I'm more sensitive now because I've just spent a few months with a shaman in California." A waitress places a carafe of water and a bowl of lemon slices on the table. My eyes swivel back to meet hers. "I guess the stillness of the desert has taught me more than I realized." I squeeze lemon in my glass and hold it above her glass, tilting my head. "Want some?"

She nods. "I see Karl has given you his lemon talk too." She waits for me to squeeze a few drops, then takes a sip.

Lili looks up as I reach over and pour water into her glass. In the light, her eyes are as black as onyx. One day she will have the same laugh lines around her eyes as Eugen did. She catches me studying her, so I give her an embarrassed smile.

"Sorry. It's just you remind me so much of Eugen."

She reaches up and plays with a strand of hair from her ponytail. "That's the best compliment anyone has given me for ages."

I look at her. "It was meant as a compliment."

She bites her lip. "Did you really not know he was ill?"

"Hard to believe, isn't it?" I sigh. "Otto Sinsky says secrets are a Vasoy tendency."

Lili looks away. "He knows our family well."

"Did you know?"

"No," she says. "I only found out when Mami told me. I knew something was up with Mami after he died. She spent hours ransacking your apartment. I know because I saw lights on."

"Do you know what she was looking for?"

She shakes her head. "His will, I suppose. Mami told me he died intestate."

I pull out my phone and scroll through it, looking for the photo of the birth certificate that Christiane sent me. "Well, she is wrong. I met Otto at his office yesterday. Apparently, Eugen left a few things with him for safekeeping. One of them was this."

As I give her the photo of her real birth certificate, I keep my eyes glued on her face.

Confusion clouds her eyes as they scan it. "But why is my name on it?"

I take a breath. It's now or never. "Because it's your birth certificate," I say. My voice echoes in my ears. "Your real one."

She raises her eyes to meet mine. "And Eszther Szabo?"

In the silence that follows, I can hear everything around me as if it's being projected by a speaker. Someone shouts to close the

173

windows. A bus eases around the corner. A door bangs in the distance. My mind spins, trying to find an easy way to explain things. But every time I can only come up with the most important word of all.

"She's your mother," I find myself saying. "Your real mother."

Lili folds her napkin, slowly, crease by crease, as if she's sweeping away her old self with each measured swipe of the hand. When she next speaks, her voice is barely a whisper. "And my father?"

"Eugen." The word comes out of my mouth like a stone.

"Eugen is my —" She stops and looks up at me. "— father?"

By now tears are rolling down my face. "If only I'd known. I could have done so much more for you. Supported you. Helped you. Been there for you. If only I hadn't listened to Eugen. I should have told you about what we were planning on doing in India. Who knows, maybe he would be here now, telling you himself, rather than having me do it." I look at Lili with tear-stained eyes. "Oh Lili, I'm so sorry. So very sorry. I was a coward, always hiding behind Eugen when I knew better. I saw your mother manipulating you, and it made me so angry, and yet I did nothing about it until it was too late."

"She's not my mother," Lili snaps. Her eyes are flashing with a fury I never knew she had. "I always knew that something wasn't right between us. Mami," she stops and corrects herself. "Maria Eugenia— I'll never call her Mami again—had eyes for only one person in her life, and it wasn't me."

Lili takes a tissue out of her purse and dabs it under my eyes. "You have already gone through so much. Not knowing that Eugen was ill. Not knowing he was my father. Not knowing that Maria Eugenia hated you. She hates everyone. I could never understand her hatred." She stops speaking and looks up to the heavens. "And to think that she isn't my mother after all." She looks at me with shining eyes. "I'm so happy I'd like to scream from the rooftops."

Of all the things I had imagined she'd say, it wasn't that. No rage or denial. I pull a tissue from my purse and blow my nose, then sit back in my chair to tell her the story of her birth. As my words wash over her, I watch the image of Lili Vasoy, daughter of Hans Georg and Maria Eugenia Vasoy, crumbling in front of me. I can feel the emotional swings and memories flipping like dominos inside her head, dismissing some, rejecting others, remaking her past so that she can stand in the present. A waitress places our dishes in front of us, and hands us a cup with the knives and forks and spoons wrapped up in paper napkins, but we are in so much emotional overwhelm that all we can do is stare at her like two cows chewing our cud.

"Do you know," Lili says, scooting her chair closer to mine once the waitress leaves. "The night I found out Eugen died, I took a tram up to the Kahlenberg—you know, the hilltop on the Danube where you can see all of Vienna—so that I could gaze down at the city. It was so beautiful that night. The air was crisp and clear. And the moon—I saw it rising over the Danube." Her eyes latch onto mine. "Maybe you'll think I'm crazy, but I could sense Eugen next to me. He wanted to comfort me. To tell me that he was OK." Her mouth stays slightly open, as if still in wonder at the miracle that had occurred. "Do you know what I did? I put my head back and howled. Just like a wolf." She drops her head. "I think he was ashamed of himself. He didn't know how to tell me."

I nod. "So he didn't say anything at all." I pause, letting my emotions settle within me. "Oh Eugen." My voice trails. "He lost his mother when he was too young. And that wizened old bat who has been calling you her daughter and treating you like a slave doesn't know how to give love. I suppose it's not her fault. She probably didn't receive it from her mother, either."

She nods. "No wonder I was always looking for a mother's love. I think that's why Venus of Willendorf moved me so."

There it is again. Venus of Willendorf. "Karl showed me a photograph of her."

Her eyes light up. "Isn't she amazing? She is called the Great Mother."

"The Great Mother. I like that."

"Mother of us all. She's so proud. So unassuming. So unashamedly accepting of her body. So happy. Unlike me."

"What do you mean, unlike you?"

Lili tucks a loose strand of hair behind her ear. "I'm never happy

175

with myself. Always wanting to fix something. Thinking if I could just do a little more, strive harder, I'd make things better. But when I saw this tiny figurine, it was as if something inside me came alive." She wipes her fingers on her napkin. "It was as if she was calling me to break free. I wanted to know more about the people who created her. That is what led me to get a job at Vienna's Natural History Museum. I wanted to learn everything about her."

I tap my phone a few times and pull up an image of Venus of Willendorf. "The Great Mother," I say, running my finger along the screen. "A Great Mother feels so much more reassuring than the image of God I was brought up with."

She leans over to stare at the image. "That's because back then, God wasn't a man. God was a woman."

The moon and the stars seem to do a dance in my head when she says this sentence.

I put my phone back in my purse. "She was the goddess of what?"

She shakes her head. "There was no goddess of what. She was *the* Goddess. The Queen of Heaven who reigned for tens of thousands of years. The civilizations who lived under her rule are referred to as the Goddess civilizations. They weren't matriarchal, by the way. It drives me crazy when feminists want to romanticize these ancient civilizations and make them out better than we are today. But they were matrilineal, which means they were more egalitarian and peaceful. That's why anthropologists have such a difficult time understanding these ancient societies. It's because there aren't any images of heroes violently slaying monsters or conquering evil. They didn't worship death as we do."

"We worship death?" I ask.

A sudden rumble of thunder makes us both look up. I glance at my phone. "I've got to go. I'm going to be late."

She looks embarrassed. "Have I been speaking too much? Boring you as usual."

"Not at all. Exactly the opposite."

We quickly get up and gather our things. "Where are you going?" she asks as she waves away my offer to pay the bill. I let her, knowing that this is a way she can get rid of some of her guilt for what happened back at the palace. She pulls out a few notes and leaves them under the plate as the sky rumbles again.

We both look up. Dark clouds are gathering above us.

"The symposium with Percy the South African shaman," I say. "It's going to start any minute. You can join me if you like."

She smiles, and I see, for the first time, pure, unadulterated joy shining from her eyes. She pulls off her scrunchie hair tie and locks of auburn hair tumble onto her shoulders. "If he's that sexy shaman with the furry hat lined with cowry shells, I'm in."

The clouds are gathering low in the sky by the time we find our way to Percy's forum. The classroom, a long wide room on the ground floor of the Schloss, is full when we walk in. Sitting cross-legged on the floor at the back of the room, we look around, but Percy is nowhere to be seen. In his place is a blond American dressed in a furry fez-like hat and wearing a belt of shells and bones. I retreat into my skeptical self as I listen to his story about how he had been adopted as an African sangoma. I can't help it. I find the African costume on him ridiculous. I don't want to hear someone talking about the culture of the South African sangoma when the real thing is lurking around somewhere. Why do we Westerners feel the need to adopt the dress of other nations? Rather than wearing costumes from other cultures, we ought to find our own authenticity. To me, Westerners wearing indigenous costumes is like Japanese people wearing cowboy hats.

Just then Percy appears. Shaking his sandals off at the door, he strolls in and instantly his energy fills the room. He walks erect, rolling on his bare feet as if he were a cheetah stalking the savannah. Graceful. Proud. Lithe. He has such a wonderful connection to the earth that I can hear the unspoken rhythms and dancing of the planet underfoot. Percy has jet-black skin, a crinkly gray beard topped by kind eyes, and a fur fez he wears with great dignity. He stands in front of the crowded room and, in a quick movement, drops down onto his haunches and gazes at us. "I did not want to be a sangoma."

I perk up when I hear this sentence. I haven't heard a lot of "how I became a shaman" stories, and I realize that it's the becoming bit—the process—that interests me most. He tells us that he spent time in jail. That it took four times to find his wife. That he didn't want to be a sangoma, but he didn't have any choice when the master of witchcraft called him. His master took his clothes and burnt them while he was bathing, and then sent him to bed, telling him that from now on he needed neither food, nor family. He was dead. It took many years to learn his craft, and slowly his life began to turn around. Although he is a powerful man, he is no longer the master of his own fate. From that moment on, he is fated to serve his master. And his master is mankind.

I glance at the room and in my mind's eye I feel all of us in a grass hut on the African steppes. Outside the rain is coming down in sheets, the gusts blowing the raindrops against the windows. I rub my hands together to warm them in the cool afternoon air, enjoying the spectacle. All of this—the storm, the gathering of the people, even this magnificent sangoma—is a symphony of the divine. Percy stands before me, his heart bleeding, and I understand him. The depth of his truth reflects the pain in his eyes. Did pain make him into a shaman, or was it the other way around? In that moment, I know that I can't think about spiritual things in a linear way. There is a matrix that connects us all. It is so perfect and so grand that it is impossible to grasp its entirety. And this matrix has us all in its plan.

By the time he finishes, the storm is over. There are still a few rumbles of thunder, but the wind and the rain have passed. Large, puffy clouds, now empty of rain, dance weightlessly in the sky as we watch Percy kneel on the floor and roll out a reed mat. He lifts a leather pouch for all of us to see. This is his oracle, he explains, and when he turns the pouch upside down, a rush of bones, sticks, shells, and stones spew out and clatter as they hit the mat. Every object, he explains, represents something symbolic: job, family, love, children. All he needs is for a person to sit in front of him, to tell him their name, and he whispers into the pouch. Throwing the bones, he explains, creates a map of the person's spiritual journey. They help him read what needs to be done to make that person whole.

At the end of his talk, I feel humbled by his story. Lili and I stand up, I observe Percy. He smiles and nods, patiently speaking to one person, then the other, for a good fifteen minutes. Finally, a woman in a white shirt and jeans arrives, offering to take the names of those who would like a session with him. Thinking that this would be a good time for me to leave, I follow Lili to the door. But when I reach it, something makes me turn around and look once more.

Just then Percy looks up and our eyes meet. "I'll see her," he says.

To my amazement, he is pointing to me.

In the afternoon, I'm on my way to meet Percy the sangoma, but the lake beckons to me to go for a swim. So I do, jumping with a one-two-three and dousing myself underwater, quickly, before I change my mind. The snow on the mountaintops tells me the water will be cold, and I'm right. But the lake water is so silky, the coolness so refreshing, that I jump in again, enjoying the tingles that race up and down my limbs as I towel myself dry. Tossing my wet hair from my face and doing a quick change inside my car, I drive to the address he gave me, bumping down a long dirt road on the other side of Mondsee just on time.

Percy's hotel is a farmhouse bed-and-breakfast. The cluster of old wooden buildings has ducks waddling about and a cat playing with her kittens under an old oak tree. As I park and get out, one of the kittens, a black one with emerald eyes, scampers toward me. I've just picked it up when I see Percy waving at me. He looks different without his costume, less imposing and more human. He glances at the black kitten in my arms and bursts into laughter.

"Come," he says as I place the kitten on the ground and watch it run back to its mother. "Let's go upstairs."

At the top of the stairs, Percy kicks off his sandals and I slip my shoes off before we walk into his room. He unfurls his reed mat and, with a graceful thump, sits on his heels at one end, gesturing for me to sit at the other. Then, just as he showed us in his demonstration, I tell him my name. By the time he whispers it into his pouch, my legs are beginning to tingle. Then, with one quick movement, he turns the pouch upside down, and all the little objects come tumbling out. He sighs and leans forward to study the scattered bones and twigs.

"I see," he says, slowly moving his finger along the bones. "Yes, I see."

When he looks up again, his eyes have an otherworldly sheen. "You are a large energy. But you carry the burden of your ancestors. Their unresolved lives are mixed within your own."

It makes me think of something that happened years ago when I was living in London. I kept getting sick. Conjunctivitis. Colds. Yeast infections. It was endless. When I left Brazil, my new spiritual viewpoint didn't match the conservative world I came from, so I had put all that mumbo-jumbo, which is what I called it, into a box within me and forgotten it. The idea of seeing anyone except for a fully qualified medical practitioner was anathema. But my body finally won. I wouldn't be able to work until I did something, so I finally relented and agreed to see a doctor who specialized in alternative medicine.

As part of his diagnostics, the doctor told me he wanted to measure my aura. He placed me in the center of his office, pointed a lozenge-shaped device at me, and began to back away. About five feet away, the light on the machine flickered off. My front aura was normal, he said, making a notation in a booklet. He then walked behind me and did the same thing over again.

But this time, no matter how far away he was, the light never went off. He turned the machine on and off, tapped it against his wrist, tested my front aura again, then opened the door of his office and backed into the corridor. About twenty feet away, the light flickered off. He shook his head, moved me to a different part of his office, and tried again. When it gave him the same result, he stopped and stared at me as if I were an exhibit in a zoo.

"Well," he said, puffing to himself. "Well."

"Well, what?" I asked, nervously.

"You have the largest back aura I have ever seen."

"But what does that mean?"

"It's your past lives," he answered. "You have an extraordinary number of them."

I wish he had been more explicit. I wish he had told me what I know now. That the back aura is a person's foundations. That my past was holding me back and that I couldn't go forward until I had resolved it. A friend once told me I must be a very old soul, and that suited my ego just fine because it didn't require any self-reflection. But now, nearly two decades later, when a sangoma tells me the same thing, I'm ready to listen.

"Why are ancestors important?"

Percy looks as if I have just said something blasphemous. "Your ancestors are your lineage. It's where you come from. They give you roots into the earth and insights into your life that are far greater than any of us understand."

I pick at a loose thread from the mat and twist it between my fingers. "I don't have any connections with my family. I was sent away when I was twelve."

Percy nods his head. "Leaving was good. There was no room for you to develop. And you have much to say."

"And that is?"

"Your unique way of seeing things. When you tell others how you see the world, you heal yourself and others. You must pursue this. But in order for you to go forward, you must heal your past. And that means connecting with family. What do your parents' families have in common?"

I can feel the back of my neck tightening. "Nothing. My mother's family were liberal academics. My father's, religious conservatives. They were like oil and water."

Percy bends down to examine the objects on the mat, then he sits back on his heels again and shakes his head. "That is not what the bones say. There is something you are not seeing."

I wrack my brains. "Well, I guess you could say they were immigrants. Both of my mother's parents emigrated from Germany and Norway just after they got married. My father's parents emigrated from England after the war."

Percy makes a low noise that sounds like *hunh*. "You do not see what they have in common? Your ancestors died where they were not born."

I raise my eyebrows in recognition of this truth. "But most of America is that way."

He nods. "Yes. America is the land of unresolved ancestors. So many people cut off from their lineage, and they wonder why they're hungry even though they have enough to eat. They consume to feed their hunger, but a new home or a new car will never satisfy it because it's internal. And internal hungers cannot be satisfied by external things."

I cede the point. "And why is this important?"

"Your ancestors were not able to resolve things before their death," he says. He points to where some of the figures are clumped together. "So you must travel to the countries of your ancestors and do a blessing."

I start to calculate the cost of traveling to all of these countries. My stomach begins to knot. The last thing I want to do is spend money flying around the world on a wild goose chase. "Because?"

His eyes become stern. Once again I can see that I'm asking a question that is so obvious to him that he can barely comprehend it. "By freeing them, you'll free yourself."

"Can someone else do this for me?"

He shakes his head. "No. It must be you, and you alone. Say that you are there to bring healing. For yourself. For the family. For the greater family. When you have completed your task, you must create an altar for your ancestors in your home."

The idea of inviting my family into my life is a frightening supposition.

"What's wrong?" Percy must have noticed my expression.

"My parents won't understand," I say, quietly.

"Come," he says. "You must expand your interpretation of family." He pronounces each syllable: fa-mi-ly.

"And what will that give me?"

He smiles. "Roots, madam. It will give you roots." When I don't say anything, he puts his hands over his heart. "My name is Percy. It's my father's name. I feel my father every time I hear my name."

My spirits lift when I hear this. "That's my grandfather's name," I say.

Percy gives a deep, throaty laugh. "You are full of good stories. We both have ancestors named Percy. And your name?"

"Annabel Larissa. Larissa was my great-great-grandmother's name. From Norway."

He smiles. "And you say that family is not important to you?"

My eyes open wide. "How could I never have noticed this before?"

He gathers the objects from the mat and puts them in the pouch, then we stand and he begins to roll his mat up. "We are blind until we can see. Wherever in the world I travel, I always know that my family is close when I see a black cat."

"A black cat?"

He nods. "It's a sign to comfort me. It makes me not feel alone."

Images of the black cats I've spotted the past few months flash by in my mind's eye. Mandu in Joshua Tree. Olive in London. In Austria, too. "Black cats," I say, slowly.

He throws his head back and gives a deep-throated laugh. "You are a black-cat person too. That is why I laughed when you arrived. I saw the black kitten in your arms, and I knew." When he sees the confusion on my face, he puts a wrinkled hand on my shoulder. "Do not worry, Annabel Larissa. The world is in conversation with you all the time. All you need to do is listen."

I'm standing on Christiane's balcony, a cup of steaming tea in my hand. In the distance, I hear the clang of the cowbells and the high-pitched calls of a hundred starlings streaking across the sky. I breathe in deeply, enjoying the cold air swirling in my lungs. The Attersee shimmers in the early morning light, promising me a last invigorating swim before I fly to London tonight. I turn my head to the north to look at the mountains tickling the sky. Just there, only half an hour's drive away, lies Germany. Where my grandfather was born.

I don't know much about my German past. All I know is that my mother's father Hermann was less than a year old when his parents, Wilhelm and Marie, emigrated from Bavaria in the second half of the nineteenth century. Great-grandfather Wilhelm was disinherited by his wealthy father—one mystery—and emigrated to the United States with his wife and son to become a gentleman farmer in Kansas. But the land was poor and full of rocks, so, after buying three farms, he gave up and returned to Germany, leaving his wife and children behind. Twenty years later, he returned, got his wife pregnant again, then fled back to Germany. He returned one last time to see his family.

But by then, he was a sick old man, and his wife, who had been raising five children on her own, wanted to have nothing to do with him. Neither did his children. He loitered in front of a synagogue—another mystery, as we aren't Jewish—wearing a black coat and hat and a long beard. Finally, word got out to his son Hermann, by then a successful doctor, that his father was ill. Even though Hermann didn't want to have anything to do with his father the Hippocratic oath called, so when he examined his father, he knew that he was very ill and insisted on operating right away. But it was too late. Wilhelm, disinherited by his father, dismissed by his son, died on the operating table. His death was mourned by no one.

A decision like this needs breakfast. I make my way down the stairs, my bare feet sliding across the wooden floor, to find Christiane pottering in the kitchen, wrapped like a cocoon in her overly large blue robe and fluffy socks.

She disappears behind the refrigerator door and I hear a cheerful clank of bottles. Her head appears from behind the door as she shows me two small eggs.

"From the farmer's chickens," she says. She places them into a pan of boiling water, pops two pieces of bread in the toaster, and hands me a cup of tea.

"Enjoy this because it will be your last. I've been reading up on why Karl drinks celery juice." She gives me a wistful smile. "No eggs, gluten, or dairy. No pork, either. How will I survive?"

For a second, neither of us speaks. I had the same reaction when I learned that this is food that feeds pathogens in the body. "Is that bread non-gluten?"

Her eyes give a naughty glint. "Tomorrow be damned. Today, we're going to celebrate all that we shouldn't eat."

And so, we have it all: warm soft-boiled eggs on brown toast, plates of crispy bacon, grilled tomatoes and mushrooms, muesli, yoghurt, fresh fruit, and even warmed croissants with pads of butter from the local farmer's cow. As we both lean back in our chairs, hands on our over-stuffed bellies, Christiane looks at the clock. "Aren't you going?"

"To do what?"

"To do your ancestor blessing."

"Do you think I should?"

Christiane gives me a look of incredulity as we clear the table. "You meet an African shaman in Austria, of all places, then discover you have a father and a grandfather named Percy, and that you are both followed by black cats. How can you contemplate not doing it?"

"But I don't know what to do. What's a blessing, anyway?"

Christiane, who has been loading the dishwasher, stands up and turns to me. "Do you think any of us knows what we're doing?" For a moment we gaze through the kitchen window at the delicate fingers of fog floating on the lake's glossy surface. "We are all trying to make our way through life. So if you have been given an instruction booklet, use it. Even if it doesn't follow the normal path."

When I still don't say anything, she smiles and gives me a hug. "You've been given a magical life," she says. "So you might as well enjoy it."

An hour later, I have gathered enough for an excursion into the wilds: a map of Bavaria, a map of Salzburg, a bottle of water, a backpack, and just about everything I can possibly imagine I'll need to do an ancestor blessing—including a few small bottles, in case I find something worthy of an ancestral altar.

The weather is exquisite, the air cool with the sun warming my shoulder as I exit the highway and cross the border into Germany. I'm not using a GPS because I don't know where I'm going. Not knowing what to do, I decide that I might as well pretend to know what I'm doing. So when I see a beautiful church on the horizon, its white steeple piercing the blue sky like a balloon, I drive toward it.

I remember Percy telling the story of how he first met his teacher. He left his house one morning and walked in the wrong direction, then took a bus and a train and hitched a ride in a car, not having any idea where he was going. But he followed his instincts, which led him a day later to his master's house, who had been calling him all along. And so, I decide to do just that. Zone out and follow my nose.

I drive along a small road, wiggle right and then left, up a hill, through a village and up another hill. All around me are small towns nestled in the valley, each a cluster of pastel buildings surrounding a whitewashed church. In the distance, the craggy peaks of the Alps soar into the sky, still topped with snow.

The road passes the church and winds its way farther into the valley, then forks. I brake hard, not knowing which road to take. I squint. Something is sitting by the left-hand road. It's a black cat. The lithe figure runs across the road, low on its haunches, and disappears into the bushes. Without thinking twice, I throw the car into gear and turn left. The road winds up the hill and ends abruptly in a field. I park, gather my collection bottles, and begin walking toward the top.

I continue, through one field, then another, until I arrive in a field full of cowpats. This can't be right. I haven't even started my first blessing and I've failed already.

Looking around just to make sure that I'm alone, I lift my hands to the sky and yell in German, "*Ich kann es nicht!* I don't know what to do. If any ancestor of mine wants me to bless them, then come now."

I wait for something to happen, like a black cat to show me the way, but there's nothing except the sound of the rustling grass. I turn my jar upside down, scattering the bits of sticks and earth that I thrust into it during the walk, and watch them flutter in the breeze. I'm more embarrassed than I want to admit. My legs give out and I collapse in a heap on the grass. What a fool I am. How long have I been walking? In which direction? Worse still, I have no idea where I left the car. Frustrated and tired, I take a breath. And another. With each breath, my mind starts to calm. The breeze blows through my hair. I take yet another deep breath, exhaling in a long, weary sigh. And that's when I feel it.

Something shifts, so subtly that I don't sense it immediately. The beauty around me becomes sharper; each blade of grass, each tree, each cluster of red roofs and spiky steeples in the distance becomes clearer. It's the energy. It's shifting, becoming thicker, like pudding. And when I look at the scenery around me, I'm aware that something else has changed. I've never seen the world this way. And with a start, I understand why. It's not me who is looking at the scene. It's someone else.

It's great-grandfather Wilhelm.

I've never met my great-grandfather. I've never even seen a photograph of him. I don't know how I know it's him, but it is. To my surprise, I like him. He's sensitive. Creative. Fun. There he goes, grouping everything I'm seeing in terms of colors on an artist's palette. That's it! He was an artist—not the loser he was branded by the family. I'm still tuning into his energy when my ears begin to hum. And when I let my jaw drop slightly open, I find that my ears can relax. That's when I perceive it—a voice drifting on the breeze. It's so soft I can barely hear it.

The voice, in German, is so gentle that it makes my eyes fill with tears. It was the wildflowers that I missed. *Es waren die Wildblumen, die ich vermisst habe.*

Wildflowers? What is he talking about? I look at the tall grass dancing around me. And that's when I see them. Hundreds of them. Wildflowers, waving amongst the long blades of grass. They sway delicately in the breeze. I ask the flowers if I may pick a few, and they bob their heads yes in the wind. I collect one or two flowers of each

187

kind—bellflowers, cornflowers, poppies, daisies, and clover—and place them delicately in one of my bottles. When I finish, I sit down on the grass again to rest in my great-grandfather's energy.

Wilhelm was born surrounded by mountains and lakes and onion-domed churches. I can only imagine what the flatlands of Kansas must have been like for him compared to this. In the early twentieth century, travel was expensive and difficult—and yet, he returned to America twice. There must have been a reason he did that. He must have missed his family. A lot.

Compassion. Understanding. Forgiveness. It rolls within my breast, as powerful as a roaring stream. Before, it was easy to loathe Wilhelm. But now that I know him, it's impossible. He is family, I tell myself, and that says it all. With the ease and grace of an old hand, I say my blessing and gather my things. Then I slowly walk in the direction from which I came.

WOOD

London

Summer has arrived. Everywhere I look, people are taking advantage of the beautiful weather while it lasts, and they're doing it with gusto, walking dogs, riding bicycles, strolling in the parks. Everyone is going somewhere, anywhere, and I'm one of them, gazing through the windscreen of a double-decker bus heading to have a bite to eat with Chloe before going to the theater on the Strand.

Sitting in the front seat on the upper deck makes me feel like a mahout riding an elephant, heaving and sighing through an urban obstacle course. Swaying and jerking in tandem with the other passengers, we seem to be close to running people over but narrowly avoiding them at the last minute. The bus beeps and sighs as we lumber around corners, trundle by pubs, bounce around roundabouts, and huff and puff against red lights. On either side of me, buses whoosh by like fellow elephants. As the bus barrels down a wide avenue flanked by plane trees, a branch from the suspended leafy carpet above us thumps the roof, making me jump. I can hear the tinny sounds of rap coming from the earphones of the skinny man in a hoodie behind me. He's keeping the beat by tapping one foot against the back of my seat. It's hot, the bus is stuffy, and I've stepped on something sticky but don't dare look at the sole of my shoe to see what it is.

No wonder I'm stressed.

But life is that way, isn't it? One moment I'm in Salzkammergut, the next I'm on a bus in London. One minute I'm planning my life with Eugen in Austria, the next moment I'm wrestling with the unknown in California. One minute I feel as if I'm treading water in a stagnant pool, the next something happens, something as implausible as meeting a South African sangoma in Austria, and life surges forward again.

The Savoy feels like the country clubs my father insisted on joining but rarely had time to attend. This is the world I was raised to strive for. Conservative values built on the stability of the past. A staff member, solicitous and discreet, directs me with a tilt of his head toward the American Bar, which is where Chloe said she'd be.

The American Bar is an art deco jewel box, large enough for a dozen round tables and an old-fashioned bar with dripping icicle lights. The buzzing atmosphere reminds me of the Oyster Bar in New York's Grand Central Station. Chloe is sitting at a table in the far corner of the room, wearing in a tight-fitting blue dress and heels. Holding a cellphone to her ear, she looks up, sees me, and waves. We blow each other a kiss, and I sit down.

By the time Chloe hangs up, a waiter has set bowls of potato chips and nuts on our table while I tell her about my Austrian adventures. "Which is why," I say, leaning back as a waiter arrives with a glass of sparkling water for me, "You should come to Provence. Jeanette told me that often we do things for one reason, and then it turns out that the reason we are there is completely different."

She stares at the potato chip between her fingers as if wondering what to do with it. "Don't take it personally, but spending a month with you and a woman I don't know who does things I don't approve of doesn't sound like a holiday to me. I'd prefer a week with Jean Luc

190

on the Riviera."

We sit back as our food arrives. I reach over and pinch one of her fries. "Has he offered to take you to the Riviera?"

She puts her hands protectively around her plate. "Order your own. Not yet."

I give one more longing look at her plate, then decide it's not worth it and focus on my club sandwich. "So take what's on offer. That's what I'm trying to do, even if it does come with black cats."

Chloe gives me an annoyed look. "Not *more* black cats."

"They were in Austria, too," I say, poking at the sandwich mess on my plate. "Sitting on windowsills. Lying under chairs. It feels like there's a stagehand somewhere, hurrying the cats into place so that they can appear on cue. Even when I met a South African sangoma called Percy, I was holding a black kitten. When he saw me, do you know what he said?"

She gives me an innocent smile. "You've got a black kitten in your arms?"

"I'm not joking. He told me he was a black-cat person too."

Her eyes glaze. "You met a sangoma in Austria who said he was a black-cat person, too?" She stares at me for the longest time as she twists a lock of hair around her index finger. Round and round it goes, the red lacquered nail glinting in the pale light of the bar. Finally, with an external sigh, she raises her hand into the air, waggles it about like a handkerchief in the wind, and then, as it catches the eye of someone, the hand drops onto her lap with an air of resignation.

In a few moments the maître d'hôtel appears. "Thierry," Chloe says, gazing at him through half-lidded eyes. "Be a darling and introduce my friend to Kaspar, will you?"

He inclines his head in my direction. "Are you planning a dinner here, ma'am?"

"For thirteen guests," Chloe adds.

He bends slightly from the waist and tells me to follow him.

I throw a glance of incomprehension at Chloe, but she motions for me to go on. We walk into the lobby, then thread through the hotel guests until we reach a glass vitrine. It's about the size of an aquarium.

Whatever is inside is clearly something the Savoy regards highly.

"This is Kaspar," he says. "If you have thirteen guests, he will sit on the fourteenth chair. He even wears a napkin when he is served food."

I crouch on my heels and bend down to look inside. There, behind the glass, is a statue of a black cat. The head is bent, looking coyly backward. The tail is curled so long it almost forms a circle.

Until this moment, somewhere in me I was still doubting. Thinking that I was making things up. Inventing stories, which is what my mother used to say when I told her about the Native American chief who used to appear at the foot of my bed at night. But now, as I stare at this statue, I'm forced to recognize that I'm not exaggerating. I'm not trying to draw attention to myself. I can now see, as clearly as I can see my shocked reflection in the glass of the vitrine, that I'm not going crazy. This isn't about forging a path through the unknown jungles of my life, it's about following one. And right now, black cats are showing me the way.

Chloe's eyes follow me like a hunter from the moment I walk back into the bar. When she sees the look on my face, she starts to laugh. Really laugh. Her shoulders shake, and tears begin to run down her cheeks. Soon the giggles catch on, and I let go and allow myself to do something I've been wanting to do for a long time but haven't dared—laugh. Who ever heard of a person surrounded by black cats? It's as absurd as meeting a Viking in Dorset. Or a sangoma in the Salzkammergut. Or a long-dead great-grandfather on a hilltop in Germany. Whoever has written the story of my life has a great sense of humor. Far better than my own.

"Life is infinitely stranger than anything which the mind of man could invent," Chloe says, then adds, when she sees I'm not following her. "Arthur Conan Doyle." She wipes away a tear with a cocktail napkin. "God, that has cheered me up enormously." Her eyes are twinkling in a way that I haven't seen for ages.

With her giggles now under control, she reverts to work mode and reaches into her purse. It takes her a second to find what she is looking for, then pulls out a tablet, places it on her lap and starts typing. "You need my help."

I must not have heard her correctly. "I need your help?"

"Let me translate Chloe-speak for you. When I say you need my help, what I really mean is I need your help."

"With Jean Luc?"

She nods. "We can't talk. I end up attacking, he becomes defensive; and one of us ends up hanging up. Our relationship can't continue like this. We both know it. I don't understand what's going on with your life. But I do know that flouncing about, pretending I know what I'm doing when I don't, is not helping me at all. I'm far more of a mess than I let on. And you're far more together than you let on." She pauses. "So let me help you. I'll even go to Provence, though I'm petrified. I know. I will be your assistant."

"You'll be my assistant?" I ask, folding my arms. "That's funny."

She looks hurt. "What's funny about it?"

I unfold my arms. "I didn't mean it that way. I mean, you have a good job, a beautiful home, a glorious husband. Money in the bank. I've got nothing."

"And yet, you've got something. I don't want to be —" She purses her lips. "— a Neanderthal, like all those chinless wonders at that drinks party."

"Didn't Neanderthals have protruding chins?" I wonder, pulling my earlobe.

Chloe puts her hands up in mock frustration. "Argh! Don't make fun of me. Do you know how frustrating this is for me? There is an entire world that you are in touch with that I can't grasp. I want you to help me find it."

"I'm not sure if you are ready for it. It will pull you out of your comfort zone."

"You've been living out of your comfort zone since Eugen died," she says. "And look at the good it's done you." We stop as the waiter arrives with an espresso for Chloe and a cup of verbena tea for me. Chloe downs the espresso, picks up her iPad, and readies herself as if she were a secretary taking dictation. "So. How can I begin? I know. I want to learn that neti pot thing."

I nod. "Deal. Then there are things you can't do or eat."

193

"Such as?"

"No gluten, dairy, or eggs."

"I'm regretting this already."

I shrug. "You asked for it. What else do viruses and pathogens eat? Oh. No corn. Soy. MSG. Canola Oil. Citric acid. Artificial flavors and sweeteners." I pause. "Oh yes. And no alcohol either."

She takes a last guilty swig of her martini. "What *can* I eat? And if you say rabbit food, I'm going to kill myself right here and now."

"You can eat all sorts of greens," I say. "Spinach. Salad. Parsley. Cilantro."

"Fruit?" she asks hopefully.

"Lots of it."

She wrinkles her nose. "Thank God for that. What about meat?"

"Up to you, but no pork. Oh! And get a slow masticating juicer. The horizontal kind."

"Slow masturbating juicer? Now that's a thought."

"Chloe!"

She tosses her hair. "How long will this insufferable diet be for?"

"Till August. I'll do it with you. We can finish by the time we go to Provence."

She nods. "Fair enough. I couldn't imagine anything more torturous than being in France without wine and baguettes." She taps her pen against the edge of the table. "Now it's my turn. Your ancestor blessings. Do you have everything you need for your Norwegian expedition?"

I study my friend for a moment. Once she has decided she wants something, she's like a horse racing toward the finish line and won't stop until she gets there. Pulling my notebook from my purse, I flip through the pages. "I've written to my fourth-generation Norwegian cousins. They said yes right away. They even offered for me to stay."

She nods. "And Germany's been taken care of. So that leaves England."

"And that's my problem. I've been to the house where my father was born. But the idea of doing a ceremony in a busy street in London doesn't feel right at all. Then again I suppose we can do the blessing anywhere."

Chloe begins typing with a practiced air. "You need something symbolic." Her eyes scan the screen. "There aren't any towns called Jones, but wasn't your grandfather called Woodham? There's a village with that name. It's near Byfleet." She turns off the iPad and places it in her bag. "Done. Anything else?"

"A job?" I say, hopefully.

"Contact Jackie," she says. "Her husband approached me about a book deal not long ago that had to do with shamans. Maybe you can work on it."

Jackie! I've known her since I first arrived in London. When it comes to investigative reporting, they are as good a team as it gets. "Why didn't I think of that?"

She gives me an irresistible smile. "Because you wouldn't need me if you had," she says and calls for the bill.

A few days later, I'm walking along the labyrinth of walkways, bikeways and footpaths that lead me away from Chiswick Park underground station on my way to the Thames. The further I go, the urban noises fade, gradually replaced by the sound of birdsong and branches whispering in the wind. Then the river, in its muddy glory, appears. The Thames is teeming with life. Boats of all kinds plough its surface, sleek pleasure boats, kayaks, loud tugs. Even a needle-like rowing scull gracefully skims by, all oars in syncopated rhythm.

I stop to absorb the scene with all my senses. It's good to feel the warmth on my skin, to hear the lapping of water against the quay, to smell the lime blossoms in the air. I breathe in deeply and let the air slowly out of my lungs, noticing the feeling of peace when I do this. Breathe. Slowly and consciously. In twenty seconds, I've forgotten the underground ride and am more relaxed. I head down the pedestrian path hugging the river, pass pubs spilling lunchtime guests onto patios, dodge a few joggers and bikers and, after a twenty-minute walk, arrive at a large white Georgian house covered with purple wisteria. This is where my journalist friend Jackie lives with her husband Max, a documentary television producer. Before I have a chance to knock, Jackie flings the door open and gives me a long, teary hug.

"Who would have imagined shamanism would be your thing," she cries. Her eyes bore into me with laser-like precision. Apparently satisfied, she pulls me through the door. I drop my bag on a table in the foyer and follow her into the kitchen.

Jackie pushes her black glasses up on her head and focuses on making tea.

"Do you know what crossed my mind when I heard that Eugen had died?" she says as we pile the tea things on a tray. "I'm afraid to say it, but I thought, finally." She gives me a plate of spelt bread and jam and we head upstairs. At the top step, she turns to me. "Don't get me wrong. Max and I saw how happy you both were. But there was always something I couldn't put my finger on. Something not right."

"What do you mean by that?" I ask.

"Call it a sixth sense. We knew it wouldn't last forever. You weren't born to take care of a crumbling castle." She pauses a moment, letting the words go where they need to go, and when we next speak, the past is behind us. She sits down on the sofa next to me and places the tray on the table. On the other side of the open window, trails of wisteria wave to and fro in the afternoon breeze.

"I haven't done research in a while," I start, but she stops me.

"Once a professional always a professional." Shaking the crumbs from her fingers, she gets up and returns with an armful of books and a large manila folder. "When Max heard that you've spent time with a shaman, he was beside himself with excitement." She opens the folder up and pulls out what looks to be a television series proposal and hands it to me.

"The Return of the Feminine," I read. On the cover is a small statue of a naked woman. It's Venus of Willendorf. This is getting ridiculous. Wherever I go, there she is. "The Great Mother herself."

She nods. "We don't have a name for her in our religions, but Hinduism calls her Shakti and the Chinese call her Yin. We decided to call it the Feminine because what we are talking about is an energy that both men and women carry with them."

"Do you have the production schedule?"

"Not yet." She unfolds a map of Europe peppered with sticky notes. She runs her finger over the map as she speaks. "The main locations are the Lascaux Cave in France. Vienna, to see the Venus. Çatal Höyük in Anatolia. The palace of Knossos in Crete. It's hard to choose because there are so many anthropological sites where these figurines have been discovered. Every month new statues are being found."

"So how does shamanism come in?" I ask as I help her fold up the map.

"Because shamans also see the planet as the Great Mother."

I stop, holding the map in my hands. "So what happened to the Goddess societies? If these ancient civilizations were so advanced, why did they fall?"

"It was a number of factors," she says. "Climate change was one. The domestication of the horse was another. The geologist James deMeo blames the massive climatic changes around six thousand years ago. The earth heated up so much that the grasslands turned into desert. As soon as the horse was domesticated around 5,000 BCE, wave after wave of pastoral nomads from Central Asia invaded what we know as the fertile crescent. The archaeologist Marija Gimbutas called these people Kurgans. The invasions lasted well over two thousand years."

"Why couldn't the Goddess cultures defend themselves?"

"Because they were agrarian and peaceful," she explains. "Their cities were in valleys, not on hilltops, so they were easily overwhelmed. The invaders were brutal. They not only understood war, they thrived on it. There was massive spiritual and archeological destruction. Slavery began. Temples were burnt. And so, slowly, over thousands of years of being hunted, purged, burned, destroyed, and oppressed, the Goddess—and the peaceful societies who worshipped her—began to lose power and eventually fell."

I start to take notes. "But why did they have to destroy everything?"

"Because of one word," she says. "Fear."

She takes the proposal back from me and flips to the back. One of the pages is a photograph of a statue of a sleek black cat sitting regally, ears pointed forward. "This is Bastet. This Egyptian cat goddess ruled home, fertility, and childbirth. Now watch."

She turns to a page with two pictures side by side. The first is of witches with warts on their noses and sinister eyes. Dressed in black robes, they stir a bubbling cauldron. At their feet is a black cat, tail puffed like a toilet brush, back arched in a full hiss.

"The witches from Macbeth," she says. As I'm studying this, she pulls out a photograph. It's an image of men stirring a massive brass pot on a coal fire. She places it side by side with the photo of the witches. "This is Ayurvedic medicine being made in Kerala."

I look from one photo to the other. Both have people stirring something in a cauldron. The only difference is that one is peaceful, the other an illustration of evil. The penny drops. "Those woman weren't witches," I say. "They were herbalists!"

She nods. "Demonization is often done during campaigns of war, where leaders need to goad their armies to hate the enemy. The Nazis did this by stirring up fears of the Jews in World War Two. The Kurgan peoples demonized the Goddess because it was the only way that they could convince the people who loved her to abandon her."

"Fear is that strong," I murmur as Jackie takes the photos from me. She then pulls a book out from the pile and opens it. "As patriarchal attitudes began to rise, the Goddess was lowered from Queen of Heaven to merely being the wife of the ruling God. As myths and legends are ways to reflect what is happening on the spiritual level of humanity, it shows that women, too, were losing their status. But it wasn't just that. Everything that was associated with her, such as black cats and serpents and everything to do with healing, became symbols of death and evil. The Goddess' consort, the Bull God, became the hoofed and horned devil. The half-human, half-bull Minoan minotaur became a monster who ate Athenian youths. The ancient snake goddess became the Medusa. The bird goddess the Harpies. The Titans ate children."

I pull off my jacket. "I feel like my head is being turned upside down."

"That's exactly what happened to these ancient societies," she answers. "Their world was turned upside down. The Minoan bull dance, or bull-leaping, which is depicted in frescos on the walls of the palace of Knossos, was a peaceful dance of dexterity and skill where an acrobat grabbed the bull's horns and catapulted over its back." She pauses theatrically. "Do you know what happened to that innocent dance?"

I shake my head.

Her eyes flash. "It became the bull fight. And what do we do with the bull? We torture and kill it. That's because we are a warrior culture."

"What about the ritual of sacrifice?"

"That, too, was twisted as time went by. Agrarian societies wouldn't spill blood to appease a gentle goddess. It was the nomadic invaders who killed animals to appease an angry God." She snaps the book shut and drops it on the coffee table in front of her. "Sacrifices were symbolic, Annabel. If blood was used, it was freely given female menstrual blood. So once again, something that was peaceful became an act of violence."

I look beyond her. "I don't believe it. Violence has been part of humanity forever."

"That's not true. Our violent and warlike attitudes stem from the warlike attitudes from the desert."

"But surely when they arrived in more fertile lands, they could relax."

"But they didn't. Even when they moved to fertile lands, they couldn't let go of their old ways because of something DeMeo calls the institutionalization of violence. The techniques they learned to survive had begun ingrained as a way of life."

"But what about the Aztec sacrifices? They ripped people's hearts out."

"That, too, is a twisted interpretation that stemmed from a simple ritual of connecting to the heart," she explains. "As the Kurgans were herders, expansion was part of their structural make-up. Once they became mobile, they moved into Europe, down through the Indian subcontinent, across the straits into the Americas and into South America."

"The Kurgans invaded the Americas?"

She shakes her head. "It wasn't the Kurgans per se. It was *a shift of a mentality.* Everything became about power and domination. Military might was glorified. Weapons were worshipped. Heroic warriors idealized. Death, rather than life, became the focus. The Aztecs were the same. What was once a peaceful ritual of heart connection became a bloody rite to appease an angry god."

It feels like she is taking a hammer to my precious beliefs and destroying them, one by one. "Are there any of the older peoples left?"

She nods. "What do you think indigenous cultures are?" She pauses to let me think about this. "Places that were harder for the invaders to reach, such as islands, retain some of the old ways. That's why Celtic and ancient European cultures can be found in Sardinia, Crete, Great Britain, and Iceland. But in time, even they became warlike and aggressive."

I stare at her for a long time, waiting for all these images to settle in my brain. "What happened to the invaders in the end?"

She gives me a peculiar smile. "You haven't gotten it yet, have you?"

"Gotten what?"

"Annabel. It's us."

I rub my eyes. "*We* are the descendants of those people?"

"Our society is based upon a scarcity mentality. Our nomadic ancestors established a cultural dynamic that concretized their dominate-or-die attitude." She picks up the proposal and waves it under my nose. "But we've come to the end of the road. We can all feel it in our bones. This old-fashioned war-like attitude no longer works because there is nowhere else to go. It's time we learn to live with each other and the planet, not destroy each other, or we'll be toast. We need to change our ways, Annabel. And this series can help

200

show the way."

Water is everywhere. It's on the floor of the bathroom. In the tub. On the walls. On my T-shirt and legs. On my arms. In between my toes. In my hair. It's soaking Chloe's shirt, running down her face, and making her hair look like she's dashed through a sprinkler. It's gathering in puddles around the faucet, dribbling off the marble countertop, falling in lines that run down the cabinets. In fact, water is everywhere except where it's supposed to be—up Chloe's nose.

We've been in Chloe's bathroom for the past half hour. For the third time, I lift the neti pot, which looks like a miniature watering can. "It can't be that difficult. Lean over the sink. Tilt your head, open your mouth, and breathe. When I start to pour, let gravity do its work. The saline will naturally flow into one nostril and out of the other."

She leans over the sink. Her hair falls like snaky tendrils into the basin. I hold the spout against her nostril. "Tilt your head," I say. "Don't forget to breathe."

As I start to pour, she gags and leaps up in the air. One hand hits the neti pot and it flies out of my hand, arcs in the air and lands in the bidet with a clang.

Chloe leaps up and pulls it out of the bidet and shakes it. "Shit. I need to hear it again. Why am I doing this?"

I watch the droplets fall on the floor. "It clears your sinuses. Helps you sleep. You'll breathe better. Catch fewer colds." I pause to wipe her forehead. "And because you said you'd do this if I went to that singles party with you."

"And we know what happened there," she says, patting my forehead with a towel. "You were supposed to meet a man. What happened instead? You ended up having your third eye blasted open. Lord, give me a normal friend. Instead, I have Guru Ma herself."

I fill the pot with water and mix a quarter teaspoon of salt in it, then give it to her. "You have one more chance. If you succeed, I will sit at your lotus feet."

Chloe brings her elbow up as if she's about to serve a tennis ball, places the neti pot against one nostril, and breathes like a locomotive through her mouth. After a second, a dribble of water drains out of the other nostril. She blows her nose, then, as she inhales, her eyes widen.

"Oh my God! I can smell. Everyone should use these things." She hugs me so tightly I can barely breathe. "Cup of tea in the crow's nest at four?"

As she releases me, I gasp, grinning. "I thought you'd never ask."

The crow's nest is at the top of the house, reached by a winding stairwell. It's an intimate room, with a small window on every wall and French doors leading onto a small patio lined with flowering sweet peas. A sea of rooftops stretches as far as the eye can see. The room is just large enough for two wicker chairs, a low table, and a small bookcase. A Buddha sits in one corner and a dancing Shiva graces the other. A Moroccan lamp. A few candles. And not a sign of flowery chintz.

Chloe is sitting on a chair with Olive curled up on her lap. In front of her is a tray with a pot of tea, dainty porcelain cups, and a small Moroccan blue and white bowl. Next to the tray is a stack of books and a neat pile of papers, some with paperclips on them.

Chloe hands me a cup. "Here, take a throw and curl up. I've brought Jeanette's candied ginger." She lifts the bowl. "Try some."

I flick off my shoes and settle into the other chair, then pop a piece of ginger in my mouth as she picks up a blue folder and sifts through the pages until she finds what she's looking for. "You do know that Jean Luc and I were doing a book on tantra, right? " She waves her hand at the bookcase. "I wanted to share our research with you. I think it might be something Jackie might not know."

I take the folder and open it and am surprised to see photos of vaginas. Lots of them.

She doesn't bat an eye. "As you know, for tens of thousands of years, the earth was seen as feminine. She gave us food. Home. She birthed us, just as a woman's body births a baby. Therefore the yoni—

202

you remember that's what tantra calls the vagina—was honored. It is nature's gateway of all births. Which is why cave entrances, watery ponds, even the inside of flowers, were worshipped. Because they look like the yoni."

"And why we build skyscrapers that look like penises, or vajras," I say, remembering the Tibetan word that tantra uses. "I remember this from tantra. We worship a masculine culture and therefore build our homes in the form of phallic symbols."

"Haven't you come a long way from the sexual nerd I used to know and love," she says, smiling. "So. It's not surprising that there is so much toxic masculinity around. That's because women hold the key to the greatest pleasure of all."

I grin. "Sex."

"My favorite subject." She takes the book from me. "The Goddess cultures didn't consider sex shameful or titillating. For them, sex was healing. How could anything that feels so good not be? Women's bodies were revered. They were considered fertile soil, so they fertilized their crops with menstrual blood. Just like in farming, a man ploughed his seed and life appeared. Sexuality, and more specifically, a woman's yoni, was a sacred gift of the gods. That's why the symbol of a V, which is everywhere in prehistoric cave paintings, is a symbol for a woman's yoni. And that, my dear Annabel, is why their societies were so peaceful."

I rest my chin on my hand. "How did you come to that conclusion?"

She pulls out her phone. "By studying our closest relatives."

She swipes at her phone and brings up a YouTube video of what look to be chimpanzees playing in a jungle.

"They aren't chimps, they are bonobos," she explains. "They are known as hippie chimps because they have sex all the time. Males with males. Females with females. Males and females. It is their main occupation. Do you know why?"

"Because they like it?"

She laughs. "Because they use it to keep the peace. And do you know how?" She stops the video.

"You are going to say it's because of sex," I say.

She gives her hair a toss. "Thank goodness you studied tantra or you would have been writhing on the floor by now. You see, just like the ancient Goddess cultures, the bonobos are matrilineal. The females hold the power. And guess what? No tension. No aggression. Just harmony and cooperation."

"But one thing doesn't necessarily produce the other," I say.

She shakes her head. "No. But by observing the bonobos, we can understand how the Goddess cultures also diffused the natural tensions that occur." Her eyes glitter with excitement. "The ancient Goddess cultures understood that when males get together, they can be whipped into a fury of breast-beating. So they created social structures that didn't allow this to happen. Instead of war or competitive sports, testosterone-filled youths, angry and lonely old men could go to the temple instead."

"And visit temple prostitutes?"

She goes crazy when I say this. "Just because women made love to strangers didn't mean they were prostitutes. That shows how warped our understanding of sex is today. This was part of their temple duties. They were married, as well as single, and they came from wealthy and royal families. They resided for a period within the temple as *qadishtu*, or sacred women of the Goddess. They were free to come and go as they wished. They were free to marry at any time. Dedicating themselves to the temple was their way of giving back to society."

I fish a leaf of tea out of my cup. "And this was respectable?"

"It was beyond respectable. Remember, there was none of the shame or blame or distorted perversions that we have around sex back then. To them, sex was something that felt good. It gave pleasure. It created children. Why wouldn't they see it as sacred?"

Sex has always been Chloe's subject more than mine. "Are you sure you aren't putting a feminist overlay onto this?"

She takes a sip of tea. "I have to admit, it took me a while to get my head around this too. But think about it. Until recently, it was perfectly acceptable for half of humanity to dominate the other.

Don't you think that's odd? Why do men hate us so much? The answer is because of sex. It's woman's greatest power over a man." She stares into my eyes. "These societies weren't stupid. There was an excellent societal reason for having these temples. When you have sex with someone, it creates an intimate bond. It's hard to hate, much less fight, a person you have had intimate relations with. They harnessed the power of sex to act as a glue to bring people together. Sex, not fear, was the underpinning that brought peace to their society."

She runs her hand through her hair. "Well. You can imagine what happened when the sex-starved desert nomads, who treated women like passive wombs with legs, arrived. They must have freaked. These nomads had formed societies based upon hardship and war. There was no time for love. Their leaders realized that if men started to enjoy life, their power would collapse. So instead of adopting these gentler ways, they set out to destroy them. And that they did, with relish. You can still read the harrowed harangues against the temples of Babylon in the Old Testament, smiting the Lord's wrath against people for returning to the old ways."

"You mean the old ways were the peaceful ones?"

She nods. "These old ways, with their communal, ritualistic practices involving sexuality as divine, were labeled as prostitution. Even then, it took repression and violence to stamp out the ways of the Goddess. Remember this was long before Christianity and the Bible. But once it happened, these ideals spread like a virus." She closes the folder with a snap. "Our entire culture, Annabel, is permeated by cruelty and fear, especially toward women. It's so accepted that we don't even see it anymore."

"That's the type of mentality I was brought up with," I say, quietly.

"Misogynistic?"

I lower my eyes. "Very."

"Violent?"

My voice drops to a whisper. "Yes."

"I take it you were raised to marry well?" The tone of her voice makes it perfectly clear what well means.

"I had it pounded into my head," I say. "I remember once asking my father what I could do to become successful in his eyes, and he responded I would need to get married and have children."

"But what did that have to do with you?"

"Precisely. But still, deep down, that message took root inside me."

"So that's why you dropped your career and moved to Vienna to marry Eugen," she muses. "It was the culmination of what you had been raised to achieve."

I nod. "It's embarrassing to admit, but it's true. I was taught I had no value."

Chloe tosses her hair in disgust. "A woman doesn't become a queen because she married a king. A woman crowns herself. I learned early that on we don't need men. Just look at this family tree nonsense. Why docs a woman take a man's name in marriage when she is the one who gives birth? Until DNA was discovered, the only parent you could guarantee was your mother, not your father."

"Is that why you kept your name when you got married?"

She nods. "And Jean Luc uses his own. Think about it. We don't need men to procreate. A woman can implant sperm into her womb. But a man can't have a baby without a woman. We don't need men. They need us, and for that, they hate us." She stands up abruptly. "No wonder our planet is a mess. Our race needs to evolve or we are going to become extinct."

"Aren't you exaggerating?"

"You need a history lesson," she says, pointing to the bookshelf. "It took me months to assimilate a wider, more open understanding of our species as a race. It's time to bring you up to date on the real history of humanity and not the polished version we've been taught." Her eyes flash. "But I warn you. It's going to make you angry."

I spend the next few weeks reading through the books on Chloe's bookshelf. At first, I tell myself that it will help with my research for Jackie's documentary. But soon I realize that this is for myself. I comb through archives. Spend days in the British Museum, where I examine sacred objects, reliquaries, deities and demons from thousands of years ago and thousands of miles away. I am struck by a sense of disconnect, from our past, and from ourselves, as I see these objects jockeying for space, comically lost and frozen in time. The society in which I live is so shallow that the sacred has become entertainment. Where are the magic and the mystery? Everything has been interpreted literally. Not knowing the true value of our past, we have no choice but to see objects as things. Why? Because we have lost our roots within ourselves.

The author Riane Eisler helped me see history through a larger prism than just man versus woman. The Goddess societies were based upon partnership and cooperation, not domination and submission. And yet there is a lot to get angry about, especially when I learn the atrocities women were subjected to by these dominator societies. Even my view of the Greeks, whom I had been taught to admire, dimmed once I began to see how misogynistic they were. Although whiffs of the Feminine appear in Greek and Roman cultures, it is only an aroma left behind in an empty glass of fine wine. The Greeks were virulently warlike. Misogynistic to the point of being a phallocracy. Erect penises were everywhere. Homosexual sex in Greek times was not a loving act but a dominating one between males with submissive slaves or young boys. And where were women? Curtailed to women's quarters, forbidden to speak or appear in public, denied status to go to court, forced to be under the legal guardianship of men. Female children were sold as slaves. Slave girls were used as prostitutes. Women were barred from public office. Had no birth records. Were considered ovens to produce babies for men. And this was because, as Aristotle said, women by nature were inferior.

Rage burns within me. A sadness so deep it swallows me whole. How can I be upset at events that happened thousands of years ago? Because it has never been acknowledged. By the time the Middle Ages arrived, women were considered chattels. Sex, which used to be the glue that bonded men and women together, became shameful and dirty. The body was vilified. Healers were branded as witches and burned. Thousands of years of herbal medicinal knowledge was destroyed. Life became so painful that the only thing religions could offer was hope of a better life in the afterworld.

A blindfold is being ripped from my eyes. I'm emerging from the darkness of Plato's cave, and the reality I discover is so bright I can hardly see. I give up applying for jobs I don't want, stop seeing friends I don't have much in common with, and spend days locked up in the crow's nest, sailing above the sea of roofs as one book after another opens doors to a new worldview that includes everyone, men and women, equally in its embrace.

This is the second time I'm making this journey. The first time, I threw off the chains of my misogynistic upbringing to free myself from the shame I had around being a woman. Now I'm doing it again, seeing what happened to me through the perspective of history. It transports me into the dark recesses of my being, and when I emerge, weeks later, I feel as if I'm rising from the underworld back into the light again. I see that the disconnect and pain of my childhood are a microcosm of the larger story of humanity. My struggle to open my heart and embrace my natural tendency toward kindness is not an individual battle. It's a reflection of what the entire world is going through right now.

I'm sitting in the crow's nest, surrounded by books, a pen in one hand and a glass of lemonade in the other, when my phone rings. I scramble through the papers to find the source of the sound. When I put my phone to my ear, a voice makes my heart sink.

It's Maria Eugenia. "I assume you have read the will."

Instantly I feel like a rat in a cage.

"Have you? Because if you have, you should know I have the legal right to the apartment you are living in."

She exhales sharply. "Don't patronize me," she snaps. "Pretending to help others when all you care about is yourself. My son ruined his life trying to please you. No matter what he gave, you always wanted more. You pushed poor Vandana out of that marriage and you know

208

it."

"You didn't give a damn about Vandana until she was dead."

"Neither did you," Maria Eugenia answers. Her voice reverberates in my head like a church bell. "We are more similar than you would like to admit."

She doesn't belabor the point. Everyone has an ouch spot, and this is mine. Sometimes, when I can't sleep, I wonder whether Eugen's guilt over his divorce didn't trigger his illness. "I loved Eugen."

"I never said you didn't," she says. "People said the same thing to me when I married Georg. They said I took advantage of a man in a weak moment. Beguiled him with my beauty. Did everything I could to ensnare him. They spread poisonous stories about me that said everything except the truth."

"Which was?"

"That I loved him," she says. "Dearly."

In this instant, the strangest thing happens. Until now, I saw Maria Eugenia as an archetypical evil character. But I realize she's human like me. She knows what it is to love. And knows what it is to lose that love.

This moment of connection leaves us both disoriented, like two warriors who pause and put their weapons down. "My daughter is everything to me."

"You mean your step-granddaughter," I say.

The moment that held us in its embrace breaks like a brittle cord. "I had entertained the hope that you would be able to see beyond the narrow confines of your upbringing. You will bring this family to ruins. I hope this weighs heavily on your soul."

My face burns. "I didn't write the will, Eugen did."

She makes a *pah* sound. "Eugen would have expected more from you than to take revenge on a poor widow. Out of the kindness of my heart I have let you keep your things in the palace. And what do you do? Turn my own daughter against me."

"You wouldn't know the truth if it were staring you in the face," I snap. "I want my home back."

"Then go home," she says, her voice dripping like saccharine. "Back to where you belong."

"I belong in Vienna," I cry, but I know it's no good. The moment my anger flared, she knows she has won the battle.

"You don't belong here. You never did. And you never will." The line goes dead.

I'm no longer in the crow's nest, but back floating in my last memories of Brazil. The family has just finished lunch. The aroma of cafezinhos, the small cups of sweetened coffee, wafts through the house. Hearing the front door open, I assume it's Dona Mathilde. But when I stand on the landing and look down, I see Dona Mathilde's eldest daughter, Paula. I'm just about to ask if she has forgotten something when she runs up the stairs.

"Go home." There is fire in her eyes. "You are no longer welcome."

Her words feel like a sword in my heart. "What are you talking about?"

Paula jabs a finger into my chest. "You aren't part of this family and never will be."

I run to my room, slam the door, and throw myself on the bed. I am still sobbing when I hear the front door slam. Then silence. Outside my window, chattering birds flit from vine to vine. Thunder crashes and the first drops of rain plop on waxy leaves. I used to love all of this—Brazil, the forest, my family—but now the jungle seems ready to swallow me whole.

I had secretly hoped that if I could just pretend to be one of them, I, too, would be a part of the family. My heart aches to think that I would cause Dona Mathilde pain.

And so, without ever telling Dona Mathilde why, I take leave of it all—the magic, the mystery, the spiritualism, and the healing—and return to Kansas. It's only years later that I learn that Paula was mentally ill. I was not the first, nor the last, recipient of her anger. But by then it was too late. Dona Mathilde died in a car crash a few years after I left. I never saw her again.

It's midnight. I'm still in the crow's nest, sitting on the floor, when I hear Chloe's voice. She's calling my name. I try to move, but my limbs creak like the timbers of an old house in the wind.

I hear footsteps, then silence. If Chloe is surprised to see me sitting alone in the darkened room, she doesn't show it. Without saying a word, she puts her arm around me and walks me down the stairs to my room. Pulling back the bedcovers, she helps me slip inside, and disappears upstairs. Moments later she returns with a steaming cup of miso soup.

I sit up and hold the cup in my hands, staring at the liquid inside. "What a fool I was. All these years I believed that just because they had a title and a palace and a place in history, they were better. More civilized."

Her voice murmurs like the ocean. "You were chasing. You've been doing that since I met you. Chasing families who will never accept you. Chasing countries where you don't belong. Chasing a life that doesn't suit you."

I'm silent for a long time. "I chased my family, too. Been chasing them ever since I was sent to Brazil. Blaming myself for why they pushed me away. Thinking I'm damaged goods." My shoulders slump. "I did everything I could to be accepted by Eugen's family. I so wanted to belong."

"Belong," she says. "To a family like that? You would be tolerated at best. The sooner you accept that, the freer you will be."

"Free to do what?"

"To begin your future," she says.

"And how do I do that?"

"By letting them keep their past. Remember. It's all they have." She tiptoes out the room and turns out the light.

The early morning sun streams through the windows announcing a new day. But when I pull my arms out of the duvet, every muscle from my neck to my toes aches. I think back to yesterday, remember

211

Maria Eugenia, and groan.

My body feels heavy as I get out of bed and get dressed. The house is as silent as a tomb. It's Saturday, which means Chloe is gone and Jeanette won't be here. With nothing to do and nowhere to go, I decide to fill the emptiness by going for a walk.

First comes Hyde Park, then Green Park, then St James's Park. Two hours later, I'm still going, along the Mall and into Parliament Square, until I find myself in front of towering spires piercing the sky. Sweeping past the tourists pressing against the iron railings, I enter a door and am embraced by a thousand years of history.

Inside, the vaulted ceiling of Westminster Abbey draws my eyes upward like a magnet. Rays of pale sunlight glimmer through the carved windows, highlighting honey-colored arches and multitudes of memorials carved in stone. Seeing a stand with guide phones, I rent one, hoping the information it will give me will spark my curiosity. I've always loved sacred places. It doesn't matter what religion they are, the more ancient they are, the better. However, now all I can see is repression. Like a broken record, I remember the church's horrible past, its endless announcements, edicts, and laws that have oppressed women for centuries.

Wandering the corridors, my mind swirling in indignant anger, I walk too close to an exit and set off the Abbey's alarm system. As I stand, trying to pretend that the screeching whine is not emanating from the object in my hand, a woman in a red mantle swooshes toward me. With a benevolent smile, she takes the phone and presses a few buttons. The piercing wail cuts abruptly and I could swear the entire church breathes a collective sigh of relief.

She looks into my eyes and blinks. "I know you."

Trying to shake the buzz from my ears, I shoot an uncomprehending glance at her.

She smiles. "It's Mary. You know, from Herefordshire."

I look again. Her body is stout, her skin clear. But it's her eyes, a bright piercing blue, that jog my memory. "Mrs More-Hamilton?" The absurdity of it all begins to sink into my consciousness as I gaze at Chloe's mother in front of me. "What are you doing here?"

"The countryside bored me," she says with just enough of the Irish lilt to give away her roots.

My eyes wander along the stone frieze of one of the most beautiful religious monuments in the world. "But aren't you, um, Catholic?"

"So I am, so I am," she answers. "And they say that God doesn't have a sense of humor." She waves at me to follow her. "Come with me to put this back where it belongs."

The heaviness that has been following me since I left Chloe's begins to lift. In that discombobulated way that happens when two people meet in extraordinary circumstances, we chat about our lives as we walk along the main aisle, Mary's robe fluttering in her wake like the gown of a queen. "Isn't it gorgeous here?"

"I had religion forced down my throat when I was young," I explain. "It's put me off the church for good."

"Don't look down upon organized religion, my dear," she says, handing the guide phone to an attendant. "You may not need it, but it gives many people a set of values and a sense of community."

"But how it treated women," I begin, but she puts her hand on my arm.

"Don't let the past color the present. See the church as it is now." We watch a young woman with blond hair sitting on a pew, head bowed in contemplation. Behind her, a couple walks, heads tilted toward the ceiling, rapt expressions on their faces. "This is a sacred space that gives people the space to reflect. But if you're like me and want to know the larger picture, let me show you a few of our secrets."

She points to an elaborately carved neo-Gothic canopy. Underneath, reclining on a sarcophagus, is a statue of a man with his elbow resting on books. "That's Sir Isaac Newton," she says. An angel reclines on a golden globe that hangs above his head. "See those books he's resting on?" She points to what looks like a black marble bathtub underneath him. "Those are tomes of classical mechanics. Calculus. The laws of motion and universal gravitation."

I gaze at walls jammed with architects and artists, writers and

213

poets, politicians, explorers, and scientists as her words wash over me.

"In the Age of Enlightenment, curiosity was king. That's why Sir Isaac was so interested in alchemy. It was a particular fascination of his. He was a little unorthodox, which is what I love about him."

"No one could turn metal into gold."

"Don't take it literally, my dear," she says. "It was mystical. Alchemy was deeper than just turning lead into gold. It is what happens when a person begins to transform."

I stop in my tracks. "Alchemy is another word for the spiritual journey?"

Her eyebrows rise. "That's exactly what I'm saying. It was as peaceful as the teachings it was based upon. That's why Jesus' message was called the Gospel. It was good news. Frankly, after those thousands of years of brutality and torture, I would have called it good news too."

"I just can't get over my anger about what happened to women," I say. "They destroyed the Goddess."

But my reaction only makes her laugh. "Who said she was destroyed? She is alive and well." She lowers her voice. "She's just gone underground. Like over there. Hidden in all that foliage." Mary points to an elaborate carved panel shaped like a gothic arch. Carved curlicue tendrils wave every which way like a jungle. "Can you see it?"

For a moment, all I can see are leaves. Then, as I focus on the screen, I can see, peering out from its jungle home, a golden face. Growing out of the face are five vines.

"Who is he?"

"He's called The Green Man." She tuts to herself. "Keeps us on our toes, he does."

"But he's a man. The Goddess is a woman."

"If you ask me, the Green Man is her consort." She winks. "Just like all things mystical, the Goddess is hidden in plain sight. Even in a man's face." She indicates for me to follow her to the shop. There, she picks up a book. As I turn the pages, I see hundreds of Green Men, with foliage for hair, beards of leaves, and vines sprouting from open

214

mouths. Sometimes, the entire face is made up of leaves, sometimes it peers out of a jungle. Other times, the tendrils sprout from ears and even eyes.

She points to one. "He's a touchstone to remind us of something we have forgotten."

Before I can ask her any more, the bell rings. The cathedral is about to close.

"So what are you doing on the solstice?" she asks as we make our way to the exit.

"I want to do a blessing for my English ancestors."

Mary beams. "You couldn't have chosen a better day. I love the solstice. It's so powerful I can hardly sleep. For a few days I just feel the sun hovering like a golden disk above us, just about to tip over and head south again." We stand by the doorway as people thread by us. "Are you going with Chloe and Jean Luc?"

"Jean Luc works in San Francisco now."

She stops walking. "Are they having troubles?"

"More than either would like to admit."

"How is she handling it?"

"Soldiering on."

She turns to me, her eyes like steel. "Then we must do what we can to help." She fluffs her red mantle and pulls out a card. "Come to Herefordshire," she says as she gives it to me. "There's a church in Kilpeck I want you to see."

"Does the church contain a Green Man?"

"It does," she says. "And he's friends with a certain woman named Sheela."

The solstice dawns bright and clear. The day is going to be a scorcher. I pull on a sun dress and sandals and head in Chloe's car south of London, my collection of glass bottles rattling in the passenger seat next to me. Avoiding the M25, the beltway that surrounds London like a girdle, I wiggle along country roads sunk so deep it feels like a leafy tunnel. I pass Kingston upon Thames, Esher and Hersham and the village of New Haw, and there it is—a small white sign with WOODHAM in black letters.

Leaving the car idling by the side of the road, I get out and walk around the sign, and when I look up again, I see a black cat sitting by the edge of the tarmac, staring at me. It's as large as a bowling pin. By now, I know what to do. As the cat gets up, stretches, and turns away, I lock the car and follow it into the woods. Ten minutes later, I see a canal. By the time I reach it, the cat has disappeared into the dense underbrush, and in its place, I feel Percy. No, not Percy the sangoma, Percy my English grandfather.

I'm surprised to find my grandfather Percy. I hadn't been expecting him. I had been expecting—well, I'm not sure what because I'm not used to ancestors making sudden appearances in my life. But of all my English ancestors, I hadn't thought of Percy. I have no memory of him because I never knew him. He's different from the black-and-white photo of a wiry man with a long nose I remember seeing in a silver frame on my father's chest of drawers. Percy was something of a rake when he was young, leaving England to travel the world on a sailing ship. He apparently loved to dance and sing pub songs from his wasted youth, but he was always overshadowed by his wife, a battleax of a woman who was determined to leave the ruins of postwar London behind and make a life for themselves in Minnesota. It must have taken a lot of courage to emigrate to America when he and his wife were in their sixties. She had the drive and the ambition, so people never talked much about Percy. But now, with him in front of me, I can sense that he is gentle and kind. He is thin too, like Gandhi. He also has a wonderful sense of humor. As I walk along the canal with him, he regales me with stories about fairies and water sprites and the magical people of the forest, whom I could see if only I would slow down enough. *Connect with nature,* I hear him say. *She will nourish you whenever you need it.*

Percy tells me that even though he emigrated to America, he always considered England his home. This is why he passed on this love of England to his own son, my father. *The world is playing music all the time,* Percy whispers. *Sometimes it's loud and jarring, sometimes it's sweet and soft, but it's always there. Follow life's rhythms. Find the music within you, and you'll dance to all that life gifts you.*

As I walk along the canal listening to wise words from my grandfather, my heart speaks in return. Half an hour later, I recognize by the soft tears running down my cheeks that the blessing is done.

I bend down to scoop a little earth into my collection vial. This will be a touchstone to remind me, whenever I look at it, of my grandfather's wise words. I then retrace my steps along the canal to my car, get in and close the door, and sit in silence. I have just had an hour with my grandfather, speaking more heart-to-heart with him than I probably could have done had he been alive. I've spent half my life in search of family, only to discover that I have them inside me.

Just like mystery and magic. They're in me, too. The earth is alive. Each tree, each flower, each blade of grass, each pebble. It's in the tales that my father told me at my bedside; it's in the constellations that my brother showed me when I was young, as we lay on our backs trying to make sense of the blanket of stars above our heads. It's in the nature that surrounds me everywhere I go. Wherever I am, all I need to do is be still, and that is how I can nourish my soul. I'm home wherever I am, as long as I connect with myself. That is the gift of my grandfather Percy.

EARTH

Herefordshire

The two most important days in your life are the day you are born and the day you find out why
—Mark Twain

It's morning. I'm lying on my bed, waiting for my latest energy episode to be over. I'm observing my mind trying to make sense of it all: the prickling sensations, the effervescent bubbles racing up and down my limbs, the heaviness that makes my body feel like a sack of soft cement. During these moments, my mind spins uselessly, like a tire in mud. It presents me with a list of chores, each task more imperative than the next. It reminds me of all the things that still need to be done. It tells me I'm wasting my time. It bullies me. And if that doesn't work, it threatens me with existential questions that I never can answer. It wants me to do everything except what I'm doing, which is lying in stillness, feeling my chest rising and falling with each breath. Just me observing myself.

My inner battle is cut short by the ring of a phone. Like a diver at the bottom of the ocean, I swim upward toward the bell that's bobbing on the surface. But my arm feels so heavy I can't pick it up, so I ignore it, letting the sound wash over me instead. Time rolls by, slow and steady. Thoughts come and go. I'm resting in stillness. Then the phone rings again. The incessant sound flickers in my awareness, and finally, I fumble under the pillows and find it. It's Chloe. With great difficulty, my finger presses the answer and speaker buttons and my head hits the pillow again.

"Why didn't you pick up?" A voice demands.

I'm still trying to find my mouth. Ah there it is, just where I left it, right in the middle of my face. "Mm," I answer.

"Ah, you're having one of those spells. Never mind, I'll just talk. You won't believe what's happened. My mother called me today, inviting us to Herefordshire. She has someone she wants us to meet."

"Ermphh," I mumble.

"She told me to tell you she has a lot of information on the Green Man. When I asked her how she knew you were in London, she told me you ran into each other last week. What was she doing in London?"

I find my mouth muscles and force them to form a word. "Westminster."

But Chloe can't contain herself. "What does Westminster have to do with anything? Well, never mind. I've got to do three days' work in one day so we can get to Herefordshire by Friday. And hey. Don't panic about trying to get another job. I can see you can't work. Not in the state you're in. Rest up and relax. This will be fun."

As I hang up, I'm thinking I haven't heard Chloe sounding so excited in ages. I sit up on the bed, groggy and confused. My mind finally does something useful and points out that my doubts about letting Chloe help me were unfounded. She's a part of the puzzle, and so, it seems, is Mary.

For as long as I've known Chloe, her mother has been living on a family estate in Herefordshire. It's a forgotten part of England, a few hours west of London and a stone's throw from Brecon Beacons National Park. With our weekend bags in the trunk, we leave London in the early afternoon, pass through the Cotswolds, and enter a world of dramatic rolling hills and market towns built in local red sandstone. Although geographically not far from London, Herefordshire is a place lost in time.

The sun is low on the horizon by the time our car turns up the long drive leading to the house. We park, then roll our bags up the gravel path that leads to the heavy oak door. Above us, a brick chimney pokes out of the roof. A thin curl of smoke rising from it tells me that Mary has lit a fire for dinner.

More-Hamilton Manor is a beautiful L-shaped house, too large for one person, but Mrs More-Hamilton, or Mary, as she insists everyone call her, has been a widow for years and has adapted well to living on her own. The sixteenth-century manor, with its steep gabled roof, Tudor windows, and white-washed half timbering, is comfortable in a relaxed English way that makes everyone feel at home. It's a magical house painted a beautiful cream color that complements the soft green of the surrounding forest. The daylight is just fading as I press the bell, which tingles merrily as Chloe leans her shoulder against the door and pushes it open.

Within seconds, Mary bustles into the foyer, Ben the Labrador by her side. For the next few minutes, it's all smiles as Ben, with his slobbery black muzzle, wags his tail and bounces between the three of us. Mary, dressed in jeans tucked into gumboots and an apricot sweater, air kisses us both and ushers us inside.

She puts me in the main guest room upstairs, with windows overlooking a small burbling brook that runs at the back of the house. It has a large double bed covered with a pale rose-colored bedspread, a squashy yellow daybed under the bow window, and piles of books on every table.

I open the window and lean out to breathe in gallons of fresh, country air. Seeing a few bats swooping in the early evening light, I shut the window and draw the drapes. On the bedside table, Mary has left a selection of books, some of which I already know: *The Green Man*, by Kathleen Basford; *The Chalice and the Blade* and *Sacred Pleasure*, by Riane Eisler; *When God was a Woman*, by Merlin Stone; *The Gnostic Gospels*, by Elaine Pagels; and *Echoes of the Goddess*, by

Simon Brighton and Terry Welbourn. I briefly flip through them, note her thoughtfulness, then walk downstairs.

The kitchen, where supper is served, is a large open room with windows that run nearly from floor to ceiling, pots of herbs on the ledges, a massive black Aga stove, and a solid, oval antique-oak table in the middle. A large old-fashioned refrigerator stands next to the windows, covered with magnets: green shamrock-shaped ones from Ireland; smiling Labradors; and, to my surprise, black cats. The table has been set, the candles lit. Chloe and Mary are sitting across from each other at the table, sipping Mary's famous homemade gooseberry wine.

"This isn't really alcohol," Chloe says, raising her glass at me. "Want some?"

I accept a small glass as I join them and we sip our wine happily while catching up on small talk. Every now and then Ben, curled up in his wicker basket against the Aga, lifts his head, thumps his tail, then falls back asleep.

Dinner, Mary tells us, getting up and going over to her stove, is a medley of vegetables from the garden. She pulls a casserole of roasted vegetables from the oven and places it on the table.

"I'm giving up gluten and dairy soon," Mary says, as she serves heaped portions of vegetables on our plates. "Although I can't resist a good pat of butter from the neighbor's cow now and then. Everything you're eating comes from the garden."

Over dinner, Chloe doesn't say much, but I do, talking about my experiences in California and my shamanic blessings, which fascinate Mary to no end. Her curiosity is catching. It unlocks doors and opens windows in my being, and I feel my soul expanding and receiving a full airing. It's the way she looks at me when she talks, eyes twinkling, nodding her head, that teases one story after another out of me.

But the more I talk with Mary, the sulkier Chloe becomes. She's always this way when she's around her mother. For the millionth time, I wonder why.

222

After dessert, we retire to the conservatory with a tray of lemon balm tea. The large glass room is comfortably furnished with oversize wicker chairs and soft throws. It will be a full moon tonight, Mary tells us, which means none of us will get much sleep, but she wants us to stay up and see the partial eclipse forecast for later this evening. She lights a candle in a glass hurricane lamp and tells us to sit wherever is most comfortable. The night is dark and clear, the stars are twinkling all around us as we curl up, each taking a warm blanket and wrapping it around our shoulders. Mary pours us tea and we pass the cups around, then sit in silence as the moon appears over the horizon.

"Look," Mary says, as the large silver disk climbs into the sky. For a few moments, none of us speaks as we watch the earth's shadow pass across it. "You see? The moon looks as if someone has taken a bite out of it."

How often have I looked at the sky? Before Joshua Tree, not often. But now, I can't seem to open myself wide enough to take it all in. Chloe, on the other hand, is examining her nails.

"What were you doing in London?" Chloe asks.

"Oh, I go in to help out in the church."

"Not just any church," I add. "Westminster Abbey."

Chloe turns to her mother. "You work at Westminster Abbey?"

Mary's face, shining in the moonlight, looks highly amused. "Isn't that a lark? I was thrilled when my application to be a church marshall was accepted. I thought it would be a way to make good use of my doctorate."

Chloe frowns into her cup. "Most mothers don't get a degree in theology at the age of seventy."

"I'm not most mothers, dear," Mary says, as she stirs a teaspoon of honey into her cup. "Does anyone want honey? It's raw. From the neighbor's bees. You must always check that honey is raw. If it's been heated it loses its healing properties."

She passes a teaspoon and the pot of honey to Chloe, who scrapes the spoon against the edge of the jar and places it in her mouth with a look of pure pleasure, then passes the pot and the spoon to me. I

223

follow suit and put a small spoonful in my mouth. It's the perfect consistency; smooth and silky with a touch of sandy granules. "Delicious."

Chloe gives me a strange look as I pass it back to Mary. "I don't get it. How did each of you know that the other was there?"

Mary takes the pot from me. "We didn't. Annabel's guide phone set off the alarms. You should have heard them, wailing like a banshee right into those glorious ceilings. I rushed over to turn it off, and I said, 'I know you,' and that was it." She puts a spoonful of honey in her mouth and smiles. "I just love synchronicity, don't you?"

Chloe rolls her eyes. "Don't tell me you still believe in coincidences."

Mary places the pot and spoon on the table. "Everything is interconnected, my dear. Surely you know that."

"Come on, Chloe, you saw that back in the Savoy. You can see for yourself that wherever I go there always seems to be a black cat."

Mary gives us both a look of surprise. "Annabel. Well bless your heart. You have black cats too?" She gives her daughter's thigh a reassuring pat when she sees the look of incredulity on her face. "They've been following me for years, dear. I'm so used to it I don't think twice about it. But I must admit, the bats took a little longer to get used to."

"Bats?" Chloe puts her head in her hands.

"Yes, bats," Mary answers. "They were all over the place for a while. It was, let's see, not long after your father's death. I wasn't in a good way and was searching for answers. They helped soothe my anxieties. Made me relax."

"Come to think of it, wherever I go there are bats, too," I say, settling deeper into the chair. "In Joshua Tree, they'd circle around my room for a few minutes each evening, then leave. They comforted me. Made me feel less frightened of the dark."

Mary's eyes glitter in the darkness. "Bats see at night, my dear Annabel. Never be afraid of the dark. It's a woman's greatest strength. We transform darkness into light."

Chloe looks up from her hands. "Can't I have a normal mother and a normal friend? You know, who can speak about normal things?"

I stare at my best friend. When she's around her mother, Chloe's breezy authoritarian manner wilts like a deflated balloon. Even though she towers over her mother by nearly a foot, she seems smaller somehow. I try everything, even chat about the weather—the one subject the British can talk about for hours on end—but no matter what I say or do, Chloe won't relax. After a few minutes, Chloe breaks in.

"Now it's *you* talking about the weather. That's what Mary does too. Talks to me about the weather. The dog. And the garden."

Suddenly I can feel Chloe's anger attaching to mine like Velcro. "What do you expect? You prickle like a cactus if either of us talks about anything you happen not to agree with."

"That's because Mary and you are talking complete nonsense," she barks back.

"Please speak to me, not about me, in my presence," Mary interjects, putting her hands in the air, palms out. She turns a placid eye in Chloe's direction. "You've been difficult to be around lately, Chloe dear. It's like being with your father all over again."

But I'm still irritated by Chloe's jab. "Why do you call your mother Mary anyway?" The words blurt out of my mouth so quickly I don't even have the time to regret them.

My question hangs, suspended in the air like a hummingbird with its beak in a flower. It floats toward Mary, then back to Chloe, then rests in the space between them, waiting for a response.

Chloe twists a strand of hair so tight I think it's going to break. "Since I found out she wasn't my mother."

For a moment, none of us speaks. I look at Mary, then at Chloe, consider a half-dozen pleasantries that I could say to ease the atmosphere, and then decide to sit this one out.

Mary reaches behind her to fluff the cushions and gives a long sigh. "Your father told you, did he?"

"On his deathbed." Chloe drops the strand of hair, and with that, the prickly anger she's been carrying within her all evening dissipates like clouds after a storm. "He asked me to keep it a secret, so I have.

225

But after that, I couldn't call you mother. Not when I knew the truth."

Mary tilts her head to the side. "Did he tell you *all* the truth?"

"All I know is that you and Daddy married when I was less than a year old."

Mary adjusts her shawl around her shoulders, takes a sip of tea, then puts the mug down in front of her, as if she has all the time in the world. "Well now. I know it's a time for truths, but I hadn't expected this one to come out of hiding this way. But now that it has, I'm glad." She settles deeper in her chair. "Your father was a charming but difficult man, as you know. He really should have remained a bachelor all his life; it would have suited his character better. A few months before we got married, he had an affair with a young French au pair who was working for the Van Daels. You know, their children have inherited the big house near Kilpeck, where we're heading tomorrow."

The silence is broken by the hoot of an owl. We look toward the garden, as the owl repeats its call. Mary looks up. "I know, I know."

Chloe's eyes narrow. "Did you just talk to that owl?"

"No, I just answered it," she answers, her eyes twinkling. When she next speaks, her voice is almost lyrical. "Now. This au pair was a most beautiful girl, with the thickest, blackest hair and the bluest eyes you've ever seen. Not the sharpest tool in the shed, I'm afraid, but she had a kind heart and was a real stunner. They met when he would go for a drink at the pub down the road in the evenings."

She pours herself another cup of tea and raises the pot toward us, as if to ask if we want a refill, but we're so taken with her story we both shake our heads. She puts the pot down again, adjusts the tea cozy over it, and continues. "Wouldn't you know, she became pregnant. Not knowing what to do, she kept the pregnancy hidden as long as she could. It was all terribly hush-hush back then, you know. Finally, when she got too large to hide it, the family paid for her to return to France. It was there that she had the baby."

"It was where?" both Chloe and I ask at once.

"A little town in the Camargue called Saintes-Maries-de-la-Mer,"

Mary answers.

Why have I heard that name? I wonder. But I'm so overwhelmed by what is happening that the thought goes right out of my mind. "Chloe," I say, trying not to smile. "I can't believe it. You're French?"

"I am English," Chloe huffs. "I just happened to be born elsewhere, that's all."

"But that's incredible. What a coincidence that you married a Frenchman."

Chloe glares at both of us, but Mary ignores her. "Don't lose your sense of humor, darling, it shows your age. Besides, your mother did become British eventually. If you were to hear her speak now, you wouldn't know English wasn't her mother tongue."

"But where do you come in?" Chloe asks.

Mary's eyes are shimmering like a night owl. "All in good time," she says. "I've been wanting to tell this story for, oh, just over forty years, so let me savor it a bit. Now, where was I? Ah. How I fit in. So. A few months before John had the affair with the au pair, he got to know me. I was studying at Hereford University on a scholarship, you see, and he was well into his fifties. I couldn't believe such a distinguished gentleman would be interested in a young art student, so it didn't take long for him to sweep me off my feet. You should have seen your father then, Chloe dear. He was so handsome in his topcoat and hat, especially when he went riding with the hounds. Smart, too. We met on one of the weekly hunts. We were married within the year."

An involuntary sound escapes from Chloe's mouth. "I didn't know you rode."

A half-smile flickers on her lips. "I think there's a lot about me you don't know. And after all these years, I'm delighted we can start to have some real conversations. Gardens, the weather, and Ben bore me just as much as they bore you."

With Chloe in check, she continues. "While we were engaged, I had to have an operation, which ended up as a hysterectomy. I was crushed I would never be able to have children. I think that's when John had the affair with the au pair. She was pregnant when she attended our wedding. Then she slipped away to have the baby in France."

"But how?"

Mary picks up her cup of tea. "You must remember that things were different then. Your father and the Van Daels were close, so when she returned, your father insisted on visiting the baby. I have to say, everyone was surprised. John was no sentimental man. It put everyone's suspicions up, including mine. I went along to see for myself. And when I set eyes on you, I understood it all." She turns to Chloe and smiles. "You were the spitting image of your father."

Both of us say almost simultaneously, "So what did you do?"

Mary runs her hand slowly over the cushion. "Knowing how much your father wanted a child and realizing that the au pair couldn't afford to raise a baby on her own, I offered to adopt you."

My body does an involuntary shudder, so I pull the blanket around my shoulders. "Weren't you upset that your husband betrayed you?" I ask. "After all, he was engaged to you when he had the affair."

Chloe frowns. "I had no idea my father was such an ass."

But that just makes Mary laugh. "My dear girls, men seem to be particularly adept at displaying asinine qualities, especially when they know they're wrong. It's far better for a woman to be wise than right, if she wants to keep the marriage together. It gives a man time to see the foolishness of his ways. He will make it up to you in his own way." She pulls herself taller. "And for me, I chose not to listen to my bruised ego crying for revenge, and to listen instead to that wise woman we all have inside us. Everything is a gift, I always say to myself. However, some gifts are harder to swallow than others. I wanted a child, your father clearly loved you, and the au pair was too young to take care of a baby. Just think. You even attended our wedding."

Her eyes soften. "God works in mysterious ways. Besides, it wasn't your fault you were born out of wedlock. It was a privilege to have you in our lives. You were everything I could have ever wanted: beautiful, intelligent, warm, and with the spunk and feistiness of your father."

"So rather than reject the baby, you brought her into the fold," I say. My admiration for this woman grows by the minute.

"But of course. I asked for a child, and you appeared." Mary pats Chloe's hand. "You can be a difficult, stubborn woman, but I love you dearly. You are my daughter, blessed one. It's just that you were born from another woman's womb."

"And my birth mother?" Chloe asks, pulling her hand away. "Is she still alive?"

Mary looks outside for a moment, as if waiting for another owl to talk to, but then, in the silence that follows, she turns and faces Chloe. "She is."

Chloe's hands flutter in the air. "You know my real mother? Why didn't you introduce me to her?"

The owl hoots in the distance. Everything becomes so still I can hear the humming of the water heater in a distant room. I don't dare breathe.

Mary's eyes shine like obsidian. "I don't need to," she says.

Chloe's mouth pulls tight. "And why not?"

Mary smiles. "Because you already know her."

Chloe grimaces. "I can't think of anyone who could be my mother."

Mary looks out the window. "She wanted to keep close to you in the only way she knew how. Her choice was an unusual one, but we agreed to respect it. She has seen you nearly every day of your life."

Chloe frowns. "But how can that be?"

Mary smiles. "Because she works with you."

The wheels of my brain, which have been whirring like the blades of a lawn mower, suddenly stop as if someone has thrown a stone into them. Of course. Jeanette told me she is from Saintes-Maries-de-la-Mer. The silence is so loud I can hear my heart beating in my chest.

"It's Jeanette," I whisper.

I glance at Mary, then at Chloe. Although Mary looks as calm and peaceful as a lake after a storm, Chloe looks as if she is experiencing an inner tsunami. To be fair, I don't know what I would do if someone had just told me that my mother was my cleaning lady.

229

Chloe practically bounces out of her chair. "Cleaning lady Jeanette? You mean the woman who *works* for me?"

Mary nods. "She works *with* you, not *for* you, dear. Yes, that Jeanette."

Chloe stares at Mary. "Of course she's not my mother. Where did you come up with such a harebrained idea?"

Mary crosses her legs. "I know it is difficult to take in. Your father gave her an ample sum of money so she would never need to work again, but she wanted to. I think it's her way of keeping an eye on you." She adjusts her shawl again and indicates for Chloe to relax back into her chair. "Now don't blame Jeanette, dear. Or your father for that matter. Times have changed. But at that time, Jeanette was relieved we wanted to adopt you."

Even though Mary appears at ease, I can see she is carefully monitoring Chloe's reaction. "Try to look at it from her perspective. It gave you a legitimacy you would never have had. It gave you money. And a home. And two mothers who both love you. Eventually, Jeanette got married and had children. She's a practical soul. Always was. Just accepts things as they are and gets on with it."

"But why didn't you tell me?"

"I wanted to, dear. I always think the truth is the best way forward. But John didn't want it. It would have shown him in a bad light, see. At the time I thought the role of a wife was to follow everything a man says, but I've come to see the folly of those ways. That's why I taught you differently. To be independent. It's so much better to have two brains and hearts working together as a team rather than all this silly patriarchal nonsense." She pats her daughter's arm.

Chloe stares at her mother's hand as if it's a foreign object. She looks paralyzed. Slowly, Chloe removes her mother's hand, then wipes her hands on her thighs, as if with each swipe she can remove what she has just heard. I sense she's using every ounce of willpower to keep herself together. Finally, she looks up.

"I think I need to be on my own for a while." She gets up from the table with a slow, purposeful air. "I'm sure the two of you have a lot to say to each other."

230

Mary's eyes are wide as she looks at Chloe, but she doesn't say anything. I think she, too, knows Chloe needs this time to herself. "Of course, dear," she says. "Take all the time you need. Sleep well. We'll see you in the morning."

Without a word, Chloe turns her back on us and is gone.

Mary and I sit quietly, each of us in our own thoughts. I break the silence. "I never thought I'd see a cosmic kick equal to mine," I say. "But I think I just have."

Mary turns to me. "Cosmic kick? I like that expression."

"I learned it from a teacher of mine. You understand it?"

"How well I do," she says. "It's as if life has just taken you by the scruff of the neck and shaken you so hard that you don't know which way is up."

"It wakes you right up, doesn't it?"

"It certainly does. And if anyone were to say to you, even one second before, that you weren't awake, you'd argue with them all the way home." She unwraps the blanket from her shoulders, puts her hands on her knees, and pushes herself up. "Let's get another cup of tea and go into the snug, shall we? I'm sure the fire is still going nicely."

In the kitchen, Mary puts on the kettle for more tea. As she places everything on a tray, I start to clear the table, but Mary shakes her head, telling me a girl from the village will do it in the morning. She picks up the tray and walks out of the kitchen, disappearing like a ship in full sail down the dark corridor. Ben and I follow in her wake.

The snug is a cozy room at the back of the house that doubles as a library. A bookcase, which lines one entire wall, is filled from floor to ceiling with higgledy-piggledy piles of books, magazines, and mementos. A puffy sofa in soft yellow and pink is perfectly placed in front of the fireplace, just far enough from the embers for us to feel the heat without getting too hot. The draperies are open, and the moon, now high in the sky, shines through the French windows, bathing us in a soft white light. With the red and orange flames from the fire, the room is bright enough that we don't need lamps.

I put a log on the fire, and Ben drops next to the sofa and falls asleep, his nuzzle between his paws. Mary pours the tea, and we sit down on opposite ends of the sofa, propping needlepoint throw pillows behind our backs so that we can comfortably face each other. As Mary turns to me, the embers highlight her profile. In the firelight, I can see she was once—no, still is—a beautiful woman.

"Poor Chloe," Mary says, as she hands me a cup. "I feel for her. When she started calling me by my Christian name, I knew John must have said something to her. I tried to broach the subject, but up came those stop signs and back we went to the conversations of old. The weather. The garden. Ben." Mary gives a little laugh. "I think I embarrass her. She could never understand my unconventional ways."

"Were you always this way?"

"You mean different? I suppose so. My Irish roots are far too whimsical and not grounded enough for her. John's had a history Chloe could be proud of. And to be fair, his side had the money, too. I think that's why she leaned much more toward her father's family." She sighs. "Money and status have always been important to her, poor dear. I think it's because they give her a sense of self. Since she was born with both, she's never had to dig very deep inside. She doesn't know what makes her tick. But this could be the making of her. I always knew that underneath that Sloane Ranger—I believe you call that preppy—facade lies a woman of substance. Goodness knows, we need all the substance we can to get the world back on track again."

"What do you mean on track?"

"Come now, you can't say you don't feel it in the air. That's why all these bats and black cats are about. She is on the move again, gathering everyone she can into the fold to help her."

The conversation is going so fast I can hardly keep up. "She? On the move?"

She puts her cup down. "My dear! The Feminine is back. Humanity has been running on fifty percent capacity for too long. Those of us running on both cylinders will need to help the others who are still only running on one."

There is so much in those few sentences I don't know which question to ask first, so I choose the most obvious one. "I'm surprised you know about this."

"Of course," she says with a matter-of-fact air. "I was educated by nuns, so it took a while for the Catholic drama to wash away, but luckily I had a broad-minded theology professor who challenged me to look at history with fresh eyes. I think the hardest thing of all was to grasp just how dreadfully women have been treated for thousands of years. The more I learned, the more I realized how deep the biases and prejudices we all carry, and when I say all, I mean both men and women. They are ingrained so deeply it's hard to spot just how much they affect the way we think and act. Just think, half of humanity has been subjugated by the other half for thousands of years. Boggles the mind, doesn't it?"

I don't need to ask the next question, but I do anyway. "Was the destruction and subjugation of women throughout the centuries really that bad?"

Her eyes deepen. "Yes." For a moment her face falls. "Yes it was. Probably worse than we can imagine."

For a moment, neither of us speaks. I cast my eyes around the room and notice the embers dying, so I get up and poke them. The orange-red sparks dance in the blackness.

"You know, when I was doing my shamanic journey, I touched a space in consciousness that felt like a wound. It was so deep and so dark that I had to lie down or I would have thrown up. The pain was so intense it throbbed. Initially, I thought it was my own wounding, but when the shaman asked me about it, I realized that although it was me, it was also much bigger than me. The shaman called it the pain of the Feminine."

Mary studies me. "The pain of the Feminine. I know it well. It is held deep within all of us. It's part of our cellular memory. What did the shaman tell you to do about it?"

"The shaman told me to feel it," I say, pushing the burning ends of the logs into a pile. "As deeply as I could. Not intellectualize it. Or avoid it. But feel it. By feeling this pain, I was helping to heal it."

233

"She is wise," she says. She points to the basket of wood and asks if I could put another log on the fire. "All these angry feminists aren't helping much. The world doesn't need one more angry woman. Women need to own our anger, not dump it on other people. Anger is mental pollution. We already have enough pollution in the world, don't we?"

"It's hard not to feel angry when you see how badly we have been treated," I say, pulling out a log from the basket and placing it on the fire. It splutters and spits, and in a fit of sparks, the log catches fire. Instantly, the room becomes brighter, so I return to the sofa and sit down, feeling the cushions sinking underneath me.

Mary wraps her shawl tighter around her shoulders. "It's helpful to know about our past. Because this universal pain is one and the same with my own. But a person needs to move beyond the anger, or they are part of the problem and not the solution."

I turn to her. "What did you do with your anger?"

"It took some time, but I finally owned it," she says. "All of it. To recognize that we are all to blame for our current situation. Men and women."

I tilt my head. "What do you mean?"

Her eyes gleam in the firelight. "Who raises these misogynistic men? Who pours burning water down a baby girl's throat to scald and kill her because they wanted a boy? Who insists on sexual mutilation—cutting off a female's clitoris—in the name of tradition because it was done to them? Whose hands help break their daughters' toes and bandage their feet so they can never walk properly again, just so they can conform to society's twisted views of beauty?"

"Women," I say, quietly.

She nods. "The same hands that nourish and love are the same that cause pain and deformation. Both men and women have shadow. Masculine shadow acts out in anger, feminine shadow plays the victim. The deepest shadow was around the Middle Ages. That was when the Feminine was eliminated from the church entirely."

"But that was the age of chivalry. Knights in armor worshipped their damsels in distress. Women were placed upon a pedestal."

"True," she says. "But what happened to sex?"

"Sex?" I say, not understanding. "They couldn't have much sex. Not with those chastity belts some women had to wear."

"Many of those chastity belts were for show," she says. "But it did show just how screwed up society was back then. Just think. Those magnificent knights in shining armor never had sex with the women they venerated." When she sees I'm still not following her, she says, "They turned their damsels into a Madonna, whiter than white, motherly, chaste, and innocent. All the other parts of a woman, her sexuality, her anger, her ability to throw a good storm when necessary, were removed from the church. Placed upon women that were considered of ill repute, even though the men who visited these women were never judged with the same harshness."

I never thought of it this way. "So that is when sex came to be seen as sin."

She nods. "You can blame the Middle Ages for that ridiculous perception. The Feminine had been so squeezed from reality back then that the only place for it was in romantic novels. But you can't get rid of sensuality and sexuality. It is the building block of our existence. As there was no room for it in a real relationship between a man and a woman, it was absorbed into the spiritual quest."

Now I really don't understand.

"Where else could they put their sexual energy? Have another look at a few spiritual texts from the Middle Ages. Spiritual ecstasy sounds just like a person having an orgasm." Her eyes glitter. "Oh my, those poor souls, trying to make their bodies conform to a spiritual ideal. You can see it in the myths and stories of that age, like Tristan and Isolde. Those chivalric romantic notions impacted our Western culture until today. But it was all because the Feminine was removed from our culture. Oh the self-punishment that occurs when sexual gratification is squashed. No wonder people turned to sadomasochism. All those hair shirts and torture." She raises her hands to the sky. "Life was so miserable that people could only hope for death. No wonder the Green Man looked sinister back then."

"But you told me he was the husband of the Great Mother."

"I still think he is," she says. "He became the expression of the inner torture caused by the suppression of the Feminine. Some even had tongues sticking out, like—what's the name of that black goddess you both learned about in tantra, you know, the one with the lolling red tongue?"

"Kali?" Images of the black-faced Indian goddess, a necklace of skulls around her neck, dancing on corpses with their heads chopped off flits through my mind. Suddenly, the moon and the stars come together. "The Green Man is the Western variant of Kali, isn't he?"

"That's how I interpret him," she says, tapping a hand lightly on her thigh. "Kali is my type of goddess, bless her wild heart. Didn't you see how she just handled Chloe?

The moon is now high in the sky. It shines so brightly into the snug it almost looks like pale gray rays of sunlight pouring through the roof. "What do you mean?"

Mary's eyes flash. "Kali is the unruly, dark side of the Feminine. She is going to keep throwing storms at us until we all wake up and recognize that there is enough."

"Enough of what?"

"Enough of everything. There's enough love. Enough time. Enough money. Things that our nomadic ancestors couldn't understand."

"Of course," I say. "Fighting over scarce resources, they must have developed a fight-or-flight mentality that came from fear. Fear that there isn't enough."

She nods. "So even though life became easier in the Fertile Crescent, they were chained to their traumas. They continued to live in the harsh desert of their minds." She puts her cup down with a decisive tap. "So after John's death, when I was wallowing around in my own inner desert, I decided to create three tenets to help me remember the larger truth. I remind myself of them every time I let myself slip into the never-never land of self-pity and fear that we have inherited from those desert ancestors of ours."

"And they are?"

Her eyes sparkle. "We are all one. There is enough. And love heals

236

all."

I gaze into the fire, testing each of them to see how they resonate. "The first two come easily. But love heals all?"

Mary, who has begun to gather the pot and the cups, puts a hand on mine. Her voice sounds soft and soothing in my ear.

"Don't lose hope, Annabel dear. You've been dealt a hard blow. To have your husband taken away on the day you sealed your marriage vows would have broken many women. Love will come again to you when it's the right time. But right now, you are shedding parts of yourself that no longer serve you." She tilts her head. "Are you having a lot of things happening to you on a physical basis?"

"Am I ever," I say.

She laughs. "I had that too. People never truly believe that waking up is a physical process until it starts happening to them. Are you getting lots of bodywork?"

I nod. "As much as I can afford."

She nods. "Good. And make sure to make time to sit in stillness. Listen carefully to what the wind whispers to you at night. Learn to follow that little voice within you, no matter how odd it may seem. Be kind. Be caring. Love everyone, especially those who have closed their hearts, like my daughter. They are the ones who most need it."

The next day at breakfast, I've never seen Chloe so quiet. I would have expected her to be furious, but I think that what she has discovered has hit her so deeply she doesn't even know what to say. She responds with monotone answers and disappears back to her room. For a quintessentially upper-crust Englishwoman like Chloe, where image is all important, discovering that she was born out of wedlock in France to a mother who works as her cleaning lady must have turned her world upside down. The illusions propping up her identity are gone.

Kali is transformation, which is an essential part of healing. And for healing to work, things need to get worse before they can get better. And so, rather than jollying Chloe out of her mood, I respect her silence, busying myself instead with Mary in the garden. We rummage through old bits of plastic and terra-cotta pots in the shed to find a pair of garden shears and gloves and then weed through the rows of vegetables, talking about the Green Man, healing, and an infinite number of subjects that interest us both. I had no idea Chloe's mother could be so interesting. We could be together for a month and still have things to say. She is as fascinating to listen to as to talk with, and that's because she's curious—about me, about life, and about herself. Best of all, she accepts me, black cats and all.

Long after Mary disappears up into the house to do a few chores, I continue to work in the garden, then take a break and lie on my back, enjoying the feeling of the earth beneath me. Ben lies by my side, basking in the warmth of the sun. By the time Ben and I return to the kitchen, it's nearly lunchtime. After a quick bath, I knock on Chloe's door.

Her voice is faint. "What is it?"

"It's me. Can I come in?"

When I don't hear a response, I open the door and peer in. Chloe is half-sitting, half-lying on the floor, gazing out of the window. She reminds me of Andrew Wyeth's painting of a paraplegic sprawled in a semi-reclining position, *Christina's World*. She pats the space next to her without turning around and asks me to close the door.

"It's introspection time," she says as I sit down next to her. Her eyes are puffy and swollen; her breezy, devil-may-care attitude gone, replaced by a serious woman whom I hardly recognize, but to my surprise, I like. "I'm watching all these parts of me, or rather, all the parts that I thought were me, disappearing into thin air. I keep pulling out sentences that I would have used to describe me to myself, and one by one, I'm realizing they aren't true."

"That's neti-neti," I say, and when she frowns, I explain that neti-neti is a spiritual process that means not this, not that. "You keep peeling away parts of who you *think* you are until finally you get to the truth of who you *really* are."

She pats my hand. "Who I am is the daughter of my cleaning lady."

My heart goes soft. "And that matters? I love Jeannette. So do

238

you."

She pulls a strand of hemp from the carpet and rolls it between her fingers. "OK. That was a stupid thing to say. How she must have felt all these years. I was unbearable."

I lightly touch the pockets of my jeans, looking around for my phone and realize I've left it in my room. Then, spotting a tiny daisy caught on my sweater, I pluck it off and give it to Chloe. "You're softer now. More human." I bring my legs up so that I can rest my chin on my knees. "Besides, we all have shadow."

Chloe tucks the daisy in her hair. "What's shadow?"

"Shadow is the parts of ourselves that we desperately hope aren't true but probably are. I'll give you an example of a piece of my own shadow. Being friends with you nourished my own insecurities. If I was accepted by a snob like you, then it made me feel as if I mattered."

"Of course you matter." She pulls the daisy out of her hair and looks at it. "What was I thinking of? Of course I should have told Jean Luc about the miscarriage." Her eyes start to mist. "Oh Annabel, what an ass I've been." She leans her head against my shoulder and runs her fingers through her hair. As she does, I see a few gray roots peering out from the tawny curls. She may not need to color her hair as much as she used to. She's worked hard for those gray hairs.

I stand up and hold out my hand. "Come on, girlfriend. It's time for lunch." I pull her up and put an arm around her and give her a little hug. "I'm sorry you're having to go through this. But it's worth it, I promise."

"Time will tell," she says. And we walk downstairs.

Lunch, served on the table under a pergola at the back of the house, is a massive salad in a roughly hewn wooden bowl, with slices of smoked trout and warm new potatoes tossed in olive oil and chopped dill. After lunch we rest in our rooms and before I know it, it's already afternoon and the three of us are squeezed into Mary's green Citroen 2CV heading toward the village of Kilpeck.

Chloe, sitting in the back, must be feeling more energetic because she's pelting Mary with questions. They come so fast and furious that it reminds me of a tennis match at Wimbledon. Mary fields each question with answers that are just long enough to satisfy Chloe, and then she serves the next question—and off they go again. I hear it all, from Chloe thinking it's a conspiracy against her, to how emotionally betrayed she feels, to her panic about what to say to Jeanette, and finally, with both a little flushed from the effort, we arrive at the church.

It's a blissful summer afternoon. The weather is warm but not too hot, the air fresh but not too cool. When Mary pulls up near the church, we all get out, stretching our limbs.

"This, girls, is the Church of St Mary and St David," Mary says, adjusting her wicker basket on her arm as we make our way through the tombstones. She points to two massive yew trees. "Do you see those yews? You'll often find them in ancient churchyards. They were sacred to the older religions and frequently predate the churches themselves."

When we arrive beneath the church, she puts her wicker basket down by her feet and rummages around until she finds what she is looking for; a laser pen. Clicking it on, she points it at the side door of the church and a tiny red dot dances against the wood. "There. Can you see it? On the doorway."

Chloe and I gaze at the heavy oak door. Every inch of its surface is covered with carvings. I see dragons, grotesque heads, a phoenix, and angels with trumpets. Even a riot of snakes slithering up and down the pillars.

"Good," she says, then points it at the serpent that makes a figure eight. "What about on the archway? Do you see the Ourobus?"

Chloe squints. "Is it the serpents swallowing their tails?"

She nods. "It symbolizes wholeness. Many of these mythological creatures stem from the pre-Christian era. In the olden times, religion was esoteric, which means it followed the inner transformation of the individual. That is why the older, goddess-based cultures had so many mythological creatures. They were symbols that helped reveal a person's inner world. You see, the past thousand years was all about humanity separating itself from nature. But you know what transformation is like. The pendulum swings too far in one direction and it needs to come back to the center again. Instead of the right and left brain, or the Feminine and the Masculine, or Yin and Yang or Head and Heart or goodness knows what you want to call these two opposites that work together, the Masculine took over and tried to erase the Feminine entirely. Everything became literal.

The Christian religion did the same. It took the story from the tale of a gentle Jew from Nazareth who could perform miracles and linked it with the ancient Hebrew prophecy of the coming of the Messiah. The story was an overlay of earlier myths that were co-opted from previous religions. But the importance of all this is that we are waking up to both sides of reality: the masculine and the feminine parts of ourselves. We need both our heads and our hearts. We need to individuate and yet to understand that we are all one."

Mary has given us so much to think about that we all stand, lost in our thoughts, as we stare at the figures in front of us. Dampness is in the air, so Mary pulls her sweater on.

"I thought you were a strict Catholic," Chloe says quietly.

Mary's eyes soften as she looks at her daughter. "I was. Learning to see the stories that I was taught are most likely myths shattered my reality. I didn't know who I was. But when I did begin to let go of who I thought I was, and began to access who I really am, it was like a breath of fresh air opening the doors of my soul. It put layers of meaning into the stories and traditions I was brought up with. It freed me to love the religion I was brought up with for all the traditions and solid values that it did give me." She brushes the front of her pullover and looks at Chloe as if seeing her for the first time. "I've saved the best for you, my dear daughter. Something you'll find fascinating."

Mary asks me to reach in her basket and pull out a small pair of binoculars. As I do this, Chloe pulls out the walking cane seat and sets it up next to Mary.

"Here," she says, quietly. "Rest your legs."

241

"Thank you, my dear," Mary says, sitting carefully down. In that split second, their eyes lock and I see a world passing between them. It may take some time, but all will be forgiven. Their relationship is being officially rebooted, this time without secrets.

From her seated position, Mary hands me the binoculars and picks up her laser pen and points it to the roof. "There is a Green Man here, too, but he's not as nice as ours in Westminster. But what I want to show you is this. "

The carving she is pointing to is rudimentary, with a large head, no hair, and bulbous eyes. She has thin arms and legs and a tiny body. The arms are reaching down and pulling something open with both hands. I twiddle the knob of the binoculars to get a better view. She's holding something open. When I recognize what it is, I lower the binoculars. My eyes must look like golf balls.

"Is that woman doing what I think she's doing?"

She beams with pleasure. "She is, she is."

"And this is on a *church*?" I can't help emphasizing the last word.

She nods. "It is, it is."

Chloe pulls at my sleeve. "Let me see."

I give her the binoculars and watch as she points them at the roof. She stares at it for a long time. When she drops the binoculars, she gives me the first smile I've seen all day. "Well, I'll be damned. She's smiling, too." She looks at her mother. "Who is she?"

Mary is clearly amused. "She's called a *Sheela na gig*. This is perhaps the most famous of them all."

"There are more?" Chloe and I ask at the same time.

"About sixty in England, but there are more being discovered all the time. There are a lot of them in Ireland, hence the Irish name."

"Sheila? S-H-E-I-L-A?"

She shakes her head. "No, Sheela with two 'e's. Sheela is the Norman form of Cecile, which means heavenly, and that's what she is, especially that gaping gig of hers." She laughs when she sees we aren't following her. "*Gig* is Celtic for a vulva."

Before I know it, my hand has reached into my pocket and has pulled out my phone and I begin to take photos to show Jackie. "Why

242

haven't I heard about them?"

Mary switches off the laser pen. "Because no one knew what to do with them. If they are hard enough to accept now, you can only imagine how people felt about them in the past. Archeologists ignored them. Museums locked them away. If anyone did write anything, it tended to be pejorative and lewd. It's only in the past few years that people have begun to talk about the Sheelas in a scholarly way. Some claim it's medieval anti-morality teaching. But to anyone who sees the bigger picture, it's obvious they are a symbol of the Feminine."

"I assume they began to appear around the same time the Green Man turned into Kali?"

She nods. "By the time the Middle Ages arrived, there was nothing soft and feminine left. That's why Sheelas are old hags. Oh it was dark times. Imagine. Sex as pleasure had disappeared. Pain was celebrated. Carnal love in disgrace. People didn't have to worry about going to hell. They were living it. The only thing women had that men couldn't own was a vagina. What do you call it in tantra, dears?"

"A yoni," I say.

"That's such a nicer word for it, isn't it?" Mary says. "Not so clinical. I'll have to remember that. Now. Let's go inside before it gets too dark."

I gaze in wonder at this diminutive woman in welly boots, sitting with authority on her portable throne. Chloe reaches out to help her stand, then folds the chair and gives me the wicker basket. Dusk casts a golden light on the reddish stone as I push the heavy door.

"Worshipping the Goddess often took place in caves," Mary says as the door creaks open. "So. Shall we go into the womb?"

It all makes sense once Mary says it. The inside of the church is as snug as a womb. Mary lights the candles on the altar, on the window ledges, and in the corners while I place three oak chairs in the center so that we can sit in a circle. We hold hands.

"If you were to excavate under this church," Mary says, "You'd find ruins. Then more ruins. And even more. People have been coming to these sacred spots to recharge their batteries for eons. Can you feel the energy? I'm already buzzing like mad."

Closing my eyes, I feel the familiar warmth at the soles of my feet. I sit quietly for a few moments, absorbing the atmosphere, when I hear Mary's voice.

"Now. Men make great warriors. Protectors of the house and of the home. But this idea of man as the master of the universe and woman as his submissive slave is over. Even though we women have a lot to be angry about, we can't continue to blame men for the past. So don't go the way I see many feminists heading and become angry. Learn to work with men as equals even if they don't see us that way. The most important thing is to understand that our true nature is not violent. It's loving. It's only fear that separates us. We are all one, my children. Understand that, and the universe is yours." She squeezes our hands. "And when you leave here, I want you to remember one thing."

"What's that?" Chloe says.

"That you were once as ignorant as everyone else. Keeps one humble, that."

She turns to Chloe. "And you, my beloved daughter. I can only imagine how painful that miscarriage of yours was. But don't think that you are any less if you do not have a child. You don't need to be mother of one. You can be mother of many."

The tears in Chloe's eyes mirror my own. Mary bends down and pulls out matches and three small votive candles from her basket and gives us each one. We light them and hold them in our hands.

"Remember," she says. "We are all one. There is enough. And love heals all. That is the key to how we change the world. It happens one person at a time."

A week later, it's time for my last ancestor blessing. In England I blessed my father's side, and now I have five days to bless the land of my mother: Norway .

As the Norwegian Air flight circles the small seaport of Ålesund, I'm surprised by the dramatic scenery below: the soaring mountains with their jagged edges covered with creamy white snow, the endless green forests, the fjords stretching their sapphire fingers inland. This is the land of the Vikings, the craggy ancestors of mine who raped and pillaged along the coasts and inlets of Europe and traveled to America five hundred years before Columbus.

My hotel in Ålesund, with its soaring white plaster walls, sloping slate roof, and rounded eaves enclosing two windows at the top that look like eyes, reminds me of a smiling face with raised eyebrows. Once in my room, I open the window to breathe in the salty tang of the sea. The blue sky beckons me to explore, so I wrap a sweater around my shoulders and go out for a walk.

It feels as if I've landed in a Norse fairytale. Ålesund isn't just a town of red and white wooden houses, but a sophisticated, architectural marvel of Art Nouveau, with painted soft pastels, turrets and spires, and rounded windows. I gaze at a statue of a fisherman overlooking the harbor, then buy a bag of shrimp from a real live fisherman with bushy eyebrows and ruddy cheeks.

Suddenly, I have this funny feeling as if time has slowed down so that even banal moments such as eating a shrimp seem meaningful. My feet lead me toward a tourist train, then, realizing that I'm supposed to be on that train, I leap into a seat just as the train takes off. Picking up a pamphlet on the seat, I read that we are heading to Fjellstua, a cliff with a panoramic view of the archipelago. Fifteen minutes later, we chug up a steep track that zigzags up the back of a stone cliff. Once we get to the top, the train stops and the driver tells us it's a ten-minute photo break.

Still lightheaded from the plane journey, I drift toward a café, but when I gaze at the view, a shiver runs up my spine. In front of me is a landscape that I recognize. There are three islands, a hump-backed one, followed by two smaller ones petering out into the water. It's the landscape I witnessed during my breathing course in Dorset.

I raise my hand to my cheek. It feels strange to the touch. As my hand drops to my side, my vision drops to my tennis shoes. But they,

245

too, look out of place. In a daze, I walk back to the train and tell the driver to go on without me, barely listening as he points out the steps that I can take back into town. I'm already walking back as fast I can to feast my eyes on the view I thought I'd never see again. *It's real*, I think. The words loop around my brain again and again. *It's real. It's real.*

I split into two people at that moment. There's me, Annabel, and then there is another me, a larger me, absorbing the view with every pore of my being. Images flood my memory banks. I begin to understand what happened on that night: It wasn't nighttime, it was autumn. I remember wondering how the Viking could have climbed so quickly, but now I see how he did it. Fjellstua is a rocky outcrop that springs like a skyscraper from the edge of the peninsula. It's a natural watchtower. I must have come up here often.

I take in every tiny detail—the shape of the mountains, the rugged edge of the shoreline, the shimmering sea—until I am so sated that I can't absorb any more. Peering over the edge of the cliff, I can see steep and twisty slate steps heading back into town. Those must have been the steps I climbed as a Viking.

I take one more look at the sweeping vista of mountains and sea and sky, then start to walk down. I haven't descended more than a dozen steps when I hear a loud meowing. I stop, confused, and then, coming around the corner, I see a black cat running up the steps. Its tail is straight and fluffed like a toilet brush. I step back as it continues along its way, leaving a trail of insistent meows behind it. This happens so quickly that I stop in my tracks, my mouth open, and have to sit down. Gobsmacked, as they say in England. I don't remember what happens next because I enter a space where logic can't go, and unfortunately memory can't either.

I am all there is. I am the elements of this earth. I am the fire and the darkness, the space and the wind, the stones and the water that flows like blood. I am the wood and the water, the rocks and the soil, the air, and the light. My essence grows in each tree, my blood flows in the veins of every person that has lived. Consciousness is not static, nor is it linear. It expands, and this expansion includes every

246

experience lived by every sentient being. I, just like the Viking, come from this earth, and at the end of my life, I will return to it with the ease of a child falling into its mother's arms. I will never understand the infinite wisdom of this planet, and I am glad for that, because it is the magic and the mystery that make it so wonderful.

I sit on that stone for what seems like ages, working these truths through me, and when I am done, I pull my sweater around my shoulders. I get up, feeling the ache in my bones that comes from sitting cramped in one position for too long, and slowly walk down into town and back into the twenty-first century.

In the afternoon, I pick up my rental car and zigzag down the watery coast on my way to spend the weekend at my cousin's home. The car zooms over land and through tunnels, onto ferries and around hairpin bends as I head south through Ørsta, then Dalevegen, beyond Hovdenakk, and finally east into a valley. My family's valley.

I pass industrious farmers, blond-haired and brown-skinned, taking advantage of the beautiful weather to bring the harvest in. I pass Rekkadal, a cheerful red farmstead that must have been my great-grandmother's farm. And then, when I don't think I can absorb any more beauty without stopping and rolling with happiness on the soft grass on either side of the road, the valley widens and the blue waters of the Hjørund Fjord appear. Just beyond the ferry boat landing is a white clapboard two-story house. This is home to my fourth cousin, Bjarne, and his wife Ruth.

Bjarne, who looks much younger than his eighty-odd years, greets me with a warm *Hej*. I hug his wife, who shows me the guest bedroom, placing a small vase of wildflowers on the chest of drawers like a welcome gift. My cousin and I steal glances at each other when we think the other isn't looking. Even after four generations, it is easy to see the family resemblance. I look like his daughter Kari, Bjarne tells me, pointing to a photograph on the dining room table.

From my cousin's living room window is one of the most beautiful views I have ever seen in my life. Conversation is kept simple, with

Ruth speaking in Norwegian and me pretending to understand. Outside, the midnight sun casts a pale golden light upon the green lawn, making the fluttering insects dance like golden sparkles. Although it's late, we join others from all parts of the valley making their way toward the tiny clapboard church. Each person raises a hand in greeting, and Bjarne and I do the same back. I observe the high cheekbones and blue eyes, the lines of the jaws, and I see myself walking toward me in myriad forms. We walk up the creaking steps, and Bjarne pulls a massive iron key from his pocket and unlocks the door. It swings open with a reluctant creak, and we're blasted by a warm, musty smell. The wooden floorboards groan as people enter the church just as they must have done for centuries.

Everyone gazes at me, the long-lost cousin from America. Leather-bound books containing family history far back to the sixteen hundreds are fingered and discussed. Watching my cousins' strong fingers flip through the lovingly constructed family tree, I feel honored by my Norwegian family's vast knowledge. I come from a long line of Larissas. Eleven generations, in fact. I smile and nod and shake hands, while Bjarne sits next to me and beams. I don't have to do anything to receive this love, just be me.

These people don't know of the years of abandonment and sexual abuse that I suffered when I was young. They probably have never heard of the eye procedure that helped me start the long journey home to myself, and they would be incredulous to know that I am here because I am following the instructions of an African sangoma who told me I need to heal my past through blessing my ancestors. All they know is that I am Annabel Larissa, whose grandmother left this valley many years ago, and that I've come back. It's one of those moments, as I find myself in a beautiful old church in a valley, sitting with family members that look just like me, that I feel special, the chosen one, as if the entire world has come together at this precise moment to give me a flash of insight.

I belong. It's as simple as that.

The next morning, as the seagulls circle above me, I slip away after breakfast to walk along the edge of the fjord to collect a few white pebbles from the shore while whispering a blessing. I enjoy these quiet moments. I like this gentler way of being with myself. I'm going to continue to do this, wherever I live.

When I return to the house, Bjarne is standing in the doorway. "You collect dirt?"

I stutter a reply, but he interrupts me.

"I do the same in America. I bring a rock back to Norway. Journeys home go both ways. You are practical. My rock was so large I pay overweight."

Later that evening, as the midnight light streams in through the window, I pull out the stationery that I took from my hotel and begin to write. Soon, I realize, I'm not just journaling my experiences, I'm writing . . . a letter.

To my surprise, it's a letter to my parents. I tell them about Percy the sangoma and about my mission to bless my ancestors. I tell them about Wilhelm's love for wildflowers and Percy's love of nature. I tell them about the Viking and about how Bjarne and Ruth have introduced me to every family member in our valley. I tell them that it makes me feel connected to my family in ways I never expected, and because of that, I conclude that what I've done is a good thing to do. I tell them that they should ignore it if it makes them feel uncomfortable, but these shamanic blessings have brought me peace at last. And lastly of all, I tell them how much I love them. I look at that last sentence, amazed that such words could flow out of my pen.

It's dark outside when I finish writing. I place the letter inside the envelope and turn it over to lick it shut, and that's when I see it. A pen and ink drawing of the hotel printed on the envelope. When I look closer I see, in the left-hand corner, two black cats.

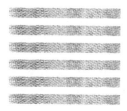

AIR

Provence

We are all just walking each other home
—Ram Dass

The silver nose of the French TGV high-speed train slides past me with a pleasantly pitched hum and slows to a stop with an exhausted sigh. In a little under three hours, the train has traveled four hundred and fifty miles from Paris' Charles de Gaulle airport to this platform in Avignon. Behind me, the ultra-modern train station, a sophisticated low-lying structure of steel and glass, hugs the embankment like a transparent worm. The compartment door opens with a hiss, and Cassandra appears on the top step. She's dressed in layers of her favorite colors, black and brown, and carries a cane in one hand. Her eyes brighten when she sees me, and she calls out, "Hey!"

I help her maneuver herself, then her heavy bag, onto the platform, and we give each other a warm hug. She looks tired but happy. As we leave the platform, I'm glad to see she's walking on her own, without her cane, her arms swinging to keep her balance. I match her pace, carefully keeping an eye on how she's faring. When I'm with Cassandra, so many things I usually take for granted, like

251

rolling a bag onto an escalator, running to catch a train, or even standing on a platform, take on a new dimension. I become aware of how many steps it will take to get somewhere and how difficult it will be to take them.

We get in the car and soon leave the station behind, driving past ploughed fields and villages baking in the August sun. On either side of us, rows of plane trees, their trunks flashing mottled colors of gray, olive, and cream whip by, their soft pastels blending with the caramel-colored landscape.

Cassandra turns to me. "How did it go with your parents?"

"I can't say our relationship is better for it. But something has shifted."

She rests her hands on her lap. "These things don't resolve themselves at once. It may take a few times to sort things out. Just keep showing up."

I don't believe that anything can change between my parents and me so I focus on the scenery. We wind along the banks of the Rhone, then head east and drive past endless vineyards bursting with purplish grapes. Eventually we turn off the main road and carry on up a gravel drive passing between two ancient stone gateposts. On either side of us, silvery-green olive trees wave a greeting as we drive by and park in front of the house, the dust from our wake floating behind us.

Cassandra peers through the windscreen. "How beautiful!"

I know what she means. Nestled in the heart of a valley, facing south to offer protection against the Mistral—the local wind that can blow so hard it has been known to drive people mad—the Mas de la Val is an ancient farmhouse—*mas* means farmhouse in French—divided into two wings overlooking an inner courtyard. Ivy runs up the weathered limestone façade, forming a leafy wall with lines of large windows framed by grayish-green shutters.

I ring the bell and Albin, the caretaker, appears, telling us that Jean Luc and his uncle will be back by dinner. He carries Cassandra's bag as lightly as a sack of leaves on his back and deposits it in front of a large room at the back of the house, then disappears with a wave of

252

his hand.

When she sees her room, Cassandra gasps. The room is painted a most beautiful beige-pink, the same color as a sunset. It contains just what she has asked for: a comfortable bed with no steps to negotiate and easy access to the kitchen so she can slip in and out for her morning chaga latte.

She examines every nook and corner, her cane thumping this way and that on the wooden floor, then bends down and picks up a pebble. "Look, even French stones are beautiful." I think she's joking until I see her luminous eyes.

Jean Luc and I have worked hard to get things ready, renting a wheelchair, stocking the kitchen, and arranging the schedules—which is a good thing because we're booked solid. We have participants coming from France, Switzerland, Austria, Germany, and even the US. Chloe, who has been helping with the logistics, will arrive tomorrow, and two days later, our first client arrives. It will be an intense month.

I show Cassandra the living room, which is now set up as our journey space, then go into the kitchen to meet Michelle, Albin's wife, who is elbow deep in the sink stuffing a fish with dried fennel for tonight's dinner. Outside, we take a tour of the garden, lush with heirloom tomatoes falling off the vine and rich wine-colored eggplants hanging like large teardrops from their stalks. Behind the house, we peer into the swimming pool, deep and cool and begging for us to take a dip, then visit the pond, home to large frogs that croak persistently every night. Returning for a quick bite at the wobbly cast-iron table in the courtyard, we go over the work schedule, until finally Cassandra, dopey with jetlag, disappears to her room to rest.

The relaxed atmosphere is so enticing that soon I, too, decide to take a nap. Each room in the mas is named after a color; Cassandra's is the Orange Room, Jean Luc's is the Beige Room, and mine is the Blue Room, called this because the walls are painted the most beautiful shade of robin's-egg blue. This is Emil's favorite room, Jean Luc told me last night over dinner, filled with ethnic furniture that his uncle has collected on his travels to the Far and Middle East. It reminds me of the furniture that Eugen and I bought in Rajasthan and had sent to Vienna. By now, my life with Eugen feels like a faraway fairytale. Sometimes it seems so unreal I catch myself wondering if it wasn't a dream.

Ever since Eugen died, I've become a nomad. Everything I have with me, from my stretchy cotton clothing to my sneakers and flip-flops, must be worn with everything else. A couple of outfits to dress up, another for when it's cold, and another for when it's warm. Every new piece of clothing means I must give something away: My suitcase can only carry so much. I've been on the move so long I'm forgetting what it feels like to live normally. I feel like a turtle carrying its house on its back.

When I lie on my bed and shut my eyes, I still long to sleep in my own bed. Live with a full wardrobe. Make plans for longer than a month.

But now, as I snuggle against the soft sheets, I recognize I'm happy. I listen to the frogs in the pool playing their evening concerto, feel the breeze through the open window brush against my cheek, and before I know it, I'm asleep.

It's evening by the time Cassandra and I walk into the courtyard for dinner. Jean Luc and his great-uncle are already sitting at the table under a plane tree, enjoying an aperitif. When we arrive, both men stand up to greet us. Jean Luc, dressed in a loose cotton shirt and jeans, looks more relaxed than I've seen him in months. He introduces Cassandra to Emil, who kisses her on both cheeks with a hearty *bienvenue*.

Uncle Emil, as he is known by everyone here, is a distinguished gentleman of a *certain age*, as they say in France, with impeccable manners and more charm in his little finger than most men have in their entire body. Even though his white hair has thinned with age, it's easy to see the family resemblance with Jean Luc. Both have the same high forehead, broad smile, and strong Gallic nose. His open countenance puts us all at ease. We are just sitting down when

Michelle arrives with a tray of drinks and bowls of green picholine olives.

"An unusual name, Cassandra," Emil says as he pulls out a chair for Cassandra. "Do people not believe your prophecies, either?"

Cassandra's eyes sparkle when she hears this. She gives her cane to Jean Luc, who rests it against the wall behind him, then carefully settles into her seat. "Cassandra isn't my real name."

Emil helps bring her chair closer to the table. "So why do you call yourself that?"

She glances up at him before picking up a napkin, fluffing it and placing it on her lap. "Because not many people are ready to hear what I have to say."

He studies her. "Glad to hear it. I find teachers focus too much on making people feel good about themselves. It's like putting a bandage on a wound. Far better to clean the wound so it can heal."

Cassandra raises an eyebrow as she watches Emil walk to the head of the table. "Sounds like you are talking from experience."

Emil sits down and picks up the bottle of wine. We all shake our heads, so he shrugs and pours himself a glass. "When my wife passed away, I knew this part of my life was over. As my friend Hubert de Givenchy once said, 'Life is like a book. One has to know when to turn the page.' So I sold my business in Paris and moved here. I wanted to take time off. Ponder my own existence. Write a bit."

"Emil is the author of a number of books on Provençal legends and myths," Jean Luc interjects. By the way he is looking at his uncle, it's clear to see he adores him.

We all stop talking as Albin arrives with a platter holding a large grilled fish nestled on top of a bed of roast vegetables. Albin places the dish in front of Emil, who begins to filet the fish with slow, careful movements. "To me, Provence is the most healing place on the planet," he says. He stops talking to concentrate on removing the spine, then sits back as Albin takes the platter from him and walks around the table so that we can all serve ourselves.

"*Bon appétit*," he says, and as we tuck in, he continues with the conversation. "It healed me, anyway. I suppose that's why Mary

Magdalene came here."

I look up from my food. "Mary Magdalene?"

Emil nods. "According to the legend, yes."

Cassandra picks up her knife and fork. "What is this legend?"

Emil rubs his finger along the rim of the wine glass. "It's a lovely story, really. Apparently, after Jesus died, Mary Magdalene, her Egyptian servant Sara, and several followers were forced into a boat without rudder or sail. After weeks in a storm-tossed sea, the boat landed near a small fishing town on a broad expansion of marshes we know as the Camargue."

"But that doesn't make sense," Jean Luc says between bites. "There are no currents from Palestine to France. A boat without rudder or sail couldn't get there."

Emil gives Jean Luc a broad smile. "Legends should never be taken literally, my nephew. However, the location where the boat landed is real. It's called Saintes-Maries-da-la-Mer or Saint Marys of the Sea."

That's Chloe's birthplace, I think. But before I can ask anything further, Michelle arrives to light the candles, and soon a soft light springs up from the hurricane lamps placed in strategic positions all along the windowsills. As she disappears back into the kitchen with our plates, Emil pours himself another glass of wine.

"Once the boat landed, everyone headed in different directions to spread the gospel throughout France. Martha headed north. Lazarus went to Marseille, where he became the first bishop. Maximum became the first bishop of Aix-en-Provence. And Sara, Mary's black servant, stayed behind and became the canonized saint Sara the Black."

I lean toward him. "And Mary Magdalene?"

Emil places a piece of bread on his fork and mops up the juices from the platter before Albin whisks it away. "It is said that she spent the last thirty years of her life living in deep prayer in a lonely grotto."

Cassandra's eyes shine like onyx in the night. "Does this cave exist?"

"It does," Emil answers. "It is halfway up a tall cliff face in the Sainte Baume mountain ridge. It's not far from here. Five Dominican monks live in solitude there. I met one not long ago. His name is Father Henri Dominique."

"How far of a climb is it?" Cassandra asks, quietly.

Emil's eyes rest on Cassandra for a moment. We know what he's thinking. "It's a thirty-minute gentle stroll. It's not strenuous at all."

She gives him a gentle smile, knowing he has said this to reassure her. For the next half hour, we talk about farmers' markets and shopping and lavender fields and the many artists who used to live here. Then, just when I think the dinner is about to end, Michelle arrives with a platter of fresh goat cheese with tiny tubs of honey and sprigs of wild thyme, followed by Albin holding the biggest wooden salad bowl I have ever seen. As we all clap and say thank you, the two of them flash embarrassed smiles, then disappear back into the kitchen.

I place a wedge of goat cheese on some bread, dab it with honey, and put it in my mouth. "Oh my God," I say between bites. "Honey and goat cheese. Who would have imagined they would taste so well together." I wipe my finger on my plate to catch a drop of honey that fell there, then pop my finger into my mouth. "The Camargue. Jeanette, Chloe's housekeeper, tells me that is where *fleur de sel* comes from."

Emil nods. "It is indeed. One of the finest salts in the world. But our honey in the Luberon is better."

Cassandra studies him. "Isn't there a black Madonna around here somewhere?"

Jean Luc wipes his fingers on his napkin. "Sara the Black."

"The Black?" I ask.

"That's the English translation," Emil explains. "The Romani people—she's their patron saint—call her Sara la Kali."

I don't know where to put my focus, on Emil's words or my plate. "There is a Catholic saint in Provence named after a Hindu goddess?"

Emil laughs when he sees the look on my face. "Isn't that extraordinary? But when you stop to look at it, everything makes sense. The Romani are descended from a wave of Dalits—better known as the Untouchables—who emigrated to Europe from

Rajasthan in the 1100s. They would have brought their goddess Kali with them. Kali is black, and so is Sara, hence the name Sara the Black or Sara la Kali."

"I thought Black Madonnas got their name because they are as black as the earth," Jean Luc says.

We all sit back and watch Michelle place a tray with a pot of mint tea and little bowls of dark chocolate on the table. She then wishes us a good night and disappears into the house and closes the door.

"The truth is," Emil says as he pours us all cups of tea, "we will never know for sure why Black Madonnas are black. For years, the church said they were darkened through age. But we now know Black Madonnas were intentionally made to be black. Sara la Kali is so popular that thousands flock to see her on her feast day."

All of us sit, mulling over his words. "I'd love to see her," I say quietly.

"You should," Emil says. "She's only an hour west of here. And Mary Magdalene is an hour east of here."

"How strange to have both a Black Madonna and Mary Magdalene in Provence," I say, pulling my sweater around my shoulders against the evening chill.

Emil, watching me, gets up and goes into the house, then returns a few minutes later with a pile of ecru blankets, which he gives us to wrap around ourselves. The gesture is so thoughtful I understand why Jean Luc adores his uncle.

"Provence is special," he says as he settles back into his chair. "It's soft and gentle and feminine, so it's not surprising the Cult of Mary Magdalene began here. The ancient pagan ways were so important here that no matter what the church did, it couldn't erase this devotion to all things feminine. So those in charge did something very intelligent. Instead of trying to erase the habits of a people who adored a Great Mother over the story of Jesus, it simply swallowed up the ancient pagan ways into a biblical story."

"I take it this was around the Middle Ages?"

He nods. "By far the most repressed and twisted era of our history. Everything that the church considered feminine attributes—softness,

258

maternal instincts, compassion, even gentleness—became enshrined into the Madonna and Mary Magdalene. Everything else—sensuality, unpredictability, and sexuality—became Sara the Black."

"You mean it eradicated them," I say, pushing my cup away. "The church did everything it could to destroy any traces of the Goddess cultures."

His eyebrows raise. "I'm glad you know about that. But here's something interesting. No matter what the church did to try to erase Her, she wouldn't go. She keeps re-appearing everywhere. Even the great European cathedrals, which were being built on top of sites where the Great Mother had been revered, ended up being dedicated to a woman."

Jean Luc's eyebrows raise. "Notre Dame. Our Lady. The Blessed Virgin Mary. I never thought of that."

Emil gives his nephew a mysterious smile. "She's always been here, hidden in plain sight. All you need to do is open your eyes and you'll see her everywhere."

Jean Luc wipes his hands on his napkin and places it next to his plate. "So the veneration of Mary was a form of ancient worship of the Goddess."

"No, it was the last gasp of the Goddess," Emil says. "But here in France, she was so powerful that the only way they could topple her was to cut her into two. It's a typical divide and rule military tactic."

"But there wasn't a war," I start to say, but Emil cuts in.

"There was very much a war," he says. "Although it wasn't war in the sense that you and I know it. The church was amalgamating its power, so it had to wipe out any traces of the ancient cultures."

When Emil sees we have all finished, he looks at his watch, murmurs about having to get a good night's sleep before he leaves for Paris, then stands up. "But no matter what the church did, she never went away." He raises his glass in a toast. "So here's to the Goddess and all she represents. Healing happens one person at a time. Here's to you for helping to do just that."

259

"Come on, Annabel. It's time to go."

Cassandra's voice is calling me from downstairs. After last week's peace and quiet, I'm surrounded by a whirlwind of movement. Emil is packing, Cassandra is waiting for me to take her into the market, Jean Luc has just left in a cloud of dust to pick up Chloe from Marseille. And I've got my knickers in a twist, as Chloe would say, because I've just received a panicky call from Lili and I can't find enough signal to call back. I walk into the kitchen, where Michelle and Albin are preparing the last of the packages for Emil to take to Paris, then rush outside, but that isn't any better, so I run upstairs, open a window, and lean outside just as the phone rings again.

It's Lili. She's practically screaming. "How can she do this?"

"Wait a second." With one hand I try to balance myself on the window ledge. She doesn't need to say whom she's referring to. We both know.

"I hope you're sitting down."

I press the speakerphone. "I'm hanging out of a window."

"Well hold on then." I hear a rustle of paper. "Just listen to this headline: *American plots with Vasoy scion to remove widow from her family home.*"

If I could put my head in my hands, I would. "Oh no. Just ignore it."

"I *can't* ignore it. You have no idea what the Viennese are like."

"Annabel we've got to go!" Cassandra's voice floats up to me from downstairs.

But I can't answer her. My mind is spinning. I hadn't thought about the psychological impact this fight must be having on that poor girl. Confronting Maria Eugenia alone must be hell. Ignoring Cassandra, I close my eyes and focus on the conversation at hand. "You are a Vasoy. You're stronger than all those stupid people who want to spread lies about you."

"That's the entire point. I don't know who I am any longer," she whimpers. "That's the question that goes round my head at night. Was I conceived in love? Or was I just the product of a fling? Who

260

ever heard of a person discovering that her mother was her step-grandmother? Or that her brother was her father? I'm falling apart, Annabel," she whispers. "I need you here."

"I'll be back in September," I say, but all I hear is a wail that dwindles into a muffled sob. My heart feels as if it wants to lunge out of my chest. "Just come here." The words pop out of my mouth before I even realize that I am saying them. Then, before I can say anything more, the line goes dead.

"We'll make it work," Cassandra says when I tell her. I'm rolling the empty wheelchair in front of me—Cassandra has so far refused to sit in it—as we head along a narrow street in the center of Aix-en-Provence. Swallows dart and swoop around us, their cries echoing against the stone walls. "Remember that this is for your healing, too."

Aix-en-Provence, which is about a half an hour's drive south of the mas, is one of the most charming small towns I have ever seen. Its local markets are some of the nicest in Provence. Today the market is held along the Cours de Mirabeau, which is Aix's equivalent of Paris' Champs Élysées. An exquisite tree-lined boulevard, framed by elegant mansions with wrought-iron balconies, the Cours is a lovely boulevard to walk down on any day, but on market day, it feels like an outdoor party. The atmosphere is jubilant and free, with locals and tourists jostling for space with food and clothing and music in a continuous movement of color and sound.

We weave our way through the food market at the Place de Precheurs, foraging for fresh bread and cheese and fruits that are soft to the touch and taste like heaven. The produce looks, feels and tastes so good we buy bag after bag of almost everything. We then hit the textile area, meandering through a sea of quilted placemats and napkins and long, sausage-like rolls of ecru and white linen, and finally spend a good hour trying on inexpensive but chic clothing in the most delectable silky cottons and crisp linens that are so feminine I feel like a butterfly. Cassandra chooses a few pieces in black and cocoa and a dark grayish blue and, with the wheelchair filled with produce, we sit at Les Deux Garçons café, tired but happy, to enjoy a croissant and *café au lait* before returning to the mas for lunch.

"You want to go on that pilgrimage, don't you?" I ask, as a waiter places a plate with two croissants and two large bowls of coffee in front of us.

"Well," she says in a tone I recognize she uses when she wants to do something but is afraid it may be beyond her body's capacity. "Maybe I can come along and sit on a blanket."

I wrack my brains as to how I could make this work. "But you've got to reach the cave. That's the point of the pilgrimage."

She pulls a bit of croissant apart with her fingers. "Who says that's the point?"

I hand her the butter. "Well, you heard Emil. It's where the pilgrims were heading."

She slathers a pat of butter on the croissant and eats it with a look of pure pleasure on her face. "Pilgrimages, like all great traditions and teachings, started out with one person searching for truth."

I take a sip of coffee, then look at Cassandra from over my cup. "I guess I never thought about how these traditions began."

She shakes the crumbs from her fingers. "Well, I did. A lot. There are common denominators. One is solitude. Another is self-inquiry. The third is some form of retreat. That is probably how this pilgrimage began. With one person who did find their truth, maybe by sitting up in that cave. But if I can't do it physically, it won't matter. I can still feel the energy."

"It must be so frustrating," I start to say, then stop and look at my hands in my lap.

"To have a body like this?" Cassandra picks up my sentence where I left off. A smile plays on her lips as she sees my embarrassment. "It used to be." Her eyes shine a deep caramel color in the sunlight. She finishes her coffee, leans back in her chair and gazes at me. "Let's go back to Maria Eugenia. She may be an angry, shut-down person, but I suggest you try not to make her wrong."

My fingers start to twitch. "What do you mean don't make her wrong? She kicked me out of my home. She is in the process of doing

262

the same thing to her daughter. Whom she stole, by the way, from her own mother." I push my plate with the rest of the croissant over to her. "And you are trying to tell me I shouldn't make her wrong? Why do I have to be the good one all the time?"

Cassandra tilts her head and picks up my croissant with her fingers. "Because whoever has the largest consciousness is responsible for the room."

I kick a pebble out from under the table. "I hate when you do this."

Cassandra bends forward as someone jostles behind her seat to get to the next table, then pops the last of the croissant into her mouth. "Remember, this is all for you. Besides. Aren't you trying to steal her daughter from her?"

Her words pull me up short.

Cassandra nods when she sees I've understood. "You stole her son's heart. Now you are doing the same with her daughter. She is desperate to save what she has left."

"But this is my home."

She wipes her fingers carefully on her napkin, then crushes it into a ball and places it on her plate. "Who knows, maybe it isn't your future to stay in Vienna."

Suddenly I'm so hot I press my napkin to my forehead and see it come away damp. What she is saying is so destabilizing that I can't even think of it without getting the sweats. Not live in Vienna? Not have my home again? "But where would I go?" I say, dropping the napkin on my plate. "I don't have a family of my own."

"Of course you do," she says. "And you are in the process of making things right with them." She takes a last sip of coffee, then places the bowl carefully on the table. "I'm not saying that this will happen. You may resolve things and stay in Vienna. But what I am saying is you need to be clearheaded. Don't act from fear, but from love. Every decision made from love will be a good one."

Irritated, I raise my hand for the bill. "I can't see how that will help anything."

Her eyes deepen. "This is doing the work, Annabel."

I'm having an inner tsunami. Everything I have worked so hard for,

for so long, to create barriers and protection, shoring me up against those who I perceive are in the way, is being torn asunder. "I don't get it. It won't help if I do my work. Or if Lili does, for that matter. It's not going to change Maria Eugenia one bit."

"Maybe. Maybe not." She dusts the crumbs from her croissant on the plate. "There is so much out there about divisiveness. What makes us separate and different. But it's not what separates us but what unifies us that heals."

"But what does my healing have to do with the Vasoys? Or my family, for that matter?"

The waiter comes with the bill, so Cassandra waves away my offers to pay and hands him a ten-euro note. "When we heal ourselves, we are healing others. I see that with families. Even yours."

I bend down to pick up her cane and hand it to her. "How can that be?"

She takes the cane from me. "When we heal our own imprint from family, cellular memory almost, we are healing our entire lineage."

We both stand up. I unlock the wheelchair with a flip of my foot on the lever.

"That would be impossible," I say as we start to slowly make our way to the car. "There are some things even black cats can't do."

Cassandra and I are pouring out a cornucopia of food from our market baskets onto the kitchen table when we hear a car driving on the gravel followed by the slam of a car door. Moments later, Chloe's face peers round the door, her hair floating behind her like a mane. When she sees me, she flings herself into my arms.

"I made it!"

"You and your luggage," Jean Luc grumbles as he walks in. "What did you pack in here, bricks?" He then disappears down the hall and I hear a scraping sound. I wonder how many of her extra-large suitcases he's going to have to lug up the stairs.

"Harrods had a summer sale," Chloe says, as if that explains everything. "Don't be a wuss, JL. Just a sec. I just need to take my heels off." She puts a hand on my shoulder, bounces a few times as she slips off her shoes, throws us a kiss and runs into the hallway.

"That's Chloe," I say as we watch her retreating.

"She exceeds expectations," Cassandra says.

We've just finished putting the food away when Chloe returns wearing a pair of shorts and flip-flops. "So," she says, putting her hands out for us to see. "Here they are. Two hands. Count them. One. Two. And they are all yours. How can I help?"

If I hadn't been leaning against the wall, I would have toppled over. I don't know what's more shocking, that Chloe would wear shorts and flip-flops or that she would offer to help. I'm still staring at her, agog, when she begins to pull plates and glasses from the cupboard. "Lunch is inside or out? Please say out. It was raining when I left London and I desperately need some vitamin D and a glass of wine." She puts her hand to her mouth. "Oh. No wine. That's right. Well then, let's hurry up and get everything on the table. I'm starved."

With a turbo-charged Chloe behind us, lunch is ready in no time. We start with salad, then move onto grilled vegetables, followed by melons from Cavaillon, succulent grapes and small rounds of goat cheese served with thick slices of fresh bread. The meal passes in a leisurely fashion, with everyone sitting around long after we've finished. Mulling over cups of mint tea, I disengage from the conversation, suddenly aware of my surroundings. I feel like I am sitting in an impressionist painting. No wonder it has attracted artists from the world over. In the center of the courtyard is the largest plane tree I've ever seen. Its branches, towering above us, cast a soft, dappled light on the table. All around me, on the floor, on the steps, and in the windowsills, terra-cotta pots of geraniums flash red against a palette of buttery cream. As I sit, taking it all in, Chloe rests her head against Jean Luc's shoulder, fingering the soft cotton of his shirt.

"Our journey's tomorrow night, right?"

"Correct," he says. "So no more food after tonight."

She sits up and turns to look at him. "Why aren't you afraid?"

Jean Luc tugs at his sleeves. "Because I'm not."

She turns to me. "And you?"

"I'm not going to journey," I answer. "I'm still trying to integrate Joshua Tree."

"I'll never forget what happened to you there," Jean Luc says, turning to me.

Chloe's eyes widen. "Annabel. What *did* happen to you?"

I glare at Jean Luc. I had tried my best to answer her questions but had studiously avoided that one. "Don't frighten her, Jean Luc."

Chloe looks at Jean Luc, then back at me, and when she realizes she isn't going to get an answer from either of us, she stands up. "Well, just so you know. I'm officially petrified. So emergency measures override rules." With a flick of her hair, she marches into the house. A few seconds later, she returns with a bottle of pale pink wine in one hand and two glasses in the other. She puts both glasses in front of Jean Luc, then drops as lightly as a handkerchief next to him.

"Wine, anyone? This rosé is divine."

Cassandra gives me a questioning look. We all know that before a journey, it's not a good idea to drink alcohol. I want to kick Jean Luc under the table as I watch her take a long sip before turning to Cassandra.

"You see, I'm nervous, and when I am, I need to drink. You'd do the same if you found out your cleaning lady was your birth mother."

A silence descends around the table. I don't know who looks more shocked, Jean Luc or Cassandra.

Jean Luc takes the bottle of wine from her. "Jeanette? Cleaning lady Jeanette?"

She nods. "That's right. Cleaning lady Jeanette. Apparently my father knocked her up when she was an au pair just before he married Mary. So I was born right here."

"In Saintes-Maries-de-la-Mer," I add, as if this little tidbit will help them understand.

"But why Saintes-Maries-de-la-Mer?" Jean Luc asks.

"Jeanette's French," I explain.

"But I thought you were English," Cassandra says.

"So did I," Chloe answers, plonking her wine on the table. "This has blasted away prejudices I didn't even know I had."

266

Although Cassandra's body hasn't moved, I can see that she is watching Chloe with eagle eyes. "It seems your journey has already begun."

Chloe looks into the distance. "If to journey means being blasted out of your comfort zone, then yes. You see, Jeanette has worked for me." She stops. "*With* me all my life. And in all that time, she never told me that she was my mother. No one did until about a month ago." She turns back to us and her eyes focus on Cassandra. "Well, as you can imagine, it has been haunting me ever since I found out. I haven't spoken to her yet because she's on summer holiday but when she gets back, I know I'll have to, and I don't have a clue how I am going to do this." Her eyes deepen. "I'm ashamed of how I've treated her all these years."

"Don't be so hard on yourself," I begin, but she shakes her head.

"No, I need to be tough, or it won't penetrate my delusions. I've been putting on a show all these years to assure myself of just how good I am. How special I am. How *British* I am. Everyone says I'm so generous. But do you know why? It's because it makes me feel good. I thought I was so altruistic. But when I really looked at myself, I discovered that it's nothing more than covert self-interest." She picks up a crumb from lunch and squeezes it between her fingers. "What did you call what happened to me again?"

"A cosmic kick," I answer.

She nods. "That's it. My ass has been kicked so hard I'm not sure if I'll ever be able to sit down properly again. I can tell you, this neti-neti thing is hard. Peeling away parts of myself like an onion. Examining what is true. Every time I get down a layer, there is another one." She turns to Cassandra with haunted eyes. "Will this ever end?"

Cassandra nods. "It gets more subtle."

But Jean Luc isn't hearing anything Cassandra is saying. He is so busy staring at Chloe it is as if none of us exist. "*You* are doing self-inquiry?"

Chloe stands up, gathering the plates and cups in one hand. "I don't know what you call it. All I know is that I'm going to help a lot more around the house than I would have before." She turns her back to us, puts the dishes in the sink, and starts to scrub them as if she's scrubbing her own soul.

Jean Luc spends the following morning walking through the olive grove, micromanaging a grumbling Chloe claiming she is faint with hunger. By the time I do my yoga, cook the journey soup, prepare the journey space, and have a bite to eat, the day is nearly over. Just before sunset, we're ready. I'm sitting next to Cassandra in the living room, while Jean Luc and Chloe are on their inflatable mattresses on the floor. Candles are burning around the room. The shutters are closed. Streams of evening light filter in from between the wooden slats, painting geometric designs on the stone floor.

Jean Luc and Chloe each light a match, then hold it over their candle while speaking their intention. Jean Luc goes first, reciting his intention in a deep, thoughtful voice. Chloe speaks hers with a gentleness that is surprisingly firm. I'm moved by what they say, which is to connect with a deeper love within themselves.

Cassandra hands them the ayahuasca and two glasses with the mushrooms and pours a little water in each glass. Chloe stirs the mushrooms into the glass of water and then swallows the ayahuasca pills. She seems to enjoy the taste of the mushrooms, scooping them all out from the bottom of the glass and licking the spoon. After they lie down on the mattresses, Cassandra and I tuck them in with quilts and blankets, the music begins to play, and the journey begins.

Monkey mind, the Buddhists call it. All those thoughts flying around the skull like monkeys bouncing around a tree. I'm so busy trying to tame my thoughts that I nearly miss it, that inner shift in energy that means the ayahuasca is taking effect. Even though I haven't taken ayahuasca, I can sense it as clearly as night turns to day. As time warps and expands in all directions, I feel an inner sigh, as if all of us who are imprisoned in linear time can relax into a deeper sense of reality. Beads of sweat appear on my forehead, and in that instant, my thoughts stop zinging around my head and begin to sink like grains of sand in a glass of clear water.

I hear a rustling noise. When I open my eyes, Chloe is pulling the blankets off and swinging her feet onto the floor. She sits up and announces, in seigniorial English, "The islands and lagoons of Venice are my home."

Jean Luc, lying next to her on the floor, opens his eyes. "What a coincidence. We have a trip planned to Venice this autumn."

"Uh, Jean Luc," Cassandra whispers from the sofa across from me, "I don't think Chloe is in this century."

Each journey has a theme, Cassandra explained to me later, and Chloe's is one of past lives. Because she's describing everything in detail, it allows me to follow her dance across the centuries. Sometimes, like the Venetian nobleman, her reincarnations stay a long time; others make cameo appearances, such as a cowboy.

"Pewee! Ooohh I stink!" she cries, roaring with laughter as she raises both legs in the air and slaps those ole thigh bones. In another life, she's a World War Two pilot who was shot down over the English Channel. She experiences so many lives I can't remember them all. It's amazing to see Chloe relaxing and being herself. Her words aren't slurred; her mind isn't sluggish. It's the opposite: Her thoughts are clear, her mind is at ease, and the tension she habitually carries in her face is gone. Her journey seems to go on forever until, after what must be a few hours, she stops, as if someone has pulled a plug. Her eyes close and I can practically feel her sinking into the depth of herself.

"It's so beautiful inside me," she says. "It's like an ocean."

"The vast ocean of consciousness," I can't help saying.

"And now," Chloe continues, "I'm accepting Jeanette as my mother." The moment holds and shimmers, and when she opens her eyes again, she has done it. There's a look of peace in her eyes that wasn't there before. In a matter of seconds, Chloe has achieved what might have taken decades of therapy.

Jean Luc, on the other hand, is having a hard time being present. Every time Cassandra checks with him, he can barely open his eyes. His body is so heavy and cumbersome, it takes ages for Cassandra and me to get him sitting upright and across from Chloe.

"Can you look each other in the eyes?" Cassandra asks Jean Luc.

His eyes keep fluttering shut. "My stomach is churning."

Cassandra's eyes soften. "Is there something you want to say?"

Jean Luc licks his lips and clears his throat. Minutes pass before he can find the words.

"Val," he whispers, and Chloe's eyes fill with pain.

"She left me because I couldn't handle the intimacy of a real relationship. But the reality is, I had already left her. Inside myself. I had already run for the hills."

Chloe's voice is so quiet I can barely hear it. "You want to run for the hills again, don't you?"

Jean Luc hangs his head. "I do."

Chloe pauses. "Do you love Val?"

Once again, Jean Luc pauses before answering. "Yes. Can you live with that?"

She closes her eyes. When she opens them, her voice is soft. "I'm trying."

He struggles to straighten himself up. "If you hadn't gotten pregnant, I never would have had the courage to marry. Not you or anyone." He closes his eyes, as if his own truth is hard even for him to bear, then he opens them again. "But that doesn't mean I can't love you, too. I do love you, Chloe. Deeply."

I see Chloe's eyes widen. It's as if the scales are falling from them. I don't think I've ever seen her looking so beautiful. Gone is the spoiled and demanding kitten, replaced by a woman, tenderhearted and as strong as a lioness. "I love you, too."

This is where I see Cassandra's work is far more than just shamanism. It's more than visions of cosmic serpents and past lives. It's using ayahuasca as a tool to deepen a person into this life, right now. I see before my eyes a couple at the brink of separation now surrendering into relationship. I don't know where things will go between them, but right now my heart is melting. I watch them hug each other for a long time. Soon after that, I bring bowls of soup, and we sit, eating happily in the flickering candlelight.

From the next day onwards, I surrender to one of the most remarkable months of my life. Days turn into weeks in an endless, flowing river of healing. As the clients' journeys go by, I become increasingly aware of just how unconscious I am. I learn to walk without making a sound, or disturbing the currents of air. I learn to drink slowly, because people in the journey space can be so sensitive they can feel the water sliding down my throat. I learn to sense, even with my eyes closed, what is happening around the room.

But most of all, I learn to observe energy. Watch how it works. What brings me closer to myself, and what triggers me to go into fight-or-flight syndrome. Watch how I want to manipulate it and therefore others. Watch how I, a little drop in the ocean, have been telling myself that I'm more than the ocean.

In the journey space, all that is required is for me to be present, but it isn't easy. I fall asleep. Cry so much that tears stream down my face. Battle with Maria Eugenia in my head. Worry about my finances. Replay Eugen's death over and over again. Sometimes I spend the entire night mute. Sometimes I translate like crazy until I don't know which language I'm speaking. Sometimes I don't like what people are saying, but I have to translate it anyway. Sometimes people don't want me near them. Sometimes I must clean up if someone throws up. When the journey is done, one of us brings in a big pot of soup and we eat, tired but content, on cushions on the floor. Then it's breakfast, integration, which is when Cassandra helps the person bring this new awareness into their daily life, the client leaves, sometimes the next one arrives right away—and we start all over again. It is endless, exhausting, and unbelievably fascinating.

The more journeys I participate in, the more I realize how little I know. I watch clients arrive unhappy or dissatisfied. They lie down and five hours pass—they either need my help or not—then Cassandra tries to sit them up to work with them while they are still in a state of expanded awareness—and that's it. In the morning, they are a changed person. The interior baggage that weighed them down is gone.

When the clients leave, there is even more work to do. Jean Luc is responsible for airport and train pick-ups and grocery runs; Chloe and I cook the meals, prepare the journey space, and do the housekeeping. On journey days, which are mostly every other day, Cassandra stays in her room, so we make sure there's enough food in the fridge and give her the space she needs. Journeywork takes a lot of juice, Cassandra says.

As time passes, I begin to realize the visions that ayahuasca produces—which is what most everyone who has had a shamanic journey talks about—aren't the focus of the journey. I learn from Cassandra that there aren't too many variations on a human theme. What she's doing, day in and day out, is helping people to deepen their awareness into their bodies. Embodiment, she calls it. It means to relax into your life, as it is, right now. And to open your heart. Life is all about how much love we can hold.

Jean Luc is professional, kind, and efficient, but the person who impresses me the most is Chloe. She's there when she's needed and leaves the person alone when she's not. And when it comes to Jean Luc, she's as solid as a rock. Their relationship moves from the starry-eyed, fireworks, romantic type of relationship into one that feels more serene. Respectful. And loving.

Gradually, the pace of life slows down. We talk less, sleep soundly, laugh more. On the occasional free day, dazed and trailing magical stardust behind us, we forage through markets for food, go for a swim in the pool, and cook; chopping and dicing and beating and slicing the market produce into a symphony of mouth-watering delicacies. Time takes on a different rhythm, not of days and nights, but of one long continuous expanse of healing—not just for those who come to work with us, but for ourselves. We hardly sleep and yet we aren't tired. We eat twice as much as normal, and yet we don't gain an ounce. We hardly talk, and yet we're closer than we ever have been. None of us gets much rest, but the energy is running so high we don't need it. Even though the work is intense, we don't complain. To experience healing at this level is a once-in-a-lifetime opportunity. We enjoy it

272

like a fine wine, savoring it in small sips until one day, the magic comes to an end.

Jean Luc has no interest in visiting Chloe's birthplace. In fact, he hasn't been interested in anything much since his journey. Something is up between them, I can feel it. So I'm not too surprised when he prefers to stay behind with Cassandra on the morning we have planned to visit Saintes-Maries-de-la-Mer. Seeing Chloe so disinterested and listless, I have to entice her into the car with promises of café au lait and croissants on our way before we go.

After stopping for breakfast in Saint-Rémy-de-Provence, we head south through the Alpilles, a lunar landscape of limestone rocks, groves of silvery olive trees and ancient stone villages, and then we enter another world. Framed by the two arms of the Rhone Delta, the Camargue is filled with marshy plains and brine lagoons. For the next forty minutes, our car bumps along a narrow road that cuts through 360 square miles of emptiness. There are no towns, no shops, in fact, no people at all. Just wilderness stretching as far as the eye can see. We glimpse flamingos bobbing like corks on shimmering salt flats. Admire a black bull with an egret on its back. Gawk at herds of white Camargue horses, one of the oldest breeds in the world, galloping along the horizon.

As I approach a crossroads, Chloe lowers the passenger window and then, in one swift movement, takes a manilla envelope out of her purse and empties it out of the window.

"Hey," I say. "What was that?"

"Jean Luc's supply from Amsterdam. It arrived in the post about a week ago." She shakes the envelope, peers inside to make sure it's empty, then stuffs it back into her purse. "Remind me to toss this when we get to Saintes-Maries." When she sees my face, she shakes her head. "Don't worry. It was biodegradable."

"*What* was biodegradable?"

She props her Jackie O sunglasses on top of her head. "You didn't know he microdoses?"

So that is what that was. "I suppose he picked up the habit in California."

She shakes her head. "He started after we got married." She gazes at the sawgrass whipping by for what seems forever. Long tendrils of tawny hair whip around her face like a Medusa. "Do you know how long you'll be in Vienna?"

My mind is still on what she has just said, so I struggle to answer her. "What do you mean? I've got nowhere else to go. Besides, it's home."

Chloe taps a lacquered nail on the dash. "I don't see you returning to live in that palace again. Or in Vienna for that matter."

My hands tighten on the wheel. "But what will I do with all my furniture? I can't continue to live with all my beautiful things in storage. It's just stupid."

I can feel Chloe's eyes on me. "I've got a better idea. Rather than searching for a place to put your furniture, why not get rid of the furniture?"

My breath exhales as if I've been punched in the stomach. "But that will take me in the opposite direction of what I want. I crave stability so much it hurts."

Her answer surprises me. "We all crave stability," she says. She presses the button on the dash and watches the window roll shut. "But sometimes things have to break apart in order for the situation to settle in a new way."

I turn to her. "What about you? Will you be following Jean Luc to San Francisco?"

"No." She stares at the horizon with a fixed expression. Her mouth opens and closes once, as if it is searching to find the right words. Finally she speaks, her voice so low I can barely hear it. "We're separating."

Her words so shock me that I lift my foot off the pedal too early and the car jerks. I put the car into gear again and slowly speed up. My hands feel clammy. Taking them off the wheel one at a time to wipe them on my jeans, I try to keep my voice steady. "But you were so loving towards each other."

"I love that man with all my heart," she whispers. "Who would have imagined that loving him means letting him go? We married under false pretenses. That wasn't the right way to start a marriage. How you start a relationship is how you finish it."

"So you are starting your relationship by finishing it?"

She nods. "It's the hardest thing I've ever done. Besides, I can't be with a man who loves another woman."

This time it's me who is quiet. What she is saying is true.

"You knew about Val?"

I look at her out of the corner of my eye. "She did come up once or twice."

"I need time. We both need time."

"Is that why he stayed behind?"

She nods. "To work with Cassandra. She's the one who helped me make the decision."

This time I see the bumps in the road before we hit them. I shift into lower gear and drive around them. As I speed up, I gaze at the endless landscape. It feels as if we are driving in a dream. "I'm so sorry. Maybe I should have told you about the microdosing. But he told me he was going to stop."

She pulls the Jackie O sunglasses down over her eyes. "That's what he told me, too. Again and again and again."

I swerve to avoid another pothole. "I shouldn't have pushed for you to come here."

She dabs a tissue under her glasses. "Stop right there. It was my decision." She opens the visor, glances in the mirror to make sure her mascara hasn't run, then drops the glasses back onto her nose and throws the crumpled tissue by her feet.

Just then, far off in the distance, a bell tower rises defiantly above the marshes. Beyond it, the Mediterranean sparkles in shades of gray, blue, and gold.

"There it is," she says. "To think I was born here. Flat. Desolate. Abandoned."

I shake my head. "Just like Kansas."

She gives me a bitter smile. "No wonder we are friends."

After nosing the car through the narrow streets of Saintes-Maries-de-la-Mer, we park. The sun, a pale orb hanging high in the sky, pelts down upon our backs as we get out of the car. Gone are the chic stores and fashionable people. The stone houses and tree-lined avenues. Instead, we are surrounded by crowds of restless teenagers and elderly couples shuffling by in tracksuits and leggings with beach umbrellas. Unlike sophisticated Provence, Saintes-Maries-da-la-Mer is a holiday destination for the working class.

We meander through a maze of squat stucco buildings with peeling paint and chipped terra-cotta roofs, past stores selling cheap clothing, past migrants holding out begging bowls. Scruffy dogs run between our legs, searching for scraps of food. Restaurants with open porches have plastic menus fluttering in the breeze.

"What a dump," Chloe says as we arrive at the courtyard surrounding the church. It sits in the center of a square like a well-polished crown. Built in the ninth century, the building is far older than the unkempt town that surrounds it. Small but dignified, the Romanesque fortress contains a belltower with five bells that rises above the roofs. The curved entrance doors at the front of the church are closed, so we wander to the back where a tiny side door beckons.

Chloe frowns as we walk inside. "Now what?"

The truth is, I don't have a clue. With Chloe huffing at my side, I stand, trying to look as if I know what I'm doing.

A cough. Turning, I see a woman in black leggings crouched on a pew nearby, her head bent in prayer. Her provocative clothing and hooped earrings make me wonder if she isn't a prostitute. She pulls a shawl over her shoulders, but not before I see the telltale needle marks of a drug addict on her arm. And something else. A symbol made from an anchor, a heart, and a three-pronged trident. It's the Camargue Cross.

Just then, I feel that underlying pull that tells me that whatever I have been waiting for has begun. At that moment, the woman slips off the pew and disappears down the steps and through a door which

I did not see before. Without thinking, I grab Chloe and follow her.

It must be the crypt, I think, as we bend down to walk into a small, subterranean room. It's stifling hot. There are so many votive candles I can hear them burning all around us. They sound like the hissing of a snake.

At the far end of the room I spot a statue, no larger than a child, draped in a profusion of colorful robes. They hang in sheaves, one on top of the other, and so voluminous I can barely see Sara la Kali's head sticking out of the top. Doe-eyed and dark-skinned, her delicate features are framed by long black hair. A mishmash of necklaces hangs around her neck, a diamante tiara crowns her head. But it's her eyes that stand out. They are large and penetrating. At her feet are dog-eared photographs, paintings, and plastic flowers. The garish colors and saintly bric-a-brac make me feel as if I'm in an Indian temple.

I watch the woman in black leggings prostrate herself in front of Sara. She then places a small photograph at her feet, stands up and crosses herself, and, with her eyes glued to the ground, slips up the stairs and is gone.

Prostitutes. Our own untouchables. We blame them, arrest them, make it illegal for them to work. But never touch the men who are their clients. Prostitutes are marginalized by society. Just like the untouchables from Rajasthan. Of course the untouchables would bring their goddess Kali with them. Kali is pure compassion. And here she is, the pure, dark Feminine, dressed as a Catholic saint. The gypsies are the true nomads, with no ties to any homeland. Theirs is a world where what is yours is mine and mine is yours, where calendar time is ignored, where rules and boundaries are unthinkable.

Chloe's face has taken on the eerie glow of the red votive candles. Pulling out some coins, she puts them through the slot of a metal box by the candles. They make a tinny clank as they fall inside. "Let's light a candle and get out of here," she whispers, lighting hers. I swivel my eyes from where the candles are, but she's gone.

Holding myself back from following her, I light my candle and hold it in my cupped hands. A tiny flame splutters and grows into a

277

small golden teardrop. Whispering my blessing, I place it on the rickety iron stand and feel my wishes become one with a thousand others. Looking around, I see that I'm the only one here, so I take advantage of the moment and sit in front of Sara and close my eyes.

At first, I feel nothing. The candles continue to hiss. The muggy heat surrounds me like arms. I take a breath, then another, trying to follow it deeper into myself. I do this, again and again, trying to let my awareness drift deeper into my body. Time and time again I take a breath. Then, just as I'm about to give up, I sense an inner whoosh, and my energy drops lower into my hips. As I do, I feel the subtle energy of the land beneath me. And in that moment, I understand there is a reason why the church was built here. It's because of the land. The energy is dark, deep, and compassionate, just like Sara. In other words, Sara is only a symbol of this energy, not the source of it. The more I connect with the energy, the more at peace I feel. I open my eyes. Sara is staring at me.

What's your dharma? she whispers. Her eyes are as deep as the sadhu I met in Agra.

"To serve the planet," I whisper.

The compassion blazing from her eyes is almost more than I can bear. *Finally, you've understood.*

By the time I emerge from the darkness, I know exactly what I need to do. I find Chloe leaning against the wall of the church, smoking. I can see she is desperately trying to keep it together and failing miserably. The sound of starlings surrounds us, their calls echoing against the church walls.

"What a waste of time," Chloe says, throwing the cigarette on the ground. She stubs the butt out with her heel. "I have about as much in common with this place..."

"As I do with Kansas."

I see a flicker of understanding in her eyes. "Yes."

I hook my arm in hers. "We are all homesick for kindness," I say. "Maybe by letting Jean Luc go, he'll come back in a new way."

When she turns to me, tears are in her eyes. "I hope so," she whispers.

278

I'm surprised to feel her frailty. I squeeze her arm. "Do you know what I used to do when I was sad?" I say. "I would get on my horse and ride through the fields as far and as fast as I could go. The feeling of the wind on my cheeks and in my hair always made me feel better."

She tilts her head. "You did that back in Kansas?"

I smile. "It could be in Saintes-Maries-de-la-Mer, too. They do have cowboys, you know." I pause for a moment, then ask, "Do you still ride?"

Her eyes take on a glint I haven't seen in a long time. "Do I ever."

Soon, we're standing in front of a whitewashed stable a few miles outside the town, watching a cowboy untie two horses from the hitching post. When he sees both of us swing into our saddles with ease, a grin spreads over his face as he gives us each our reins, then slaps his hat on our horses' rumps and cries, *Allez!*

In no time we are in the Camargue gazing at a band of wild horses galloping through the marshes. Their white bodies with long gray manes and forelocks are a delicate contrast with the moody landscape. In that moment, I lean over my horse's neck and cry, *Giyap!* Our horses leap forward. Hooting like cowboys, we gallop as fast as we can until we are abreast of the herd. Then, in a few moments, we become part of them, a whirlwind of horse and human all racing as one. I feel the dust and hear the thunder of the hoofs and smell the pleasant scent of horse sweat, as clumps of earth spin around us like rockets in the air. The pounding of the earth, the splashing of muddy water, and the rich, grassy smell make me feel so alive that I holler into the air.

"It's just like Kansas!"

Chloe's eyes are shining, her face smeared with mud and sweat. "Who wouldn't want to be born here?"

We ride and ride until our horses cannot run anymore, and then slow to a walk and plod through the marsh toward the stable. Our horses are heaving, their legs and necks dripping with sweat. As I

279

watch my horse carefully picking through the solid ground in between the clumps of long sawgrass, I feel it. The shift that has occurred within me. It's subtle, but real. I know that the separation between my will and God's will is gone. Paradoxically, what is left behind isn't a feeling of being tied down, but one of complete, utter freedom.

Cassandra gazes upward and shakes her head. "You go on. I'll stay here."

Jean Luc hitches a rucksack on his shoulders. It's filled with bottles of water, bags of dates and almonds and a few apples, just enough for our thirty-minute pilgrimage up to the ridge and back. "We've been together for a month now. We aren't going to separate now."

In front of us is the Sainte-Baume, an eight-mile-long rocky bar shooting out of the valley like a frozen stone wave. About halfway up the rockface is the grotto of Mary Magdalene. For hundreds of years, people have traveled from far and wide to make a pilgrimage to Her, and now we are going to do the same.

We are surrounded by tall parasol pines, winding rivers, and cool green forests. As I watch Cassandra sizing up the length of the walk, I stay silent. I understand her physical limitations better than anyone and know that this will be pushing her. She is far more fragile physically than she lets on. Each of us has taken a journey these past few months. This day is hers.

Cassandra stands, hands resting lightly on her hips, and stares at the cliff as if weighing up the pros and cons of doing something which is clearly a folly. But then something changes within her and she takes off, her body floating like a silk scarf along the path. Her departure is so quick it catches us by surprise, so we gather our rucksacks and run to catch up with her.

At first the path meanders through dried riverbeds and over a carpet of fallen leaves and gnarled roots. As we wind our way through the undergrowth, patches of sunlight begin to appear through the branches. None of us says a word. We are all focused on Cassandra. There's always someone with an arm for her to hold, a shoulder for her to rest on, a smile to encourage her.

The path winds its way gently up the rock face, meandering back and forth in long sweeping strides so that it is never too difficult, never too steep. As we walk, I catch myself watching Jean Luc. I'd hoped to have a few words with him, but nothing. He's struggling with his own demons. Chloe, on the other hand, looks determined. Even though I can't say she is at peace, a decision has been made.

After thirty minutes of walking in silence, we emerge above the trees. The path becomes white and rocky and lined with sweet-smelling rosemary and wild thyme. Arms swinging wildly, Cassandra negotiates the last steps of a stairway cut into the rock face and we find ourselves standing on a small platform hewn out of rock. In front of us, undulating hills stretch like a silken green carpet as far as the eye can see.

The sense of accomplishment, not just these pilgrimages, but of having spent over a month healing others, gives me a feeling unlike any other. We hold hands and raise them into the sky, four tiny stick figures in a vast open space. The silence is so loud it's palpable.

"I wonder if it will be historically proven that Mary Magdalene was here," Chloe whispers as we tiptoe toward the entrance of the grotto.

"Does it matter?" Cassandra says as Jean Luc holds the heavy oak door open for us to file through. "I can feel her presence now."

The door creaks in the stillness, revealing a womblike cave that's empty apart from a few benches, an altar, and a few candles. Our footsteps echo when we walk in. Sitting on the bench, I close my eyes and absorb the stillness into my soul. It's a serenity rarely experienced in daily life. Within moments, I feel a vertical pull downward from the center of my body and with a whoosh, I'm inside again, resting in myself. After all these years of searching, I'm finally home.

By the time Lili arrives, our month is coming to an end, and we are

281

all weary. So is everyone in Provence after a long hot summer. The restaurant owners are crabby. The land is baked and dusty. The wind whips the dry dust into small spirals like a sirocco from the desert.

But Lili's journey is like a breath of fresh air. I'm surprised to see her so eager and open to do something that she knows nothing about. And her journey? Journeys are precision perfect, Cassandra explains. They give each individual exactly what they need to propel them further into their healing. This certainly is the case with Lili. Hers is the family tree journey. Lili spends time with her mother, Eszther Szabo, and all the ancestors on her mother's line. When Lili describes the little house where she was born in the tiny town of Balaton Almadi, on the southern tip of Lake Balaton, it is as if she were describing her own childhood. Her mother was beautiful, Lili exclaims.

"You mean you saw her?" I ask as we walk afterwards, arm in arm through the olive trees.

Lili nods, her eyes shining. "I was created in love," she says, hugging me. "That's all I needed to know."

It is night. Lili is gone, having flown back to Vienna—was it only this morning? Cassandra, Jean Luc, and Chloe are in their rooms preparing their bags, or maybe they are already asleep. And me? I've finished packing; my suitcase is by the door, and I'm in bed, listening to the night sounds of Provence. By now I'm familiar with the inexplicable noises of the ancient farmhouse. Together with the soft chirping of the crickets in the courtyard and the occasional croak of a frog, they lull me into a state of relaxed awareness. I'm at peace with myself, at peace with the world, and even though I don't know what will happen in Vienna, I'm at peace with my life. I nestle under the covers and feel the soft sheets caressing my skin, and before I know it, I'm asleep.

A strange whirring wakes me up. I could swear something has flown past my cheek. A thought appears in my brain. *Someone must have turned on a ceiling fan.* Then I stop. None of the rooms have ceiling fans. My eyes snap open. Disoriented, I reach over and turn on the light. Above me, a swarm of musical notes dances in the air. I'm watching, mesmerized, when I realize that these things pirouetting above me can't be musical notes. I'm not dreaming. Nor am I doing a journey. I'm wide awake. And above me are bats. Hundreds of tiny black bats.

I scoot out of that room so fast my feet don't touch the floor. In two seconds, I am pounding on Jean Luc and Chloe's door.

Jean Luc's face peers out. He's fumbling with his nightgown. "What's wrong?"

"Bats," I croak.

Chloe peeks out from behind him. She's wearing a sexy cotton negligee we bought together in the market. "What is it? And why aren't you dressed?"

I pull my T-shirt down over my knees and, without saying another word, I take them both by the hand and drag them to my door. "Go on, open it," I whisper.

Jean Luc opens the door and looks cautiously inside. My room is just as I left it. The lamp is on, my bedclothes pulled down, my suitcases are by the door and a glass of water with lemon is on the bedside table. The room looks like it has every night for a month now. Except that every inch of airspace is covered with twirling, whirling bats. There are so many that we can feel a frenzied whooshing in the air.

Jean Luc pulls the door shut so quickly he nearly catches the edge of his slippers underneath it. I can almost hear the thoughts spinning in his head. "It's bats," is all he can say.

I nod. "I know."

By this time, Cassandra has joined us. "What's going on?"

"It's bats," Chloe says, turning to her.

"There must be hundreds," Jean Luc says. He puts his hands on his hips and frowns at me. "You ought to know better than to sleep with the windows open."

"Uh Jean Luc," Chloe pipes in. "If you didn't notice, the windows to the room are closed."

283

Jean Luc opens the door again, peers in, then pulls his head back and closes it. He stares at the doorway for at least a minute before turning to face us. The look on his face is priceless.

Cassandra starts to laugh. "Oh Annabel, not again." She nudges Jean Luc. "Come on, be a *bon chevalier*. Go in and open the windows and let them out."

Jean Luc runs a hand through his hair. Then, tightening his dressing gown like a soldier heading off to war, he checks his slippers are firmly on his feet, opens the door again and marches into the room and unlatches all three windows and opens them wide. He then walks, desperately trying to act as if everything is perfectly normal, through the flock of bats, back to where we are all standing.

And this is how my black cat and bat episode ends, with the three of us watching an entire colony of bats circle once, twice, and then, like a swarm of bees, fly out of the window and disappear into the night.

For a moment, no one says anything. Then Chloe starts to laugh too.

"Oh Annabel," she says. "Couldn't you have been a little more original with your approach to becoming a wise woman? Bats and black cats? Really? If anyone would have written this in a book, I would have rejected it for being unoriginal."

"Do you think I orchestrated this?" I cry. "I'm having a hard enough time believing this myself."

Chloe points to my bed. Every inch of the duvet is covered with thousands of tiny black pellets. "Bat shit," Chloe says, smiling. "It's real, Annabel. It's all real."

LIGHT

Vienna

*Ever since happiness heard your name, it has been running through the
streets trying to find you*
—HAFIZ

I look out the train window at the French countryside. It's an Indian
summer. Oceans of wheat, pale yellow and russet brown, whoosh
by in syncopated waves. Summer is gone, autumn not quite here, and
everywhere I look farmers are busy turning the hay. Plastic-wrapped
bales of hay dot the landscape like white marbles. In the fields, I see
cows grazing. Tractors mowing diligently. Horses galloping, tails held
high. After the intense work schedule in Provence, it's bliss to have
nothing to do. I press my forehead against the windowpane and
become one with the train, feeling the movement in my body as we
roll from side to side in an endless dance of wheels and tracks that
connect Paris, the City of Light, with Vienna, the City of Death.

Vienna's ultra-modern Hauptbahnhof station, with its sleek glass
façade and shopping mall, is a world away from Paris's romantic fin-
de-siècle Gare de l'Est. Giving the taxi driver my address, the
German consonants sound hard on my ears after French's sultry
vowels. As my taxi winds through the narrow streets and stops at my

new address, the city erupts in an explosion of bells. Everything around me reverberates: the buildings on the streets, the wrought-iron lamp posts, the cobblestones under my feet. It is said that Beethoven discovered the totality of his deafness when he saw birds flying out of bell towers in silence. He must have been deaf because the gongs are so loud the driver and I have to shout at each other while I pay. By the time I arrive on the top-floor landing, the bells have slowed to a steady bong. It sounds just like Vienna's heartbeat.

My new home, lent to me by Christiane and Otto, is a studio with soaring white walls, shiny parquet floors, and a mezzanine just large enough to hold a bed. On the terrace, two stone cupids ponder a sea of rooftops drenched in a golden glow. The cooing of the pigeons on the roof, the starlings swooping in open skies, even the trams rumbling along their tracks are the relaxed pace of yesteryear. It feels good to be back.

I spot a note from Christiane on the kitchen table telling me she's left food in the fridge and her bike in the cellar. Wallowing in the warm fuzziness of an unexpected kindness, I find an apple in the fridge and munch it while I unpack, then tumble into bed. I fall asleep instantly, the rhythm of the train still in my ears.

In the morning, I wake up to the hollow clang of bells. After sitting with myself quietly in bed for thirty minutes—I now do this every morning—I walk to the window and gaze at the cupids on the terrace. They smile at me like guardian angels, welcoming me home. Making myself a cup of hot water with a slice of lemon, I sit on the sofa and begin opening the mail Christiane has left. Bank statements, credit card bills, a few officious letters, more bureaucracy around Eugen's death and—I turn a cream-colored envelope over to check the postmark—a letter from Kansas. I recognize the large loopy letters of my mother's handwriting right away.

I slit the envelope with my finger, pull out a single piece of beige writing paper, read it quickly, and let the paper drift from my hands. It lands as lightly as a fallen leaf by my feet. I stand up from the sofa and head for the door. It's time to go for a walk.

Vienna is a clean city, and that's just how its inhabitants like it, I think, as I wait while a road sweeper motors by. It washes the street with industrial verve, suds dripping behind it. I watch it trundle away like a bug with an enormous mustache. My mind chews on my mother's letter as I walk through the streets. In all the years I have lived here, my parents never came to visit me. Not once. But now that I have no home, no job, and no husband, they want to come for Christmas. My lower back tightens at the thought. Then again, they probably would like it here, I think, as I watch my footsteps, now wet from the soapy water, follow me. It's as tidy as my parent's home and is as full of music as their home is, too. But just the idea of having them here while my life is so unsettled makes my stomach turn. Before I know it, I am standing in front of the one place in all of Vienna where I go whenever I am in search of an answer.

Peering through the glass door of the tiny Trafik newspaper shop, I see Karl standing behind the countertop, smiling at a customer. The man's Tyrolean hat with a horsehair bristle stuck in its crown bobs up and down. Waiting patiently at his feet is a dachshund wagging its tail. I remember the dog's name. It's Hansi.

The bell tinkles as I open the door and slip inside. I bask in the familiarity of it all. The magazines lining the walls. The pungent smell of lemons. The colorful prayer flags fluttering from the ceiling. Even the wow-wow-wow Viennese–German dialect, which makes Herr Dietmayer and the man sound as if they are speaking with rubber in their mouths, comforts my ears. I watch Karl fold a newspaper like origami and hand it, together with a lemon, to the elderly man.

"Sixteen ounces of water with a squeeze of fresh lemon before you go to bed. Then again in the morning. You'll start to feel the changes in no time." As the man turns to leave, Karl slips Hansi a dog biscuit and winks at me.

I flatten myself against the wall as the customer squeezes by, but instead of greeting me, the Austrian lowers his hat and brushes by me, dragging his dachshund behind him as he sweeps out the door.

"The power of the press," I say, as I place my rucksack on the floor with a thud. I'm trying to pretend that I don't care that someone I've known for years has just snubbed me, but Karl sees right through me.

"Ignore it," he says, leaning over the counter to make sure the water bowl in the corner is still full after Hansi's departure. "Today it's the Vasoy scandal. Tomorrow it will be something else. Never worry about what others are saying. Remember, truth is like a cork. It will pop up to the surface eventually." He hoists a pile of newspapers onto the counter. "So what do you think of the changes?"

I take a closer look around me. In between his habitual magazines and newspapers, the shelves are now stocked with books on food, vitamins, supplements, yoga, and general wellbeing.

I finger through one of the Medical Medium books. "So many changes," I mumble.

Karl takes out a pocketknife and with a neat upward movement, slices through the cord holding the papers and gives me one. "So here's one more to add to that." Sliding the papers to the side of the countertop, he taps his hand on the top corner of the wall behind him. With a click, a door opens.

He smiles when he sees my reaction. "Everyone needs a little James Bond in their life." Lifting the countertop with one swift movement, he tells me to lock his front door and follow him.

I do so, bending down so I won't bump my head as I step through the doorway. It's dark. Putting one foot in front of the other, I edge forward, but the moment I'm inside, I see a line of light and can just make out Karl pushing open a door at the other end. What I thought was a tunnel is a passageway carved between the stone walls of two buildings.

I blink in the bright lights as I emerge from the darkness. I'm in a professional kitchen. In front of me, a young man in a white apron is pulling pineapple chips out of a dehydrating oven. A woman in a chef's toque is whisking something inside a copper pan. A third woman with short blond hair in a white chef's apron is vigorously chopping a large pile of celery stalks. When she looks up, her face bursts into a smile.

It's Darinka, my old cleaning lady.

"*Mein Gott!*" she cries. Wiping her hands on her apron, she comes over to shake my hand. "Welcome to Wake Up Cooking School and Café." She throws a panicky glance at Karl, but he gives her the thumbs up and tells her that her English is getting better every day. She beams at him and returns to the cutting block. "People are waiting," she explains.

I suddenly realize what this is: it's a miniature coffeehouse. A shoebox, really, just large enough to contain a half dozen tables. Everywhere I look, I see touches I like. On each table are small bowls of tasters with signs explaining the nutritional elements and spiritual lessons of each food. Fresh fruit is piled high in large ceramic bowls like pieces of fine art. Oil paintings of gorgeous vegetables are hanging on the walls like ancestral portraits. I don't need to ask whether it's popular; a line of people snaking from the counter all the way out the door gives me my answer.

"It's our double duo celery juice and Heavy Metal Detox smoothie takeaway," Karl says, when he sees me glancing at the queue. "It became popular after our restaurant review came out. Just goes to show how much people are searching for ways to become healthy."

"There are lines like this every day?"

He nods and points outside the shop. "You do know who's behind this, don't you?"

Just then a woman bustles in through the door. She's wearing a long white apron like a French baker, but instead of baguettes in her arms, she's carrying piles of celery. A bright orange and burgundy tartan scarf drapes haphazardly around her neck. She pats her determined tufts of short hair once, then pushes her glasses up on her head.

"Karl? I've got a question —" When she sees me, she stops so quickly that the celery tumbles onto the floor. "Annabel!"

It's Christiane. To say she looks good is an understatement. She's lost a good twenty pounds. But it's not just that. She's glowing. Her skin is firm, her eyes clear, her voice strong. I don't even need to ask her about her relationship with Otto; one glance at her tells me all is well. We bend down to pick up the celery stalks, but as soon as she tries to hold them in her arms, they slide onto the floor again. So we hand them to Darinka, who stacks them like pieces of firewood in her arms and marches to the kitchen. Christiane wipes her hands on her apron and we give each other a hug and stand in the middle of the café, smiling at each other. It's hard to know who's more pleased to see whom.

Christiane shows us to a table in the corner and tells us to sit down. Her exuberance bubbles over like a spring, the words tumbling over each other so quickly it's like a fast-flowing stream. She points to Darinka, who's showing a young woman how to place celery in glass vases. They look like exuberant puffs of flowery art.

"Just look at her go," she says. "She'll be manager one day if she keeps this up."

While the three of us catch up on each other's lives, a waiter arrives wearing a long white apron with *Celery forever!* printed on it. He places glasses of dark purple juice and plates of banana pancakes with wild blueberries on the table, then disappears.

Christiane watches me pour maple syrup over the pancakes. They are warm and fluffy. Sweet but not too cake-like. "Delicious," I say between bites.

She gazes over the café like a proud duck surveying her brood of chicks. "Who would have imagined I would be cooking in a way that helps people lose weight."

She stops talking as Darinka arrives and whispers in her ear. She nods and gets up. "I've got to go. Too many orders, not enough food. We're going to need to open a second café soon if it continues like this." She takes one last swig of her juice, puts the glass on the table, waves at us, and follows Darinka into the kitchen.

I place my knife and fork down at the edge of the plate and turn back to Karl. "You've become vegan? I thought you loved meat."

He looks guilty. "Still do. I used to tell myself that factory farms aren't so bad. That environmental problems are too large and I'm too small, so there is nothing I can do to help. But when Christiane came up with the idea of educating people through food, I realized I was wrong. I could be part of the solution. So instead of closing my Trafik, I expanded it and called it the Wake Up Café. It's all about changing the world one person at a time." He winks, and we both smile.

The following afternoon, I roll Christiane's bike to the Westbahnhof train station to travel to the Wachau, a twenty-mile stretch of the Danube about an hour west of Vienna. It's September, which means the summer heat is gone, the sky cloudless, the trees a quilt of green and copper and gold. It's a quick train ride, and when I arrive in Melk, I exit the station, hop on my bike and pedal across a bridge over the Danube, then coast downhill toward the river.

Above me, Melk Monastery, built in 1089, sits like a Baroque crown on a rocky outcrop overlooking the entire valley. Europe's second-longest river winds like a silver ribbon through gentle hills set in a landscape of unspoiled vineyards. Each bend of the river is adorned with a tiny fairy-tale village.

At the village of Spitz, I hop off my bike and roll it onto the *Rollfähre*, a tiny motorless ferry attached to a steel cable that traverses the river. The captain, a heavyset man with kind blue eyes, tells me I'm his only customer. As I park my bike against the boat's railing, he turns the rudder and we slide away from the shore, propelled forward by the force of the river current.

Leaning against the guardrail, I watch the shoreline become smaller. As we silently glide across the water, I wonder how a river that appears so placid on the surface can be so powerful as to push us across without a motor.

Looking into the swirling currents, a haziness overcome me, and when I next look up, I'm in that funny space where I no longer know what's real. I'm no longer on the Danube, but on a ferryboat crossing the mythical River Styx. The captain is Charon, the boatman who ferries people across the boundary between the Earth and the Underworld. I'm not seeing this, of course. Nothing in the scenery around me has changed. It's as if the physical world has faded, allowing me to see my spiritual journey shining through. And when

I recognize this, I understand that Eugen isn't the only one who died at the Taj Mahal all those months ago.

This has been a journey into the darkness of Hades and back. I've been twisting and turning on a path, trying to avoid the pitfalls, stumbling as I tried to clean up not only my life but those of my ancestors. At each step, there was always a helping hand, whether it came from Cassandra or Percy or Mary or Karl—or even black cats and bats.

As the ferry bumps against the pier on the other side of the Danube, I pull a few euro coins from my purse and gaze at them, glittering in the sunlight in the palm of my hand. They look just like the silver coins that people used to pay the mythological ferryman of Hades. The captain smiles as I give them to him and waves as I pedal away. I am firmly in the land of the living again.

Fifteen minutes later, I arrive in Willendorf. No more than a handful of houses at the edge of the river, this is where Venus of Willendorf was found. Getting off my bike, I take a few photos to send to Jackie, then, my job done, I sit down by the river's edge and put my feet in the water.

Who is my greatest teacher right now? The person who is most driving me crazy. Now that's a different perspective on Maria Eugenia. As Cassandra says, it's not what separates us but what unifies us that heals. It's not easy to pull away from all the emotional triggers and to see her as she is. She's a widow. Like me. She doesn't have children. Like me. She was brought up in a conservative family. Like me. She probably had it drilled into her brain to marry well. Like me. She was de facto queen until I dethroned her.

No wonder she hates me.

I feel the release that comes from within me every time I feel myself surrendering to a deeper truth. I know exactly what I need to do. I can see it as clearly as the water flowing over my feet. I get up and dust the leaves from my jeans, then pull on my sneakers and get on my bike. It's time to get back to Vienna. I've got a lot to do.

I'm standing in front of a glass display case. Bright spotlights from the ceiling highlight a figurine so small she could fit in the palm of my hand. Venus of Willendorf looks different in real life. She's the essence of Mother Earth; ageless, beautiful, and sexy in a soft, feminine way, which is an impressive thing to say about a woman who is twenty-five thousand years old.

"I'm glad you're finally meeting her in person."

I turn around. Lili is standing right behind me. She's dressed in black, her thick dark hair coiled in a neat knot at the nape of her neck. We give each other a warm hug.

"She's powerful, isn't she?"

"Powerful enough to make me want to work here," she answers. She gazes around the room with pride. The Vienna Museum of Natural History exhibitions are normally glass, but Venus of Willendorf's display case is in her own wooden house.

I smile. "Have you considered my idea?"

"Not only thought it over, I've spoken to the head of the anthropological department. He thinks it's a great idea. We may be able to access EU money too."

I turn to her. "That would help fill up the palace's coffers nicely, wouldn't it?"

She hooks her arm in mine. "Wouldn't it just."

"Do you know, I biked to the Wachau last week," I say as we begin to walk. "I wanted to see where Venus was found."

Her almond eyes widen. "You made a pilgrimage to Willendorf!"

"I hadn't thought of it that way, but I suppose you're right," I answer. On either side, saber-toothed tigers snarl at us from their dusty glass cages.

We stop at the entrance to the café, which is in a large airy room underneath the central dome. "I wonder why Otto wanted to meet us," she says.

"I'm not sure," I answer. "All he said is that it couldn't be in his office."

With its round walls, vaulted ceilings, and arches filled with plinths and angels and caryatids, the museum café feels like a cathedral. Statues of notables in the field of natural sciences standing in pompous repose circle the room. In the center of the geometric black-and-white floor is an open circular hole, surrounded by a marble balustrade.

Otto, dressed in a traditional linen trachten jacket and jeans, is sitting at a table next to the balustrade, peering over it down at the entrance hall, one floor below. "Now I know what God must feel like," he says, as he stands up. He clicks his heels and gives us both a Küss die Hand, then pulls out chairs for us. "I'm glad you could meet me at such short notice."

With a flick of his hand in the air, a waiter appears to take our order, then whisks himself away. Otto puts his glasses on his nose. "Welcome back Annabel. How long are we graced with your presence?"

"For good I hope," I say. "My parents are coming for Christmas."

Otto looks surprised. "I didn't realize you had parents."

"Neither did I until recently," I say. "My mother wants to find her father's birth certificate in Bavaria before she dies."

We stop talking as a waiter arrives with two glasses of elderflower lemonade for us and a *kleiner Schwarzer* coffee for Otto. He then places a piece of apple strudel with a dollop of fresh cream and three forks in the middle of the table and disappears.

"*Kein Problem*. Just go to the town hall where he was born and ask for one," Otto says.

"That's the problem," I say as I pick up a fork and take a bite of strudel. The crust is warm, the apple filling melts in my mouth. "We don't know where he was born. My mother says he was from Erdinger. But there is no Erdinger in Germany."

"That's easy," Lili says, as we all tuck in. "A person from Vienna, or Wien, is called a Wiener. So if your grandfather was an Erdinger, he is from Erding."

"That's near Munich," Otto says. "So it's settled. You can spend Christmas in Munich and visit Erding on the way. Then come to us in Attersee afterward." Otto puts his fork down. "I'm sure you want

294

to know why I wanted to meet you here."

Lili and I nod.

He rests his forearms against the table and leans forward. "The reason I didn't want to meet you in my office is because I am meeting you as Otto your friend and not Otto your lawyer." He stares at us for a moment, waiting for his words to sink in before continuing. "So, here we are, chatting away about our private lives, and lo and behind, it just happens to come out in conversation that I was approached by a Russian couple last week."

"And?" I ask.

His eyes glitter with an intensity I haven't seen before. "They are interested in purchasing a certain palace in Vienna."

Lili practically leaps out of her chair. "Mami is trying to sell the palace?" Her voice jumps nearly an octave. "I hope you showed them the door."

Otto helps Lili back into her chair. "On the contrary." He lowers his voice. "She's feeling the heat. She is desperate to do something while there is still some doubt as to who will inherit the estate."

"So why can't we settle the will right now?" Lili asks, frowning.

"Ah," Otto says, removing a cotton handkerchief from his pocket and cleaning his glasses with it. "That's precisely the point." He lifts his glasses in the air and squints through them, then, apparently satisfied, he stuffs the handkerchief back into his pocket and puts the glasses back on his nose. "Let's say everything goes smoothly. What will you do once the will is settled?"

Lili looks surprised by his question. "Annabel will move back into her old home. I will move into my old apartment."

"And Maria Eugenia?" His eyebrows wait, poised, for her response.

"Will move into the granny flat," Lili answers.

He gives a faint nod. "Didn't you try to move her there when her husband died?"

Lili pauses. "She kicked up such a fuss that after six months, Eugen asked me to move instead, which is why I bought my small apartment behind the Museum Quarter. I didn't mind." She pauses, then adds, "Too much."

Otto turns to me. "Annabel. You are a journalist. Tell me. What will the press do when you move back in?"

I run my finger along the edge of my table. "They'll have a heyday. We'll be portrayed as money-grabbing heirs usurping our rights over an innocent mother-in-law."

He picks up a crumb of strudel and puts it in his mouth. "So would I be right in thinking that this could ruin the family's reputation?"

I raise my hand to my forehead. It's started to perspire. "And if we fight her in court, it will bankrupt the family. I get it. She might as well be aggressive and reinstate herself as matriarch while she can."

"But that's not fair," Lili says, rapping her hand against the table. "She's bullied Eugen and me all our lives. We can't just let her get away with it."

Otto interlaces his hands. His eyes run from Lili to me and back again. "Maria Eugenia is heading to Styria soon, isn't she?"

Lili looks confused. "In a few weeks. It's the start of the hunting season." She pushes her hair away from her face. Her gaze goes beyond us toward the stone statues. "I don't understand anyone who hunts for pleasure. How anyone can point a gun and kill beautiful long-horned rams is beyond me."

Otto takes out a pen and a small notebook from his jacket and scribbles something inside. "Ah, Lili. I hunt in a different way. Remember softly softly catchee monkey?" He grins. "Let's catch this monkey, shall we?"

By the beginning of October, we are ready. Lili and I are in the courtyard in front of my old home, staring upward at my old apartment on the top floor. It feels like stepping into a film set where once I was the lead actress. The wavy panes glint as my eyes follow the line of windows underneath the overhanging roof. There I am in my office, looking up from my computer to stare at the patchwork of roofs stretching in front of me. There we are, Eugen and I, our heads together, laughing over a glass of wine while having supper in the

296

kitchen. And over there, behind the balustrade, is the balcony where my cat Minou used to warm herself in the sun.

Taking a deep breath, we count to five and then, like two burglars on the prowl, we slip inside the palace, making sure the heavy entrance door closes without a bang. We're about to do something unimaginable. We're about to break into our own home.

We tiptoe up the marble staircase, making sure that we make no sound. On the top landing, I pull out my old keys.

"Are you sure she's gone?" I ask before I turn them in the lock.

"I saw her car leave half an hour ago," Lili whispers back. "She'll be in Wiener Neustadt by now."

With a soft click, the door unlocks. We stop talking as it swings ajar.

As we step into my old home, the bells of St Stephens cathedral begin their noontime chorus. As their rhythm tolls through the city, I inhale, wanting to lose myself for just one second in the nostalgia of my old life: the smell of beeswax polish on the parquet floors; the pungent aroma of cut roses from the garden which I always kept on the entrance table; the mustiness of the ancient walls. But there is none of that. Instead, I'm breathing in a chemical smell. It is sharp and sickly sweet. To my horror, I recognize it is Maria Eugenia's perfume. I cough, trying not to gag as it catches at the back of my throat. So much for memories, I think, as I close the door and stare at the view in front of me.

What was once a space of soaring white walls and contemporary clean lines is now a Habsburg hunting chalet, complete with antlers in all shapes and sizes mounted on carved wooden crests lining the corridors. Massive oil paintings cover the walls. Scenes of romantic lakes and mountain gorges with tumbling waterfalls; dead stags brought home from a day's shoot; dead rabbits and quails hanging from hooks outside peasant cottages; crusty ancestors with placid eyes glaring down at me from heavy gilt frames.

Opening the French doors, I hitch my rucksack on my back and follow Lili into the drawing room, turn to close the doors behind us, then stare, agog, at what was once my drawing room. Needlepoint

297

cushions with the Vasoy family crest stare at me from dark red velvet sofas. Heavy folds of fabric in golden brocaded swirls, complete with swags and drapes, hang from windows that were once curtain-free. A boxy, old-fashioned television sits on top of a round table covered with a heavy tasseled tablecloth.

To my surprise, all of Eugen's inherited furniture has been pilfered from the storage room and placed in strategic positions all around the room. Over there are Eugen's dining room table and chairs. His Chinese lacquer commode is in the corner. Even his Ernst Fuchs and Rosa Obermeyer landscapes are hanging on the wall.

Lili pulls at my sleeve. Her face is waxy; her eyes have an abnormal gleam to them. "This place looks just like it did when I was growing up," she whispers. "There is so much past here I can hardly breathe."

I look in the direction she's pointing. For a moment the clutter overwhelms me, but then I see what she means. Silver photograph frames line the fireplace mantel, cluster on the top of the grand piano, rest in groups of two and three on every side table. They look like glittering memories, just waiting to be admired. I pick one up. It's Maria Eugenia and her husband. I pick up another. This too is of Maria Eugenia and Georg. In fact, they are all of Maria Eugenia and her husband. Cross-country skiing in the mountains. Rowing on a lake in the Salzkammergut. Standing next to each other with a dead stag at their feet. As I stare at the photos, slowly it dawns on me what is bothering me. There isn't a single photograph taken after Georg died.

"Maria Eugenia never accepted her husband's death, did she?" I whisper.

Just then my phone pings, making us both jump. I turn off the speaker, stuff the phone in my back pocket and drop my rucksack next to Eugen's empire secretaire. We don't have much time. Bending down, I run my hand along the smooth surface of the wood and slide my finger underneath the middle panel, just like Eugen's father showed me. There. I feel it. An almost imperceptible indentation. My heart racing, I press down, and hear a faint click. Like

298

magic, a secret drawer slides open.

"Bingo," I whisper. Reaching inside, my fingers creep along the polished edge of the drawer until I feel something firm. It's a blue cardboard folder. I open it and peer inside.

It's a treasure trove of our past. Eugen's pocket diaries. Love notes we wrote each other. Receipts from special meals we had together. Plane tickets from trips we made, napkins from restaurants with names I can barely remember. *My husband, the hopeless romantic*, I think, as I hold one of his love notes to my lips.

"Hurry," Lili whispers, jarring me out of my reverie.

Bending down on my knees, I sift through the contents of the folder and pull out a dog-eared Polaroid photo. It's a young woman leaning against a rock underneath a willow tree. She's laughing. Even with the faded colors of a polaroid, it's easy to see her resemblance to Lili. The long, thick black hair. Her almond eyes. Slim nose and delicate hands. I turn the photo over and read the name on the back. Eszther Szabo. No wonder young Eugen was smitten. I hand the photo to Lili with a sense of triumph.

"I remember finding this photograph in Eugen's things, but he never explained to me who it was."

She runs a finger over the face in the photo. "Eszther Szabo. My mother." Her eyes fill with tears. "It was real," she whispers. "The woman I saw in my journey was real."

I nod. "Yes. As hard as it is to believe, it was all real."

Just then, a door slams.. The folder slips from my hands as I jump up. It falls sideways, scattering a cascade of papers, then drops onto the floor. A second later, we hear muffled voices through the closed doors of the drawing room. It's Maria Eugenia, together with a voice from a man I don't know. They are laughing and speaking in German.

Lili and I look at each other, panic on our faces. "What's she doing here?" I hiss.

"You've got to hide," Lili answers.

But I can't go. That woman ripped apart my marriage certificate. She's not going to get her hands on these memories. Ignoring Lili, who is pulling frantically at my arm, I scoop up the contents of the folder and hand it to Lili. Then, looking around wildly, I throw myself behind a pair of thick swag drapes. Lili pulls the heavy folds around me with one quick movement just as the door opens.

For a moment all I hear is the sound of laughter and the click of heels on the parquet floor. Then silence. Not being able to bear it any longer, I peer out from my hiding place. My heart constricts when I see Lili holding the folder to her chest, staring at Maria Eugenia. Next to her is a beefy man with flushed cheeks. He looks like a butcher in a business suit.

I hold my breath, forcing myself not to make any sound. My stomach feels like I have swallowed a stone. I pull out my phone and text: *Come now!*

"What are you doing here?" Maria Eugenia's voice sounds like a hiss. I hear a scuffle, and when I next peer out, the folder is now in Maria Eugenia's hands.

"You see, Jakob?" she says, waving the folder under the man's nose with a smile of triumph. "I told you it would turn up eventually." She opens the folder and starts to finger through it. "Let's see. What do we have here?"

Lili's voice is so low I must strain to hear it. "That's not yours."

Maria Eugenia looks up. "What do you mean by that, my dear? This is mine."

I expect Lili to jump up. To scream. To do something. But she's standing, immobile. I'm reminded of a story by the French writer Marcel Pagnol. When he was a child, he was watching a praying mantis being attacked by ants. The mantis, its triangular face swinging to and fro, kept taking swipes at the ants with its long forearms, but every time it succeeded in throwing them off, even more climbed up its body. No matter how bravely the mantis fought, the ants kept coming. They swarmed up its stick legs, hung on its pincers, dangled from their tiny mandibles clenched around its body. As the fight continued, the mantis began to slow down, its forearms swiping emptily in the air. It looked drunk. Finally it stopped, frozen in space. Pagnol kept waiting for the mantis to react, to fight back, to protect itself, until he observed, with morbid fascination, ants emerging triumphantly from its skull. The praying mantis had become an empty shell. The ants had eaten it from the inside out.

This is what is happening to Lili. Gone is the confident anthropologist, the grown woman I know and love. In her place is a confused little girl cowering beneath a superior. Maria Eugenia's energy isn't just dominating her. It's eating her alive.

"Give that folder to me," Lili whispers.

Maria Eugenia's voice turns cold. "How dare you talk like that to me." She turns to the man. "Jakob," she says. "Please be so kind as to show my daughter the door."

Lili's body wavers like a willow tree in the wind. She places both hands on the back of the sofa, her head drooping between her shoulder blades, as if exhausted by the effort. She speaks slowly, as if each word is so heavy it barely can make it out of her mouth. "Don't call me your daughter."

"Of course you're my daughter," Maria Eugenia says in a sing-song voice of a mother chastising a young girl.

"My dear little Lili. Falling for that trumped-up birth certificate story." She laughs. "Oh dear me. How my son could have married a fool like Annabel is beyond me."

Lili's eyes narrow. "Don't you dare call Annabel a fool."

Maria Eugenia gives a little-girl laugh. "Come now. You know perfectly well she married Eugen for his title and his money and she's got neither, so she is a fool. And you will be, too, if you believe her. That's a girl," she says, reaching to hold Lili's arm. "Listen to your mother, now. Go home." She is mesmerizing Lili with her voice.

Lili shakes her head once, then pulls her arm away. "This is my home. And you aren't my mother. My mother is Eszther Szabo."

The moment that name is mentioned, it is like a shot has been fired into the room. Maria Eugenia's face turns bright red. Her voice bursts from her like a cannon. "Never mention that trollop's name in my presence again."

This sentence hangs in the air between them. It floats toward Lili, stops, then turns around and flies back to Maria Eugenia, who will have nothing to do with it. Meanwhile, something is happening to

301

Lili. Her spine straightens. It is as if her entire being fills out and becomes larger, more solid somehow. When she next speaks, her voice rings out like a bell.

"Don't you dare call my mother a trollop. Don't you dare call any woman a trollop. Or a whore. Or a prostitute or a slut or a floozy or a harlot or a hooker or any of those terms our society throws at women who don't have the means to support themselves any other way. You took advantage of my mother, offering to take me off her hands when you knew perfectly well she had no other form of income."

"My dear," Maria Eugenia says. "It was just an expression, of course. She was a perfectly good seamstress."

Lili's eyes narrow. "Do you understand?" Her words are slow and measured.

The two women face each other like two stags preparing to rut. Lili is defiant, Maria Eugenia, increasingly confused. A flicker of remorse flits across Maria Eugenia's face when she realizes that something is wrong. Deeply wrong.

"Lili," she says. "My precious Lili. I didn't mean —" She stretches out her hand to touch her arm.

Lili flinches, as if Maria Eugenia's fingers are made of burning coals. Keeping her eyes firmly on Maria Eugenia's face, she continues, "Don't come near me."

Just then, the buzz of the intercom cuts the atmosphere like a knife. Maria Eugenia throws a glance at Jakob.

"Don't answer it," he growls. Quickly, he walks over to the windows and pulls the thick drapes shut.

But of all the things he is expecting when he pulls at the heavy folds of fabric, the last thing is to see me, standing with my arms flat at my sides.

I smile. "But I will," I say, and make a beeline for the door. Dashing around Jakob, my shoes slide on the carpet and I slip onto my knees. As Lili runs to shield me from Maria Eugenia, I pick myself up, but Jakob is too quick for me. He grabs my right arm and yanks me so hard that I can feel my shoulder twisting in its socket. I cry out as my body pivots around, my arms swinging wildly. In that moment, I take a deep breath and bring my awareness from my throbbing shoulder toward my feet. It's like I've thrown an anchor into the earth and I come back into balance again. And the most extraordinary thing happens.

From all the violence in my childhood, where I kowtowed and trembled in the face of powers that were stronger than me, from all those years searching to belong to families that would or could never accept me, my body, now in line with the earth's rhythms, connects with the force of something greater. It's as strong as the mightiest of mountains and yet as gentle as a fawn. It's the planet underneath me, supporting me, holding me in her arms. This energy fills my being and centers me so that my body, instead of falling, spins on its axis and my leg, without any influence from my brain, swings around and does a karate kick so powerful it would have made Karl's Tai Chi teacher Master Chan proud. I feel the resistance that comes from my shoe meeting soft flesh and, to my horror, I see that my shoe has just landed squarely on Jakob's groin. He makes a low mooing sound and crumples on the floor.

I pick up the intercom. "Top floor," I say, then add, "Hurry."

Maria Eugenia looks increasingly the worse for wear. With Jakob down for the count, she's on her own and she knows it. She spins around, one hand fluttering in the air, her eyes flitting from side to side. I can almost hear the wheels whirling in her brain. As she turns, Lili grabs the folder from Maria Eugenia's hand. For a moment, they tussle, both pulling at the folder. Just as I open the door, the cardboard bursts and the contents shoot into the air.

If Otto is surprised to see us standing in the drawing room, surrounded by a confetti of floating bits of paper, receipts, wine labels, and love notes, with his arch enemy Jakob in a whimpering heap, he doesn't show it. "Jakob. What a pleasant surprise."

The look on everyone's faces is one I'll never forget. Jakob's face is red and sweaty, his suit crumpled and dirty. Maria Eugenia is doing the best she can to look composed and is failing miserably. But the biggest change is in Lili. She stands tall, her eyes flashing with a fire

I've never seen before. She gives her hand to Otto, who lifts it to his lips and clicks his heels.

"Otto," Maria Eugenia says. If looks could kill, he would be dead. She thrusts a limp hand toward him expectantly. "What brings you here?"

Otto takes her hand, but instead of raising it to his lips to kiss it, he holds it. "I was on my way to meet a Russian couple when Annabel texted me." He pulls a piece of paper out of his pocket with his other hand and snaps it open. "They are interested in a palace which has been put up for —" He glances down at the piece of paper in his hand. When he looks up again, the smile is gone. "— private sale by the owners."

Maria Eugenia is in a complete panic. Her entire world is collapsing around her. Getting caught trying to sell the most valuable thing an ancient family possesses—its historic home—must be her worst nightmare. She tries to pull her hand away, but Otto's fingers tighten. "Have you no shame?"

Maria Eugenia's face darkens to the most extraordinary color, a combination of a muddy red and a sickly brown. Her forehead is speckled with beads of sweat. "I was under duress," she whispers, flashing a steely glare at Jakob, who's still rolling on the floor, clutching his crotch. "Having just lost my son, it was all I could do to act upon advice from my lawyer." She wipes the sweat from under her eyes, leaving smudge marks below them. "I felt dreadful of course."

"It didn't stop you moving in here a few weeks later," he answers. "Children do things like this, Mitzi," he adds, using her dreaded childhood nickname. "Not adults." Flushed and smiling, pink bow tie practically quivering with delight, Otto gives Jakob a hand to help him up from the floor. The lawyer utters swear words as he tries to stand up. He looks so ridiculous that none of us knows what to say.

Otto is enjoying himself tremendously. He shows Jakob the door without a second glance. "I expect you to be gone from that apartment below by next week."

We all watch as Jakob, still growling obscenities, disappears down the stairwell.

Otto then turns to Maria Eugenia. "Now if you will excuse me, I have an appointment with my Russian clients. I'm going to take them to see a palace that really is for sale."

At the threshold, he turns to Maria Eugenia. "Any further expenses regarding this estate, please speak to Lili. The estate bank accounts are now in her name." His eyes become steely. "I expect you to be gone from here by the end of the year. And if you dare do anything to change this, such as contact the press, I'll sue your ass off. And you can quote me on that." Without another word, he heads down the stairs, whistling with every step.

"Maria Eugenia, a word," I say, as the door shuts.

The once terrifying matriarch leans against the wall. I don't think I have ever seen her look so disheveled. Her clothes are wrinkled and stained. Her cheeks sweaty. She has aged twenty years in the last hour.

"Pompous ass," she says.

My arch enemy's face is shiny with perspiration. Her left eye is twitching. Flyaway hairs are everywhere. When she raises her arm to put her hand against her forehead, there are sweat marks under her arms. If there is a heaven, Eugen would be waltzing in happiness right now. Lili helps me collect the last few pieces of paper from the floor and we slip them into the blue folder, which I place in my rucksack and tie the ends tightly.

"I should have known Otto Sinsky would have it in for me," Maria Eugenia grumbles as she follows us like a sullen bulldog into the kitchen. "He's had an ax to grind ever since I fired him."

We know it's not true but don't say anything. She has dug her own grave so deeply she won't be able to get out for a very long time. As Lili and I pull glasses from the cupboard, she slumps at the kitchen table and watches with dull eyes as I search in the refrigerator and pull out half a lemon. I give a squeeze into the water that Lili places on the table, and we sit down.

"I only drink water from the Kaiserbrunn fountain," Maria Eugenia says, staring at the glass in front of her as if it contains poison. "Fresh mountain water, straight from the Alps. If it was good enough for our Kaiser, Emperor Franz Josef—you know we are related, dear Lili—it's good enough for me."

"Austrian tap water is excellent," Lili says, giving Maria Eugenia a look of ill-disguised irritation. "How could you have tried to sell our family home?"

Rather than answering, Maria Eugenia stands up and staggers to the freezer and pulls the door open. Spying a large bottle of iced vodka, she pulls it out. Plonking herself down again at the table, she gives a firm twist to open the bottle, pours herself a generous slosh, and takes a good long drink. Her body does a little shiver, her thin lids twitching over her closed eyes. "What is the difference between what I did to Annabel and what you plan to do to me?" she says, wiping her mouth against the back of her hand. "As soon as I lost my husband, I became worthless. If I hadn't fought back, I would have been forgotten."

Neither of us says anything. That is exactly what would have happened, and we both know it. Maria Eugenia takes another sip of vodka, knowing she now has our full attention. The back of her hand comes up to cover her mouth as she gives a slight burp. When she takes it away, the lipstick has made a long red streak on her skin. It looks like blood.

"I'm not going into the granny flat," she says. She taps a long fingernail on the table. "It would be the death of me."

"Nonsense," Lili says, glowering at the woman she once had considered to be her mother. "I have half a mind never to allow you to live here again."

The energy between the two of them feels like a thunderstorm, but it doesn't bother me. Nothing is bothering me any longer, even the rhythmic drumming of Maria Eugenia's nails. I reach over and pour Maria Eugenia more vodka. As I watch her taking a sip, one of Cassandra's favorite expressions comes to my mind. *Whoever has the larger consciousness is responsible for the room.*

I have had it backward all along. Maria Eugenia can freeze the Arctic Ocean with one of her icy stares. But it doesn't mean I have to respond to her in the same way. In fact, how I treat her doesn't have to have anything to do with how she treats me. I'm simply in front of a woman who has a heart as shriveled as a prune. Living next to her without Eugen would feel like sandpaper to my soul. I shake my head at the irony of it all. In order to be accepted into the family, I have to leave it.

"I'll move into the granny flat," I say. The moment the words come out of my mouth, they surprise me. My truth often does. In the distance, the deep, repetitive gong of St Stephen's cathedral wafts through the windows toward me.

Both Lili and Maria Eugenia stare at me as if I've just landed from Mars. Lili starts to protest, but I shake my head.

"Besides, with the museum coming in, I won't be living permanently in Vienna."

"Museum?" Maria Eugenia asks.

Both Lili and I smile.

Her eyes narrow. "What's the catch?"

I shrug my shoulders. "There is no catch."

Maria Eugenia's icy façade wavers. Her face a mask of perplexed confusion. For the first time, she doesn't know what to say. You can't fight a war when there is no enemy.

Lili takes Maria Eugenia's empty glass out of her hand and slams it on the table. "The decision to allow you to continue to live in this palace after what you have just done is Annabel's, not mine." Her voice is icy as the arctic wind. "She has deep-fried you in kindness. But the next time you misbehave, it will be hot oil."

I hear the clock ticking. The faucet dripping in the sink. The low murmur of the hot water flowing through the heaters. Maria Eugenia may be a churlish child living in the body of a grown woman, but she forced me to move beyond a situation I wouldn't have had the courage to confront. In her hatred, she set me free. My heart murmurs. I listen to its words. And it's clear to me what I need to do. I can see it as if it is glowing like a neon light on Maria Eugenia's forehead.

I turn to her. "I want you to help me finish what you began."

Maria Eugenia gives a little grunt as she opens the door to the long low building at the end of the courtyard where my things are still stored. The door gives way with a groan and we both walk in, waiting for our eyes to adjust to the darkness. Maria Eugenia runs her hand against the wall. I hear a click and the light goes on. The furniture looks like slumbering bears in hibernation. For a few minutes, I sift through picture frames and photo albums. Lift up heavy dust sheets. Unlatch creaking doors and slide open drawers. "Everything is so unloved," I say, running my finger along a chair edge and gazing at my dusty fingertip.

Maria Eugenia's eyes narrow as she watches me. Then, without another word, she disappears. Fifteen minutes later, she returns armed with buckets of warm water and sponges, old towels, and spray wax, and hands me a dust cloth. "So let's make it loved, shall we?"

And that is how we begin. We polish the long wooden oak table and chairs from England, dab beeswax on the painted antique Austrian Bauernmöbel chest, put a little elbow grease into my grandmother's wobbly chair. I cart armfuls of scrapbooks and photographs, picture albums, videotapes, files, and books to the large waste bin and dump them unceremoniously inside.

Day after day, we clean and sort and sort and clean. I can't say we become friends—I don't think it would be possible to trust a woman like this—but apart from her begrudging stares and long sighs, she works hard, doesn't dither, makes decisions quickly, and executes them with efficiency. At the end of each day, she marches off without a word and I drag myself home and cry myself to sleep. The next day it begins all over again.

The most challenging are the objects from my life with Eugen. As I go through each box, I repeat, did he give me this as a gift or does it belong to the family? Sometimes I have to ask myself this question a dozen times before I know the real answer.

Soon, everything that belongs to the family—every object, gift, book—is in boxes with the name Vasoy written on them, waiting for Maria Eugenia to cart them off. The Vasoy possessions are no longer intertwined with my own.

By the time November arrives, my past is in order. All along the walls are beds and tables and chests of drawers and lamps and armchairs and desks, polished and clean and standing to attention like tin soldiers. Even the wooden carranca carving that followed me from Brazil to New York to London to Vienna is here, its furrowed brow and open gargoyle mouth snarling in space. On the other side of the room lie piles of things to be returned to their rightful owners: my mother's wedding dress to my parents, photograph albums to friends, my grandfather's ancient leather medical bag to a cousin. We are now ready for the next step: to sell everything to the highest bidder.

Maria Eugenia introduces me to Alexander, who heads the furniture department at the Dorotheum, the largest private auction house in Europe. Tall and lanky and soft-spoken, he can't believe what I'm about to do, so he takes me under his wing. With Alexander's help, we sort what can be sold in auction, and what can't. After I say goodbye to my furniture, Alexander arranges for it to be taken away.

The last step comes with the auction. On the day, I slip into the room where it is being held and sit at the back to watch. The auctioneer stands at the podium as piece after piece is examined, bid on, and sold. Down goes the gavel and off they go, no longer mine.

When the auction is over, I go home and spend the rest of the evening gazing onto the rooftops of the city that was once my home. All my possessions, apart from two suitcases of clothes, are now in a musical instrument box. There aren't many: a small statue for which I modeled when I was a teenager. A photo or two. A Russian lacquer box. A commemorative plaque of Dona Mathilde. A box of pottery shards from the Amazon. The three glass vials containing the stones and earth and dried wildflowers I had collected from the lands of my ancestors. And that's it. When I open the box and look inside, I burst into tears, not believing what I have just done. There is nothing of the

309

old me left. My past is gone.

It takes a few seconds to get a handle on what I'm feeling. I feel light, unburdened. Free. I smile at the irony of it all. I had to get rid of everything I own in order to understand the true meaning of abundance.

By the time my parents arrive, it's nearly Christmas. Watching them emerge from airport customs, they look small and fragile, like two little dolls holding hands. It's hard for me to see two people who were once so strong looking so frail.

I feel a pang of sadness when I see that my dream of seeing my parents in Vienna has come true just as my reason to be here no longer exists. Eugen is gone, and with him, so is my life here. Dreams are funny things. They inspire you and yet they can imprison you, too. So can anger. Yes, my parents weren't good at their job. But when I remove the label of parent, all I have in front of me are two people who wish me to love them. I can do that. My heart is big enough to love the entire world.

And, because Vienna is the city of music, we enjoy it in all forms. We tap our feet to the *Nutcracker Suite* at the National Opera House, hum to Handel's *Messiah* at the Musikverein concert house, have lunch in Hungary because why not eat lunch in another country when you can, and even drive to Bratislava, only half an hour away, to see *Un Ballo in Maschera* at the tiny jewelry box of an opera house. The music is so moving that we sing at the top of our lungs all the way home.

My parents love Karl who, in the spirit of Christmas, has tacked a sign with a quote from Ram Dass on his wall: *If you think you're enlightened, spend a week with your family.*

But my greatest pleasure is to take them to visit my healer. Mighty Mildred greets us, plastic apron and all, then winds her way through the plates of Christmas cookies and bottles of schnapps and bunches of flowers to bring my parents to the treatment room. My mother approaches healing with caution, but my father doesn't hesitate. He

310

drops his clothes on cue, lies naked on Mildred's table, closes his eyes, takes a deep sigh, and tells her with the firm words of Winston Churchill, *Keep calm and carry on!*

Mildred pats me on the back, her star pupil, but my father wins the prize, receiving a kiss on his forehead because many of his inner stop signs, as Mildred calls his blocks, release with ease. Afterward, we eat lunch at the Vienna Yacht Club, watching the ships plough the Danube toward Hungary and beyond. As I watch my underweight father wolfing down a double portion of mussels and mashed potatoes plus two desserts, I know I don't have to explain anything to him about healing.

With Christmas almost upon us, we head down the street, our shoes scraping against the slippery cobblestones, until we reach the large green gate of the palace. I take out my beeper and press it and the gate slowly creaks open.

"You lived here?" My mother's eyes blink against the falling snow as we walk into the courtyard. As she looks toward the ornate baroque façade, she reminds me of a little girl. Behind us, the heavy double gate to the street closes with a solid thud.

"Up there," I say, pointing to the windows. "But that's not what I wanted you to see. It's this."

We walk arm in arm up the steps and enter the atrium. Inside is chaos. The marble hall is covered with plaster dust. Huge carpets rest upright against the wall like long, bent sausages. Dust sheets are draped over pieces of furniture like gray ghosts. Scaffolding runs along the walls. Ever since Lili and I began to draw up the plans for the atrium, painters and carpenters and electricians and plasterers have been working day and night. A man in overalls is plastering a mural of Venus of Willendorf on the wall above us. As we walk under her, she peers down over her rounded breasts, blessing us, as she will all the guests who enter the Museum of the Feminine.

As we walk in, I feel a surge of happiness bubbling inside me. *It's going to be beautiful*, I think. All around us—on pedestals, in display cases, in interactive designs, and even painted on all the walls—are representatives of the Goddess. A hundred faces of the Green Man,

311

in all his foliate forms, are stenciled as murals around the walls. Kali, with her lolling red tongue and necklace of skulls, is here too, with her Christian equivalent, the Black Madonna. There is a historic section showing the Paleolithic cultures with the hundreds of Venus figurines, plus the Neolithic cultures of Sumaria, Mesopotamia, the Minoans, and Çatal Hüyük in Turkey.

With Lili's help, the historical museum traces, through architecture and myths and legends, the Goddess from her beginnings as Astarte in the Levant to the Sumerian goddess Inanna to the Mesopotamian goddess Ishtar to the Egyptian goddess Isis to the Greek goddess Aphrodite to the Roman goddesses Venus, Athena, and Persephone, all the way to Mary Magdalene and Mother Mary.

There is so much information that a person could spend a day and there would still be more to see. There will even be a future Wake Up Café and cooking school to teach the culinary delights of healthy eating in a way that sustains the body and the planet. I watch my parents walking around the exhibition, their faces going from dismay to disbelief to, finally, a wary acceptance that perhaps there is another way of looking at the world rather than through the fear-based way they were raised.

"I might not understand it, but I'm proud of you," my father says, as we walk out of the palace and make our way carefully across the cobblestones toward the gate.

"For living in a palace?" my mother says, wrapping her sable around her.

I press the bell and the massive gate opens. We walk through it onto the street. My father gazes one last time at the scene in front of him before the ancient gate closes with a bang. The creaking wood gives one last shudder and stops. As we turn and walk away, he puts one arm through mine. "No. For leaving it."

EPILOGUE

23 December

The week goes by in such a flurry of activity that the birth certificate hunt is upon us sooner than we expected. Tired from the late nights and rich food, my parents are subdued as we set out for Munich. The westbound Autobahn highway is clear; snow has fallen lightly on the ground, dusting the winter fields with a whiteness that accentuates the crispness of the day.

"Why are we leaving Austria? I *liked* Vienna," my father huffs from the back of the car, as we drive along the A1 highway toward Munich. "I don't know what happened to you after that eye operation of yours. Giving up your career and all that. You used to be someone. Now you're no one."

"I'm turning my story into a book," I say. My voice sounds lame, I know it.

"You'll get sued," my father snaps.

I look at him through the rearview mirror. He is in commander-in-chief mode, and great helmsmen do not like being in the back of a car driving into the unknown. "No, it's fiction," I say. "I'm calling the heroine Annabel Jones."

My mother looks up. "Will it include the black cats and all those passed-up lives?"

"Past lives," I interject.

"Past lives then," she says. "I know that's impossible. Just look at it mathematically. With the population increase, where do the new souls come from?"

313

I sigh and change gears a little too quickly. I wish I had kept my mouth shut a few nights ago, when, feeling expansive after one glass of champagne too many, I shared one story too many.

She reaches over and pats my knee. "Now now, dear. Don't fret. I was this way during menopause, too."

I raise my eyes to the ceiling. As my mother gives me an innocent smile, I turn my gaze toward the sun, low in the sky.

The light has already faded by the time we reach Munich. The hotel is a bit too modern for my father's taste, making him more on edge than usual; my mother has reverted to her perennial worry that her father Hermann never had a middle name, which implies to her just how much his father Wilhelm cared about his eldest son. Over dinner, an elaborate affair offering lobster to foie gras, my father glares at the waiters.

"Look," he whispers loudly, ordering the most expensive bottle of wine. "He looks like a Nazi."

"He's German, that's all," I answer, in a low voice.

"Never could trust a German," my father growls, following the sommelier with his eyes.

"You married a German," I say, but the joke falls flat. We keep quiet after that. Parent sitting is exhausting. I very much look forward to crawling into my bed and closing my eyes on the world. But as I see my father totter over to help my mother up from her chair, then walk out of the restaurant hand in hand, I realize that they are simply tired. And so am I. I wish them both goodnight and we disappear into our rooms.

24 December

As soon as I wake up, I call Erding Town Hall. I doubt anyone will pick up. It is 24 December, Christmas Eve, after all.

The phone is picked up on the first ring. I hear a male voice. "*Grüß Gott.*"

"*Grüß Gott,*" I answer, unfurling the piece of paper my mother gave me. "I'm not sure if I have the name, the town, or the date right, but do you have *Geburtsurkunde,* a birth certificate for Hermann

Kesting?" I read out the few details from my mother's note.

"*Einen Moment, bitte.*"

I hear a metallic click. I sit, twisting the piece of paper around my fingers as I wait. After a minute, the clerk picks up the receiver. "*Jawohl,*" I hear. "What would you like me to do with it?"

The piece of paper flutters from my hands. "What did you say?"

"Hermann Kesting. I have his birth certificate in front of me. If you get here before noon, we can give you a copy."

"We're coming right away," I nearly shout. "Don't close without us!"

I pound on my parents' hotel room door and we race to Erding. Now it's no longer just a small German town, it's Erding—our town—my grandfather's town. We find the town hall, a modern efficient building off the main square, and wait impatiently in a small room until a squat man arrives with a large parchment in his hand. I squint at the thick black letters and read, "Frederic Hermann Kesting."

My mother can hardly contain herself. "Oh!" she whispers, hugging her hands to her chest. "Frederic Hermann. Imagine. He did have a middle name after all."

We take down the name and address of his birthplace, then take photographs in front of the house. To celebrate, we go for lunch at the Hotel zum Erdinger Weissbräu, the oldest restaurant in town, built in 1537. We all imagine Wilhelm eating *Weisswurst* sausage and washing it down with beer.

"I had to choose between going on a lion hunt with an Arab Sheik or marrying your father," my mother says, gazing at my father with adoring eyes.

My father, who suddenly looks forty years younger, puffs up like an army corporal and blusters, "You're darn right!" Story leads to story, and over bowls of steaming hot chocolate, we conclude that finding Hermann's birth certificate is the best Christmas present ever.

We duck into the cold as the snowflakes flutter around us like thick white cotton puffs. "Do you smell that?"

315

My mother lifts her nose to the air and shakes her head.

"Roses," I say. "I smell roses."

I see from my parents' faces that they can't smell anything, so I say no more. But when I get in the car and the pungent, fresh-as-dew smell of roses follows me inside, I think, *It's happening again.* The fragrance isn't coming from out there, but from in here.

As the windshield wipers flip back and forth, I pull onto the highway and head toward Austria. I am in my own world, listening to the wipers doing their flic-flic-flic like a metronome, when I hear my father speaking from the back of the car.

"Dachau isn't far from here. I'd like to see it." His voice sounds hollow.

"Now?" my mother asks. "But it's Christmas Eve."

I'm about to agree when I glance in the rear-view mirror and see my father's face. His eyes are shining with wartime memories as a young man growing up during the Blitz. Too many close friends and relatives were lost. Germany is a country he never wanted to visit, and yet he is here. We all have a journey to make and this is his. Although we are all tired, I change direction and pull back onto the highway without another word, heading east through the snowflakes. The day becomes tinted with a grayness that has nothing to do with the weather.

As my father stands on his own, ramrod straight like a soldier, deep in thought as the memories of the Battle of Britain swirl around him, I wait for the expected judgments to arise. The last time I was at a concentration camp, I wanted to throw up. But now, the feelings never come. I feel a deep, numbing pain, but that's it. No judgment. No blame. No stories. That's all it is, pain. Pain of those who killed, and pain of those who were killed.

And yet, when I breathe in, all I can smell is roses. The more present I am, the more intense the fragrance becomes. I'm carrying a million bouquets of roses in me, showering their fragrance on that pain. And in this moment, I understand. I may never know what the smell of roses means, but what I can do is choose how I interpret it. And to me, the smell of roses means that something is healing.

"We never thought we would win the war," my father says, his voice rasping with emotion. "London was in tatters. The Germans had us beaten and didn't know it."

"But you fought anyway."

"We had to," he says, quietly. He looks at me, a small, self-contained package of contradictions. "But I now see it wasn't the Germans, but the ideology we were fighting. It's never people, is it? It's fear. We were fighting fear."

"We're all human," I say. "And we all make mistakes. But one day we wake up and get over it. And that's when the healing begins."

And we walk back to the car, the smell of roses wafting in our wake.

25 December

It's Christmas Day. Cheerfully assembling my breakfast selection, I arrive at my parents' table. They aren't talking much. My mother randomly picks at her toast, while my father's nose stays entrenched in a copy of the New York Times. A number of times over the meal, I see my mother stealing a glance at my father. Finally, at the end of breakfast, she folds her napkin and lowers her voice.

"We had a visitor last night." My mother runs her hand over the tablecloth to gather the breadcrumbs together. "After dinner we went to bed as usual. Then I woke up in the middle of the night." She lowers her voice even more. "This is where it gets strange. Three men were looking at me. I don't know why I knew there were three, and that they were men." She keeps running her hand over the tablecloth. "This morning, I said nothing. Your father would have pooh-poohed my story and asked how many sleeping pills I had taken. But then, as we were getting dressed, he came in and asked if anything unusual had happened last night." She looks at my father, who's sipping his tea in silence. "Come on, John, tell her."

As my father looks up from his cup of tea, his voice is blustery and loud. "How safe are hotels here?"

I put my teacup down. "Why do you ask?"

He clears his throat. "Well. I saw a man in the room. I asked him,

317

'What are you doing here? I've locked the door!'"

"Had you locked the door?"

My father bristles. "Of course I had! I do that every night."

I keep my voice even. "This man in your room—where was he?"

My father looks as if he has swallowed a lemon. He opens his mouth, closes it, opens it again, adjusts his tie, looks as if he can find the answer to my question in his teacup. "He was, well now, how can I say this." He looks up to the ceiling. "He was floating above our bed."

I wouldn't have changed places with anyone in the world at that moment. The look on my father's face is priceless. "How was he dressed?"

My father frowns. "Old-fashioned clothes. A long dark mantle and fedora hat. Good quality. Long black beard."

I start to smile. Why, great-grandfather Wilhelm decided to visit us after all. "What was he doing?"

"He was observing your mother," he says, quietly.

I think about Wilhelm's words. It was the wildflowers that he had missed when he moved to America. For me, this isn't about seeing ghosts, but healing. I speak slowly, keeping my voice even as I tell them about how I smelled roses in Erding, even though there were no roses around us. I tell them how the fragrance followed me to Dachau, and how powerful it was for me to feel pain without blame. I tell them that it's important to heal family rifts. To accept people as they are. I pause. "Even Wilhelm." I toss his name in the space between us as gently as I can.

My mother's eyes flash. "Wilhelm never amounted to anything. He abandoned his wife. Not just once, but twice. Left her pregnant too."

"Traveling from Germany took time, effort, and money," I answer. "He might have left twice, but he returned three times. He wouldn't have done it if he didn't care."

My mother pauses. "That's true."

"He died of a strangulated hernia," I say. "On the operating table. That means he didn't expect to die. Maybe America didn't fit him.

318

Maybe he shouldn't have left. But one thing I'm sure of. He wasn't at peace when he died."

"Ostracized by his own family. That must have been hard," my father says.

"We came to find Hermann's birth certificate," I say. "Perhaps by doing this, we have just set Wilhelm free."

My mother still doesn't understand.

"We reap what we sow. Wilhelm wasn't a good parent. But he did the best he could. As long as you hold resentment against him, healing can't happen. When you release your anger, it leaves more room for love."

"I think I'm going to cry," my mother says.

"Are you afraid of death now?" I ask. I don't know why I ask this, but I know that one day I will be glad that I did.

A smile spreads toward her eyes. "No." She pats my father's hand. "When I die, my family will be waiting for me. That's comforting."

I reach across the table and take their hands and we all smile, a little teary-eyed. Family. We can't get rid of each other, so we might as well enjoy each other. I've stretched into the cosmos to embrace all of humankind as my family, which narrows into two subsets called men and women, then narrows again into countries, then again into my lineage. At the end I have, sitting in front of me, the two people who gave me life. How can I not be grateful to them for that?

In the afternoon, while my parents rest in their hotel room, I take a walk to digest all that has happened. Standing on the edge of the bridge, I look down at the water rushing beneath me and let myself go and sink into the place within myself where I can find the answers I'm looking for.

I see the image of an Oreo cookie. I expected something more profound, but when I throw away my expectations and concentrate on the image, I understand what this means. Great-grandfather Wilhelm was the soft filling between two hard biscuits. Hated by his son, a successful doctor, and hated by his father, a successful businessman, he fell somewhere in the middle, unable to be himself and unable to live on either side of the Atlantic. He loved Europe, his family was in America—and I stop.

It's not my great-grandfather I'm thinking about, but me.

Me.

I am my great-grandfather. I live in Europe but my family is in America. This isn't about healing someone in the past, it's about healing me. All the shamans and black cats and bats and ancestor blessings are no more than clearing my own life, right here and now. The first time I arrived in Europe, it was to escape my past. But as great-grandfather Wilhelm discovered, you bring your baggage with you.

Every ending offers a new beginning. We all live two lives. And, as Pablo Neruda once said, we begin to live the second one once we know we only have one.

I'm going to do just that. Starting now.

POSTSCRIPT

The Taj means something to me. It is there that my own heart shattered with an orchestration so perfect I can only call it divine.

This novel, just like *The Extraordinary Awakening of Annabel Jones*, is inspired by a true story. It covers a period of great transformation in my life. It was a time of reconciling with my past, making peace with my family, both dead and alive, and abandoning old dreams. I found letting go of my hopes of meeting my prince charming to be the most difficult of all.

Annabel is me and not me. We share the same spiritual journey. But her magical moments—the ancestors whispering in the wind, the mysterious shaman in the desert, even the black cats, are real. In fact, the entire Epilogue is real.

All lives are filled with miracles and mystery. Inexplicable wonders. Extraordinary moments. All we need to do is open our eyes and see them. That's why I've written these novels and have created a program called S.H.E. to help guide women home to heal themselves. It's all part of healing the world, one woman at a time.

For more information, please see www.andrenawoodhams.com

ACKNOWLEDGEMENTS

To Arik Shimansky, for his love, creativity, and endless patience in all things that matter including the beautiful artwork and typesetting of this book.

To Frances Stolberg for her invaluable friendship, support, and inspiration.

To my dear friends Margaret Bentham, Lisa Berg, Alexander Hamilton, Christel Ibsen, Vanessa Kastner, Sarah Lavers, John Man, Lori Miller, Abbey Peruzzi, Richard Wall, Nick Williams, Stefanie Winkelbauer, and David Wright for helping me edit out the pretentious bits.

To Gaia Imperiali for being there for me every step of the way, and for providing, together with Marcia and Robert Barclay, the most beautiful homes to write in.

To Chantal Schreiber, who encouraged me to write this as fiction, and to Jennifer Read Hawthorne, Claudia Shaffer, and Fiona Brown for making the book a pleasure to read.

To Mildred Cabanero, Percy Konquobe, and Bjarne and Ruth Hustad for being themselves.

And lastly to Lorraine Weiss, whose teachings are sprinkled throughout this book, for helping me to shed the parts of myself that no longer served me so that I could grow into the woman I am today.

BIBLIOGRAPHY

Ayahuasca and Shamanism

Castaneda, Carlos. *The Teachings of Don Juan: A Yaqui Way of Knowledge.* New York: Washington Square Press, 1985

McKenna, Terence. *Food of the Gods.* New York: Bantam Books, 1993

Pollan, Michael. *How to Change Your Mind.* New York: Penguin Books, 2018

Walker, Julian. "The Red Pill Overlap." www.medium.com. May 21, 2020

Health and Healing

Harari, Yuval. Sapiens: *A Brief History of Mankind.* New York: Harper Perennial, 2018

—— *Homo Deus: A Brief History of Tomorrow.* New York: Harper Perennial, 2018

Pollan, Michael. *The Omnivore's Dilemma: A Natural History of Four Meals.* New York: Penguin Books, 2007

—— In *Defense of Food: An Eater's Manifesto.* New York: Penguin Books, 2009

Sams, Jamie, and David Carson. *Medicine Cards: The Discovery of Power Through the Ways of Animals.* New York: St. Martin's Press, 1999

William, Anthony. *Medical Medium: Secrets Behind Chronic Illness and Mystery Illness and How to Finally Heal.* Carlsbad: Hay House, 2015

—— *Medical Medium Life-Changing Foods: Save Yourself and the Ones You Love with the Hidden Healing Powers of Fruits & Vegetables.* Carlsbad: Hay House, 2016

—— *Medical Medium Thyroid Healing: The Truth Behind Hashimoto's, Graves', Insomnia, Hypothyroidism, Thyroid Nodules & Epstein-Barr.* Carlsbad: Hay House, 2017

—— Medical Medium *Liver Rescue: Answers to Eczema, Psoriasis, Diabetes, Strep, Acne, Gout, Bloating, Gallstones, Adrenal Stress, Fatigue, Fatty Liver, Weight Issues, SIBO & Autoimmune Disease.* Carlsbad: Hay House, 2018

—— *Medical Medium: Celery Juice.* Carlsbad: Hay House, 2019

Woodhams, Andrena. *The Extraordinary Awakening of Annabel Jones: A Tantric Fairytale.* Naples, FL: Yinbound Books, 2022

The Feminine

Basford, Kathleen. *The Green Man.* Cambridge: D.S. Brewer, 1978

Bonobo Love: Wild Wives of Africa. Nat Geo Wild, 2011. Video

Brighton, Simon, and Terry Welbourn. *Echoes of the Goddess: A Quest for the Sacred Feminine in the British Landscape.* Surrey: Ian Allen, 2010

DeMeo, James. Saharasia: *The 4000 BCE Origins of Child Abuse, Sex-Repression, Warfare and Social Violence, in the Deserts of the Old World.* Ashland: Natural Energy Works, 2011

Eisler, Riane. *The Chalice and the Blade: Our History, Our Future.* San Francisco: Harper One, 1988

—— *The Real Wealth of Nations: Creating A Caring Economics.* San Francisco: Berrett-Koehler Publishers, 2007

—— *Sacred Pleasure: Sex, Myth, and the Politics of the Body—New Paths to Power and Love.* New York: Harper One, 1996

Keen, Sam. *Faces of the Enemy: Reflections of the Hostile Imagination.* New York: Harper & Row, 1992

Kurlansky, Mark. *Salt: A World History.* New York: Penguin Books, 2003

Man, John. *Searching for the Amazons: The Real Warrior Women of the Ancient World.* London: Bantam Press, 2017

Pagels, Elaine. *The Gnostic Gospels.* Vancouver, WA: Vintage Books,1979

Sheela na Gig Project. sheelanagig.org.

Smoley, Richard. *Inner Christianity: A Guide to the Esoteric Tradition.* Boulder: Shambhala Publications, 2002

Starbird, Margaret. *The Woman with the Alabaster Jar: Mary Magdalen and the Holy Grail.* Rochester, VT: Bear and Company, 1993

Stone, Merlin. *When God Was a Woman.* New York: Harcourt, 1976

Wolkstein, Diane, and Samuel Kramer. Inanna, *Queen of Heaven and Earth: Her Stories and Hymns from Sumer.* New York: Harper Perennial, 1983

LOCATIONS

Black Madonna Sara la Kali: Notre Dame de la Mer; Saintes-Maries-de-la-Mer; Camargue, France.

The British Museum: London, England.

Fjellstua Aksla Viewpoint: Ålesund, Norway.

The Green Man: Westminster Abbey Quire Scree; London, England.

Grotto of Mary Magdalene: Starting Point Hotellerie de la Sainte-Baume; Var, France.

Kaspar the Black Cat: The Savoy; London, England.

Rathaus Townhall: Erding, Bavaria, Germany.

Rollfahre Ferry: Spitz on the Danube; Wachau, Austria.

Sheela na Gig: The Church of St Mary and St David; Kilpeck, Herefordshire, England.

Venus of Willendorf: Vienna Museum of Natural History; Vienna, Austria.

ABOUT THE AUTHOR

Andrena Woodhams is an author, speaker, and expert in international travel events. She has lived in seven countries, speaks six languages, has written travel articles for The Times and Tatler, was a presenter and reporter for BBC World Television, assisted a modern day shaman for over a decade, and learned to play the bagpipes— although not exactly in that order.

Andrena writes with a fearless honesty that comes from living an adventurous life with an open heart. Whether she is scaling mountains in Norway on a quest to heal her ancestors or confronting her sexual fears by studying tantra in France, her search across continents and countries for love and a place she can call home offers a real insight into the human psyche. It inspires readers to reach within themselves and discover the magic and the mystery that is available to us all.

BOOK CLUB QUESTIONS

1. What did you learn from reading Annabel's story?

2. How did this book compare with other novels like this you might have read?

3. Did you reread any passages? If so, which ones?

4. Would you want to read another book by this author?

5. Do you find the author compelling?

6. If you could ask the author anything, what would it be?

7. Are there any areas you wish the author had elaborated upon further?

8. Did the book feel real to you? Do you think it's true?

9. How did it impact you? Do you think you'll remember it in a few months or years?

10. Who do you most want to read this book?

11. Were the couples' connections believable? Would you fall for either man?

12. Did this book melt your heart? Make you believe in love again?

13. Are there lingering questions from the book you're still thinking about?

14. How did the setting impact the story? Would you want to read more books set in that world?

15. Are there any people or therapies in the book that might interest you?

16. Are there any characters you'd like to deliver a lecture to? If so, who? What would you say?

17. Has this book affected the way you go about your life? If so, in what way?

18. What are some passages that you underlined, or that touched you?

19. How did this book make you reflect on your own life?

20. Has this book sparked an interest to delve deeper into yourself, and if so, what do you think you'd like to do?

S.H.E.

If you have enjoy Andrena Woodhams' books and want to go deeper within yourself, why not take her online course S.H.E.

This 6-month personal program forever transforms how you see yourself and your place within the world aound you.

For more information about Andrena Woodhams and S.H.E., or for inquiries for book club and speaking engagements, please visit:

www.andrenawoodhams.com